A QUEST OF SEA & SOIL

A QUEST OF SEA & SOIL

THE SEOD CROI CHRONICLES

BOOK 3

S. USHER EVANS

Sun's Golden Ray
Publishing

PENSACOLA, FL

Version Date: 9/26/25
© 2023 S. Usher Evans
ISBN: 978-1945438561

Cover Design by Bianca Bordianu | www.bbordianudesign.com
Cover Typography by Sun's Golden Ray Publishing
Map Designed by Frederick Kroner with Stardust Book Services
Line Editing by Danielle Fine, By Definition Editing
Proofreading by Lisa Henson, Capitol Editing

Sun's Golden Ray Publishing
Pensacola, FL
www.sgr-pub.com

For ordering information, please visit
www.sgr-pub.com/orders

THE FAE REALM
PENNLAN
KONEVELL
SUDAEMOR
DRIWANIA
NESURIA
N

Chapter One

Ayla

Dear Cade,
You're an ass.
Love, Ayla

I stared at the words, wishing there was a way to get them to the stupid wizard who'd left without a goodbye. But we weren't even sure where he'd gone, and I had a feeling that even if I *could* reach him, he'd probably toss my letter without reading it.

"And I've loved you for years. I just… I never had the courage to say it."

"I love you. But as a friend. As my brother. Not as…"

Our conversation echoed in my mind and guilt washed over me. The very last thing I wanted was to hurt Cade. He was one of a handful of people I could still trust. But I couldn't lie to him about how I felt. He was a brother, my comfort, my security. The one constant in a world gone mad. Romantic love, however…I'd never felt that for him. And I knew in my heart I never would.

So I'd been truthful, and he'd made some excuse about seeking the third piece of the *seod croí* and vanished.

One fragment of the magical stone hung from my neck, given to my many-greats ancestor after a fierce battle against Laughlan, the wizard who'd created it. Another piece was now in the hands of Eoghan, who'd bartered with the trolls for it—something we hadn't realized until we were entrapped in a stone prison by the two-faced King Edric. But we'd escaped (barely), Edric was dead, and his trolls would be returning to their homeland after a thousand years. And while I was grateful we were safe again, it was merely a brief respite. Eoghan had several months of a head start on finding the final two pieces. For all we knew, he already had them.

Don't even think it.

No, he couldn't have the other two stones. If he did, he would already be back, breaking through the banishment spell and taking my piece for himself.

Therefore, if Cade wanted to have some "space" by searching for the missing piece, it was perhaps for the best. The banishment spell seemed to be holding well and there was no imminent danger to Pennlan.

I glanced to my left, where an open letter sat unfolded.

Ayla,

I'm sorry to use this box, but I thought it would be the fastest way to get a message to you. Cade's left in search of the third stone. I hope this isn't news to you, that he stopped in to say goodbye as he promised, but I'm not confident. Either way, I wanted you to know.

As well, the Erlking has given us permission to resettle the trolls in the wildlands. Lynton's on his way back to you to gather the trolls and take them with him, so expect him within the next day or so. I'm not sure how fast he can travel through stone.

Since Cade is gone, I figured I'd continue what he started, looking in the Erlking's library for any mention of the aether stone. If you have any ideas, I'm all ears.

Again, I apologize for using this box you and Cade shared.

- Riona

I hated how apologetic she was—and that I'd made her feel she had to be. In the chaos after the troll kingdom had fallen, I'd only had time for a few rushed apologies for my abhorrent behavior.

I pulled a fresh page from my stack and dipped my quill in the ink.

Riona,

No apology necessary. Cade clearly doesn't want to talk to me right now anyway. He didn't stop in before leaving, so your message was the first I'd heard of it.

We will keep an eye out for Lynton. In the meantime, let me know if Pennlan can be of service to the Erlking in any way. I wish you the best of luck searching in the library. We need all the good news we can get.

I paused, chewing on the end of the quill, then added:

I eagerly await your next letter.

Sincerely,

Ayla

I reread it a few times then folded it, sealed it, and put it inside the magical box. It glowed gold for a moment before dimming to its normal color. I imagined Riona's face when the box glowed on the other side, and hoped she'd stuck around to get a response.

After a moment, I crossed my office to tug on the small cord, ringing my attendant, Bronwen.

"Can you fetch Ward for me?" I said softly when she appeared. "I think he's down with the trolls."

She rubbed her hands together. "I don't like them. They're creepy. Why isn't their skin all the way…?" She shivered. "Are you sure we can trust them?"

"As much as anyone, I suppose," I said. "But they're in our debt for the moment. So I think we've got the upper hand."

She bowed and scurried away, and I returned to my desk, leaning back in my chair and looking out the window. I didn't blame Bronwen for being nervous. We'd all been conditioned to hate all manner of fae—even ones who'd been hidden for a thousand years. But as I was starting to unwind my own prejudices, I hoped the rest of my kingdom would as well.

A soft knock interrupted my thoughts. "Come in."

Ward, my soon-to-be-captain, walked inside, dashing in his uniform. I'd almost gotten used to him wearing his plain traveling clothes and sporting a thin layer of black hair along his jawline. But in the blue tunic, which he filled out better than anyone else in my royal guard, his rust-colored skin and deep brown eyes painted a striking portrait of a man I had no business noticing.

"Ayla."

I jumped, realizing he'd been talking to me. "Sorry. I received a note from Riona. Cade… Cade's already left for the south."

"I had a feeling he might," Ward said. "He can get there faster than any of our riders. Probably for the best."

"Yes, probably." My gaze fell to the table and I pushed papers around. "For several reasons."

"Are you all right?" His tone was softer than I would've expected.

"I'm fine," I said, though my throat had thickened with unshed tears. "Riona also mentioned Lynton was coming to retrieve the trolls soon. Their meeting with the Erlking was successful."

"Good," he said. "They're restless down there."

"Have they all recovered their memories?" I asked.

"Mostly," he said. "Some aren't talking much."

I could understand. For many of them, they'd gone from fighting and barely surviving a bloody war against Laughlan to hiding in a mountain to…waking up in a field a thousand years later. Any friends and family they'd left behind were gone. It was a lot to take in.

"I'd like to go visit them," I said. "Riona wasn't sure how quickly Lynton would return, but if it's anything like the rest of the fae…"

"It'll be soon," he said with a nod. "I'll go with you."

>–» >–» >–» >–»

We walked side-by-side, close enough to touch, but my arm hanging limply. Our friendship had taken a beating in the troll realm, and for a few hours, he'd resigned his post. But thankfully, his ability to forgive was on par with my sister's, and we seemed to be on the mend. Assuming, of course, I behaved myself.

"Thank you for keeping an eye on them," I said.

"There's not much to keep an eye on," he replied. "They're pretty resourceful creatures."

That was an understatement. There hadn't been much thought put into where they'd stay. We'd been too focused on getting them out of the crumbling mountain alive. But almost overnight, the trolls had built themselves a makeshift shelter using their earth magic. The sun was high overhead, so they were mostly huddled in the shade, although several hopped to their feet to bow as I entered the collection of rock huts.

"Your Majesty."

"Welcome, Your Majesty."

"So glad to see you again, Your Majesty."

I smiled at them, hoping to put them at ease. As soon as they'd paid their respects, they dashed back to the safety of their shade.

Elodia and Rutley, Ward's most trusted soldiers, were patrolling the village, and gave me a terse nod as we passed. Unlike Ward, they hadn't quite forgiven me for my behavior in the troll realm. I gave them a small wave, and Rutley cracked a smile, but Elodia kept her stony-faced glare.

"Looks like we're right on time," Ward said, pointing to the distance.

In the bright sun, it was difficult to see, but the spark of white light became more visible as it drew closer. It stopped right in front of us then materialized into the imposing figure of the king of the trolls, Lynton. He had the same translucent skin as the rest of his kind and long, silvery hair that hung loosely around his shoulders.

"Your Majesty," he said, bowing.

"Your Majesty," I said, a gentle reminder that we were now equals and a bow wasn't necessary. "Riona tells me you've been given approval to resettle in the wildlands."

"Indeed." In our journey up the mountain, I'd barely seen him crack a smile, but now he was beaming. "Erlking Birch is as generous as Riona described. We are grateful."

"We won't keep you," I said, holding out my hand.

He began to bow then stopped himself and took my hand in a firm grip. "You are most kind. Pennlan will forever be a friend to the trolls."

"Likewise." I smiled. "Safe journey."

He left without another word, disappearing into the ground the same as he'd arrived. And one by one, the stone structures that had sat on the plains dissolved into nothing, along with the trolls who'd built them. Within minutes, the village was gone—and so were the trolls.

"So that's that," I said with a soft sigh. "It seems quiet now."

"I think we could use a little quiet after all the excitement of the past few weeks," Ward said. "Let's just hope no more magical creatures show up asking you to come visit."

"I won't be making that mistake twice." When he chuckled, I stopped him, placing my hand on his arm. "I mean it. Lesson learned.

Stay in the castle where it's safe." I shook my head. "Suppose Eoghan was right about that."

His hand covered mine, sending shoots of electricity up my arm. "That damn wizard was right about nothing. Yes, you had no business traveling halfway across the continent to a people we'd never met before. Yes, you nearly died—several times—thus jeopardizing the kingdom. But..." He stopped. "Hm. I forgot where I was going with that."

"Funny." I should've removed my hand, but I didn't. His heartbeat pulsed against my fingertips, his hand warm and calloused over mine, reminding me of the times I'd gripped it in fear. There was no one else on this desolate plain except the two of us, the cool fall wind blowing my hair against my cheek. Even so, my body was warm and ready.

But he ended the moment, removing my hand from his chest and letting it drop, cold, against my side.

"I don't have all the answers," he said, looking away from me. "But there's a large space between putting yourself in overt danger and locking yourself up in the castle. Your kingdom stretches from the coast to the mountains—and it's yours to explore, if you want."

I barely understood what he said, too distracted by my pulse skipping in my throat. "Would you take me?"

The question dangled in the air, and even I couldn't pretend it was innocent. I did want to explore my kingdom—until we'd traveled to the troll kingdom, I'd been no farther than the village outside the castle—but it wouldn't be nearly as interesting without Ward by my side. What we might do under a starlit sky...

"I should be getting back," he said, tripping over his words. "Work to be done." He strode away briskly, his back straight and movements stilted.

My hand tingled as it rested against my skirt, missing his warmth already. But even though I was alone, I didn't feel quite so lonely on my throne.

Chapter Two

Ward

I desperately needed to stop having these "little moments" with Ayla. But she would get these looks like she was hanging on every word I said—and the sensation was addicting. I wanted to smooth every worried wrinkle from her brow, hold her hand as she navigated the difficult waters of being queen. But my job wasn't to be her knight in shining armor. It was just to be a knight—her captain.

I replayed our conversation, and the look on her face when she'd asked me to take her across the kingdom. We'd been in something of a fight in the troll kingdom—first, she was mad at me, then I was mad at her—but all seemed to be forgiven now. I hated her for creating these encounters that left me breathless and wishing I could throw decorum out the window. But the weight of my position was a heavy reminder.

"Are you lost?"

I tripped over my feet. How I had already made it back?

Elodia crossed her lanky arms over her chest and cocked her hip to the side. She was tall, brown-skinned with rope braids tied back at the nape of her neck, and she kept me on my toes. Next to her, her best friend Rutley—her opposite with a short, stout frame and pale, ruddy skin—also wore a knowing grin. I glanced behind me to where Ayla was still standing, looking out over the plain.

"What?"

"I asked if you were lost," Elodia said. "Because you certainly looked like it."

"Just thinking," I said, running a hand over my short hair. "Trolls are gone."

"I can see that," Rutley said. "You just gonna leave the queen out there by herself?"

"W—" I licked my lips. "She's within sight of the castle."

"Uh-huh." Elodia sniffed. "You two certainly looked cozy just now. All's forgiven, I suppose?"

"Leave 'em alone, El," Rutley said with a hearty chuckle. "He's gotta get in those moments while the wizard's otherwise occupied, eh?"

I shifted uncomfortably. "Cade's gone. He's left to search for the third stone."

Their heads snapped to me in unison. "He's *gone*?" Rutley said.

"Isn't there still another dangerous wizard out there?" Elodia said. "Why would he leave us unprotected like that?"

"I suppose he thinks we're safe enough without him," I said, a little annoyance falling into my voice. "And perhaps we are. Eoghan hasn't been seen these past six months. We still don't know where Ayla banished him, or what the parameters of the spell she cast are."

"We do know he could travel to the troll kingdom," Elodia said. "That's not too far from Pennlan's border."

That was certainly true. "We would've heard something if he was hiding out in the other kingdoms, I'm sure."

Rutley made a noise but didn't argue.

"So what do we do now?" Elodia asked.

"Riona's picking up where Cade left off, searching for information in the Erlking's library," I said. "And we've got enough to get on with here. Captain Gabhann will be leaving soon, and—"

"Speak of the devil," Rutley said, pointing toward the castle where Captain Gabhann was walking toward us. She was a hard woman, with lines chiseled into her pale, stern face and her gray curls kept in a bun behind her head.

The three of us snapped to salute. "Captain."

"At ease," she said, before turning to me. "Lieutenant. My office."

I nodded my silent goodbye to Elodia and Rutley and followed the captain back. She led me into the barracks in silence, and my heart thudded. Had she seen the look between Ayla and myself? Was she rethinking my taking over of her position? Or was there something else… something worse—

I stopped as soon as I entered her office. The space was empty, the walls void of tapestries and the shelves without the trinkets Gabhann had accumulated over the years. Just behind the desk, a large chest stood open, containing all that had been on the walls, as well as a few pairs of unfolded clothes.

"What's this?" I said.

"The time has come, Ward. I'm leaving for my retirement." She walked to the chest and picked up one of the tunics. "I'll be letting Her Majesty know shortly, but I wanted to tell you first so you could begin moving your things in here."

I swallowed hard. "Are you sure it's wise to leave…right now? The border problem is still a problem, Eoghan's out there—"

"And what's an old soldier to do against a wizard?" she asked.

"As much as a young soldier," I said, stepping forward. "You can't abandon us in our time of need—"

"For all we know, the wizard could be searching for the other two pieces from now until eternity," she said. "Pennlan's safe as long as Her Majesty keeps her piece."

"But Eoghan *has* a piece."

"I wouldn't be leaving if I didn't think Her Majesty was in excellent hands," she said. "Between you and the fae and the wizard—"

"Cade's gone."

"Then you and the fae," she said without missing a beat. She scanned my face and shook her head. "Ward, I'm old. My bones ache. The only thing I'd be good for against the wizard is as fodder and a reason for the queen to mourn—and that's the best case. I've already faced him once and…" She shook her head. "I'm lucky to have lived to tell the tale."

I licked my lips, searching for an excuse, any excuse, to keep her in that chair. "I'm not ready."

"You are more than ready." She closed the chest. "You're more ready than I was when I accepted the job, I'll say that." She chuckled. "But back then, the only thing we had to worry about were border squabbles. Magic and mystery were kept to the books, where they belong." She sat in her chair. "I will give you one piece of parting advice, though. I want you to keep Platt. At least until you have your legs under you."

"Are you *kidding?*"

Platt had been her lieutenant for at least a decade, and there was a reason I'd been chosen to succeed her instead of him. He did just enough to skirt by without attracting attention, and yet my promotion had affected him deeply. He'd already started trouble the moment he'd heard I was taking over for Gabhann, and I was planning to axe him the moment I became captain.

She smirked. "I thought you might say that. I'll give you my reasons, and if you still think he's wasted space, feel free to do what you wish." She steepled her fingers on the table. "When I leave, the guard will shift under the weight of new leadership. Cracks you might not have seen before will appear. There'll be soldiers more allied to Platt than to you."

"Then I'll get rid of them, too."

"And find yourself without anyone to protect Ayla," she said. When I blanched, she held up her hands. "I'm saying… Perhaps give it time to settle, for the rest to see your abilities as the queen and I have. Then, when the time is right, you can reassign him somewhere else."

"You hear how he talks," I said. "Keeping him around wouldn't settle anything."

"Then give him something to do," she said. "I can't count the number of times I sent him on an errand or scouting for soldiers. Remember, *he* was the one who nominated potential soldiers to me." She tilted her head. "Including you, once upon a time."

I sat back, considering her words. Gabhann wouldn't lead me astray; she was as invested in the success of Pennlan as I was. I could see why she'd want Platt to remain around. He did have the ear of some of the soldiers, and it might be a much-needed continuity. *If* I could get him to my side.

"Fine. He stays."

"Good. You're well on your way to becoming a strategic thinker. And that's what Her Majesty needs."

I nodded as I stood. "Thank you for trusting me."

I was halfway out the door when she called my name.

"Her Majesty also needs a captain who knows his place," she said, her gaze steady on me. "Trust and friendship are important. Make sure it doesn't go farther than that."

My heart skipped. "Absolutely."

>→ >→ >→ >→

The next morning, the entire guard gathered on the green to say goodbye to our beloved captain. She wanted no ceremony, no celebration. Nothing except a new traveling cloak to wear over her civilian clothes. Her gray hair was loose down her back—the first time I'd seen it in anything except the tight bun. She seemed a different woman, older than I'd thought. Perhaps even a little frail as she stood next to the carriage Ayla had gifted her.

"Well, I guess I owe you a gold coin," Elodia muttered to Rutley. "I didn't think she'd actually go."

The queen couldn't hide her tears as she hugged the captain. "I can't believe you're really leaving," she said, wiping her cheeks.

"Well, I've already packed, so it would be too much trouble to fill the office again," Gabhann replied, a little misty-eyed herself.

"I don't know what I'm going to do without you," Ayla said.

"You will continue ruling, as you've done," Gabhann said. "And you'll make mistakes. But you're a smart woman, Ayla. And most importantly, you *care* about your subjects. You want what's best for them. I have all the faith in the world that you will be a successful queen."

They embraced again, and Gabhann whispered something into Ayla's ear that made her shift uncomfortably and catch my gaze. I quickly looked ahead, hating that I knew *exactly* what they were talking about. But neither Gabhann nor Ayla needed to worry. There was nothing between us, and there never would be.

Then, without another word, Gabhann climbed onto the carriage and snapped the reins. The carriage rolled forward, and the former captain disappeared under the front gates.

Soft crying reached my ears, and it took everything I had not to comfort Ayla. But she took several calming breaths and wiped her cheeks again.

"Soldiers," she said, her voice still thick with tears. "Please join me in welcoming our new captain: Ward."

At once, every eye was on me, and the back of my neck burned. I straightened my shoulders as she walked up to me, forcing my gaze away from her face so I wouldn't betray any emotion. But when I could no longer avoid it, I was both heartened and sad to see no emotion on hers.

"Congratulations," she said. "I know you'll make us all proud."

"Thank you, Your Majesty."

It's Ayla. The words were on the tip of her tongue, but she knew better than to say it aloud in front of this audience.

"Captain, you may dismiss your soldiers," she said. "I'll see you in the morning for our first meeting."

I waited until she left the green to do so, barking orders to remind the soldiers of the duties of the day as they dispersed. Perhaps a quarter walked away without emotion, another quarter eager for the new chapter. But at least half—the older half—meandered away, talking amongst themselves and casting longing looks toward the east. Those were the ones who'd revolt if I got rid of Platt.

Speaking of...

"End of an era, I suppose," he said, sidling up next to me. "I'm sure gonna miss the old girl, you know?"

"We all are," I said, hoping for a neutral tone.

"I see those monstrous trolls have finally left," he said. "Glad they've found somewhere else to terrorize. Hopefully, we won't see them again."

"We'll need their help if Eoghan returns."

"And when's that gonna be?"

"Hopefully never." I turned to him, debating if I was going to follow Gabhann's advice or not. He exuded apathy, from his wrinkled uniform to the long cut of his hair. "We should plan a trip to scout for new soldiers."

He scoffed. "Sending me away so soon?"

"It's been a few months since Elodia and Rutley came," I said, nodding to them as they watched from a distance. "Probably time to get some more new blood."

"I'm not interested in finding my replacement, thanks." His scowl had deepened, and it had caught the attention of some of the soldiers.

I swallowed, thinking quickly. "What do you want, then?"

The question took him by surprise. "What do you mean?"

"You clearly want something," I said. "What is it? Do you want to be captain? Do you want recognition? Do you want to be fired and sent away?" I paused. "Or are you content to make snide remarks and undercut me for the fun of it?"

He opened and closed his mouth.

"Think about it," I said. "I can be your friend, if you'll let me. You can continue your cushy lieutenant's job, without anyone expecting anything of you. But if you'd rather be more than just the butt of everyone's jokes, I can make that happen." I shrugged. "Your call."

There I left him, hoping my strategy would work and bring him to my side. Because otherwise, I had bigger problems than him talking behind my back.

CHAPTER THREE

RIONA

I kept a wary eye on the horizon, looking for any sign of incoming troll magic. Per Ayla's last letter, Lynton was on his way with the trolls. But that had been hours ago, and they should've arrived by now. I paced the bleak landscape of the wildlands, glancing to the south and feeling like I'd rather be anywhere else.

And it had *nothing* to do with the *aos sí* staring at me from a healthy distance.

That damn cemetery. It had been the site of a legendary bloody battle for the *seod croí*. The first time I'd laid eyes on it, every fiber of my being had told me to turn around and go home. Even sitting at a great distance to the north, it mocked me, promising to release all manner of evil creatures to hunt me after the sun went down.

I shivered, glancing at the sun again and tapping my foot impatiently. The sooner the trolls returned, the sooner I could get back to the Erlking's castle and start looking for information on the final piece of the *seod croí*. Or maybe I'd waited long enough, maybe I could just head back—

I winced as my neck burned. My grandfather, the Erlking, had given me the task of ensuring the trolls were settled. Hadn't just granted it to me, but he'd made it a damn *edict*. Unbreakable by anyone except him.

I rubbed the sore spot, annoyed. It wasn't my fault the trolls were taking their time. There were other things to worry about. Bigger problems in the world. The trolls were lucky my sister was such a nice person.

Lucky isn't the word I'd use.

More like…innocent victims. Their king had kidnapped them to hide in a mountain for the past thousand years, and they'd just woken up from the spell to find a completely different world.

But they were taking too long. Perhaps time to investigate.

With a grunt, I pulled my magic and dissipated into butterflies. The world grew smaller under my fractured sight, seen through the lens of the swirling mass of magical insects. I traveled west until I found the never-ending patch of trees that comprised the forest realm. It was very far out of the way, adding at least an hour to my journey, but it was worth it.

In time, the forest realm ended in favor of the *daoine maithe* lands, long stretches of green fields and dots of villages here and there. I was close to the Erlking's castle, but even without a corporeal neck to itch, the reminder of my job was there. So I pressed southward.

My hackles raised when I came to the Pennlan border. The gates were wide open, but there was a group sitting just on this side of it. A streak of white-blond hair told me that my damned uncle was in their midst.

I guess I had my answer as to what had delayed the trolls.

Lynton was gesturing wildly to Aldrick, with a couple of trolls behind him. The others, I supposed, were still waiting in the rock until told otherwise by their king. Hovering above, I caught wisps of their conversation, and it was as I'd expected.

"…given permission by the Erlking himself…"

"As border guardian, I'm overruling him."

"You can't overrule the Erlking!"

I landed and rematerialized next to Lynton, who apparently hadn't noticed me coming as he jumped back in surprise. Aldrick, however, seemed not only to be expecting me but was…amused by my presence. I would've rather seen any other emotion.

"Your champion has arrived," Aldrick said, lifting his hand. "I suppose you're going to protect these poor, innocent creatures, Riona?"

I took a step forward. "The Erlking gave them permission."

"Not with all this filth. We have enough mouths to feed."

"They're going to the wildlands," I said. "They aren't even going to be in this realm. Now, let them pass."

He narrowed his gaze. "Your status as the second-most disgusting creature in this realm has made you cocky. It would be a shame if I had to put you back in your place."

Lynton shifted, but I shook my head to keep him quiet. "And it would be a *shame* if we had a repeat of our last sparring session," I said.

His nostrils flared but only for a moment. "A fluke."

"Care to test it?"

I held my breath, hoping he'd say no. I'd been nearly on death's door when something had come out of me, something I'd thought was the result of a mad wizard in my brain. But instead, it was some strange *second* magic that lived deep in my bones, different than my butterflies. How, exactly, I called upon it, I hadn't a clue. The only thing I knew was that being around my sister and pieces of the *seod croí* made it come out —or being on the verge of death.

And since I didn't have my sister, nor a piece of the *seod croí*, that left letting Aldrick beat me up until I managed to fall too close to the land of the dead again.

Thankfully, Aldrick seemed to remember he had an audience. "Get these vermin off my land. If they set a foot outside the woodlands, I will obliterate every single one of them the way they should've been. Is that understood?"

⤜⤜⤜⤜

Fearful for their safety, I followed the trolls from above, but I needn't have worried. Aldrick and his band of lackeys went the other direction and the trolls were a few hundred little bright lights zipping through the rock. As we came closer to the *aos sí*, I thought about zigzagging to the forest realm the way I'd done before. The trolls just continued as if they didn't have a care in the world.

I held my non-corporeal breath and followed, keeping my gaze on the northern horizon and not looking down at the darkening cemetery below. Hopefully, moving through the ground wouldn't wake anything up.

Relief shimmered through me as we passed the border between the wildlands and the *aos sí* and it seemed all trolls arrived intact. They popped out of the ground like mushrooms, craning their necks to take in the sight of their former homeland. I landed near Lynton, reforming and keeping my back toward the *aos sí*.

He tapped his foot on the ground and every head turned to him.

"First things first," he said. "We will construct our homes. Be mindful of our numbers and don't be selfish. Take only the space you need."

"When has that ever worked?" I muttered.

But before my eyes, small houses formed out of the rock. The trolls spoke with one another, discussing where to put roads and shops. Others negotiated more space for farmland and smaller gardens. In a matter of minutes, the empty wasteland became a thriving little village, complete with chimneys with twirling smoke.

"Well, that's…impressive," I said with a small sigh.

"It's nothing like it used to be," Lynton said, walking through the newly formed main street. "So much has been lost. Needlessly, I might add." The venom for his cousin was palpable.

"We should've saved more books from the castle before the mountain fell," I said sadly. There'd been quite the library.

"We could still salvage them," he said, a little dreamily. "But now's the time for moving forward. There was nothing in those books that we need to build our new way forward."

I shrugged. "Seemed to be a bunch about gardening and soil management. Which I found a bit…odd, considering."

"Considering what?"

"You're trolls," I said. "You should just know how to use the magic, right?"

He chuckled. "Are you not taught the basics of how to wield the aether?"

I rubbed the back of my neck. "I mean…kind of. Not really. I'm sort of self-taught."

"The granddaughter of the Erlking—"

"The *half-fae* granddaughter of the Erlking, who nobody *really* knew was his granddaughter until about six months ago," I said. "So it's not as if I got a lot of special treatment."

He gave me a once-over. "Your uncle made that obvious."

"He's not going to be a problem," I replied, trying to keep the worry off my face. The Erlking had made an edict—those were supposed to be binding. Aldrick shouldn't have been able to stop them from crossing the border the way he had. As soon as I got back to the Erlking's castle, I would let him know.

"We're grateful to you for your assistance," Lynton said. "Even if you are the *half-fae* granddaughter of the Erlking. You and your sister have shown us immeasurable kindness in our hour of need." A troll girl no older than me materialized in front of him, and an unrecognizable, warm smile grew on his face.

"Da, the house is ready," she said quietly. "It's not exactly the same as it was, but—"

"I'm sure it's perfect," he said, sounding nothing like himself. He turned to me and bowed. "If you'll excuse me, Princess. I've got to spend some much-needed time with my daughter."

"Of course." I waved him off. He was one of the lucky ones. Most everyone else was completely alone.

But before he could get far, another female troll appeared, looking worried. They spoke in hushed tones before Lynton turned to me for a moment then shook his head.

"We can't ask for more," he said. "Not after what happened at the border. Do your best, Fiadh."

"We can try," she said. "But it's... Lynton, we can't make something from nothing. We need food."

"Wait, what's going on?" I asked, stepping forward to join them. "You need food? Can't you...grow it in the soil?"

"Of course, but the growing season has passed," Fiadh said. "Too little sun and not enough warmth to grow anything."

"Maybe I can help," I said. "I don't know how, but..."

"What about the wizard?" Fiadh asked.

"The wizard is gone," Lynton said, his translucent skin actually getting some color. "And we can't ask anything more of the greater fae. They've already given us more than we deserve and—"

An idea popped into my head. "Why not ask Ayla?"

He stopped. "What do you mean?"

"At the southern border with Konevell, there's a big backlog of stuff—I think it's mostly goods, but probably some food and wine. I know Ayla wanted to negotiate with Edric..." That was before he'd tried to take all my blood and kill me. On second thought, he might not have been serious about any sort of trade negotiation. All they'd wanted was to get me under the mountain, and Ayla was just...

"If the queen of Pennlan is willing to sell to us," Lynton said, a little quietly, "we will surely buy it. But for a fair price."

"I mean..." I laughed nervously. "You guys can make gems and diamonds and stuff, right?"

He nodded.

"Just make a couple of those, and I'm sure that'll suffice," I said, before realizing I'd probably spoken too hastily. Ayla had already been furious at me for all manner of things in the troll realm. Might have to make sure I wasn't overstepping. "Let me write her a letter and see what we can do."

"A letter will take weeks," Lynton said with a small growl. "We need food—"

"We have something of a quicker path to each other." As long as she didn't mind me using Cade's letter box. "She should get back to me quickly."

"Your uncle," Lynton said, "he threatened—"

"Leave him to me," I said. "I'll make sure he doesn't mess with your goods."

He nodded. "Once again, Riona of the Fae Realm and Pennlan, we are in your debt."

Chapter Four

Cade

"Fish for sale!"

"Nets! Weights!"

"Fresh from the sea! Just pulled up yesterday!"

I wove through the marketplace, my staff clacking against the ground as I used a little magic to keep from accidentally tripping or hitting anyone in the crowded market. The stench of seafood and people was exacerbated by the hot sun overhead, much hotter than it had any right to be this late in the year. But perhaps I was just spoiled by the seasons in Pennlan. This far south in Driwania, I doubted they had as much as a cold breeze in the winter months.

I finally made it away from the throng of people and onto the docks. I squared my shoulders as I walked up to the first ship.

"Good morning," I said.

The sailor looked at me and snorted. "We already paid our dock tax."

"No, I'm not here for that," I said. "I'm on the hunt for a ship to take me somewhere south—if they've seen what I'm looking for."

I pulled a drawing from my pocket—one I'd magically sketched based on my memory of what the *fuath* looked like. Though I could've just said, "Have you seen a fae creature with a fish for a head in your travels?" and the message would've been the same.

"Er...nope. Can't say I've seen one of those before," he said, scratching his head. "You might want to go north to the fae realm. I hear they have all kinds of weird creatures up there."

I sighed and folded the paper. "Appreciate your help. Thanks."

Although I could conjure a portal and go anywhere, in order to do that, I had to have a clue where to go. Creating a portal over land was easy. I'd venture into the recesses of my mind, casting a magical view over the world and using landmarks, roads, rivers to guide me to my destination. But the ocean was vast, and once I lost sight of the coast, I couldn't tell where I was, how far I'd been traveling—any of it. I'd ended up on the floor of my small room more times than I could count, dizzy and exhausted from the effort.

After a few days of failed portal attempts, I stalked the docks, asking sailors whether they'd heard of the *fuath*—the water fae who'd supposedly stolen a piece of the *seod croí*. My hope was if I found someone who'd seen them, they might be able to take me to them.

Edric had mentioned the *fuath* had gone south, perhaps—but his guess was as good as anyone's. It had been a thousand years, after all.

Still, there was another, more personal reason for my presence in this southern port. Before he'd betrayed us, my former master Eoghan said he'd found me somewhere in the southern islands. It must've been pretty remote, because as many different types of people as I'd seen come and go from these docks, I'd never seen anyone with my shade of reddish-brown skin, silky black hair, and sharp cheekbones. The longer I lingered here, the more I was beginning to suspect Eoghan had found me in some other land and lied. It wouldn't have been the first time.

Still, the primary goal was to find information about the *seod croí*, and the fish-headed creatures that might've taken it. But after two weeks, I was starting to doubt the brilliance of my plan. There was a constant influx of new sailors from all corners of the known world, and none of them had seen what I was looking for.

It was starting to feel like a hopeless effort. It might've been smarter to return to Pennlan and…

"I love you. But as a friend. As my brother. Not as…"

My skin itched, and I gripped my staff as a wave of anger and hurt washed over me. No, I wouldn't return to Pennlan. I'd just keep looking elsewhere. Maybe forever.

Today, though, my motivation was gone, so I resolved to have a rest and continue my questioning later in the day. But as I walked back toward the city, I spotted a ship I hadn't noticed on my way in, and a large sailor who looked like he'd been through a passage or two.

"Good morning," I said. "Where are you coming from?"

"Is this an interrogation?"

"N-no." I frowned.

"Are you from the king?"

"No," I said. "Just asking—"

"Then buzz off."

He almost knocked me off the dock as he prowled away, chewing a stick between his teeth. No one else on the ship seemed eager to talk, either. In fact, they all seemed keen to avoid looking at me. Odd. Most of the sailors I met had been friendly.

I was almost ready to move on to the next ship when a figure emerged from the captain's quarters, and my heart stopped.

She was a few years older than me, perhaps, her black, silky hair braided in a single plait down her back. Her reddish-brown skin was complemented by the shade of green on her tunic, and her boots stretched up to her knees. She paid me no attention as she directed her sailors to remove this crate and that crate, and to expect so-and-so to come to pay for the goods.

When she turned around, I was staring at her. "Hi! I'm Cade. Who are y—"

She gave me a once-over then jumped off the ship and briskly walked away.

"Wait!" I called, rushing after her. But she disappeared in the crowd before I could stop her. And when I spun around, all her crew members were gone, as if they'd evaporated into the morning air.

>→ >→ >→ >→

I waited hours for the crew— or at least their mystery captain—to come back. I used magic to try to find her, but there were too many people in this port city. It was as if she'd vanished.

The sun was starting to set, but I didn't move. She would have to come back eventually. Surely, she wouldn't just abandon her ship. While I waited, my heart pounded with questions.

Was she from the same place as me?

Did she know how to get back there?

Would she have the answers I was seeking?

Questions about the *seod croí* took a distant second in my mind, though I hadn't lost them completely. But I couldn't let this opportunity go to waste.

Finally, after the sun was gone, she reappeared, though she seemed to be sneaking around, hiding between boxes and nets as she approached her ship. She hopped on and adjusted the rigging as if getting ready to set sail.

"Let's try this again," I muttered. I created a portal from where I stood on the dock to the deck and stepped through.

She cried out, and to my absolute joy, she used a word that I *recognized*. A curse that had been on my tongue since before Eoghan took me. I could've cried. Or kissed her.

"Where are you from?" I babbled. "What's your name—"

"Clearly, the same place you're from," she said, annoyance piercing her voice. "And I'm not in any hurry to go *back* there, so how about you just go on your way and forget you saw me." She tossed a bag of gold toward me. "Whatever bounty the queen put on my head—"

"I don't know what you're talking about," I said, pushing the gold back. "I'm just...I'm looking for something, and I found you, and I don't know..." How should I phrase this? "I haven't been there since I was a boy. I don't even know what home is. I just wanted to talk with you about it."

She watched me, as if she were able to see into my soul. *Does she have magic as well?* "You're just a lost kid, huh?"

"How lost?" I asked. "Could you tell me how to find it?"

"You won't get there unless they want you there," she said. "It's a path not known by many."

Sounds familiar. The trolls had done the same. "In this land, are there…things known as *fuath*? Fae creatures with fish heads?"

"No idea what you're talking about."

But there was something…something about the way she denied it. Hope rose within me like a beacon. Could my home be where the third piece of the *seod croí* was hiding? Had Eoghan been so close to a piece he could've taken for himself but took me instead?

The thought was at once exhilarating and terrifying.

"Take me there," I said, grabbing her hand. "Please."

"I'm sorry, did you not hear me say there's a *bounty* on my head?" she asked, ripping her hand out of mine. "And it's not just a slap on the wrist either. My life is over if I set foot on that island again."

"The whole world might come to an end if you don't," I said.

She snorted then threw her head back and laughed. "You certainly have a lot of drama for an orphan *re'nal'sef*"

"*Re'nal'sef?*" The word was foreign, and yet… "Is that what we're called?"

She sighed as she crossed her arms over her chest. "You really don't know anything, do you?"

"I'm grateful for anything you can tell me," I said, taking a hesitant step forward.

"*Re'nal'sef* is our word for…" She hesitated. "People who live here. On the main continent. Or really anywhere that isn't H'sipotu. *That* is the name of our island. And our people are called *e'potu*."

E'potu. I turned away from her so I could savor this moment. Finally, I knew where I'd come from. Even having the name felt like a huge step forward.

"Look, kid." She rubbed the back of her neck. "If you want to get to H'sipotu, you're going to have to get far away from this city—from the *re'nal'sef.* You won't find a soul who even knows they exist, let alone how to get to the island. And you aren't going to make it there unless you know the way." She shrugged. "And you'll be hard pressed to find someone who does."

"You," I said.

"I already told you, I'm not going *near* that place. I love my life too much," she said with a wry smile. "Now are you going to leave me alone, or do I have to get my muscle involved?"

Behind her, the crew moved menacingly. Against my magic, they'd find themselves defeated without much of a fight. Still, it was better to keep things friendly than resort to violence so early.

"Maybe I can help you," I said.

"I doubt it."

"I'm a wizard."

Her eyes widened. "You're a…what?"

"A wizard," I said, nodding to my staff, which had started to glow. I dimmed it before anyone else on the dock noticed. "I'm not sure if those are common in H'sipotu, but—"

"They're not." She watched my staff with a wary eye.

I held my breath. "Maybe…maybe you know who I was, then? I was just a boy when I was taken—"

"No." She rose. "No, I don't. And I don't know how you ended up so far away from home. I hope you get back there soon, but I'm not the one to take you. Good night." She walked away.

"Wait!" I called, scrambling to follow her. "I can be useful. I can triple whatever you're selling so you can make more. Calm the seas—"

"I don't need a wizard's help," she said. "I get by just fine on my own."

"Please." I took a step toward her. "Please, I'm desperate—"

"Find someone else. And leave me alone."

She turned and walked up the stairs to the deck, and her crew advanced, albeit a little less confidently. I was still hoping to avoid violence or threats, so I lifted my hands in surrender and walked off the ship.

But I didn't go far. Once I was out of sight, I doubled back and hid amongst the crates to watch them. The captain barked orders to get the ship ready as quickly as they could move, and they obliged without complaint, perhaps sensing her worry. Why she was so afraid of me, I hadn't a clue. But she didn't have a reason to be, and perhaps if I just had more *time* with her, she might see that.

I glanced north, indecision creeping up my spine. This seemed to be…a detour. I was supposed to be looking for the third piece of the *seod croí*. To find it before Eoghan and take it for safekeeping. Going on a seafaring adventure with this mysterious sea captain and her grumpy crew wasn't in line with that.

And yet…she'd reacted when I'd mentioned the *fuath*. It could've been a trick of the light, or maybe even wishful thinking, but my gut said there was something there. More than anything else I'd seen.

Besides that, a petty voice murmured, *Ward can search for the third piece. He and Ayla can go together and have a grand time.*

It was immature, but my heart was too broken to chide myself for thinking such things. And the chance to know who I *really* was? I had to jump at it. Ayla…Ayla would want me to.

Without another thought, I opened a portal and stepped through, finding myself in the bottom of the ship. Then I cast a spell to hide myself amongst the crates and sat down, readying myself for another adventure.

CHAPTER FIVE

AYLA

Ayla,

After some trouble, Lynton has returned with all the trolls, safe and sound. But we have a new problem. They aren't able to work the land to grow food until next spring, and they have very little. I think I remember you saying something about having a surplus at the southern border. Would it be possible for the trolls to have some? I'm sure they could figure a way to take it off your hands.

Sincerely,

Riona

Riona's timing couldn't have been better. Shortly after Gabhann's departure, I'd received a message that three of the most powerful merchants in the coastal city of Orapus were on their way to me to have another chat. We'd last met before I'd left for the troll realm, and I'd promised to work through the border issue for them. Three weeks later, I had very little to show for my efforts, except to say I'd written a letter to Queen Ramira that, so far, had not been answered.

"Well, I did tell you not to go."

"Shh." I waved Ward off, though he wore a little mischievous smirk. He'd been in my office for our daily meeting when both messages had arrived. "I thought you weren't going to say I told you so anymore?"

"Just a few more times," he said, looking at Riona's letter. "But this looks win-win, doesn't it? The trolls need food. Orapus needs to offload some stuff."

"Not exactly." I watched the window, expecting the merchants to arrive at any moment. "At our last meeting, I'd told them I was working with the Erlking, and the response wasn't…great."

"Why?"

For the same reason I was horrible to Riona.

They, like most everyone in this kingdom, had been fed a steady diet of fear and prejudice from Eoghan about the fae and all magical creatures that dwelled up north. Though, technically, the trolls were a different race, and they'd lived a thousand years under a mountain, I was sure the merchants wouldn't notice the distinction.

"They could go for it, I suppose," I said, after a moment. "But it's just a temporary fix. We need to normalize relations with Konevell again."

"They're the ones who wanted you to marry a kid, right?" Ward asked.

"That's putting it lightly, but yes." I chewed my fingernails, though there wasn't much left of them now. "They said they'd remove all the restrictions if I did, but I wasn't about to be bullied into a marriage." Though perhaps I should've given it more thought, considering…

The door opened, Bronwen poked her head in with a half-smile then disappeared again.

"I suppose it's time," I said.

"It might not be as bad as you think."

>→ >→ >→ >→

The onslaught began before they even sat down. The merchants had arrived in separate carriages, but their grievances were so similar, they might as well have spent the entire ride grousing with one another. Cormac was the loudest, barking that he'd had to throw an entire warehouse of crates in the river because the produce had gone bad, and asking me if the crown would be reimbursing him for my failures. Then Pádraig chimed in, arguing that he'd run out of room to store *his* wares, and that he was getting charged an arm and a leg to rent whole boats that were sitting unused in the bay next to Orapus. Finally, Róisín, the sole woman of the group, joined in, telling me that half her sailors had quit because they hadn't been paid in months.

I let them yell at me, casting silencing looks to Ward, who seemed eager to jump in. But they needed to get their anger out before we could have a conversation.

When Cormac stopped long enough to take a breath, I held up my hands.

"May I speak?" I asked.

"It's your office," Róisín said with a sneer. "Or have you forgotten that in your *journeys*?"

"I understand you're angry," I began. "And that you think my trip to the troll kingdom wasn't in your best interests. But there was a reason for it—"

Pádraig sneered. "It had better be a *damn* good reason."

I explained briefly that Lynton had come with a request to discuss the stones, and how important it was that we get the pieces of the *seod croí* before Eoghan did. As I told the story, Ward looked more and more uncomfortable, and it wasn't until I was nearing the end that I remembered why.

"And did you accomplish what you set out to do?" Pádraig asked. "Get an alliance between your kingdoms?"

"Not exactly." Nerves skittered down my spine. "Turns out their king had given Eoghan their stone months ago in exchange for—"

The rest of my words were drowned out by a new onslaught of angry yelling. I sat back in my chair, staring at the space just beyond my stack of letters and waiting for the storm to pass, until a new voice rang out.

"Will you three *shut up* long enough for her to tell you the good news?" Ward snapped, having gotten to his feet. "In case you forgot, she's your queen. Show her some damn respect."

"Ward," I said, but it was too late.

"And who the hell are you?" Cormac asked. "The queen's new courtesan?"

He sputtered. "I'm the captain of her guard."

"Then you have no business here," Pádraig snapped, turning back around to me. "Our audience is with the queen and nobody else."

"Precisely," Róisín barked, turning back to me. "Ayla, you've shown a complete disregard for your position here. We're losing thousands of pounds of food every single day, and you think it's time to go on an adventure."

"I didn't *go on an adventure*," I said, though the argument hit a little too close to home. "I was invited to meet with the troll king to discuss an alliance with our stones—"

"Frankly, girl, we're tired of hearing about this little gem," Pádraig said. "You have real issues to deal with in the here and now. Your people are suffering because you've been otherwise occupied. But it's time you put aside those silly concerns and focus on what you need to do."

"And what is that?" I asked.

"You declined a *very* generous proposal from Lord Galliford…"

I couldn't help my snort of derision. Generous wasn't the word I would've used. "It wasn't a serious proposal. I'm not in the business of marrying children."

Róisín tutted. "You're still a child yourself. I hardly see the problem."

"The problem is that I'm not going to be bullied by the Queen of Konevell or her envoy or anyone else," I snapped. "It's clear to me all they want is access to the Pennlan stone."

"They wouldn't have been so brazen if that's all they were after," Róisín replied. "The border is closed."

"What?" I blinked. "Closed?"

"We haven't been able to offload a ship or even enter the country in over a week," he continued.

"And my ships have encountered a blockade to the south," Róisín said. "Cutting us off from the other nation as well."

"Not even your own seal passes muster." Cormac pulled an envelope from his pocket and flung it on my desk. Queen Ramira's name in my handwriting looked back at me—and my heart sank as I ran my finger across the unopened wax on the back.

"Well?" Pádraig said. "What are you going to do about it?"

I turned the letter over in my hand a few times, waiting for a brilliant answer to come to me of what to say.

"I don't know," I said before my brain could catch up with me. "What do you want me to do?"

The yelling began anew, their insults melding together and paling in comparison to the guilt already hanging around my shoulders. Ward got in on the action, keen on defending my honor. The soldiers down below could surely hear the yelling through the cracked window.

But all I could do was turn the letter in my hand, worry threatening to consume me. How in the world was I supposed to negotiate a border opening if I couldn't even speak to the other side? And more importantly, how did an official royal seal not have enough weight to bypass whatever restrictions Konevell had in place?

I barely noticed when Bronwen arrived with an announcement that pre-dinner wine was waiting in the library downstairs. The three merchants, still red-faced and breathing hard, left me alone at that point. But Ward stayed, watching me with his fists balled.

"I shouldn't have let them talk to you like that," he said, watching the hallway as if the merchants would come back for another round.

"I deserved some of it. They're right. I have been distracted." I sat back in my chair and took a few deep breaths to keep emotion from welling in my eyes. The last thing the merchants needed to see was my tears. Ward, though… He'd seen them more times than I could count.

"Honestly, Eoghan's plot to destroy the continent seems a *bit* more pressing than them losing some money." He sniffed, craning his neck. "You didn't even get a chance to tell them about the trolls wanting to buy their goods."

"I will," I said. "When they're good and drunk."

He looked at me. "Are you okay?"

"Of course." I offered a half-hearted shrug. "It's good to be the queen."

"Ayla."

The sound of my name on his lips was a small balm to the rawness I felt. "They don't scare me. Not like…not like the news that the border's closed. That's… It's…" I swallowed as I handed him my unopened letter. "She's not even letting my own correspondence past."

He rose and gently took the envelope from me, staring at it as if it were a challenge he needed to solve. "I can take it for you."

"What do you mean?"

"I'll go to Orapus, help the trolls get the goods. Once that's done…" He turned the envelope over in his hand. "I'll sneak across the border and hand-deliver this note to Queen Ramira." His deep brown eyes met mine, ensnaring me. "What do you think?"

Hope mixed with sadness in my chest. "It sounds like a worthwhile and dangerous quest."

"Most quests are." He stood. "I should get down to the barracks and start preparing to leave. Unless…" He hesitated. "You'd rather I stay and protect you from the merchants?"

I wanted him to stay. But after what Gabhann had said to me, it was perhaps better if he started on his journey.

Remember your place. You don't have the luxury of giving your heart to just anyone.

The words had snapped me from the daydream I'd been in since Ward had held my hand on the field. I was becoming attached to him again. We needed some space between us, even if my heart wanted otherwise.

"I can handle them." I lifted the stone from my chest. "I've got this, remember?"

"I thought you were still working out how to use it?" he asked.

I chuckled darkly, turning it over in my hand. That was certainly true. In the troll realm, we'd nearly been crushed to death under a mountain. Ward's leg had been pinned, and I'd tried with *everything* in my body to get the dull gem to light up. But it hadn't sparked to life until Riona had touched it with her magic. And when she'd left for the fae realm, it had fallen back into its usual dull blue.

"Be careful," I said softly. "I don't know what you'll find when you cross the border."

"Can't be any worse than the fae realm," he said. "Are you sure you don't want me to join you for dinner?"

"No." I smiled. "You go."

>�;>⇥ >⇥ >⇥

It took nearly four bottles of wine, but the merchants agreed—in principle—to the sale of their goods to the trolls. They had questions, as none of them had seen a troll or understood what their magic was capable of. And they wanted assurances that the so-called "magical gold" was the same. But at least we had something.

I sent word down to the barracks via Bronwen, as I couldn't bring myself to see Ward myself. He would most likely leave first thing in the morning, eager to get a head start on smoothing things over in Orapus before embarking on his quest. It might take him weeks to make it there and back.

And perhaps when he finally returned, he'd be erased from my mind.

Chapter Six

Ward

"You can't be serious, boss."

Elodia and Rutley watched me incredulously as I stuffed my meager things into my traveling pack. I'd left Ayla's office and immediately set to preparing. I wasn't sure how long the trolls would take to get from the wildlands to Orapus, but considering they could travel through rock and stone, it wouldn't be long, so I'd summoned the duo to my office to tell them the plan.

"I'm serious," I said. "I'm headed to Orapus, and once the trolls are situated with the goods they need, I'm going to sneak across the border to Konevell and hand-deliver this letter for Ayla." I turned to look at them. "What's the problem?"

"Several things," Elodia said. "Starting with the fact that *the captain of the royal guard shouldn't be sneaking anywhere.*"

"Why not?"

She threw her hands in the air. "Because you're needed here. In this castle. Overseeing your soldiers. Not halfway across the continent playing the hero."

I looked at Rutley, who always seemed to have my back, but he grimaced. "She has a point, boss. Things are a bit...tricky since Gabhann left. Hearing a lot of complaints about you—especially from Platt. Might be smarter to stick around."

"Send us instead," Elodia said, putting her hand to her chest. "We can handle the transfer of goods to Orapus then figure a way across.

Nobody will care if we're gone for a month."

But I stared at Rutley, remembering what Gabhann had said about Platt and sparking an idea. "No. I'm going. And I'm taking Platt with me."

I thought Elodia's eyes were going to fall out of her head and Rutley just stared at me, slack-jawed. "Come again?" he said.

"I think you've lost it," Elodia muttered.

"Hear me out," I said. "Gabhann told me I needed to get Platt on my side, and the best way to do that was through a mindless, but important task. I can bring him to Orapus, get him set up with the trolls, *then* sneak across without him noticing—"

"Are you listening to a word I'm saying?" Elodia said. "You *can't* sneak across the border. What if you're captured? Caught?"

I scoffed. "This isn't my first closed border, El."

She looked at Rutley and shook her head, as if she had nothing more to say. He took a step forward. "Why is it so important that *you* deliver this message?"

"Because..." I reached into my pocket and felt the envelope, recalling the hope on Ayla's face as I told her I'd take it. "Because I doubt Ramira would see a regular soldier," I said, scrambling for an excuse that wasn't the truth. "If I go, I'll be able to speak for Ayla in an official capacity."

"Right. And this has nothing to do with you two making ga-ga eyes at each other?" Elodia asked.

"No." But I couldn't look at her as I said it. "Look, I don't intend to be gone long. It's two days to Orapus if we keep a good pace. Then a day or so to get things set. From there, it's four days to the capital of Konevell—"

"Assuming you can even get across the border," Rutley said.

"Meet with the queen," I said, ignoring him. "Then come straight back. Two weeks—tops."

"Unless you're captured and killed," Elodia said. "That's always a possibility."

Again, I ignored the barb. "I trust the two of you will handle things while I'm gone. Hopefully, with Platt gone, things might settle a bit."

"Or get much worse in your absence." Elodia shook her head. "Fine. You want to go on a suicide mission? Great. But *don't* bring Platt. He'll probably knife you in your sleep on the first night."

"Then I won't sleep." I brightened. "Look, maybe it'll be a chance for the two of us to bond. Get to know each other. And maybe when he comes back, he'll be more willing to cooperate."

From the look on their faces, I was the only one who thought that was even a remote possibility.

>→ >→ >→ >→

Obviously, my preference for a partner to Orapus would've been Elodia or Rutley. But Captain Gabhann's advice about Platt was hard to ignore. And sitting in a town and making sure things got from one place to another was mindless enough that not even Platt could screw it up. I didn't actually think we'd emerge friends, but maybe he'd have a smidgeon more respect for me.

I found my would-be partner in the dining hall, surrounded by a cadre of adoring soldiers. He was sitting atop the long table, regaling the crowd with a profane story about a whore in the village nearby. Although alcohol wasn't permitted within the barracks, he was making no attempt to hide the flask in his hand. Others, too, had followed suit and, based on the volume of the laughter, they'd all come from the pub.

Platt stopped his story when he noticed me then took a long sip from his flask. "Evening, cap'n. Is there a problem?"

It took everything in me to keep from knocking the flask from his hand. "I need to speak with you. Now."

A chorus of "oohs" came up from the crowd as Platt stood slowly. "Well, friends, looks like my time is over here. It's been fun—"

"You're not getting fired, you idiot," I snapped. "I have a job for you."

"Reassignment then." Again, he turned to the crowd. "As I said, it's been—"

"A *temporary* task," I snarled through gritted teeth. "I don't want to tell everyone what it is, so can you *please* come with me so I can tell you about it?"

"I'm bu—"

"*Now.*"

I all but dragged him away from his adoring fans, now second-guessing my decision to leave *at all*. Gabhann had been right; there were certainly cracks in the guard that I hadn't noticed before.

"Ow, quit pulling, will you?" Platt shoved me off, adjusting his tunic. "What's so important that—"

"Pack your bags," I snapped. "We're going to Orapus in the morning."

He did a double-take. "We? What do you mean we?"

"I'm coming with you," I said.

He sighed dramatically, as if he were still in front of his crowd. "I don't need a babysitter, you know. I'm quite capable of—"

"I'm sure you could handle it, what with your drinking and stories about your local whores," I said with a scowl. "But this is important to the queen. I need to be there to facilitate the initial conversation. After which," I gestured to him, "it's all you."

He eyed me. "The queen, hm? And with whom are we facilitating this conversation?"

"The trolls." When he showed a little fear, I felt somewhat victorious. "Oh, don't be like that. They're lovely people."

"Didn't they try to kill you last week?"

"Only their king, and he's dead." I waved him off. "Be ready at sunup. We've got to move quickly."

>→ >→ >→ >→

"Was it really necessary to leave so early?"

I chewed my tongue instead of responding. Our definitions of sunup were different, it seemed, because the sun was quite high in the sky by the time Platt appeared in the stables with a large satchel. He wore his official uniform, which I was sure to hear about later when he complained about the heat.

"I mean, it's *so* early," he continued, sighing heavily in his saddle.

"If we make good time, we can rest," I said, turning back to the castle growing smaller behind us. My gaze landed on the tallest tower, on the window of Ayla's office. "But we're running late, so hurry up."

He sighed again. "You know, when *I* traveled the kingdom for Captain Gabhann, I used to set my own schedule. It wasn't a breakneck pace to get to the next town. Slow and leisurely, that way I was in the best mental condition to assess candidates such as…well, yourself."

"And aren't you so glad you picked me?" I replied, not catching his gaze. "Otherwise, Eoghan might've been successful."

I smirked as he clammed up.

But the peace didn't last long. We were taking a well-traveled road, which meant far more small villages and cities along the way. At each one, Platt made the same noise—perhaps expecting me to announce that we would be stopping. And when I didn't, he would sigh loudly and sadly.

"Look at those folks, doing the smart thing and taking a break from the unrelenting sun," Platt said, nodding to a trio of travelers peeling off the main road toward a small town situated next to a lake. "Might be nice to get something to wet my tongue."

"You didn't bring your flask?" I asked, retrieving my own water skien and taking a sip. "Maybe if you were less fond of it last night, you might not feel so poorly today."

I waited for him to respond, but he didn't. I sighed, cursing my luck once more. Between Cade, Ayla, and now Platt, why did it seem I was always stuck traveling with naive idiots?

"I noticed you aren't wearing your new uniform," he said. "Did you have to send it off to get tailored?"

"I find it good practice not to draw attention to myself when I'm out on the road," I said. "When we stop to rest the horses, I suggest you lose the uniform."

"Well, *Captain*, I'd love to, but you see, as a soldier traveling through my own country, I assumed we wouldn't need to be incognito, so all I have are uniforms."

I shifted in the saddle. "How long's it been since you've left Pennlan castle?"

"Oh, you know, I get out on occasion. Not much excitement, though, these past couple months. Just been sitting around, being... well...overlooked for certain tasks."

"Then aren't you so pleased I hand-selected you for this one?"

I couldn't see his face, but I could hear his snort of derision. Platt would have to work harder if he wanted to get under my skin.

"I find it odd that you did, as you say, *hand-select* me for this task," he said. "Wouldn't you have been better served by your lackeys?"

The company would've been preferable.

"You're my second-in-command, and this is an incredibly important task from the queen." I paused. "Besides that, I thought it might be a chance for us to get to know one another. Since we'll be working closely together for the foreseeable future."

I waited for the argument, for him to proudly state that he would be seeking employment elsewhere, but instead all I got was an, "I see."

We continued in silence, keeping the horses at a quick, but steady pace. Out of the corner of my eye, I could see Platt wince with every bob and jostle. He hadn't spent much time in the saddle, it seemed.

As the sun set, a village appeared over the crest of a hill. Platt started to turn his horse toward it, but I cleared my throat.

"We have to keep moving," I said. "As we got a late start."

"And if I fall off my horse from exhaustion, I'll be of no use to anyone."

"Then don't fall off."

I snapped the reins and kicked my horse into motion, making a point to gallop by the village. A part of me didn't care if Platt was behind me, and I was a little disappointed when I checked and he was. It would've been a great opportunity to fire him if he'd gone to the village instead.

The moon was full and cast a bright glow across the road. I'd studied the map of the road well—not that there were many roads from Pennlan castle to the border town—but at the third horribly sad sigh from Platt, I decided to throw him a bone.

"We can rest here," I said, leading my horse toward a nearby tree. "I'll take the first watch."

"Watch for what?"

I sighed, glancing at the stars overhead. "For anyone who wants to take our things. You do know there are thieves out here, right?"

"The Pennlan captain should do something about that."

I didn't respond, yanking my bag and saddle off my horse and brushing her sweaty coat as I counted to ten.

"What do we have to eat?"

"Whatever you brought," I said.

"I thought we would be staying in villages," he said. "That's what civilized people do."

I reached into my bag and tossed him a piece of dried meat. "Get some rest. We'll be moving on soon."

CHAPTER SEVEN

RIONA

Ayla's letter was met with much relief. Lynton, of course, was grateful his people would have food, and I was relieved I hadn't done anything to muck up our newly repaired sisterly relationship.

As quickly as they could assemble, Fiadh and ten other trolls headed south once more, with me trailing overhead. Yet again, we had to cross over the *aos sí* and yet again, the ghosts remained quiet. Better yet, Aldrick didn't bother us as we crossed over the border with Pennlan.

I landed in the grass just beyond the city of Críoch on the Pennlan-fae border, though only Fiadh materialized to meet me on the other side. She nodded her thanks as she gazed at the wall a few steps from us.

"It seems your uncle saw fit to leave us alone," she said. "I'm grateful."

"Hopefully, it stays that way." I conjured a map made of butterfly magic. "Ayla told me that Ward will meet you in Orapus. Based on the map," I pointed to a spot, "it's all the way down here. Remember, most humans haven't seen a troll in a few hundred years, so maybe stay hidden until Ward arrives."

She nodded. "Ward was the male human with you in the troll realm?"

"Yep, that's him. Brown skin, curly black hair, tall-ish, but not as tall as the wizard," I said.

"I'm familiar. He's the one who pulled me from my stupor," she said. "What if your uncle causes me trouble on the way back?"

"I'm hoping I can nip that in the bud," I said. "I'm going to the Erlking's castle to see why he was able to skirt the edict. Maybe get it strengthened a little. But I'll keep a butterfly here looking out for you."

"Fae magic has always been so powerful," she said.

"You guys kept up a mountain for a thousand years," I said. "Power's in the eye of the beholder, I guess."

"I will be back as quickly as I can," she said, bowing. "Thank you, Riona of Pennlan and the Fae Realm."

I didn't love that title they'd started to give me, but I didn't want to argue with her. Instead I waved her off as she disappeared into the ground and zoomed away. Then I turned my attention back toward the north. Aldrick might not have shown his face this time, but I couldn't count on him ignoring Fiadh on her return visit. The Erlking needed to know that Aldrick was skirting his rules, and that needed to end.

⇥ ⇥ ⇥ ⇥

Something felt *different* about the Erlking's castle. It was like the walls themselves were whispering quiet warnings about storms to come, ignored by everyone except me.

Even the servant fae seemed on edge. I passed a group of *bwdbachon* who spent their days sweeping, dusting, and wiping and who seemed more agitated than usual. They were the size of my pinky, with brightly colored wings that looked more like glowing halos as they beat to keep them afloat.

No, they were agitated because they were being bombarded by tiny little magical flies, and were effectively frozen in place.

I searched the hall until I saw a young fae child giggling behind his fingers.

"Knock it off," I barked at him. "They have work to do."

"I don't have to listen to you, fae bastard."

I glared at him. "Do your parents know where you are, kid? Or do I have to bring you to the Erlking so he'll see you defying his edict?"

I didn't know if there was a specific edict about not screwing with *bwdbachon*, but I didn't expect this child to know that either. With a scowl, he pulled his magic back to him, releasing the small fae from his clutches.

"Stupid halfling," he sneered, skulking away.

"Watch your manners," I called after him. I hadn't a clue about his name or parents, but my guess is, they wouldn't mind hearing their son was terrorizing the so-called *lesser* fae.

"Are you guys all right?" I asked the buzzing group.

"Thank you, ma'am," one said, bowing. "Back to work!"

They flitted away, surrounding a patch of wet floor and drying it before disappearing around the corner. I shook my head and hung a left, headed toward the Erlking's chambers.

Even before I reached his doors, there was a crowd spilling out into the hallway. Though only a select few actually lived in at the castle, the Erlking had always welcomed everyone who lived in the fae realm to come to him with any sort of grievance they had.

The downside of all this open-door policy was it being damned near impossible to get an audience with the Erlking. I'd known people to wait months—even a whole year—before finally getting my grandfather's attention and their grievance resolved. Today, it was even more packed than usual, thanks to a collection of rowan, forest fae whose heads scraped the ceiling and whose broad shoulders encompassed three of mine. No fewer than twenty of them stood near the front of the room, pushing everything else toward the back.

But it wasn't just people interested in talking to the Erlking. Many of the *daoine maithe* in the room were who I liked to call "hangers-on," the sort of court watcher who seemed to live on gossip and hearsay. They sat in the corners, sipping wine and talking to themselves as they not-so-silently judged the rest of the room's inhabitants.

"Psh," a tall *daoine maithe* woman said to my left. "Look at all these vermin allowed to walk freely."

I thought she was talking about the collection of nymphs standing a few paces from us. It wasn't unusual to see all manner of creatures, big and small, flitting around the castle. Most of those who needed the Erlking's help fell into the *lesser fae* category.

Lesser fae. The term had been so casually thrown around my entire life. It wasn't until Edric had told me about how life *used* to be under Erlkings past…about how it wasn't just a category, but a way of life. The greater fae of years past thought the other fae that lived among them to be lower than dirt.

And based on the way this *daoine maithe* was looking at me, she'd put me into that same category.

I returned her glare with gusto, daring her to speak directly to me. When she didn't, I turned toward the front of the room, pushing my way through those gathered and ignoring their cries of protest. It took some time, but after the rowan had been heard and moved their bulky bodies out of the throne room, it was considerably more spacious and I was able to get closer.

My grandfather sat on his throne with a crown made of golden twigs. His gray hair curled around his ears, his cheeks were rosy, and when he spoke, it was with a deep, booming voice. He was listening intently to two fae who looked to be in some kind of stalemated argument, each of them pointing at the other with silent accusation. Conversations with the Erlking were private, so I didn't know what they were upset about, but based on the quirk of his mouth, their squabble amused the Erlking. He spoke, and they both touched the back of their necks. A small edict then—just for them.

Then he rose and held out his hands. "Who's next?"

The room exploded into voices, each clamoring for his help. I pushed as hard as I could, jumping up and down and waving my hands to get his attention, but he selected another *daoine maithe* who strode forward confidently, and the bubble of silence descended again.

"At least he's picking a real fae," said another disgruntled voice to my left. "Can't believe the Erlking would entertain an audience with rowans, of all creatures. Filthy things."

"I think he's going senile," came the response from the forest fae next to him. He looked like the personification of autumn, with red, curly hair and two short horns sticking out. He made a sound as he chewed his nail. "I think it's affecting his magic, too."

"Erlkings grow old and die, same as us," the first one said. "Maybe he's coming up on his death."

I felt compelled to step in. "He's *not* dying. He's perfectly fine."

They turned to look at me, their gazes drifting up and down my body as they took me in. The forest fae snorted. "You must be his bastard granddaughter."

"Bastard would imply my parents weren't married," I replied sweetly.

"Would you prefer abomination?" the *daoine maithe* said. "It's a wonder you weren't drowned at birth."

Early in life, I'd learned it was smarter to keep my mouth shut than to let devils run my tongue. I slipped away from them, searching for another way to the front of the room, and took a spot next to a *sidheog*, this time a tall man with puffy white hair. He looked down at me with disgust, rose, and walked away. I watched him go, a little sadly, until something else caught my eye.

Two of Aldrick's favorites, Onora and Haslett, were lounging on the side of the room. They seemed in no hurry to be seen, if they even wanted to be seen at all. They weren't part of the usual crowd of gossipers, so their presence was odd. The Erlking was otherwise occupied, so I inched closer to overhear what they were talking about.

But they weren't talking, not really. One of them had a journal in his lap, his quill ready to write. The other was craning his neck, frowning.

"Do you hear anything yet?" asked the one with the quill.

"I think they're still blathering."

"I hope it's not another useless edict. We need something specific. Something we can—" His gaze narrowed when he spotted me. "Looks like the filth has returned."

His partner found me as well and cracked a smile. "I wonder if the Erlking would notice if we gave her a few bruises."

"I guess Aldrick didn't tell you what happened in the sparring ring," I said.

"He said your wizard stepped in to save you," Haslett said. "I don't see him around anymore, do you, Onora?"

"No, I sure don't," he replied with an evil grin. "Perhaps—"

But whatever he was going to say was drowned out by the Erlking asking for another volunteer. I cursed my luck and timing—it would be a bit longer until I could finally sit down with him, I guessed—but at least the distraction was enough for me to slip through the crowd and away from Aldrick's goons.

Still, the conversation left me uneasy and I made more of an effort to push to the front of the room. It was hard, especially when I was nearly thrown to the ground by a *puca* who snarled he'd been waiting for weeks to be seen, but I got close enough.

The Erlking rose and held up his hands.

"Who's next?"

Again, a hundred voices exploded around me, mine barely a whisper amongst them. But I jumped and waved my arms, tossing a few purple butterflies into the mix so I'd be seen.

Luckily, my grandfather took the bait. "So!" His voice boomed across the room. "The summoning spell finally worked, eh? I was about to bring Aldrick here to see if he'd skirted his responsibilities again. He's becoming good at that these days."

Ignoring the chorus of not-so-nice mumbles, I approached the throne nervously. I'd been *summoned?* And Aldrick was supposed to have told me? It should've been the first thing out of his mouth, or else his tongue would've twisted and choked him to death.

"I wasn't aware I'd been summoned," I said.

He made a noise. "You didn't run into him at the border when you were moving the trolls?"

"I...did," I said softly. "Grandfather, I'm worried about him. He seems to be flouting your edicts—"

"Oh, don't worry about that," he said with a mild wave. "How are things in the wildlands? Are the trolls settled?"

I huffed. "I think I should worry about it. If he's not telling me about a summons and ignoring your directives—"

"Leave it alone and tell me about the trolls."

The words came with a shimmering feeling across the back of my neck. I glared at my grandfather, but even *thinking* about Aldrick made my neck burn.

"Fine. Yes. The trolls are *great*. They're seeking an alliance with Pennlan for their goods," I paused, again wondering if I'd overstepped. "Um...do you want an alliance with Pennlan, too?"

He chuckled. "We've gotten along fine without our human neighbor's wheat and wine for this long. What's another twenty years?"

I wasn't sure what to make of that.

"You've done well at the tasks I've set you," he said. "Now, I expect you'll continue to help the trolls as they need."

I nodded. That wasn't news.

"And in the meantime, you will be here and return to your studies and training."

My throat went dry. "T-training? With...Aldrick?"

He chuckled. "The border guard is otherwise occupied at the moment, so you will have a reprieve from him. But Clíodhna has agreed to take another few weeks from her lands to spend time with you. You will meet her in the training room. Dismissed."

I turned to leave then thought better of it. "Erlking, I'm...I'm concerned about—" My neck began burning again. "You know who I'm concerned about."

"You don't have to be concerned about anything where your uncle is concerned," he replied, his face losing some of that characteristic warmth. "Your only concerns are keeping the trolls content in their new lands and learning as much as you can from your grandfather. Is that clear?"

As clear as the burning on the back of my neck. "Yes, but—"

"Dismissed."

Chapter Eight

Cade

Seafaring was not for the faint of heart. Or stomach.

No matter how many spells I cast, I couldn't shake the sense I was about to be sick all over myself. I closed my eyes to try to steady the rocking, but all that did was make me dizzier.

Above me, the sounds of the crew walking on the creaky boards echoed all day long. No one sat still on this ship, that was for sure.

The ship gave another lurch—and my stomach went with it. I swallowed hard, steadying my breathing and glancing toward the deck again. Fresh air would certainly be welcome.

I'd been watching the sun through the crack in the door, and it had moved from one side to the other, so we were at least far enough away from land that she wouldn't turn around and head back to port. The farther we were, the more reasonable she might be to letting me stay.

Another big lurch and this time, my stomach came to my throat. I quickly rose to my feet and marched toward the staircase that led to the upper deck.

As soon as I popped my head up, a cry came from the crew, but the captain didn't seem all that surprised to see me. The gnarly bunch of miscreants advanced on me with whatever weapons they could grab, but the captain held up her hand to stop them.

"I guess you can't take a hint, kid," she said. "How the hell did you even get on board?"

"Magic, remember?" I said, waving my staff around. Her crew

cowered backward a little—a good sign. "Now, perhaps we can continue our conversation."

"No." She crossed her arms. "Magic yourself back to port and get off my ship. Or I'm tossing you overboard."

"I would love to see you try." I planted my staff on the ground and allowed the tip to light up menacingly.

None of the crew moved, their beady little eyes focused on my staff. I'd never been *feared* like this before, and it made me more confident in my position.

The captain let out a sigh. "I'm not taking you to H'sipotu. It would be the end of my life."

"I can appreciate that," I said. "Maybe we can compromise. There must be somewhere you can take me that will get me closer? An island they frequent?"

"If it's an island they frequent, I won't be there." But something in her tone gave me hope. "But I'll see what I can do. In the meantime, just stay out of the way."

I smiled. "Excellent. I'm Cade, by the way."

I expected her to ignore me, but she offered the smallest of nods. "Aldonza."

>⇥ >⇥ >⇥ >⇥

It was much nicer above deck, though the company was decidedly less friendly. As instructed, I kept away from the crew's work, moving from this spot to that as they went about their day. Pull this sail, mop this floor, adjust this rigging. They purposefully ignored me, refusing to meet my gaze as they walked by, perhaps thinking themselves hostages to my magical whims. There were five of them besides Aldonza, and as the day progressed, I caught all their names.

Cluny—who was short but strong, with ebony skin and gray curls in his black hair—seemed to be Aldonza's second-in-command. Volker sat in the crow's nest most of the day, a telescope perched beside him. Perhaps he'd once had pale skin, but now it was a deep golden brown, offset by his bleached blond hair. Iga seemed to be the brute strength of the bunch. She was the tallest (save myself and Aldonza) and had large muscles that rippled under her shirt. There was almost something supernatural about the way she was able to hoist heavy ropes and shift things around. More than once, I scrambled out of her way before she picked me up and moved me.

Next was Cai, who must've come from somewhere far away, because her accent was so heavy I could barely understand her at times. Her hair was almost purple in the sun, spilling down her back in a mess of curls. The carpenter of the crew, she carried woodworking tools around her waist. Onor had a spare white sheet draped across his lap that he was sewing back together with a needle and thread. He and Iga perhaps hailed from the same place, though he wasn't nearly as large. The more I watched them, the more I wondered if they weren't siblings.

Aldonza remained at the helm, her hands perched on the large wheel as the ship moved through the water. She hadn't said a word to me since allowing me to remain onboard, but I hadn't given up hope that I could convince her. There had to be *something* she valued more than her stubbornness. Maybe if I promised to protect her from whatever bounty had been laid upon her head. She could drop me off, and I'd portal her entire vessel away before anyone was the wiser, assuming I figured out how to navigate the seas.

"What's our port, Captain?" Cluny asked, climbing the stairs to join her.

"Gorenza," she replied, her gaze sliding to me. "We'll see if our new friend enjoys living amongst the most cutthroat ne'er-do-wells on the southern seas."

"Can't be worse than the trolls," I called to her with a genuine smile. "Or the fae. Or the griffins. Or—"

She scowled, and my grin widened as I rose and walked the short length of the deck.

"I could tell you about my travels, you know. If you'd tell me a little more about—"

"No. I liked you better when you were just in the way."

Volker, in his usual perch, let out a whistle. "Off the stern, port! Incoming ship!"

Aldonza narrowed her gaze and grabbed a nearby telescope, running toward the back of the boat and gazing through. If I squinted, I could see something in the distance. Perhaps a ship? But it was hard to—

"They found us," she said, glaring at me for some reason. "We need to move."

Her words set off a firestorm of activity. I gripped my staff and stepped backward to avoid being knocked over by Onor as he ran to pull the sail. Others went belowdecks and returned with weapons—swords, knives, a few bows, and quivers of arrows.

"Who's chasing you?" I asked.

"The Driwanian navy," she said. "They don't take kindly to our line of business."

"We also didn't quite pay our dues when we were in port," Iga replied with a grin.

"And we might've stolen some stuff while we were there."

My stomach sank. "Are you…*pirates*?"

"I prefer privateer, but whatever you like," Aldonza said before turning to the crew to bark orders. "Onor! Cluny! Find me a current or a wind to get out of here before they blow holes in our ship."

As if on cue, a loud explosion echoed in the distance—a cannon. The puff of smoke came from the ship that was quickly approaching.

I turned back to Aldonza, realizing this might be my golden moment. "Let me help."

"No," she snapped. "Stay out of the way!"

I sat down and watched them scurry around the ship, trying desperately to gain speed against the aggressors. I'd no idea if they were doing well or poorly, but they were certainly moving quickly.

Another cannon blast, this one much closer. I didn't know why the other ship seemed to be moving faster than we were, but the thought of us sinking made me quite nervous.

"You know, I can help," I said as Cai ran by. "Get you out of trouble. I can create a portal and—"

"Can it, wizard, or I'll—"

I turned as an odd whirring sound echoed in the air. Barely in time, I jumped out of the way as a large iron ball collided against the side of the ship, leaving a gaping hole in the wood.

"Fix that before we sink!" Aldonza barked.

"Please, let me help," I cried. "Otherwise we'll all be in trouble."

She ignored me to run toward the gash in the ship. But before she could get there, I waved my staff and the hole fixed itself.

"See? Helpful."

She balled her fists, looking at me over her shoulder. "*Fine*. Do what you must."

"But I want something in return," I said, waving my staff to block another cannonball headed toward the ship. The crew gaped at me in awe, but Aldonza just looked mad.

"And that's why I didn't want your help." She turned back to her crew. "What are you standing around for? I said *move*!"

"But he can save us," Cluny said, pointing at me.

"I'm not drowning because you're too stubborn to listen," Iga replied.

Onor nodded. "Either he helps, or it's you we throw overboard."

Aldonza let out a growl of frustration as she turned back around to me. "Fine, Wizard. What is it you want in return? And *don't say* to take you to H'sipotu."

"I know you won't agree to that," I said. "Just take me to a port where *someone* will be able to."

She made a face. "No."

"Then I guess you'll sink, and I'll just make a portal to safety." I smirked and sat on a crate as I easily deflected another cannonball.

"Unless…"

She looked at the approaching ship, which was now close enough to see their flag colors and some of the crew. The wheels in her head were spinning, and I held my breath, waiting for her to come up with some way out.

"Fine. Get us to safety, and I'll take you to a port where you can find someone to help you."

"Help me what?" I pressed. "I've spent many months around fae. I know how tricky words can be."

"Help you get to H'sipotu." She gestured to the air. "Happy?"

"Very."

I walked to the front of the ship, gathering magic in my staff as I drew a circle. It became wider and wider until the tall ship mast could fit underneath it. Then I cast a burst of wind toward the sails to push us forward, sending everyone but me flying forward. Within seconds, the ship was clear of the aggressor, and I closed the portal behind us.

The ship slowed without the magic behind it, and I turned, smugly, to the captain. "Well?"

She strode to the front of the ship, looking left and right as if she could tell the difference between the ocean where we'd been and the ocean where we currently were. Then she turned to scowl at me. "Where are we?"

"W-what?"

"How far did you take us off course?" she asked, then narrowed her gaze.

"I…" I cleared my throat, straightening and pressing my staff into the ground. "I'm not sure how to communicate where we are. I'm not a seafarer, and—"

She threw her hands in the air. "Useless wizard. Keep this heading until nightfall. Then I'll figure out exactly where this idiot dropped us off. For all we know, we could be on the other side of the world."

CHAPTER NINE

AYLA

Gloom fell over the castle, and I could do little to dispel it. Ward had taken my letter to Ramira, and I hoped—prayed—he would be able to get past the blockade and deliver it. Then, perhaps…

But that was weeks away. In the meantime, I walked the halls of my empty castle, wondering what everyone else was up to. After the second full day of moping, Bronwen all but kicked me out, saying my constant pacing was getting in the way of her keeping things clean. So I ventured out to the green, where my soldiers were running their drills in two separate groups led by Elodia and Rutley.

"Morning," Elodia said, stopping to bow. "Your Majesty."

"How goes it?" I asked.

"The same as usual," she said. "Don't want Ward to think we let anyone rest while he was away from his post. He's got to prove himself a hardass, like Gabhann."

I didn't doubt it. "I think I'd like to go for a ride later," I said. "If you can spare a couple soldiers to accompany me."

Elodia eyed me suspiciously, denial on the tip of her tongue. "Ride to where?"

"Just around," I said. "Stretch my legs a bit. Maybe venture into the village." I gestured up to the castle. "Not much to do up there. Might be nice to see my kingdom up close instead of making decisions from afar."

"That sounds fine—" Rutley began, but Elodia was faster.

"Ward told us to keep you in the castle," she said. "So no."

"He did?" I stuffed down my annoyance. It was…understandable, considering. But I couldn't help testing the waters. "Even to the village? It's just down the road."

"C'mon, El," Rutley said. "*It's just down the road.*"

I knew I liked that Rutley. "I promise, just a quick visit. It's been so boring since the trolls left—and Ward as well."

"Boring is welcome," Elodia said, but her resolve was weakening. "*Fine.* To the village. But only for a short bit. And you'll keep your crown and jewels in the castle."

She wouldn't have to twist my arm; I hated wearing those things anyway. "I'll be back in a few minutes!"

>⇢ >⇢ >⇢ >⇢

I opted to wear a basic tunic and pants, braiding my hair quickly as I descended the stairs. I hadn't even visited my horse since returning from the troll kingdom, and I was sure she missed me as much as I missed her. Riding on the green was the only thing Eoghan ever let me do without his overbearing presence. It was my small bit of freedom, the one thing that still felt the same.

"Ready?" Elodia asked as I climbed atop my saddle.

Rutley rolled his eyes. "We haven't even left, Elodia. Calm down."

I didn't want her to change her mind, so I knocked my horse in the barrel and we set off under the front gate and out onto the road. The wind in my hair was freeing, and I took a deep breath. The sun and cold breeze took turns warming and chilling me, as if the weather couldn't make up its mind what it wanted. The thundering of the hooves behind me told me my soldiers weren't too far, so I urged my horse faster, lowering myself as the wind picked up. My horse neighed in appreciation and broke out into a full-on gallop.

But the ride was short-lived, as the village really wasn't that far. My horse slowed to a trot then a leisurely walk, and I turned, grinning at Elodia and Rutley. The latter joined me in amusement; the former gave me a scowl.

"Were you trying to run off?" she asked.

"No," I said, exasperated. "You were right behind me the whole time."

She tutted and dismounted. "Ward told us to keep an eye on you. Don't make it harder than it has to be."

"Elodia," I dismounted as well, "I'm *trying* to be a good little queen. I asked permission. I kept you with me. I promise I'm not going to…going to…" I threw my hands in the air. "Gallivant to the troll kingdom and get myself killed."

Rutley snorted as Elodia glared at me.

We walked the village square, pausing at each of the tables to inspect the wares. There were farmers who'd brought their goods, though this late in the season, there wasn't much to share other than gourds and some root vegetables. Still, the wares seemed lighter than usual.

"Trade's all messed up. Would be nice if the queen would get out of that castle and do something about it," the farmer said when I asked why.

"I…um…" My cheeks heated, but I swallowed any protestations. Perhaps it was for the best she didn't recognize me, based on her tone. "I'm sure she will."

The woman snorted with a hearty roll of her eyes. "Never even seen her out and about. She just hides up there, same as she did her whole life. I think she's scared of what's coming."

"What is…coming?" I asked, leaning in.

"Storm." She wrapped her cloak tighter. "Now if you aren't going to buy anything, move along."

I did but turned to watch the lady as I walked away. The skies above were blue, so the storm she was talking about must've been metaphorical. I glanced behind me, torn between going back to ask more and wanting to give her space.

"Are you okay?" Rutley asked. "What did that woman—"

"Nothing," I said with a shake of my head. "Don't worry about it." I nodded toward the local tavern. "Do you think we could pop in for something to eat? I'm famished."

"Why don't we head back to the castle?" Elodia asked.

"I'd rather go inside," I said with a weak smile. "Please? I've never… I wasn't ever allowed."

The pity ploy worked, and Mother Elodia gestured toward the tavern. Rutley took my arm, giggling like a little boy as we made our way over. Elodia tutted to herself, following behind, probably mentally writing a letter to Ward about my mischievous behavior.

The moment I stepped inside, I was hit with the smell of stale ale and bread and the roar of a lively tavern. Immediately, I understood why Eoghan had never let me go in. There were so many conversations and different people, one of them might've told me he was manipulating me.

Through the din of conversation, I gathered that Rutley wanted me to follow him to sit down at a table, but there wasn't one to spare, so we crowded in at the bar. It was enthralling to be among so many people after the silence of the castle, and I listened to as many conversations as I could.

"That damn queen, I should walk up to the castle and give her a piece of my mind!" The man railing looked to be a few tankards deep, his cheeks ruddy with anger.

Elodia moved to take my arm but I shook my head, wanting to hear what he had to say.

"Letting Konevell walk all over her. Closing the borders—her father would never let such a slight go unpunished. She has all these soldiers wandering the country. Why not send them to open things back up, eh?" He took a long sip. "Because she don't care. She's got that stone. That's all she needs. What does she care about the rest of us idiots?"

"I'm sure she's doing all she can," I said, raising my voice over the noise. "I hear she's enlisted someone to move the goods out of Orapus."

The man turned to me, and for a brief, terrifying moment, I thought he might've recognized me. But he just snorted, giving me a once-over. "If you ask me, she spends too much time with magical creatures and not enough time handling her own kingdom. Did'ya hear she skipped town to play with the trolls? Came back with a whole group of 'em. Living out in front of the castle for two weeks." He shook his head. "That wizard needs to come back and put her in her place."

"You mean Cade?" I asked, though I wasn't optimistic.

"Naw, the other one. The one who ran things while she was playing dress up." He shook his head. "Things were better when he was in charge."

It was hard to keep my mouth shut, but I managed it as Elodia tugged at my arm. But I wasn't ready to leave. I wanted to hear more of what my people thought of me. I wanted to know every single complaint.

"What do you recommend, then?" I asked. "What would you have her do?"

"Give up her throne to someone who knows what they're doing." He rubbed his nose and threw his arms as he rose and swayed. "Bah. I might just leave Pennlan for Sudaemor or one of the other kingdoms," he said, pushing himself to stand. "This country's going to be run into the ground sooner than later. Might as well get out while I can."

"What does that mean?" I asked.

"Means there's some funny business afoot," he said. "I keep hearing things from my friends who travel down the river. Lots of Konevellian ships filled with people—soldiers, from the looks of it."

My throat went dry. "For what purpose?"

"What other purpose is there? War."

The word echoed between my ears. "There hasn't been war in centuries," I said, though my voice lacked conviction.

"Time for everything, you know? I'm sure the young queen will send her soldiers to die on her behalf before losing spectacularly." He chuckled. "She'll hide away in her castle, safe and protected, while those young people sacrifice themselves on the altar of patriotism."

"She wouldn't." I balled my fists under the bar. "She would stand with them. She has the stone, remember?"

"Bah. Fairy tale, that is. Like I said, she spends too much time in magic and beasts like the fae to pay attention to what really matters." He rose and tipped his hat. "Good luck to you, missy. I hope you can get out before the chaos reaches this far north."

>→ >→ >→ >→

The ride back to the castle was quiet. I stared off into the distance, ruminating over the complaints, unable to rebut them in my mind.

"He was a drunkard," Elodia said, after a moment. "Ignore him."

"He's not wrong, though," I said, staring at the darkening sky above. "Things really were better when Eoghan was running the show. At least to the outside world."

"But they weren't," Rutley said. "You said he made a mess of everything."

"They didn't know that."

"They would've figured it out eventually," Elodia said.

"What he said about the Konevellians, though," I said quietly. "About war…"

"Why would they do something so dumb?" Elodia said. "Besides that, he's a merchant. What he knows about the military couldn't fill his tankard." She waved her hand. "Like I said—ignore him. We know you're doing everything in your power to make things right."

The problem was I didn't have any power. Not to open the border, not to force people to respect me as the queen. Even the one piece of magic I had was useless without my sister nearby—and when I did wield it, I was uneasy and haphazard.

And yet…

I turned the stone over in my hand. What was stopping me from inviting Riona here to practice with it? It wasn't like there was much else for me to do, and practicing with my stone would at least make me feel like I was doing something constructive. And maybe spending more time with Riona would help me learn how to use it *without* her, too.

"What are you plotting over there?" Elodia asked.

"Nothing that requires me to leave the castle," I said with a sly grin. "Just thinking it's time I invite my sister for a proper visit."

Chapter Ten

Ward

Even with Platt's whining, we made good time. I allowed him a few hours to rest here and there, but knowing the clock was ticking on my absence, I kept us moving.

As we crested a hill, a fast-moving river sliced through the land, parallel to the horizon. If my map-reading skills were correct, this river came down from the mountains and formed the border between Pennlan and Sudaemor to the east and Konevell to the west. Here, at least, it was a fair distance from shore to shore, and the currents seemed to move quickly downstream.

"This river goes all the way to Orapus," I said to Platt, by way of confirmation. "Right?"

He made a noise. "You can read a map. Good for you."

The road we were following came up right beside the river. Every so often, a ship would float by, white sails buffeted by the wind. They didn't stop at any of the small villages that dotted the river, but there wasn't a place for them to, either. Everything was headed toward Orapus.

Since Platt wasn't good for conversation, I let myself think about where they might be coming from, what they might be carrying, and did they know the border was closed?

The answer became obvious as the boats became more numerous in the river, to the point where they seemed to be bobbing in the current, anchored to the bottom. As Orapus came into view, the reason why became obvious. Every inch of the expansive bay was filled with ships, and there was no more room.

"Wow." Platt let out a breath and looked honestly concerned. "This isn't good."

"I take it this isn't normal?"

He seemed to debate whether answering me was worth it, but the sight must've shaken him a little. "No. It's busy, of course. But ships come and go quickly. Sitting stagnant like this? Waiting in the river? That's…"

I twisted in my saddle and nodded to the villages on the opposite bank. "Why not just sidle up to the other side and unload there?"

"What, like smuggling?" He snorted. "That's illegal."

"Maybe not smuggle," I said with a look. "But this can't be the only way to get things in and out of the country?"

Platt muttered something that sounded too much like "farm boy" for my liking, but I let it slide.

"I'm more familiar with the northern part of the country," I said, hoping a little sugar would help him open up. "Please excuse my ignorance."

"I suppose they left this off in your *extensive* training to be the captain," he drawled. "There are more places to cross where the river passes by Sudaemor, but once it reaches the border between Pennlan and Konevell, there are no passable spots until Orapus. Maybe intentional, you know, more money and control that way." He paused. "The city changed hands a lot until some queen of one and king of another got together and decided to split it down the middle. Pennlan gets to control what goes in the river. Konevell decides what goes into the sea." He gave me a look. "Ergo, nothing goes beyond Orapus unless Konevell says so."

"Pennlan has a long coastline north of here," I said. "Why not move the goods up there?"

"It's not just about the ships. There's a whole operation in Orapus. These people have warehouses and ships and people who work in 'em. It's not something they can just pick up and move overnight." He cracked a grin. "'Course, if the queen fails to figure a way to reopen the border, maybe they'll leave."

That was a threat that Pádraig had thrown around when he was berating Ayla.

"Another problem with using the ocean is, if you want to reach any of the other nations, you gotta go *around* Konevell. And my guess is, the Konevellian queen's got her navy out there waiting to sink ships with the Pennlan flag." He adjusted himself in the saddle. "Suppose that's why these merchants are all hot and bothered at the queen."

"Yeah." I twisted the reins. It certainly was a mess.

Up until now, the road had been outside of the villages, but it zigzagged between a pair and seemed to become the main road—complete with cobblestones and lamps. The ever-present scent of salt water was pushed by a nice breeze. The buildings were constructed of a light-colored brick, perhaps bleached by the constant sun and spray from the nearby ocean. Even the shops were different; there were cobblers and dressmakers and candlemakers, as in other villages I'd been to, but far more numerous and specialized. The variety seemed to be necessary as the people walking down the street wore fine clothes with detailed trim and wide-brimmed hats with flourishes. Even the buckles on their boots were shiny and new.

I glanced down at my worn traveling tunic and pants, and boots covered in mud.

"So, as much as I'm enjoying this walkabout in Orapus," Platt said, his voice carrying, "where, exactly, are we going?"

"Find who's in charge." Each city had its own set of soldiers, led by a head soldier who supposedly answered to me. After riding around for a few blocks, I finally spotted the telltale uniform of a pair of local guards.

"We're searching for Captain Treen," I replied. "I'm—"

The soldiers saluted, but not to me. "We've been anticipating your arrival, Lieutenant Platt."

Platt wore an amused smile as he looked at me expectantly. "Yes, I suppose you have. But you might want to salute my—er—friend here… He's your new captain."

The soldier did a double take, looking at me as if she thought it was some kind of joke. "Where's Captain Gabhann?"

"Just take us to your superior," I said with a scowl. Perhaps I should've changed back into my uniform, but it was too late now.

As we walked along the streets, I mentally practiced what I'd say to the local captain. I was sure there would be questions once the trolls arrived, and even more sure the merchants would give me trouble as their crates of goods disappeared into the earth to points unknown. This was all wholly out of my realm of experience, and based on how Platt was preening next to me, he knew it, too. He wouldn't let me forget they'd addressed *him* first.

The soldiers led us to a fancy brick building near the docks. They took our horses to be tended to as a stout woman walked out of the building—Captain Treen. She brushed right past me to Platt, took his hand, and shook it firmly.

"I hear we have a new captain. Congratulations."

A smile curled onto Platt's face as he took the handshake then chuckled. "I'm afraid you've been misinformed. I'm still a lieutenant. *He's* the captain."

The Orapus captain turned, looked at me, then searched beyond me.

I cleared my throat and stepped forward. "Name's Ward. We're happy to be here."

"You're so…" Treen slowly took my hand then seemed to think better of whatever she was going to say. "Well, we're glad you're here. Lots of concern for what's happening. We're running out of room to house all these goods."

"I understand, and I do come bearing a solution," I said. "If we can step inside."

The building was two stories, with wide-open windows letting the cool sea breeze in. Her office was large and inviting, with a perfect view to the bay beyond.

And sitting in three chairs on the other side of the desk were the merchants who'd been in Ayla's office a few days before. How they'd beaten me to the city, I hadn't a clue.

"Nice to see you again," I said, forcing myself to keep a steady face. "I see you made better time than I did."

Róisín's lip curled over her teeth. "So it's true, then? The queen really did replace her long-serving captain with a boy. I thought she was joking back in Pennlan."

Behind me, Platt snickered, which seemed to embolden the merchant.

"Tell me, what incredible reason did she have for giving you this position?" Róisín asked.

I knew she was expecting me to say something, and perhaps I could've gone on and on about how I'd saved Ayla from Eoghan then again with the trolls. But nothing I said would've placated her.

"The queen—and Captain Gabhann—thought it was the best choice, considering Gabhann had decided on her own to retire," I said, after a moment. "Now back to the matter at hand. Ayla informed you the trolls were eager to buy your wares, correct?"

The merchant smiled cruelly. "*Ayla*, hm?"

Her name had slipped out, and perhaps from a different person, it wouldn't have been such an interesting moment. But something about the way I said it garnered more attention than I wanted. Róisín's eyes seemed to glitter with malice, almost like she was spinning a story of how I came to be in my position. Platt was practically wetting himself with amusement. The room began to feel stiflingly hot as I felt all eyes on me.

"*Her Majesty* is confident this will alleviate the pressure," I said through gritted teeth. "And as soon as the trolls arrive—"

There was a loud scream from the street below, and before I knew what I was doing, I dashed down the stairs, my hand on my sword, ready to jump into action. But the voice was the soldier at the door, and she was staring at…

A troll.

"Please, calm yourself," the translucent-skinned creature said, her voice low and velvety. She was tall and lanky, with pointed ears and golden eyes. She wore no weapons, though her tunic was long-sleeved and she was wearing a peculiar hat that shielded her from the sun.

The soldier was still shaking as if he'd seen a ghost, so I stepped forward and put my hand on his arm. "At ease, soldier. This is an ally." I stepped forward. "Welcome, I'm—"

"We have been acquainted," she said with a small nod. "I believe you're the one who saved my life. My name is Fiadh."

I'd dragged hundreds of trolls from their houses in the chaos after Edric died, so she didn't pique my memory. "I'm glad you made it. Are you alone?"

"No," she said. "Ten others made the journey with me. But given the…" She craned her neck to look behind me. The three merchants had followed me downstairs, keeping their distance but watching warily. "The reception, I thought it better to come into the city alone."

"Well, this is…" Pádraig said. "This must be a troll."

"Fiadh is her name," I said. "And if you'll be so kind as to give her directions to your stores, we will begin the process of moving the goods."

"Wait a moment," Cormac said, holding up his hand. "Before we leave this place, I want to make sure this money or whatever it is you'll create is the real deal. We will need a few hours to confirm the validity."

"Very well." She turned to me. "Would you be so kind as to grab me a few rocks from outside? It's quite harsh out there."

"Platt," I snapped. "Go get some rocks."

He hesitated for a moment, his piggy eyes still focused on her, but stumbled outside. When he returned, he had a handful of small pebbles, which he dumped on the floor instead of into Fiadh's outstretched hands.

"Sorry," I muttered.

She bent down to pick up the pebbles, rolling them around in her hands. A collective gasp rose from the group as they turned from dull gray and brown to emerald, ruby, purple, blue.

Pádraig, all fear forgotten, rushed over to take the jewels from the troll's hands with greedy glee. "Amazing," he breathed.

"*If* they're real," Cormac said, plucking an emerald from his friend's hands. "We'll send word once the deal is finalized."

They left us standing there, Pádraig oohing and aaahing over their new gems, and even Cormac looking somewhat impressed as he pocketed his emerald and disappeared down the street.

Róisín, however, stayed behind, turning to me with that same scowl on her face. "And what about me?"

"What about you?" I said. "Do you want more jewels?"

She sniffed. "*My* industry is shipping. I have hundreds of ships and sailors sitting stagnant in the bay, unable to offload and unable to be paid. What do you plan to do about it?"

I blinked. "I...uh..." I couldn't quite tell her that I was planning to cross the border. "We're working on it."

"Work faster."

She grabbed the fabric of her skirt and huffed off toward where the other two had disappeared.

"You know, they *are* real jewels," Fiadh said with a scowl. "Trolls don't lie."

"Don't worry about them," I said with a wave of my hand. "Something tells me even if their so-called 'experts' find some fault with the jewels, they'd be content to pass them off as genuine regardless." She glared at me, and I added, "Of course, they're actually genuine. Just saying."

"We are desperate for these supplies," she said, a little darkly. "Otherwise, our people escaped the mountain just to starve in the harsh winter."

"I promise you," I said, turning to her, "you'll get your supplies.

Even if you have to take them and leave jewels in their places."

"Um."

Platt was back, this time with a larger handful of pebbles—and a cobblestone he probably pulled from the street. "Do you think you could make these into jewels, too?"

She stepped toward him, but I stopped her. "Finish the job, Platt. Then you can have all the jewels you can carry."

CHAPTER ELEVEN

RIONA

I attempted to speak to my grandfather about Aldrick again, but every time I walked into his throne room, my feet stuck to the floor and my neck burned so hot I was sure it would leave a mark. After three or four times of this, even my stubborn mind finally admitted defeat. The Erlking was much older and wiser than I was, and if he said he had a handle on his son, then I'd just have to trust that he did. Still, I didn't trust him *entirely,* so I left a butterfly at the border to keep watch for Fiadh.

The next morning, I was summoned to the small classroom where Clíodhna had given lessons to Cade. The last and only lesson we'd had was disastrous, where she'd pointed out all the magical skills I lacked.

A fact she reminded me of when she materialized.

"I hope you're ready to be serious with your studies now."

Clíodhna was queen of the *sidheog* people who lived in the very northernmost part of the fae realm. I'd never discovered the exact details of how she and my grandfather got together to make my mother, nor did I want them. I *did* know was it was pretty rare for a *sidheog* and *daoine maithe* to have come together at all. But I supposed it was good to be the Erlking and queen.

"I hear you had quite the adventure in the troll realm," she said, tilting my head up to stare at her. "Your eyes have light in them again. That's good."

I wasn't sure about that, but I was certainly more willing to use magic these days than last time we'd trained together. "I learned a bit from Cade when we were gone, but I'm sure there's much more to cover."

"Yes, indeed there is." She smiled, but there wasn't much warmth in it. "We will be going to the training ring first, so I can really assess where you are."

"Training ring?" I squeaked.

"You won't be facing your uncle," she said. "You'll be facing me. I'd like to see what you can do, and my methods are a bit less..." She exhaled. "Controversial than Aldrick's."

I opened my mouth to tell her about the border, and blessedly, the burning didn't come. "I have to tell you about him. I think he's found a way to skirt the Erlking's edicts. He wasn't supposed to stop the trolls at the border, but he did."

"Did he stop them or just delay them?" Clíodhna asked.

"I guess just...delayed. But had I not shown up, he wouldn't have let them pass."

"But you were instructed to see to their settling, were you not?" She gestured to the air. "He probably assumed you'd show and wasn't actually planning on stopping them. Just a show for his little group of friends."

I considered that, pursing my lips. "I suppose that does make sense..."

"Your uncle has many, *many* years of learning how to skirt around his father's edicts. He's made it something of an art form." She chuckled. "It's quite extraordinary, what he's able to accomplish when he puts his mind to. Shame that it's all for his own benefit rather than for others."

"But he had friends in the Erlking's chambers, taking notes about edicts. They wanted one they could test—"

"Riona, I promise you your grandfather knows exactly what his son's up to. And if memory serves, he also gave *you* explicit instructions to leave it be. Which I see didn't include conveying your concerns to me." She tapped her chin. "I suppose I'll have to talk with him about that."

"I'm not trying to get into it with the Erlking or anything," I said with a huff. "I'm concerned because the trolls... He *told* me to keep an eye out for them. And Aldrick seems to have it out for them. Ergo..." I gestured to the air.

"I promise, it's under control," Clíodhna said. "Now, let's get you to the training ring to see what you've got."

⤞ ⤞ ⤞ ⤞

I didn't know if facing my grandmother would be better or worse than Aldrick. He was, at least, predictable. He clearly wanted me dead. Nothing surprising.

My grandmother was much harder to read. It wasn't as if we were close when I was growing up; better to keep my identity a secret than showcase my powerful connections and run afoul of someone with the same intentions as Aldrick. I didn't know what to expect from her.

"We will dispense with the formalities," she said, throwing her heavy cloak to the side. "Now. Attack."

"Erm. What?" I swallowed. "What do you mean?"

"Attack me. Fight me. Pretend I'm that wizard out to kill everyone you love. Show me your power."

She spoke plainly, almost impatiently, as she outlined my very worst fear. But while I no longer feared that damn wizard was living in my brain, I still feared *him*. Feared what he could do if he got control of me again.

"I'm not growing any younger."

I threw up my hands, my tongue burning. "I don't know how to do it."

"Just because you *can* lie, doesn't mean it isn't obvious when you do."

I huffed a breath. "I don't want to hurt you."

"You won't."

"I hurt Aldrick."

She took a breath, then moving faster than should've been possible for a fae her age, she hurled a giant, spinning ball of snow and ice toward me. I was only just able to materialize out of the way. Another came right after it, following me around the sparring ring. She was trying to goad me into responding, but there was still something holding me back. Giving into the desire to protect myself seemed almost *dangerous.*

"Riona, I don't have all day," she said.

"I don't want to hurt you."

"Another lie, even if you don't believe it yourself." This time, she opted to walk to me, scrutinizing my face as if she were trying to solve a puzzle. "What's in your mind, child?"

A lot. I was worried for the trolls, about Aldrick, how no one seemed to be taking me seriously. I worried about the white magic in my veins—dormant now, but what would it take to bring it out? I hadn't used it enough to feel I had control over it. If I were to—

"Forget I asked," she said with a sigh. "Until you're ready—"

"In the troll realm," I began quietly, "I realized I have this…other magic. White magic, not the purple butterflies. It manifested in voices but also in raw power. It's what I used against Aldrick."

She nodded. "Your mother had such power, too."

I turned sharply. "She did?"

"Perhaps it was the joining of the *sidheog* and *daoine maithe,*" she said. "Whatever the reason, she was gifted in ways neither her father nor I understood. She seemed to be able to hear things we couldn't, understand the world in ways that were strange to us. And this white magic you speak of, it complemented her fae magic. Much as, I suspect, it does for you." She tilted her head. "It's why your grandfather wanted you pitted against Aldrick. He was trying to get it out of you."

"See, that's the problem," I said. "I can't just *wield* it. I have to either be on the brink of death or…or near a piece of the *seod croí.*" I shivered. "And I'm not keen on the former every time I need to access it."

"Hm." She surveyed me. "Perhaps it's your father's human blood that muddles things a bit. Your mother had no such problem. Are you sure it's not just a mental block?"

I nodded. "It's like night and day when I'm near Ayla. And in the troll realm, they'd imbued the water in the mountain with their stone's magic, and it lingered. Every time I touched the water, my hands would glow white. But I haven't felt that same power since returning home." I looked up into her eyes. "What do you think it means?"

"I have no idea," she said, dashing my hopes. "Much of what we know of the *seod croí* was lost to time, you know."

"The trolls were able to pull memories from the *aos sí*," I said. "We were able to see the whole battle against Laughlan. Maybe they can find another memory stone with some answers."

She frowned. "What do you mean pull memories?"

I explained the basics of what I knew of troll magic, how big events tended to leave a big impression and how the trolls were able to pull the memory from the rock itself and display it for others to see.

"What other memories were there?" she asked. "And would it be possible for me to view them?"

"I didn't see any others," I said. "And as far as I know, the memory stones are buried at the bottom of the troll mountain."

"Shouldn't be too difficult for the trolls to retrieve them, then."

Perhaps not, but I didn't think Lynton would take kindly to the idea. "Maybe there's another stone they could find. One with a different memory." I snapped my fingers together, only just remembering. "Cade said he saw a second memory. One with Aoibheann talking about how to destroy the *seod croí*."

"That's a memory worth retrieving, to be sure," Clíodhna said. "Perhaps you can take your newfound charges into the *aos sí* in search of another stone. It might come in handy as we face down this new threat to our people."

I swallowed hard. "Perhaps they could go without me."

She chuckled, possibly remembering the tale of my cowardice in the ghostly cemetery. "Perhaps, indeed. You have much more training to do before you can be of help to anyone."

I sighed. "I can try to pull this magic, but I don't really control it well. And I'm worried—"

"Not with me," she said. "You said this magic becomes more potent when you're around a piece of the *seod croi*? Then perhaps you should spend some time with a piece."

"You mean…visit Ayla?" I chewed my lip. Our relationship had thawed, but it wasn't what I would call close. I didn't know how she'd react to my visiting, or if she'd freak out when I asked to train with the stone.

"She's your blood. I'm sure she'd be happy to have you." Clíodhna retrieved her cloak. "And until you do, I have nothing I can teach you."

With that, she disappeared in a puff of snow.

⤞ ⤞ ⤞ ⤞

I returned to my room, locating the magic box that sent letters between myself and my sister. It had been hers and Cade's, and I was already hesitant about using it too much, even though she'd assured me that she wanted to hear from me. But Clíodhna wanted me to do this, and it was as close to an edict as she could get.

So with nervous hands, I penned a letter.

Dear Ayla,

I hope you're well. I'm sorry I used the box again, but it's the quickest way to reach you.

My grandmother wants me to learn more about the white magic I have. And the best way to do that is to be near a piece of the stone. Would it be okay if I came to visit?

Sincerely,

Riona

I put it inside the box, and it glowed then dimmed. I sat back, nerves sliding up my back as I worried what she might say, how she might react. She'd been relieved after they'd saved me from Edric, but—

The box glowed again. I held my breath and picked up the letter inside.

Dear Riona,

Your ears must've been burning, because I was about to ask you the same thing. Please come at your earliest convenience. I'm eager to see you.

Sincerely,

Ayla

Chapter Twelve

Cade

I would've thought saving the crew and ship from almost certain death or capture by the Driwanian navy would've put me on their good sides, but they were as distant and cold as ever. Aldonza remained at the helm, her gaze squarely on the horizon. The sun was starting to set, casting an orange and pink glow across the sky and water. One by one, the crew finished their chores and descended belowdecks. The raucous sound of conversation echoed up to us from below, so they'd clearly gotten into the food and ale.

"Are you going to join them?" I asked Aldonza, gesturing to the open stairwell.

"If I do, we'll end up even farther off course than we are now." A pattern of stars had appeared in the dwindling light, and she seemed focused on those.

"Have you figured out where we are?" I asked.

She sighed. "Once the light is gone, I will."

I frowned. "How?"

No answer.

I cast a spell to look down into the hull of the ship, finding the crew sharing a loaf of crusty bread and a bit of hard cheese. I gathered a crumb of both and held them in my hand, multiplying them until I had a whole new loaf and section of hard cheese. Then I stood at the bottom of the stairs, gazing up at the helm and her captain.

"Where did you get that?" she asked, narrowing her gaze.

"Don't worry, I can make more," I said, breaking off a piece of bread. "Keep it fresh, too, until we reach our destination."

I offered her some, and she didn't even acknowledge me.

So I ate the whole thing myself. After a whole day on the ship, the rocking of the boat wasn't as nauseating as it had been. In fact, the warm breeze on my skin was calming, the scent of the ocean somehow familiar.

When I finished my meal, I ascended the stairs to meet Aldonza on the captain's deck. By now, the only light came from the moon overhead. But she wasn't looking at the horizon anymore; she had a wooden instrument with a scope attached to a round-bottomed triangle. She seemed to be moving the sliding scale slowly.

"What are you—"

"*P'okmmud,*" she muttered. "Quit scaring me like that."

"Sorry," I said. "What is that?"

"A sextant."

I coughed. "I'm sorry, what?"

"A navigational tool, you child," she said. "It helps me measure the distance between stars and the horizon."

"Why would you need to measure that?" I asked with a frown.

She snorted. "You must've been taken at a *very* young age, kid."

"I was," I said with a soft sigh. "I think I was five. But the man who took me wasn't ever truthful with me about much. So who knows what age I was?"

She lowered the machine and watched me for a minute. "I'm sorry. Do you know why he took you?"

"Because I'm a wizard," I said. "Supposedly there aren't that many still around. None on the continent where I grew up." I could've gone into the long history of how Laughlan's evil ways had caused a centuries-long shadow on the continent, but I doubted she would've found that interesting. "So the *e'potu,* they don't have magic?"

"Not like you," she said. "But they don't need it. The land, the water, everything around them is magical. All they need to do is understand and respect the life forces around them and they can bend them to their will." She brought the machine back to her eye again. "The *e'potu* have spent eons becoming intimately familiar with the way the world works. Like these stars. We know how to navigate based on their location." She pointed to a bright one low in the sky. "That one, in relation to the horizon," she lowered her finger toward the line between sea and sky, "tells me about where we are on the ocean. You put us about twenty leagues to the south of where we were."

"Is that…good or bad?" I asked.

She shrugged. "We are on the hunt for our next job, so the closest port will do. There's always something to be found."

"You left a port without a job?" I asked, confused.

"There was a very annoying *re'nal'sef* boy who kept asking questions," she replied with a look toward me. "And I was worried you were…someone you clearly are not."

She continued measuring the stars, jotting down small notes in a notebook. She was a pirate, on the run from at least one navy. On the run from the *e'potu*, too. What had made her leave the safety of her people?

"Stop staring at me," she said.

"I'm just curious about your story," I said. "About how you came to helm this ship."

"Not much to share," she said. "Found it. Liked it. Took it. Found a crew along the way who seem pretty loyal as long as I keep 'em fed and watered and the ale flowing at night. We find jobs. We do jobs. We keep one step ahead of the people who want us to stop."

"The Driwanians?" I asked. "What exactly did they want with you?"

"Oh, who remembers?"

I crossed my arms, waiting for her to continue.

"We might owe a few thousand gold pieces in taxes," she said. "Perhaps helped smuggle some goods off the mainland back to the island nations. The usual sort of miscreant behavior." She carefully put the machine back in its box and closed the latch. "It'll take us a few days to reach the next port city. Unless, of course, you want to open one of those nifty little portals and get us there faster."

"Portal travel over water is a tad more difficult than land," I said. "On land, it's easy to know where you are based on landmarks. Rivers, towns, that sort of thing. Out here…there's nothing to orient you."

She pointed up.

"Well, I'm not as well-versed in the stars as you are," I said with a huff. "So I can stand here and search the entire ocean, but for all I know, I'm going in circles." I twisted my staff in my hand. "Trust me, I did a lot of that recently."

"What do you mean?"

I licked my lips. "I'm looking for a magical object. I'd… I was hoping it might be this way, so I spent the past few weeks using magic to search. I didn't find much of anything. But I also couldn't really tell where I was going. I'd actually given up hope I'd gone the right way until I saw…well, you."

"And you think I'm the key to this powerful object?" She quirked a brow.

"Maybe." I leaned on the railing overlooking the quiet water below. "Want to tell me about the *fuath*?"

She put down the sextant. "It'll take us a few days to reach the next port—Fortenzia. Unless you want to learn how to navigate by the stars and make it quicker."

I came closer, and she handed me the instrument. She instructed me, moving the sextant up and down until I found the star she was talking about. It was brighter than the others, shimmering against the black like a beacon.

"So then you use this to measure the distance," she said, gesturing to a small table behind her where a map rested, held in place by several heavy stones. "We take the distance then look on the map and figure out where we are."

With practice, I was sure I could figure out how to magically navigate without the sextant. For now, it seemed I needed Aldonza's help to keep it all straight.

I smiled at her. "Thanks for showing me."

"Don't get familiar," she said. "Teaching you how to navigate is just helping me get where I want to go faster."

I watched her leave, sensing her guardedness. "It must be lonely to be so unwilling to make friends."

"I don't need friends out here. I need people who'll have my back —whether through gold or bribery." She looked me up and down and gestured to the map behind us. "Now, do you think you can figure out how to get us closer to Fortenzia?"

I scrutinized the map, trying to overlay the image in front of me with the blanket of stars above. Closing my eyes, I allowed my magic to work for me, gliding over the ink marks on the paper to grab a more clear memory. And when I lifted my head up, the map expanded in my mind's eye to cover the stars, aligning perfectly. There was a shining beacon where we were, slowly moving across the ocean.

"What's happening?" Aldonza asked.

"Where do we need to go?" I asked, cracking open an eye. To her, I was just standing here like an idiot, my staff glowing.

She pointed to a small dot on the printed map and I resumed my trance. The map moved with the stars, too big for me to take in at once. But after a few moments, guiding myself with the map, I managed to find the island.

"Okay," I said. "Here."

I walked out of the cabin with my staff at the ready. Round and round, I drew the circle, growing larger and larger with the destination firm in my mind, until the portal appeared, showing a small island shrouded in darkness, with small fires lighting the docks and some of the houses.

"That's..." Aldonza walked up next to me. "Amazing. You really have wizard magic, don't you?"

"Did you doubt me?"

"After the stunt you pulled earlier..." She snorted. "Putting us in the middle of nowhere. An *e'potu* who doesn't even know how to navigate by the stars. Pathetic. Your ancestors would be ashamed."

She meant it as a joke, but it hurt somewhere deep. "Well, if you uphold your end of the bargain, I'll be sure to apologize to them when I see them."

"Sure." She turned on her heel, walking back to the wheel to guide the ship through the portal. "Wake the crew. We'll be docking at first light."

CHAPTER THIRTEEN

AYLA

Seeing as I had a lot of bad behavior to make up for in the troll realm, I had Bronwen pull out all the stops for Riona's visit. She planned a multi-course dinner, setting up the nicest guest room, scheduling a full day of activities for us to do together—another trip out of the castle, for sure. I wasn't sure what she wanted to do, but with her, Elodia and Rutley wouldn't be so concerned about my safety.

The afternoon after I received her letter, I kept my gaze on the sky, looking for the telltale purple butterflies in the air. Three or four times, I was sure I saw her, but it was my eyes that were playing tricks on me. But finally—finally—as the sun was starting to set, a cloud fluttered over the land like a flock of starlings. I rushed down the stairs, smoothing my dress as I waited for her to materialize.

"Hi."

"Hi." She rubbed her hands. "Just you? Where's Ward?"

"Still gone to the south," I said, gesturing in that direction. "Hopefully, home soon."

"I see."

We stood for a moment, and I struggled to find the right words. "So… You said something about the stone unlocking your magic?"

"Maybe," she said. "I'm not sure it will."

Another awkward silence.

"Why don't you come in?" I asked. "Are you hungry?"

"S-sure." She took a few steps toward me, still holding her hands like she was about to run in the other direction. I led her inside, down the main entrance hall, toward the throne room.

"Seems quiet in here," she said, tilting her head up. "Is it always this quiet?"

"Sometimes," I said. "We haven't had any visitors since the trolls left. And there aren't that many servants necessary to keep things running smoothly." I chanced a look at her. "Is the Erlking's castle not quiet?"

She snorted. "Not even a little. There are hundreds of creatures milling about at all hours of the day. Everything is alive and moving—even the paintings. It's a miracle anyone gets any sleep there."

We walked into the throne room, and she inhaled audibly, staring at the painting hanging on the wall. "There he is…"

I followed her gaze. "Yes. That's him."

"And…your mother, right?" she asked.

I nodded but held off on a further explanation. Originally, the painting had been of Leandra and my father, but Eoghan had changed it when I started having nightmares about her. He said it was a likeness of my mother, but it could've been anyone. I didn't trust him to be truthful about anything anymore.

"He was handsome, wasn't he?" Riona said softly. "Young."

"Very. He was my age when he ascended the throne. His father was quite old and ill." I scanned his face, the voices of the townsfolk echoing in my head. "And yet, he was much more beloved than I am."

"What's that?"

"It's just something I heard," I said. "I'm not quite as popular a monarch as I'd thought. No one even knows what I look like."

"Should they?" Riona asked.

"I don't know." I shrugged. "It's not like I expect them to throw themselves at my feet or anything. But…it feels like a pattern. Even the other kingdoms think they can walk all over me. And maybe I let them, a little."

"So don't let them. Stand up for yourself. You have the stone."

"A stone that's only powerful in theory, unless you're around," I said. "My father didn't need power to get respect; neither did anyone else in my lineage. They managed to keep the peace for hundreds of years. Meanwhile, I get on the throne and less than a year later…"

"I think you're on the right track," she said. "You're getting the trolls fed, giving the merchants gold. And sooner or later, the other humans will realize they're being unreasonable."

"Will they?"

"Maybe Ward can knock some heads around."

I shook my head, imagining him walking into Ramira's court and making demands. "The last thing I want is escalation. Especially with Cade gone. Especially with my stone…" I pulled it out and did a double take.

The damn thing was glowing.

"What?" Riona asked.

I dropped it against my chest, clicking my tongue against the roof of my mouth. "Why don't we see about that dinner, hm?"

⤙ ⤙ ⤙ ⤙

Dinner continued our awkward silences, punctuated by the sound of silverware scraping on the dishes. I tried to ignore the way the stone glowed under my dress, but the warmth was distracting—and my annoyance at Riona was starting to resurface. It was hard to keep the questions at bay. *Why* her? Was I so bad at being queen that even the stone preferred her to wield it?

"This is delicious," Riona said, after a moment. "Much better than the food in the troll kingdom."

"Mm."

I pushed my goblet from side to side, lost in my thoughts as the warmth increased. And to make matters worse, I began to hear far-off voices—those same ones that—

"Did I say something offensive?" Riona asked. "If I did, I'm—"

"No, of course not," I said, forcing a smile. "It's just…this stupid thing…" I pulled the stone out and put it on the table between us. "It's been unresponsive for weeks. But you show up, and now it's decided it likes you better."

She snorted. "I'm sure…that's not what's going on." But there was something behind her eyes, something she wasn't telling me. "Maybe it just—"

"You said your grandmother sent you here to find out more information," I said, pushing it closer to her. "So take it."

"I don't…" She exhaled shakily. "I don't think that's a good idea."

"Why not?" I leaned in.

"Because I feel like it *wants* me to," she said, her voice barely audible. "And I don't know what that means."

I watched her face—she was scared. "What do you mean it *wants* you to? Do you hear voices?"

"Not voices, no. It's…it's like when we were in the troll kingdom. The magic that was imbued in the water called to me. Made my hands glow." She turned her hands over. "I was hopeful it was a fluke. But it seems the pieces of the *seod croí* are calling to this…this other kind of magic in my veins."

Holding my breath, I opened her palm and put the stone there, and it glowed so brightly it almost hurt my eyes.

"Well?"

"It feels like… It feels like…" She put the stone down quickly, as if it had scalded her. Then she took a breath, calming herself. "There was a rush of power. It dwarfs my butterfly magic to the point where it's gone completely." She frowned. "I don't like it."

"Do all fae have two kinds of magic?"

"Clíodhna said my mother…" She cast me a furtive look, and I nodded, urging her to continue. "My mother had some weird magic. They thought it was because she was both *sidheog* and *daoine maithe*."

"Is that not common?"

She shook her head. "No, not really. They all have the same…parts, you know. But there's always been this separation between the two." She shrugged. "But I guess Birch and Clíodhna couldn't help themselves."

I blanched, considering their ages. "That's…"

"Yeah, it's not great." She caught my gaze and giggled—earning a little one from me as well. But the moment faded quickly, and we were back to silence.

"Did you tell your grandfather about this secondary magic?" I asked.

She made a face. "He's been awfully cagey lately. Aldrick—my uncle—he's been acting strangely, too. And Birch wouldn't even let me broach the subject." She sat back in her chair. "Told me I don't need to worry about him. But I have to worry about him if he's messing with the trolls."

She seemed to be talking more to herself than to me, so I took a sip of my wine.

"Anyway," she said, perhaps realizing she'd lost me. "I don't know if he'd have much more to offer than Clíodhna. She seems to think this is our mystery to figure out."

I turned the stone over in my hand, watching it closely as it glowed dimly. "Did you hear any voices when you hold it?"

"Not voices, no," she said. "Was I supposed to?"

"I do, when it really gets going." I dropped the stone and it thumped against my chest. "But it's clear I'm not the one it wants."

"But you're the only one who can use it," Riona said.

"You—"

She shook her head. "I didn't *use* it when…when he was in my mind. I used this other magic, and it just…I guess it just looked like I was using the Pennlan stone." She sat back, furrowing her brow in concentration. "It's like…being in the presence of the *seod croí* unlocks something deep inside and lets it out." She nodded to the stone. "I hadn't really noticed a difference until now." She paused. "I don't know if *he* noticed either."

"So you don't think it likes you more than me?" It sounded ridiculous, but I needed to know what she thought.

Riona stared at me for a long while then broke into a smile. "No way. It definitely prefers you to me. It just needs…me to turn it on, I guess."

"I thought it was supposed to only be wielded by a member of the Pennlan line," I said.

"Ah yeah, wielded, yes. But turned on? That's not specified," she replied with a bit of a laugh. "Fae trickery, you know. Have to be specific."

Something happy settled in my mind as I turned the stone over in my hand. It was all theoretical, of course, but it *did* make some sense.

"You promise you aren't just telling me this to placate me?" I whispered. "You really think it's mine to wield?"

"I wouldn't lie to you," she said with a smile. "I mean, I could, of course. But I won't."

She beamed, but all I could think about was the troll realm, when I'd found out she *had* lied about being able to use her magic, how I'd blown up at her, and just how horrible I'd felt afterward.

"Listen," I said, my throat tight, "I need to apologize again for—"

"You don't need to apologize for that."

"I do, though," I said. "And explain—"

"There's no need," she insisted.

I looked at the ceiling. "Stop letting me off the hook."

"I just don't think…" She sat back in her chair. "We have so many other problems out there. Two pieces of the stone are still missing. Cade's gone. It seems like there's a storm brewing in the fae realm. I don't think any of us have the energy to hold grudges or be mad with one another."

I opened my mouth. "You're right. But—"

"If you want to make it up to me," she said, "let's spend some time with that stone so we can both figure out how our magic works. That's sisterly bonding, isn't it?"

I brightened. "Sounds good to me."

Chapter Fourteen

Ward

For people who were supposedly in a hurry to get the border open, the merchants took their time in determining the authenticity of the gems the troll had created. The next morning, Fiadh told me she and the other trolls would seek refuge from the unrelenting sun until dark.

"If the merchants don't have an answer by then," I said, "you're welcome to just take the stuff and go."

With a whole day at my disposal, I decided to canvass the city in search of an easy way across to Konevell. At first glance, that looked like an impossible task. The river bisected Orapus down the center, with what appeared to be a matching set of buildings, people, and docks on the Konevell side. I began my journey by walking the streets and keeping my ears open. For a city supposedly at a standstill, Orapus was bustling. I wandered the length of the main road, stopping to peer inside the shops but buying nothing. I didn't have much coin on me, and I didn't want to carry anything back. But I did spend a few minutes admiring a rather striking green dress in the window and wondering what my queen might look like wearing it.

After giving up on finding a land bridge, I thought I'd ask a local. I bypassed some of the finer-looking individuals with gold trim on their clothes and shiny shoes until I found a man who looked weatherworn. He was mending a fishing net with a serious-looking needle and didn't seem to mind the glare of the sun in his eyes.

"What d'ya want?" he grunted, after noticing me standing there.

"How does one get over to Konevell?" I asked.

He snorted. "You and everyone else would like to know that."

I pulled a coin out of my pocket and twirled it around in my hand. "Any ideas now?"

He watched the coin warily. "I might have a few if you have another one of those."

I popped the coin in the air, and he caught it. "I'll give you another if you give me something I can use to get across."

"How much stuff you got?"

"No stuff. Just me." I pulled another coin. "What do you think?"

"It'll be tough in the city. You're better off trying to find a small boat upriver," he said. "Too many eyes around here, and too many people who'd like to be in your shoes."

"Is there any kind of land bridge?" I asked. "Or anywhere it's narrow enough that it's easy to wade across?"

He snorted. "You aren't from around here, are you?"

"Not really. From up north."

"Look, the river is fast and dangerous. You put a boat in the water, you're only going one way—toward the sea. No way to get across, and no *place* to get across." He returned to his net. "There's a reason everyone's waiting on tenterhooks for these queens to fix their squabbles."

"Hopefully soon," I said, reaching into my pocket to flip him another coin. "Thanks for the information."

"Didn't really tell you nothin', but all right."

He hadn't, but he had given me an idea. There might not be a way across, but I knew someone who was quite adept at building stone bridges who might be able to assist.

⤞ ⤞ ⤞ ⤞

When I returned to the barracks, there was a note from the merchants with instructions on where to find the goods and how many gems they wanted in return. It was a ridiculous amount—way over the price they would've gotten on the open market—but since it was no big deal for Fiadh to create wealth from nothing, I doubted she'd have a problem with it.

Once the sky turned orange, I set out for the warehouses. Along the way, I stopped in at the nearby tavern to retrieve the lieutenant who was supposed to be following my every step. He rose slowly, taking his time to count out the coins he owed the barkeep. Either the prices here were through the roof, or he was able to hold his liquor better than I'd thought. He stumbled out after me, the stench of ale palpable even as I kept my distance.

"I'm going to head back to Pennlan tonight," I told him, knowing he wouldn't question. "Will you be able to handle this on your own?"

"They keep making streets full of gems, sure thing—*hic*—boss."

The door was open, and I didn't even make it past the first step before the stench of rotting produce hit my nose. As my eyes adjusted to the dim light inside, my brows rose. I hadn't really understood what a backlog meant, at least in this context, until I found myself dwarfed by crates stacked so high they scraped the ceiling. Some of them had their contents stamped on them—everything from wheat and grapes to rocking horses and chairs to crates of wool and clothes.

"How many of these warehouses do you reckon there are?" I asked Platt.

A new voice answered me. "Hundreds. All over the city."

I spun around as a group of merchants walked inside—or as inside as the crammed room would allow. Even though I now wore my captain's uniform, they watched me warily, judgment clear on their faces. Platt sat on one of the crates and leaned back, eager to watch the show.

"Well? We were told there would be someone waiting?" one of them said. "I only see two of Her Majesty's guard."

I introduced myself and Platt. "And I suppose you're with Cormac and Pádraig?"

They didn't answer, but I doubted the two bigwigs would be here to oversee this transfer themselves. The minutes passed excruciatingly slowly, and I shifted my weight from one foot to another, keeping my gaze on the ground as I scanned for the telltale light of a troll moving through it. The merchants seemed to have a short fuse and a shorter attention span, grumbling and grousing as the time ticked on.

"Well?" one of the merchants said, addressing me. "Where's this magical creature?"

"Give her a minute."

"The sun's gone," another barked. "If you brought us here for—"

"She'll be here," I said, though some part of me was plotting how I'd escape if Fiadh never showed up. The merchants were blocking my exit, and Platt wouldn't lift a finger to help. But hopefully…hopefully it wouldn't be needed. "You said there were hundreds of these warehouses all over the city? They aren't normally this full, are they?"

"Of course not," the first one scoffed. "They're intended to be temporary housing for when ships are delayed. We run a tight business here, things coming and going in a few days' time. Our ships reach all the way to the southernmost islands and beyond. But if we can't unload our wares or get them beyond the bay, we've got nowhere else to put them."

I nodded. "Don't worry. We'll be able to move your goods quickly."

"And pay us for them?"

I nodded. "Handsomely."

Again, the first one sniffed, as if not believing a word out of my mouth. "We'll see. So far I'm—"

A gasp rose from the back of the group as a spark of light zoomed under their feet, causing them to yell and jump out of the way in fear. My heart relaxed as Fiadh materialized in front of me.

"Captain," she said, nodding to me once. Her gaze lifted, and it was her turn to look relieved. "There's so much."

"I hope it'll be enough to get you through the winter," I said. "It might not all be the freshest—"

"We've been eating nothing but moldy vegetables for a thousand years," she said with a snort. "It'll be a vast improvement."

"Who is..." I'd almost forgotten about the merchants, now cowering together in the corner. "What is she?"

"She's a troll," I said. "And she'll be taking these goods and anything else you want to sell her off your hands."

"And how will she...pay for it?"

I sighed. "Fiadh, if you will..."

She turned and took three steps outside. The cobblestone street lay before her, glinting in the moonlight. She knelt to the ground and put her hands along the street, her magic releasing across each of the stones. And one-by-one, they turned to a glittering rainbow.

"My word..."

I hastily dashed out of the way as the merchants ran into the street to pocket as many of the precious gems as they could get their greedy little hands on. I walked up next to Fiadh, who was watching them with amusement, and crossed my arms.

"So tell me this: if the trolls can make gems from rock, how come they weren't respected in the fae realm? Surely, you could've bought yourselves better lives?"

"Diamonds and gems are only valuable in the human realm," she said. "In the fae one, power is the only thing worth having."

"Well, it looks like they're nice and happy," I said. "How much can you take with you today? All of it?"

She smiled. "Even with ten of us, we won't be able to take the entirety of this place. But..." She nodded. "We will have enough to last us through the winter. King Lynton thanks you for your kindness."

"I think the humans are the ones getting the better deal," I said with a smirk as the merchants continued pulling the cobblestones from the road. Even Platt got in on the action, stuffing his pockets full of gems and diamonds.

"If that will be all, I'll—"

"Actually," I turned to her, "if your fellow trolls can handle this for a bit, I have a favor to ask."

>⇥ >⇥ >⇥ >⇥

Neither the merchants nor Platt noticed me slipping away, nor the light of Fiadh traveling through stone and rock. I'd asked her to zoom ahead and find a desolate part of the river where she could create a small bridge to get me across. I followed the directions she'd left, as she would be impossibly faster with magic than I'd be on foot.

I didn't know how much time had passed when the streak of light rushed toward me and materialized into my troll friend.

"I've found a good spot to cross not too far from here," she said. "Very few humans, lots of trees on both sides. I should be able to create something that will be hidden until low tide."

"Thanks," I said. "Lead the way."

She led me toward a thick forest but instead of going through it, she constructed a stone bridge that stretched across the wide river. As the stones manifested across the divide, I smiled to myself. It was good to have such helpful friends.

"I'll destroy it once we're across," she explained. "And create something low that'll be hidden by the tide for you to return with."

As promised, the moment we set foot on the other side, the bridge fell into the water. I hated to see it go, but it was probably for the best. But as soon as it was gone, small rocks bubbled up from the water, solidifying into dinner-plate-sized stepping stones that stretched from one end to the other.

"The tide is low now," she said. "So you may have to wait for the right moment to cross."

"Are you sure I can't convince you to come with me?" I asked. "It might be nice to have someone with your abilities as I travel through enemy territory."

"As much as I'd like to help, I must return to Orapus to gather supplies." She gazed toward the north with a longing look. "The longer I dawdle, the longer it'll be until my people get to eat."

I nodded in understanding. "Thank you. This would've—"

The sound of approaching hoofbeats cut me short. But before I could even dive for cover, the ground swelled up around me, pushing me to a crouching position. Fiadh was beside me, my fingers dangling next to her arm. She must've created a boulder-like structure around us, though she did leave a small air hole at the very bottom. Which was good, because I was having a hard time steadying my breath.

You could be captured. Elodia's voice echoed in my mind.

"I thought I heard something," a new voice said.

Another voice answered. "You always think you hear something. Let's head back to camp. The captain will want a report."

Camp? There wasn't supposed to be any kind of military camp out this way. Perhaps I'd heard wrong, and they simply called their barracks a camp, but…

As the sound died, Fiadh disintegrated the boulder around us and I stood up, scanning the horizon. There looked to be something in the east, based on the aura of light hanging on. Perhaps that was where they'd come from.

"Ward?" Fiadh asked. "I really must go."

"Right." I nodded and held out my hand. "Thank you. Please give Lynton and Riona my best."

She took my hand and shook it. "Take care of yourself. The ground is unsettled here—more so than in Pennlan. Something strange is afoot."

I hadn't realized trolls had that sort of power. "Hopefully, my trip to see the queen will fix all of that and things will be back to normal in no time."

She made no response except to nod curtly then disappeared into the ground. Within seconds, her light of magic was on the other side of the river, zipping back toward Orapus. I took one final look at the small stepping stones that would be my way back home and said a quiet prayer they'd still be there when I needed them.

And with that, I headed toward the city in the distance, hoping to find directions to the capital of Konevell.

Chapter Fifteen

Cade

Considering I'd just saved them several *days* of travel, Aldonza and her crew were oddly light with their thanks. As she'd said, they approached at dawn, anchoring in the middle of the bay and taking a small dinghy to the dock. I opted to go with them, as I wasn't eager to announce myself as a wizard to this strange island just yet.

"You think we'll be able to find someone to take me to H'sipotu?" I asked.

Aldonza nodded, her gaze toward the island. "Lots of folks in and out. We'll find you someone to take you the rest of the way."

Cluny landed the boat on the soft, white sand of the island, and I stepped out, almost immediately toppling over. My legs were like jelly, my body still moving with the rolling of the waves. The crew snickered as they easily disembarked and tied up the boat. Iga, however, did find it within herself to steady me as I stumbled over the difficult sand.

"We'll get you sea legs soon enough," she said with a chuckle.

The crew headed into the collection of buildings—could it be called a city?—and I trailed behind, enamored by the new sights, smells, and sounds. Tall trees with long purple leaves knitted together across the skyline, a backdrop for the quaint little village before me. There didn't seem to be any walls on the buildings, just thatched roofs over rickety shelters. Some were shops, displaying fruits and the catch of the day, others seemed to be watering holes where weatherworn men and women sat around small tables staring into glasses. The roads were filled with people and animals, though some animals I'd never seen before.

One creature that looked like a pig—except its snout reached the floor and it didn't have any eyes—sniffed the ground as it navigated through the throng of people. It reached a pile of moldy fruit and other refuse and dug its long nose inside, using the appendage to shovel food into its mouth.

"Scat! Get out!" The shopkeeper came rushing out with a broom, hitting the creature on its thick, armored back.

The creature bared its teeth and hissed but scurried on to the next unguarded bin where it proceeded to chow down once more.

In another shop to my left, a cage full of multicolored birds squawked and hopped on their perches. They were the size of my hand with long, black beaks and claws to match. The sign next to them indicated they were used for sending messages.

"How far do they fly?" I asked the owner.

"To the other side of the island and back," he said. "You got a message?"

"Not one that needs to go there," I said, reaching a finger inside the cage—and regretting it as soon as the closest beak clamped down on the tip of my finger.

The owner chuckled. "You've got a ways to go if you're trying to get to H'sipotu."

I started. "You know where it is?"

"Nah. Just know *of* the people. You're a dead ringer, you know. Got that feeling about you. Air of magic. They carry it with them in their clothes and hair and teeth, you know."

I didn't think my teeth had magic, but I was eager to hear more. "Do you get many *e'potu* here?"

"Nah. The captain you came with is the only one I've seen in an age."

I glanced behind me, catching the top of the mast in the distance. "Do you know her story?"

"Same as everyone else here. Didn't feel quite at home where she was, so she took to the sea."

I could empathize with that feeling. "Thanks for the info."

"Didn't tell you much, but if you're thanking…" He held out his hand. "A token of appreciation would be appreciated." He cracked a smile.

I dug in my pocket, found one of the few gold coins I had left and handed it over.

There wasn't much to this place, and I wasn't interested in braving the thick forest that lay beyond, especially with the sounds of creatures unknown hooting and hollering in the distance. I walked another loop of the village, stopping at a leatherworks shop that seemed to specialize in the most peculiar fabric I'd ever seen.

"What kind of animal is this?" I asked, running my hand along the bumpy, purple hide.

"A *law'ua'b*," the owner replied. "Large sea monsters with rows and rows of sharp teeth. They'll eat a whole boat if you let 'em get big enough. Hard to kill, harder still to skin once they're fully grown. That there's a baby's flipper, so it was easier to kill. The leather's still near indestructible."

The fabric stretched from one end of the man's hut to the other. I couldn't imagine what it was to slay something like that—and it was only a baby. I certainly didn't like the idea of one of those swimming around under the suddenly-too-small ship I'd arrived on.

She was watching me, a curious look on her face. "You probably know all about them, though. Don't you?"

"Why do you say that?"

"Because of *Law'ek'ub*."

"Who's that?"

"A *law'ua'b* who rules the southern seas, near where your people live," she said. "Don't tell me he's finally been slayed."

"I'm not…" I cleared my throat. "I'm actually trying to get back to H'sipotu. I haven't been there in a long time."

"Well, that certainly explains…" She cleared her throat, but the way her gaze raked up and down my body, I could only assume she was talking about my clothes. They were wool, made for traveling in the cooler climes of Pennlan and the fae realm, and I would've been lying if I said I wasn't sweltering in the hot, muggy temperatures.

"I have some linen in the back," she said. "New shirt, pants. And maybe some new waterproof boots?"

"Thanks, but no thanks." I nodded, walking away before she could shake me down for gold like the merchant before. But once I was a safe distance away, I scooted between one of the buildings and the forest beyond. Then I cast a charm on my shirt, transforming it from wool into linen, like the ones she had hanging in her shop. I did the same for the pants, but when it came down to transfiguring my boots, I found…the leather was impossible to replicate. Almost as if it had magical properties that prevented such a thing.

I looked around the corner to where the merchant girl had returned to sewing two strips of leather together. My boots really were fine, but something made me want to go back to the merchant and inspect that magic leather further.

"There you are."

Aldonza marched up to me, practically dragging a bedraggled man behind her. "This is Jack."

"Gerrald."

"Whatever," she said. "He's well-versed in traveling to H'sipotu. He will take you in the morning. Right?"

"Yeah, yeah," he said. "For a price, of course."

"Of course," I said. But my gaze hadn't left Aldonza. Something about this seemed fishy. "He's not *e'potu*."

"No, but he's been there a lot."

That absolutely did not fit with what Aldonza had told me about the secretive people—and based on her expression, she knew it, too. But she still shoved the captain toward me. He stumbled a few steps then straightened as much as he could, flashing me a grin that was missing more than a few teeth and breath that smelled like he'd spent most of the day in an ale barrel.

"At yer service, master!"

"Well, I guess this is goodbye," Aldonza said, already turning. "Have a nice life." Before I could stop her, she walked briskly away, leaving me with the fisherman, who looked as bewildered as I was.

"So…you wanna go to *Hopitania* or whatever it's called?" he asked after a moment. "How much money you got?"

"I have enough sense to know you have no clue where it is," I replied with a look. "Now beat it."

He didn't argue, whistling and stuffing his hands in his pockets. The coins there jingled faintly—surely given to him by Aldonza for his part in the charade. I didn't want to think about what his plan was for me. Perhaps try to rob me and leave me on a deserted island.

But the better question was why did Aldonza believe that would work?

Her ship was already speeding away from the port, all sails out as they tried to outrun me. Aldonza must've thought I had to be close to create a portal or was hoping she'd have enough time to get far enough away I wouldn't be able to find her. But she was within eyesight, and even with her ship going that fast, it would've taken at least an hour to disappear over the horizon.

I sat on a fallen tree, one of the long, spindly plants that reached for the sky with dark purple fronds, and considered my options. I could return to her ship, but she might pull the same trick on me at the next island. Then I'd magic myself back, and round and round we'd go. Presumably, she would never take me to H'sipotu, not even if I waited years.

I could stay here on this island and hope I could find an *e'potu*. But from what I'd heard, that was going to be impossible.

Aldonza was my best bet, unfortunately. Even if it meant I had to be patient.

This time, I didn't even bother hiding. I created a portal to the deck and walked through.

"You're back." Aldonza didn't sound surprised. "What took you so long?" She glanced at me up and down. "Should've bought the boots, too."

"Well, as it turns out, our bargain remains unfulfilled," I said, sitting down in my usual spot. "Which means I stay on your ship."

"Fine," she said with a wave of her hand. "If you insist."

It didn't escape my notice she didn't seem as *angry* about my interloping as she had been the first time. Perhaps I was finally getting through to her.

"Wizard, why don't you create a portal again?" she asked. "See if you can't use some of that star-mapping I taught you last night to get us to the island of Al'ocasep. Beautiful place, you know. I'm sure we'll see twenty *e'potu* people there." She grinned like a madwoman, and her crew chuckled. "We got some cargo we can offload, too, if you want to earn your keep. Save our aching backs. What'dya say?

My gaze swept from Aldonza to the crew, who shared her giddiness.

"I'd say I'd earned my keep when I saved you from the Driwanian navy," I replied lightly, unsure what I was walking into.

"But see, if you create us one of those portal things, we'll get to the next port much faster. And you'll be that much closer to getting to H'sipotu." She shrugged. "I'd call that a win-win."

She had absolutely no intention of ever taking me there, that much was clear. But my chances of reaching the island were better with someone who knew the way, even if she'd sworn she would never go. Not only that, but if I could master navigating by the stars as she did, I might not even need her anymore.

"Well?"

I smiled at her. "I think I'll need another lesson before I can attempt such a thing. Perhaps several. So I suppose you'll have to sail the regular way until nightfall." I tilted my head. "Hope that's not an inconvenience."

She scowled. "Fine. You'll get another lesson tonight. But remember who's the captain on this ship and who's the stowaway. You give me another order, you'll find yourself at the bottom of the ocean—without your stick."

Clearly, she had no clue how wizard staffs worked, but I merely nodded my agreement.

Chapter Sixteen

Riona

I awoke in a strange bed, confused until I remembered I'd spent the night at Pennlan castle. The room was homey and warm, already with a roaring fire in the hearth to beat back the morning chill. On the floor, a thick rug spanned the length of the room. There was a neat sitting table and single chair near the window, which had a light sheen of frost. My room back in the Erlking's castle was homey, but this was…nice.

What might it have been like had Eoghan never shown his face? What could my life have been had my mother never been forced to murder my father, had I not been squirreled away, hidden in the fae realm?

This might've been my room. I might've known what it was to be waited on hand and foot by a human servant. Bronwen, Ayla's attendant, was kind and prompt, eager to ensure I had everything I needed. Would I have had one just like her?

Sitting back against my pillow, I imagined a childhood where I'd ridden horses with my sister, gotten into mischief I was never allowed in the Erlking's castle, and sat in the warm embrace of a father on his throne as he told me stories about my ancestors. Had my mother's hand running the length of my hair as she sang songs and taught me about the fae realm.

Wetness filled the corners of my eyes, surprising me. I'd never mourned the life I hadn't had, never stopped long enough to think about how things could and should have been different. But as I sat there in a comfortable bed, bathed in the warm morning sun, I found I missed this fantasy life.

There was a soft knock on the door and Bronwen appeared with a kind smile. "Her Majesty would like you to join her for breakfast, if you're hungry."

I dressed quickly and followed her down, eager to continue our conversations from the night before. I felt like we were finally getting somewhere. Ayla was genuinely happy to see me, although she still held onto her fear that she wasn't good enough to be queen. Her insecurities had always been easy to detect, perhaps because I had them myself. But it only endeared her to me. For her sake, I hoped she would find the confidence she so desperately needed.

As I walked into the small dining room, my gaze immediately went to Ayla, who broke into a wide smile. But it wasn't just her at the table—Elodia and Rutley were there, too.

"Riona!" Rutley jumped to his feet and swept me into a big hug. "So good to see you!"

"Put her down, you oaf," Elodia, always the more stoic of the pair, was beaming. "What are you doing here?"

"You didn't tell them?" I asked.

"Thought it might be better to hear it coming from you," Ayla said, a little slyly.

"We're going to practice with the stone," I said.

Elodia spun around, narrowing her gaze at Ayla. "You're going to… what? Practice? Practice how?"

"Not entirely sure," Ayla replied. "But it's clear we need to be in each other's presence to access our respective magics. It would be nice to have some dedicated time to really understand what's needed and perhaps even get some control over it."

"Not here, right?" Rutley asked.

"No, of course not," I said. "There are fields outside the castle that would work fine. Far enough away from anything that might get damaged."

Elodia scowled, again glaring at Ayla. "Are you sure this isn't an excuse to knock your sister around?"

"Of course it isn't," I snapped, a little irked Elodia would say such a thing. "It's important we know more about the Pennlan stone in case…" I cleared my throat. "In case we need it."

"Fine. As long as we come," Elodia said.

"Of course," Ayla replied with a sweet smile. "Why do you think I asked you to breakfast?"

>―» >―» >―» >―»

Clearly, I'd missed something between Ayla and her two soldiers, but Rutley wouldn't leave me alone with Ayla long enough to ask her what it was. He wanted to know everything about how the trolls were getting along, the Erlking's castle, and about what I'd been up to.

"In the week since you last saw her?" Elodia asked, but she smiled as we strode across a grassy plain, putting some distance between us and anyone else.

"Well, a lot happens in a few days," he replied with a scowl.

I told him about Aldrick and Clíodhna, leading up to why I'd shown up here the night before. "Then I had a great dinner with my sister and woke up here."

Ayla beamed but said nothing.

"See? The Aldrick thing was interesting," Rutley said to Elodia.

She rolled her eyes.

"I think this is far enough," Ayla said. "You two might want to give us some space."

"I watched you blow the top off a mountain," Elodia replied, giving a half-hearted salute. "I know to keep my distance."

They scurried back to stand under a far-off tree as Ayla and I faced one another.

"So…" Ayla looked at her stone. "How do we do this?"

"I have no clue."

"I mean, in the fae realm, when you train. What do you do?"

"Conjure magic," I said. "Try to inflict pain on your opponent. But I think your soldiers would have a problem with that."

"Right." She turned the stone over. "Maybe we start with just… turning it on?"

"Good idea."

I crossed the distance between us. "Do you think I just have to be nearby or do I have to touch it?"

"I think…I think touch," she said slowly. "It didn't work at all when we were walking up the mountain."

"Okay." I placed one finger on the gem and a surge of magic took me over as the light blinded me. Immediately, I pulled away. "Sorry, that was—"

"No." She looked as dizzy as I felt. "No, that was fine. It's always a bit—"

"Disconcerting?" She nodded. "Same."

"Glad to know it's not just me," she said. "I wish we could just turn it on a little, you know?"

"I think that's the downside of this being one-fourth of the most powerful object ever created," I said with a smirk. "It's all or nothing."

"Well, then…" She swallowed, looking a bit sick. "I guess we'll just have to get used to it. Together."

It was, perhaps, silly. For over two hours, all I did was touch the stone then let go. But the more we practiced, the less overwhelming the power became. It was still potent, of course, but my capacity to withstand it seemed to grow with use.

We stopped to have lunch, a picnic Bronwen had sent along with us, under the tree with Elodia and Rutley.

"So…all you were doing was just turning it on?" Rutley asked. "You nearly blinded me."

"Why were you looking, dolt?" Elodia said, tearing into a piece of bread.

"Because I wanted to make sure our queen was safe."

"You were the one who was unsafe. She's got a glowing stone capable of disintegrating a mountain."

I giggled as Ayla handed me a piece of cheese and flask of water. It hadn't escaped my notice she was the one serving everyone. Again, my curiosity about what had transpired was piqued, but I didn't ask in front of the group.

"So you're telling me this thing only works when Riona's around?" Rutley asked.

"Touching it, more specifically," Ayla replied.

"This thing has a lot of very specific needs." Rutley grunted. "Don't do this, must do this in this order—"

"Probably a good thing," Elodia said. "What might happen if the stone could just be turned on whenever? Ward might not have survived the trek up the mountain."

I snorted as Ayla's face turned beet red. "I was a bit—"

"It's fine." Elodia nudged her. "I guess we can forgive you."

"Something I've been wondering," Rutley said. "How the heck did that Eoghan get your blood, Riona? I mean, Edric said he gave them a vial of it. Did he take it when he had you under his spell?"

My initial instinct was to shudder, to shut down at the talk of the evil wizard. But sitting next to Ayla, with Elodia and Rutley casually leaning on the grass munching on cheese, warmed by the bright sun, loosened the tension in my body.

"He'd only need a drop of it," I began softly. "Cade could make more of everything—water, food—as long as he had a crumb. That's a bit outside the realm of fae magic but seems to be easy for a wizard." I licked my lips. "Maybe he had some on his clothes when he was banished."

"Maybe." Rutley shrugged. "It's just an odd thing for him to have taken."

"A lot of magic is blood-based," I said, before being struck by a horrible thought. "Maybe he thought he could use my blood to wield the

Pennlan stone and wouldn't need to control me anymore."

Ayla lifted her gaze, looking at me. "But didn't you say you never *actually* used the stone, right? You were using this other magic?"

I nodded. "I think so."

"Then even if he has your blood…" Ayla began softly as she was working through the intricacies in her mind. "He still wouldn't be able to use the Pennlan stone. He'd be able to turn it on, perhaps, but not wield it."

I watched her for a moment, running through the scenarios in my mind. Perhaps that was why he'd taken some of my blood. I hoped he still didn't have it. "Yes, I suppose that's true."

"See?" Rutley snorted. "Too many specifics for me to keep straight."

After we finished the meal, Ayla and I walked the distance back to where we'd been practicing, and I decided to sate my curiosity about the tension between Ayla and her guards.

"Well, isn't it obvious?" Ayla said, her pale cheeks growing rosy. "They're mad at me for what I said to you."

"Oh…they are?"

"Everyone was." She sighed. "Including me."

"I mean, we're okay now," I said. "All is forgiven."

"They'll come around," she said with a sigh. "Do you want to keep going?"

I nodded. "Maybe…maybe I could try a spell this time? Or you could try a spell."

She exhaled. "Might be good to start learning how to do those. Usually I just kind of…" She flicked her hand. "Tell it to do this. It's more instinct than thought." She pressed her lips together, her cheeks reddening again. "Sorry, I think I'm rambling."

"No, that's…kind of how magic is sometimes," I said. "I didn't get a lot of formal instruction growing up, but I still knew a lot. Especially when it came to defending myself."

She nodded. "What do I need to do first?"

I chewed my lip. "What do you want to do?"

"I don't know." She glanced at the stone. "I suppose…what do I do if I have to face Eoghan?"

She still spoke his name with familiarity, but there was more now, an undercurrent of pain.

"Do what you did to Edric," I replied softly. "Use the stone to destroy him."

She swallowed. "I still…think about how easy it was. How simple it was to destroy a life with just a thought. It scared me, to be honest. That I could have that much power in my hands."

"Perhaps that's why it needs me, too," I said, catching her gaze. "Because it's a lot of power for one person to wield."

She shivered. "But I think what's the scariest of all is knowing Eoghan has a piece of the stone—and he's far more knowledgeable in magic than I am. I'm worried if we go face-to-face with him, we'll lose because he's just too…"

"That's him talking," I said. "He made it his mission to keep you docile and afraid of him. Don't let him win."

She caught my gaze again and my words seemed to have shaken her from her fear. "Right. Let's get back to it."

Chapter Seventeen

Ayla

My attempts at casting magic didn't improve as the afternoon wore on. Even after practicing all day, I couldn't get used to the rush as it came over my body, or the sound of a thousand voices echoing in my ears. Each time the stone lit up, I braced myself for the onslaught, and yet it was always much more than I thought I could handle. I could only hang on for a moment or two before I had to step away and catch my breath.

"Sorry," I said, as the sun cast an orange glow over the field where we practiced. "I wish I could stand it for longer. Maybe with more practice."

"I don't think this is the sort of thing that requires practice," Riona said. "You only need to tap into the power for a short time. I doubt you'll be engaging in prolonged battles with anyone."

Eoghan. I didn't say that aloud, though. "I suppose Aoibheann didn't intend for this to be used much. Or, I'm sure, at all."

By then, it was getting hard to see, and a headache had blossomed between my temples, so we called it a day. I couldn't help but feel somewhat…disappointed by the lack of progress.

"I just want to be prepared," I said after a long pause. "For everything. And I don't feel like I am. I don't like that I can't just *use* it without you being nearby. That seems like…"

"Seems like what?"

"A glaring weakness," I said. "What if you aren't here? What if you can't *get* here? What if—"

She stared at me. "I don't think there's anything we can do about needing me, though. Unless you want some of my blood—"

"No." I shook my head. The thought made me squeamish.

She let out a nervous laugh. "Then what are you so worried about?"

It was so silly. I was embarrassed to even admit it. "I'm supposed to be the only one. It's my birthright. And I still can't do what needs to be done."

"You know…if we get all four pieces, we can destroy it," she said, looking at me curiously. "Would you let that happen?"

"Of course," I said, without hesitation. "Why wouldn't I?"

"It's just…you seem sort of…" She squirmed. "Wrapped up in the idea of the stone. Like it's the only thing about you that has value."

I frowned, crossing my arms over my chest. "I do not."

"You've asked me at least four times if you think the stone likes me better." She cracked a nervous grin. "It's not a sentient thing, you know."

I exhaled, turning it over in my hand. "Without the stone, I'm a simple human and at the mercy of the magical creatures who threaten our borders." I paused, glancing to the south. "And otherwise."

"You're the queen, though."

"Great. I have a crown and servants and a castle. What *good* does that do?" I sighed and stared at the dark sky. "Your magic is brilliant. Cade can summon and conjure anything he sets his mind too. Ward is brave and strong. And I'm just…the stupid girl who fell for Eoghan's lies —then Edric's. I suppose…" The faint glow from the stone was becoming more pronounced as the sun disappeared. "I suppose I want to know I'm more than just the damsel in distress."

"Then be more," Riona said. "Take charge. Make decisions. Don't sit by and let others do your work for you. Roll up your sleeves and get to work. Talk to your countrymen. Find out what their problems are and work to solve them."

"Easier said than done," I said. "Especially when nobody takes me seriously."

She shrugged. "I don't know. I'm not a queen. Never had any ambitions for leadership. But what I *do* know is you aren't a nobody. You've made mistakes, but we all have. And in my opinion, you've done *really* well as queen considering..." She didn't seem to want to say Eoghan's name. "...considering all *he* did to you."

I smiled. "You think so?"

"Absolutely," she said. "And I think when you stop worrying so much about the stupid stone, that's when you're really going to shine."

"You know, that's a beautiful thought," I said. "But having the stone at full strength does tend to solve our problems rather quickly."

She giggled. "True. But you get what I'm saying."

I did, and it was nice to have someone in my corner. "I think Bronwen made a roasted leg of lamb for dinner. Are you hungry?"

"Starving. Do you think she has more of those chocolates, too?"

"All I have to do is ask."

⤞ ⤞ ⤞ ⤞

After dinner, I suggested a walk in the garden to digest the obscene amount of chocolate we'd eaten. The stone glowed, lighting our path. I found myself enjoying the hum of power, instead of threatened by it. Riona indulged me with another detailed accounting of their journey to find the Pennlan stone, making sure to emphasize how often Cade and Ward argued over me.

"I mean, really...it was quite embarrassing," she said. "Two boys thinking with their other heads."

I snorted then stared at the moon. "I hope Cade is all right."

"He's a wizard. Of course he's all right."

"Maybe physically, but emotionally..." I sighed. "He was really hurt."

"But you don't... You were honest with him, right?"

I nodded. "I wished I felt differently, but I don't."

"I think he just needs some time to accept what he already knew," Riona said. "You never looked at him the way you look at Ward."

I smiled, thinking of my new captain, then let it fade as Captain Gabhann's voice echoed through my ears. "I shouldn't be looking at *anyone* like that. I know my place, and it's not one that can give my heart away to just anyone. My marriage is…" I sighed. "It's one of the most important tools I have."

"Do you think you'll marry soon?" Riona asked.

"If I can help it, no," I said. "But even though I'm queen, I'm starting to get the feeling the decision isn't really up to me. That I may have to…have to sacrifice what I want for the good of the kingdom." I shrugged. "Either way, as much as I'd prefer otherwise, Ward isn't… He isn't possible."

She was silent for a while. "Never say never, you know? Maybe something will change."

"I adore your optimism."

"I think you're the only one." She giggled and glanced at the stone again. "I wonder what it is about me that turns on the Pennlan stone. Shame we can't talk to Aoibheann and see what sort of extra charms she put on it."

I shifted uncomfortably. "I think I saw her. When I…killed Edric. She was trying to tell me something but I couldn't hear her."

Riona turned to stare at me. "I've seen her, too. But only when I'm on the brink of death. She comes to me in this space that feels between worlds."

"Can you communicate with her?" I asked.

"A little. She told me to help you," Riona replied, then straightened. "I think she was trying to tell me *I* was needed to turn on your stone."

"Not that I hope you ever get to that place again, but if you do, be sure to ask her why," I said with a small chuckle echoed by Riona.

"I'm not looking to put myself at death's door again any time soon," she said.

"Good." I smiled at her. There was another amiable pause before I asked, "Do you see dead fae often?"

"No," Riona said. "Just Aoibheann and…and my mother."

She'd told me as much in the troll realm. I tilted my head up toward the sky. "I wish I could remember her. I wish I had stories to tell you about her. But all my memories have been poisoned by lies." I turned to her. "How did… How did she die?"

"They say it was a broken heart, but…" Her face darkened. "I think she was terrified he would get hold of her again. She knew as long as she lived, she would endanger the whole world. Me, of course, I could be hidden—and I was. But she was a target as long as she was alive."

I slowed. "Wait, are you saying… She didn't… Not to herself…"

To my horror, Riona nodded. "I think it was mostly the guilt of what she'd done. It stays with you. You don't quite trust yourself."

Her tone had changed. It wasn't Leandra she was talking about anymore. The words I'd carelessly thrown at her back in the troll kingdom came back with a vengeance. "I hope you don't feel…guilty. You have nothing to feel guilty for."

She made a noncommittal sound, and my heart sank.

"Riona."

"I'm not going to off myself, if that's what you're worried about," she said. "But I can't say I don't understand why Leandra chose to. Sometimes…sometimes the good of the kingdom comes first."

I turned to her, taking her hand in mine as the stone warmed at my chest. "If you *ever* start to feel that way, I want you to come to me, okay? There's no need for you to sacrifice yourself for anything—least of all for the kingdom."

She nodded but didn't meet my gaze so I shook her harder.

"*Promise* me." She finally looked up at me. "I know I haven't been a good sister, but…but I want you here. Okay?"

Finally, a small smile crept across her lips. "Okay. I promise."

"Good." I shook myself. "I can't lose anyone else over this stupid stone."

Riona straightened. "You know… If *I* can't use the stone, I wonder if my mother couldn't either."

"What do you mean?"

She walked ahead, her brow furrowed. "I bet when that monster took over her mind, he was accessing this white magic—*not* the *seod croí*." She stopped, turning to look at me. "And my mother would've known that. So why did she…" She shook her head. "I suppose it doesn't matter. Whether it was the *seod croí* or the white magic, Eoghan would've been unstoppable with her or me."

I watched her, wishing I had some words of comfort to offer her. Was it worse to have been bamboozled by Eoghan my entire life or to have known he was a monster? I didn't know. But I felt a kinship with her I hadn't until that moment. We'd both lost so much by his hand, including a stronger relationship with each other.

With a smile, I took her hand and squeezed it, the only thing I could offer that felt right in the moment. She squeezed back and turned to keep walking when she stopped short.

A cold breeze—colder than any wind should've been—blew past my cheeks. Snow began to fall—not fall, but *blow in*. Like it was contained to a small bundle of wind. I looked at Riona, who seemed more concerned than surprised.

"Grandmother?" Riona asked. "What's wrong?"

"*Riona, you need to return to the wildlands immediately. Aldrick continues to cause trouble, and they need your help.*"

She grimaced. "I'll be there as soon as I can."

The flurry dissipated.

"Wha—" I gaped openly. "What was that?"

"I'm sorry. I have to go." She rubbed the back of her neck. "I've been ordered to protect them, and I can't—" She stopped. "I have to go."

"But why *you*?" I asked. "Why not someone else?"

"Because I gave my word I would protect them," she said. "Besides that… Something weird is going on. Aldrick shouldn't be able to mess with the trolls at all. There's an edict preventing it." She shook her head. "He's always had it out for weaker creatures, though. He's so powerful himself, it really makes no sense."

"All the more reason to let someone else take care of it," I said. "Riona—"

"I promise, I'll be fine," she said with a reassuring smile. "And as soon as I get to the bottom of what's going on, I'll be back, and we can keep practicing. But I gave them my word."

I watched her, sensing her frustration. Then I pulled her into a fierce hug. "Thank you for coming."

"Of course." She stepped away, a smile on her face. "I hope it's the first of many visits."

"Me too."

"Ugh." She made a face and rubbed her neck. "*Fine! I'm going!*" To my quizzical stare, she said, "The Erlking gave me an edict, too. It makes delaying it *quite* uncomfortable."

"Then go," I said with a laugh. "And be careful."

Then she was gone, disappeared in a puff of butterflies into the dark night.

Chapter Eighteen

Ward

I caught a few hours of sleep under a tree, in a twilight slumber that kept me still at the ready for any bandits or thieves who tried to mess with me. Then, as the sun rose behind me, I dusted myself off, ate some of my provisions, and continued along the main road I'd started following the night before.

Day brought more activity, farmers tending to their flocks in expansive green fields, sellers bringing their pelts and other goods into towns that popped up on smaller roads that splintered off. I didn't want to stop; the faster I reached the capital, the better. Not just so I could deliver the message, but so—hopefully—I could get back to my troops and get a handle on them.

Without anyone to talk to, I was lost in my own thoughts, ruminating over what Elodia had said. Part of me agreed with her. Leaving so soon after my promotion did seem like a bad idea. Leaving on a quest into enemy territory with a queen who'd closed the border was perhaps a little stupid. But in my gut, I knew it needed to be me.

No one would know I'd come from a different kingdom unless I told them. I was back in traveling clothes, but I'd stashed my captain's pin off my uniform and hidden it in the bottom of my bag, just in case I needed to identify myself. But out here in the hustle and bustle of a busy dirt road, there was nothing but smiles and nods of welcome.

When the road passed close to a thriving village, I veered inside, hoping to spend a few coppers and silvers on a hearty meal so I wouldn't need more later. I found a bustling tavern and let myself in, moving among the crowded patrons with ease until I reached the barkeep.

I ordered a stew and ale and ate my fill, keeping my ears open for any chatter about the closed border. But it was mostly agrarian talk, discussions of how long until the first cold snap, how much was left to harvest, what they thought they might get at market. No one here even knew there was a problem. But why would they? Konevell had great trading agreements with the other nations and didn't have any blockades keeping their ships from moving across the ocean.

I finished my meal and left the small tavern, rejuvenated and ready for another afternoon of walking along the busy roads. I'd asked one of the tavern patrons how long until I reached the capital and was pleased it was only a day or two if I kept a robust pace.

I was so lost in logistics—would I just walk up to the castle and demand an audience? Would I try to sneak inside?—that I didn't hear the hoofbeats from the approaching soldiers until they were right beside me then in front of me, blocking my path.

"Where are you going?" the one on the left asked, his Konevellian uniform a bright red.

"Um…" I looked around. "The capital?"

"Did you miss the queen's order?" the other asked, pointing his sword at me. "Every able-bodied person is to show up at the encampment by sundown tonight."

Encampment. "Uh…I guess I did miss that order," I said, rubbing the back of my neck. "Why are we showing up there, again?"

"You'll learn what you need to know when you get there." He reached into his pocket and handed me a scroll. I unfurled it and saw the edict with the Konevellian queen's seal. There wasn't much information about it.

"Turn around and walk a mile the way you came then head south toward Orapus," the soldier said. "You can't miss it."

"And if we see you on this road again, we'll bring you there in irons."

"All right, all right," I said, holding up my hands in surrender. "I'm on my way."

>–» >–» >–» >–»

I could've lied to them, but something told me I needed to check this out. A closed border was one thing. An assembly of all able-bodied people in an encampment near Orapus…that was a whole different story. I followed the instructions, veering south at the fork in the road and finding myself accompanied by other young men and women walking toward the camp. None of them knew why they'd been summoned either, but they were going without complaint.

"The queen is good to us," one said. "So we should do whatever she asks."

I couldn't help but think of Ayla, and how she struggled for this sort of loyalty. Maybe after a few decades, she would inspire such love from her people.

As the day wore on, the crowd thickened until we were walking shoulder to shoulder. Finally, we crested a hill and came across our destination—and I stopped dead in my tracks. The encampment stretched from one end of the valley to the other, thousands of would-be soldiers walking about under Konevellian flags.

"Move it!" Someone behind me shoved me and I stumbled but kept my footing.

I started to move toward the edge of the throng, hoping I could break away and sneak off somewhere so I could get a better look before being thrust into the middle of it, but I was unsuccessful.

The line stopped, forming a queue that started right in front of the gates. I couldn't see farther than a few feet, but there was nowhere to go. Soldiers on horseback patrolled up and down the line, perhaps to keep those with second thoughts from acting on them.

There was nothing to do but wait.

>–» >–» >–» >–»

The sun was gone by the time I reached the front of the line. There were two exhausted-looking guards taking down the names and homelands of every person who walked through the front gates. Three people were ahead of me when I realized I didn't have a good answer for either. I craned my neck to try to overhear what the person in front of me was saying, but I couldn't make out the words.

Finally, it was my turn. I stepped toward the red-uniformed officers, my hands in my pockets.

The soldier sighed and looked up at me with weary eyes. "Name and hometown?"

"Rutley," I said, thinking quickly. "And my hometown is…" I thought quickly, coming up with the first word that might make sense. "Riverside?"

"Great." She wrote down the information without question. "Sword and uniform to your left. Find a tent to sleep in. *Next!*"

"Wait a minute," I said. "What are we even here for?"

Another long sigh. "Get your sword and uniform. Find a tent. You'll get instructions in the coming days."

I tried to ask more questions but was shoved forward by those behind me. I turned to gaze behind me at the queue of soldiers and once again, my stomach dropped. There were so many in the camp, and so many still in line.

I acted like I was walking toward the sword and uniform line, but it was dark, and no one was really watching, so I slipped between two tents. I needed to find someone who knew what was going on, and something told me no one would just tell me outright.

Most of the soldiers were still in plainclothes, so I could walk around without too much trouble. I ducked between the tents so I'd emerge far from the front gates, just in case that ornery soldier was watching.

The camp was a maze, with haphazard tents set up everywhere. I glanced at the sky, spotting the bright star that had once been my guide in the fae realm. It was in a different location down here, but still worked as a navigational beacon as I ventured farther into the camp.

It certainly didn't look like a well-managed army. Some soldiers were snoozing around bonfires, others were loudly laughing with a flask between them. I still didn't know why they were assembling, but I had a hunch—though I hoped I was wrong.

But the farther I walked, the more the soldiers looked more professional, wearing the red uniforms and swords on their hips. Finally, I spotted a large tent with several soldiers positioned outside—I assumed the captain's. I kept my eyes down as I circled a large perimeter, hoping to avoid anyone asking questions. The back of the tent wasn't guarded, so I sidled up to it, listening for voices.

When I heard none, I crouched on the ground and snuck underneath.

I was right. Based on the maps, nice dinner, and uniform hanging from the tent pole in the center, this was the captain's tent. My pulse beat wildly as I approached the main table, hoping I hadn't seen what I thought.

The map was of Pennlan and Konevell. There were several pins in the spot where we were now, just south of the border. And there were pins marking Pennlan castle, as well as the nearby soldiers. Plus a dotted line across the river where we'd just walked across. How they were planning to—

I went stick straight as voices approached. Without another option, I dove under the table and held my breath, praying I hadn't moved anything.

A moment later, the flap opened and two pairs of legs came through—one wearing a dark skirt, the other the black pants of the Konevellian uniform.

"They're not an army," the first voice—male, low, gruff—said.

"They will be." This voice was female and smooth, educated. "How long until we can begin?"

"We will have completed the flotilla within the week. After that, we can begin our movement. We're still finding stragglers out in the countryside. But soon, we will have enough in our numbers to move."

"I want to be careful. The element of surprise will be our greatest asset. If we move too many soldiers too quickly, we will lose it."

They walked to the table and it creaked under the weight of one of them—they must've been leaning on it.

"We outnumber their forces. I don't see why—"

"The stone is a wildcard," the female voice replied. "Until we know what it's capable of…"

"But it'll be back in the castle, here. By the time we reach her, it'll just be a formality. We'll have taken half her country."

"And if what I've been told is true, she can blow the tops off mountains with it. Obliterating our army would be nothing for her."

"She's soft. She wouldn't have it in her."

"I don't want to risk it. We have been waiting a long time for this—and if we fail, we'll lose more than just our pride." She paused. "Slow and steady, Captain. She will break with a little pressure, but it needs to be the right kind. Trust me."

"Yes, Your Majesty."

I almost knocked my head against the table in shock. *Queen Ramira?*

They left shortly after that, and I exhaled, leaning back against the table for a moment. The letter in my satchel was oddly heavy. Ramira was here. I could announce myself, deliver the letter and…get myself killed. There was a note of finality in her voice. She wouldn't have gone through all this trouble, gathered all these soldiers, spent all this money on weapons and food and…

Konevell was going to invade Pennlan.

The thought took my breath away. My heart pounded with uncertainty, with fear, with nerves. Sure, I'd faced wizards and magical creatures before—but an army of humans? Somehow, that felt like an entirely different animal.

What the hell was I supposed to do?

I shook myself. While I was here, I needed to understand everything I could about what they were planning. I slowed my breathing and listened for voices, and when I heard none, I crawled out from under the table and stared at the map.

It didn't tell me much except they were descending on Orapus, which seemed to be a day's walk from the camp, perhaps faster over water. The captain with Ramira had said they were preparing a flotilla, so water it was. They expected Ayla and her stone to be in Pennlan castle, and to take us by surprise.

I jumped as I heard a noise outside the tent—the queen and her captain seemed to be coming back. Without another thought, I ducked under the flap as quickly as I could and waited there, holding my breath. No one had noticed me. At least not yet.

I had to get back to Ayla. Gather troops. Let Orapus know to be on high alert and keep their cannons pointed toward Konevell.

CHAPTER NINETEEN

RIONA

I hated leaving Ayla, especially as we hadn't done much more than turn on the Pennlan stone. Her worry was palpable, but at least she no longer feared the stone was somehow biased against her. It seemed a ridiculous notion, but…there was a lot we didn't know about the *seod croí*.

Still, how very fae-like to have left out the important part about needing *me* for some reason to make the thing turn on. Perhaps someone like me, born of fae and Pennlan blood, was never supposed to exist.

It took several hours to cross Pennlan and the *daoine maithe* lands. But as the troll village came into view, I saw the reason for my grandmother's warning.

At least ten *daoine maithe* and forest fae had cowed the hundreds of trolls—many of them corralled into a large magical cage. Those who remained were fighting on the ground, trying to keep the antagonizers at bay. Lynton was amongst them, sporting a cut on his face and a ferocity I'd never seen on him.

"Again!" he called.

The trolls with him gathered their magic and sent a wave of rock toward the aggressors. They easily used their magic to lift themselves off the ground to avoid it.

"Give it up, vermin!"

I recognized the smug face of Thorstan, one of Aldrick's favorite lackeys. He seemed amused by their attempts to defend themselves, and his half-hearted attacks were more the cat-and-mouse variety. As the other fae floated in mid-air, Thorstan sent a flock of magical bees toward the trolls, easily skirting their defenses and earning roars of pain and anger.

He laughed as he pulled his magic back to him. "Ready to surrender?" Thorstan called. "It's nearly breakfast, and I'd hate to be late."

"Never!" Lynton called. Another useless wave of rock. Another laugh.

My blood boiled as I flew as fast as I could. The white magic that had been at my fingertips in Pennlan was slipping away, but I held onto it as best I could. If all I had were my butterflies, I'd be as helpless as the trolls. But righteous anger placed me right between the two factions, my teeth bared as I faced down Thorstan and the other *daoine maithe* fae, who leered.

"Well, if it isn't the little halfling bastard," he said, lowering his hands. "Come to protect your little friends?"

"Go home," I barked. "The Erlking has forbidden your presence here."

"If *the Erlking* forbade it, how are we here?" Aarto, coming to land beside his friend, taunted. "These vermin need to be taught a lesson. They stole from us, endangered the entire continent, and now—"

"That wasn't them," I snarled. "And the guy who did that has met his fate." I was losing my grip on the magic as it slid through my fingers like sand. "Now go home, or I'll have to make fools of you."

They laughed, throwing their heads back as if my mere presence was the most amusing thing they'd ever seen.

C'mon, magic, don't make a fool of me.

I held my breath as I fell back into my mind, gathering the scattered tendrils until I had enough to make my hands glow. I opened my eyes, the dark world illuminated by the magic. The appearance of it alone seemed to shake Thorstan, who'd lost his sneer in favor of wide-eyed fear. Perhaps Aldrick hadn't been so mum about the outcome of our duel a few weeks ago.

"Now," my voice was deeper, echoing around me, "would you like to see what I can do?"

The fearful leader took a step back and sniffed. "Let's go. We've made our point."

One by one, they dissipated into their respective magical creatures, floating away toward the horizon, and I exhaled in relief as the white magic fully disappeared back into wherever it dwelled when I couldn't call upon it. I'd only had enough for a light show, it seemed, and I was grateful it had worked.

Behind me, the magical cage that had held the trolls faded, and the newly freed inhabitants clambered out, clutching their chests in relief and running back to their homes. I let them scatter. They'd been tortured enough for today, and my heart ached that I hadn't been here to protect them.

"Thank you," Lynton said, walking up to meet me. "Once again, we are in your debt."

"I'm sorry it took me a while," I said. "I was in Pennlan when my grandmother notified me."

"Your…grandmother?"

"The *sidheog* queen," I said then frowned. "Though, come to think of it, I guess I'm not sure how she knew they were here, either."

"She'd been by with some supplies," Lynton said, and my heart lifted. *Thank you, Clíodhna.* "We haven't yet seen Fiadh, and our stores were running low. Her generosity was appreciated but…" He licked his lips. "I can't help but feel it attracted the wrong sort of attention."

"I don't think she had anything to do with Aldrick," I said. "Those fae are his friends. I wouldn't put it past him to send them here to cause trouble." I turned to the troll village, the streets now empty of anyone except Lynton and me. "Was anyone hurt?"

"Not seriously," he said. "They were here to cause mayhem only." His face darkened. "What fun would it be to kill your plaything?"

"I will make sure that *never* happens again," I said. "I'm headed to the Erlking to let him know what happened."

Lynton made a noise. "It may not help. The Erlking's power is waning."

I scoffed, but even I couldn't fully dismiss what he was saying. "Is that…a thing?"

"It can be. An Erlking's power comes from the steadfast loyalty of the clans who call him such," Lynton said, looking out into the distance. "If there's dissent, his power weakens. Which, if history is any indication, is the first step toward a new Erlking assuming the throne. Usually the main dissenter."

Aldrick on the Erlking's throne? My stomach turned at the thought. "One person can't cause this much havoc, though."

"No, they can't." He stared at me without an ounce of emotion. "Which means he's not the only one who's decided the current Erlking has lost his touch."

My turning stomach now came to my throat. "Either way, I'm going to report this to the Erlking. See what he thinks. Maybe he can… maybe he just didn't do something when he made the edict. It's an easy fix. Surely."

I was rambling, but the pattering of my heart was making me jumpy. I couldn't see a world where my grandfather wasn't at the helm of the fae realm.

Lynton almost seemed resigned to the idea. "We will fortify our homes for the eventual return attack," he said. "We can no longer rely on the Erlking's power to protect us, so we must protect ourselves."

I bit my lip instead of responding. I wanted to argue with him, to promise my grandfather's magic was strong. But after what I'd just seen…I couldn't say it without feeling the burning on my tongue.

"I'll be back as soon as I can."

>→ >→ >→ >→

It was becoming a bit of a habit, arriving at the Erlking's castle and heading straight for his throne room. I didn't realize until I was three steps inside that the spell keeping me from coming to discuss Aldrick had worn off. I chalked it up to my subject being the *trolls* not *Aldrick*, and prayed it wasn't a harbinger of things to come.

I pushed through the crowd, noting the usual attendees and the new ones in the room. Aldrick's spies noticed me, and I was sure they'd be telling him as soon as they could. But he had to have known that the Erlking would be my first stop. Did Aldrick *want* his father to know? The thought made me uneasy.

Still, I took some comfort in the fact that the room was full of fae creatures who still wanted the Erlking's edicts, so they held some power. How much power, though?

"If there's dissent, his power weakens."

As long as I'd been alive (which wasn't very long), Erlking Birch had had unwavering support. I didn't even know *how* one became an Erlking nor how the one preceding Birch had given up his spot. Had he just keeled over? Was there a challenge? It seemed impossible that my grandfather would have that sort of ambition.

Aldrick, on the other hand…

But he was one person. Were there more? Had he poisoned someone else against my grandfather? Clíodhna couldn't stand my uncle, so the *sidheog* were still loyal. And Aldrick wouldn't be caught dead cavorting with anything other than the greater fae, which left the *daoine maithe* and the forest fae. Surely, the majority of the *daoine maithe* still swore fealty to their Erlking.

With some effort, I pushed my way to the front, having to elbow a pair of *daoine maithe* who tried to stand in my way. The Erlking noticed me right away, dismissing the trio of *sidheog* with a silent edict that seemed to be just for them. Then he waved me over, earning a chorus of groans from the rest of the room.

"Why is she so important?"

"You've spoken to her five times this month!"

"I've been waiting a year to—"

Their complaints faded as the Erlking's charms surrounded me. He smiled warmly and rested his hand on his knee as he sat back.

"I hear you were in Pennlan. Did you learn much from your sister?"

"Yes and no." I told him about how it seemed I *couldn't* wield the Pennlan stone, but it did unlock the white magic and how my white magic seemed to unlock the Pennlan stone for my sister. He nodded, betraying no hint of whether this information was new to him.

"But we didn't get long to practice because Clíodhna summoned me back here," I said, testing the waters. "Aldrick—"

"I told you not to worry about him."

I released a growl of frustration. "*His stupid people were terrorizing the trolls!*"

Finally, the Erlking looked surprised—which made me even angrier. "That's impossible."

"It's not impossible, because I just came from there." I listed the fae I'd seen there and what they'd done. The Erlking listened with a frown, but the tension between his brows relaxed after a moment.

"I think I know what the problem is," he said softly. "Things have been unsettled for a while, and I believe it's because the trolls have come back into the fae realm. They've not formally submitted themselves to my rule as Erlking."

"Lynton did, didn't he?" I said. "When he first arrived, he said—"

"There's more to submission than merely speaking the words," the Erlking said. "I must convene an *Arwein*."

"What's that?"

"You'll find out," he said. "I must ask you once again to travel to the troll realm and retrieve him for me."

"He's not...in trouble, is he?" I asked. "Because it's not his fault that—"

"No, of course not." He smiled. "Bring him as soon as you can and come straight to the throne room when you do."

Chapter Twenty

Cade

As night fell on the sea, Aldonza broke out the sextant again and patiently showed me which stars to look for and where they should be at our destination. I watched, a bit in awe, as she rattled off islands and ports and countries I'd never heard of. She seemed to be a walking atlas.

"This is amazing," I said with a shake of my head. "I don't think I have room in my head for all that information."

"When it's the only thing you do, you make room," she said with a lift of her shoulder. "Now, think you can get us to Al'ocasep?"

The stars above matched the map she'd laid out on the table beside me. I closed my eyes, mentally rising up into the stars until I could see the whole ocean beneath me and the sea of stars above. Keeping my focus on the constellation that would lead us there, I rolled over the ocean until the stars were in alignment. Beneath me was a small speck of land bathed in moonlight.

Keeping its location in mind, I opened the portal and my eyes as the island (which looked much bigger from down here), came into view. Aldonza whooped loudly, almost a cheer of joy, and the rest of the crew came tumbling out of the lower cabin.

"Did he do it?"

"That rube. We're going drinking tonight!"

"Ssh, settle down," Aldonza said. "Wizard, if you'd be so kind as to give us a push into port."

I frowned. Why would we dock at *this* port at night whereas the previous one we'd waited until dawn? But I gathered the wind to buffet the sails and pushed us through the portal.

The stench of alcohol and human odor hit me before we'd even reached the slip. The crew, bright-eyed and eager, bounded off after sloppily securing the ship, but Aldonza stayed behind to make sure everything was tight and bound. She said nothing to me about their behavior but wore a smile as she wrapped up her work.

"So you're going to stay here tonight, eh?" she asked.

"Why would I?" I asked. "What's this island?"

"Oh, well…" She cleared her throat. "It's not the kind of place a boy like you should be going."

I made a face. "What's that supposed to mean?"

"Bet you haven't even been kissed, right?"

My entire body went rigid as my face flushed. "I don't see what that has to do with anything."

"And that, dear Cade, is why you shouldn't leave the boat," she said with a chuckle as she hopped off the boat. "I don't want to be the one to shatter your beautiful innocence. So do us all a favor and stay here."

She disappeared down the docks, whistling a tune that was somehow familiar, like most things about her. I stood on the deck, gripping my staff as the waves slightly shifted the boat in the slip. I glanced toward Aldonza's cabin. It was awfully trusting of her to leave me alone here. But neither she nor the crew seemed focused on anything else but what was waiting for them ashore.

A trickle of laughter echoed, followed by the sound of drums in the distance. Another breeze blew by, this time filled with something sweet and inviting. I chewed my lip, glancing between Aldonza's cabin and the unknown village waiting.

And I chose the island.

⇥⇥⇥⇥

The first indication that I'd made a horrible mistake came moments after I'd stepped off the wooden dock—a woman wearing nothing but a skirt came stumbling by, her face painted with bright colors as she stared around, giggling and hanging off the arm of a similarly dressed man. *His* skirt was so short it left very little to the imagination. The two of them jostled each other toward the lights in the distance, talking in a language I didn't understand.

I pressed forward, holding my staff and keeping my magic at the ready for whatever evils might come about. But I seemed to be the only one on this island in my right mind. Everywhere I looked, drunk and disorderly idiots were hanging out of windows, leaning on tables, getting into fights. I was fairly sure I passed three or four people actively fornicating between buildings, the sounds bringing a deep blush to my cheeks as I sped along.

What kind of island was this anyway?

Every instinct told me to turn around, but I kept walking. The crew had gone here willingly, but I felt an obligation to make sure they were all right. That, and a bit of morbid curiosity to understand why this place had drawn them here with such eagerness.

Finally, I spotted the familiar shade of brown skin in the corner of a tavern. Aldonza was seated with Cluny, two giant bottles in front of them, and each had a companion in their lap. Cluny's was a busty woman, while Aldonza's hand was very inappropriately placed on a muscular man's lap. Neither companion seemed to mind, especially as the one in Aldonza's lap leaned in to give her a big, wet kiss before drinking more of the bottle.

And when he lifted his lips, he had a bag of gold in his hand that he tucked away in his belt.

I walked forward, intent on returning the stolen gold to Aldonza, but I was accosted before I got there.

"Hey! It's the wizard boy!"

Iga and Cai came stumbling up behind me, throwing their arms around my shoulders as if we were all the best of friends. They both reeked of alcohol and seemed barely able to stand on their own two feet.

"Are you here to taste the pleasures of the world?"

"Get a bit of hair on your chest?"

"I'm here to make sure you idiots aren't robbed blind," I said, pushing them off. "Aldonza just allowed that man on her lap to take a bag of gold."

They stared at each other for a moment before bursting into laughter. "Oh boy, what a sweet angel."

"Just the most innocent lamb."

My face heated. "What? She wanted him to take it?"

"Look, if your dad didn't tell you the ways of the world, we aren't going to be the ones to educate you."

I bristled. "You *know* I was—"

"Oi! Look, it's Crimson!"

"I saw her first, let me at her."

They scrambled after the woman walking by, her hair a brilliant shade of red. She turned to wink at them then sashayed toward a small house that had a sign with a red dot hanging over the door. They dashed inside, pulling gold from their pants as they undid them.

I let out a huff. I wasn't wholly stupid. Though I'd never been anywhere like this, there were whorehouses in some cities around Pennlan. But this seemed more... It bordered on ridiculous that everyone would lose their minds over this.

I looked for Aldonza but only Cluny was there, deep in a romantic embrace with his partner. I made a face, turning around and walking back to the ship. If they wanted to make spectacles of themselves, they could do so. I, however, had much more important things to worry about.

That, and perhaps in my heart, I hoped that if I were to kiss a girl, it wouldn't be some woman of the night. It would be—

I shook my head to dispel those thoughts. Ayla had made her choice clear. She didn't love me.

⤜⤙⤜⤙

I returned to the quiet, realizing why the crew had been so lackadaisical about their ship and belongings. The allure of the island was strong, and I was the only soul still on the dock. Everyone else was too drunk or enamored (or both) to cause any sort of trouble.

On the deck, I picked up the sextant and looked at the stars. I turned behind me to find the stars I'd used to navigate to Fortenzia. I calculated how long it would take to get there—days, probably. Perhaps a week? I still wasn't sure on the timing of these things. But it was a long way away.

I could absolutely see a future where Aldonza used me to navigate to a port to conduct business, then return her to this place so she and her crew could drink and screw away their money. It made me feel a bit dirty, and also more than a little angry. I had the power to create portals at my fingertips. I was a wizard. Why was I relying on a drunken pirate to get me where I wanted to go?

Because you don't know how to get there.

I turned, gazing at Aldonza's dark cabin. It was improbable, considering her disdain for the *e'potu*, that she might still have something to lead her back home. But it didn't hurt to look. At least I might be able to practice star mapping until they stumbled back to the ship.

Letting myself in, I crossed the room to the chest where she kept her maps. I waved my staff, opening the chest with magic and pulling the first set of maps from the collection. The first one spread out on the table, unfamiliar and practically unreadable. I shook my head. Perhaps I should take a few more lessons from Aldonza before I attempted this alone.

But then I remembered…that would result in them using me as their mule to get to this sinful island.

"C'mon, Cade," I whispered, closing my eyes. "You can do this."

Once more, I quieted the voices in my mind as I stared at the map. One star was familiar, but it had been somewhere completely different when I'd used it to navigate before. I summoned the map I'd used previously, unfurling it in the air above the other map and comparing the two. There were a couple other similarities, though most of the map was cut off.

I overlaid the new map over the old one, and they matched perfectly. Out of the chest came another map, unfurling before me as I searched for something familiar. One star in the very bottom matched, so as with the others, I overlaid it, creating a large map.

Again and again, I added more maps to the collection until I'd practically filled Aldonza's room with a map of the entire night sky. As I put the last map in her chest in the final spot, I stood back and smiled at my handiwork, gazing upon no fewer than twenty maps back to back. It was quite the collection.

And quite useless, for what I needed.

None of them mentioned H'sipotu. Not that I really expected them to, but it did feel like a lot of effort for no result. I could read a map of the stars now, but if I didn't have a map to the island, I wasn't going to get very far. Even drunk, Aldonza wouldn't tell me what I wanted to know.

I walked over to the now-empty chest and reached inside, feeling around just in case I'd missed one. It *was* empty, but I felt something odd, like the bottom of the chest was a bit higher than it should've been. It was covered in felt, so I picked at it until it came up, revealing what appeared to be another chamber.

I held my breath as I removed the lid and found three more maps. They were much older, more worn than the others. With the utmost care, I unfurled the first, revealing a set of stars that were wholly unfamiliar.

I turned to my floating master map and used magic to search every ink dot on the map for anything that matched this one. Nothing.

I tried the second. Nothing.

But the third…that had a small collection of dots that matched another collection. And there was a corner of stars on *that* map that matched the first, and lastly, the second map I'd pulled fell into place.

I walked along the three maps that seemed to be off in their own little space, searching for what they could be showing. Unlike the others in the main chest, these didn't have any sort of island or landmass associated with them. They were just maps of stars.

The last one was the most sparse, like it was missing information. But something about it piqued my attention, something...*hidden* that called to my magic. Almost as if the paper itself was holding something in its grasp, refusing to let go. I gently touched a spot on the corner that seemed alive, and my breath left my chest.

Another island appeared, almost as if someone had spilled ink on the map. Then another, another, off the map—but the ink *just settled in the air* as it kept coming up with more islands. Until finally...in a shimmering black, a large island appeared with the name H'sipotu in italics.

My breath caught as I heard voices outside the ship. As fast as my magic would move, I rolled up each of the twenty maps and stuffed them back inside the chest, including the three that led to my home island. Once Aldonza's room was returned to normal, I created a portal to the bottom of the ship where I hastily acted like I was sleeping in one of the hanging cots.

There I lay, my heart pounding as I remained still. And for the first time in a long time, I had hope.

Chapter Twenty-One

Ayla

"The Konevellians are preparing to invade."

I looked up. Ward hadn't even changed out of his traveling clothes before barging into my office, covered in dirt and dust, his brown eyes wild with concern as he started babbling. I couldn't make heads or tails of what he was saying, so I poured him a glass of water and made him drink it.

"Now," I said as he gulped it down, "what's going on? Slowly, please. Did you make it to Ramira?"

"Kind of," he said, swallowing hard.

Ward told me a long tale about crossing into Konevell, and being all but conscripted into her haphazard army. But as he described sneaking into her tent, my heart began to race nervously—and when he spoke of Ramira's plot to invade, my hand came to my mouth.

"I got out without much trouble," Ward said, his voice full of something unfamiliar—nerves. "It was dark, and I moved quickly. Fiadh had left me a small path across the river. I stopped in Orapus briefly just to tell the captain what I'd seen, but I knew it was important to get back here as quickly as I could." He finally stopped long enough to take a long breath and to look at me. "Well?"

"Did you give Ramira the letter?" I asked.

He shook his head. "Ayla, she was… They're coming. There's no negotiating with them."

"Maybe you misheard her," I said, hoping fear didn't seep into my voice as the merchant in the tavern's warning came back to me. "Besides that, why would Konevell want to invade Pennlan? We have nothing of value that they don't have. No access to anyone they want—certainly not the trolls or the fae."

Ward swallowed hard as his gaze fell to my chest. "What happens to your piece of the *seod croí* if Pennlan becomes part of another nation? Would Ramira be able to wield it?"

My breath caught in my chest and my hand closed around my gem. "You mean…if Konevell invades and claims our borders as their own?"

He nodded.

I honestly didn't know, but the idea sat unnervingly in my mind. Queen Ramira had made it clear she wanted my stone by any means necessary; she'd been willing to send her eight-year-old son to marry me, in fact. It wasn't beyond the scope of reason that she would send her army to take it—and my kingdom—by force.

"Ayla?"

I looked up into Ward's concerned eyes and laughed weakly. "Is it too late for Captain Gabhann to come back?"

He didn't look amused. "What's your command?"

I rose and walked to my window to buy myself some time. My heart pounded, and my mind spun uncontrollably. What was a monarch to do when the borders of her kingdom were threatened? That certainly wasn't covered in my studies—I doubted it would've been on the agenda even without Eoghan's meddling. Border squabbles were common, of course, but cooler heads always prevailed. There hadn't been an all-out war since… Since the battle of the *aos sí*.

In the troll realm, Edric had shown us the battle through the magical memory stones. It had left a sick feeling in my stomach. The brave soldiers were sacrificing themselves for a noble goal, but the bloodshed was… It was hard to watch.

I imagined my own soldiers—Ward, Elodia, Rutley—having to wade through rivers of blood in my name. And to think Ramira would send her soldiers to die for the *seod croí*—and not even the whole thing! Just a small piece that only worked when a specific half-fae girl was in the room.

My stomach came to my throat.

"Ayla?" Ward caught my reflection in the window. "What's your command?"

"I don't know," I whispered, turning to face him, grateful he already knew I was an idiot. "What should I do?"

He also swallowed, uncertainty on his face. "They're expecting to surprise us in Orapus, but as I said, I informed the captain to be on the lookout. The forces there won't be enough. We should send word to every soldier in every city and tell them to drop what they're doing and march to Orapus."

"How long will that take?"

He exhaled. "Longer than we have, I fear. But we'll do our best." He walked to the door. "Would be nice if Riona or Cade would show up."

I let out a half-hearted chuckle. "Riona just left."

"She…did?" He frowned. "What was she doing here?"

"A little sisterly bonding," I said, tracing my finger along the windowpane. "And trying to figure out how to wield the stone."

"Did you?" His tone was hopeful, almost desperate.

"We need to be in each other's presence," I said after a moment.

"Any idea why?"

"We have many theories," I said. "Perhaps our shared blood. Perhaps her mixed blood. Perhaps just happenstance. But nothing solid." I looked at him. "She had to return to the fae realm to help the trolls, otherwise we would've continued."

"The trolls would come to our aid if we called them," Ward said. "And the fae would, as well."

"I couldn't ask the trolls to fight in another war," I said, looking up. "They've had enough chaos to last several lifetimes. And they're still getting it."

"We've all had chaos," Ward said.

That was certainly true, too. Tears came to the corners of my eyes but I didn't let them fall. "Ward, we can't just accept that war is happening. There has to be a way to stop this before it begins. Reason *must* prevail."

"I told you," he said. "Ramira sounded firm. I think she would've sooner cut off my head than talk to me."

I licked my lips. "Would she talk to me?"

"Ayla…" He shook his head. "The last place you need to be is anywhere near a battle."

"I'm not hoping to be at a battle," I said. "But if I'm close, maybe Ramira would…send someone to talk with me. Or we could talk. Either way, if I'm in Orapus, I'm at least closer to her, and we have a better shot of communicating before things get out of hand." I turned the gem over. "They want this so badly, let's bring it to them and see what happens."

He watched me, and I was absolutely sure he was going to say no. But he let out a loud, frustrated sigh. "Fine."

My gaze shot up. "Really?"

"But *only* if you promise me that if things get bad, you'll follow my orders and leave. No matter what happens."

I saluted. "Yes, sir."

He rolled his eyes, the ghost of a smile on his lips. "Don't even start. And you're going in disguise. Let's not announce to the world that you've left the castle."

"I'm not defenseless," I said.

"You have a stone that doesn't work without your sister," he said. "And until I see her little pointy ears, I don't trust that you're safe."

"I'm confident she'll show when the time comes," I said, looking at the gem. "She has to."

Ward hesitated, as if he wanted to say something. But instead he nodded and walked to the door. "I'll get the riders out. But you are going in disguise. That's final."

And with that, he left me alone in my office.

⤙⤙⤙⤙

An hour later, I watched from my window as twenty riders took off on our fastest horses to the far reaches of my kingdom. Some were closer in and might be able to meet us in Orapus sooner. Others... It would take a week to even reach Críoch to tell them the news.

I wrote to Riona but didn't hear back immediately. I prayed she'd dealt with her uncle quickly and was on her way back, but with each passing minute of silence, my worry increased. Against an army of thousands, we wouldn't stand a chance without magical help. Would the fae want to get involved in human squabbles? Would the trolls? Did I have any right to ask them?

Was war a foregone conclusion? If so, was it better if I...

Stop it.

I was the holder of the most powerful object in existence. My sister would surely arrive, and we could put on a light show that would scare Ramira and her soldiers back to their respective villages. Cowering in fear wasn't becoming of a queen. After all, I was no longer Eoghan's plaything to be bullied into doing whatever he wanted.

I rang the bell to call Bronwen.

"Yes, Your Majesty," she said with a bow.

"The soldiers and I are leaving for Orapus," I said quietly. "I want you to pack me a small bag of traveling clothes."

"What's waiting for you in Orapus?" Bronwen asked nervously. "You seem...on edge. Captain Ward did as well." She stepped closer to me. "What's going on?"

She was my confidante, and she'd worry whether I told her or lied to her, so I gave her a quick rundown of what we were facing. She paled as I described the army and Ward sneaking into the camp, but when I was done, she nodded curtly.

"Well, then. We'll have to make sure you look the part," she said. "I recommend the *blue* dress."

My brows shot up. "The one that…?"

She nodded with a knowing smirk.

I walked to my wardrobe and opened the door, pulling out the item in question. I'd worn it once before in a move of rebellion against Eoghan. He'd once again set up a dinner with an old suitor from one of the other nations to make himself look better by comparison. Instead of the virginal pink dress he'd picked out for me, I'd opted for this daring, low-cut dress in a dark blue. With the right hairstyle, I looked ten years older than I was.

"I suppose we can bring this, too," I said.

"And your tiara."

I made a noise. "I don't want to bring more than I need, and that thing is—"

"Not the princess one," she said with a smile. "The one that troll made for you." She walked toward the wardrobe and pulled a box off the shelf. Inside was the ornate, gem-filled crown Edric had fashioned when he was still trying to butter me up. It had been on my head when we'd escaped, but I hadn't cared where it had gone. It was yet another reminder of how I'd misread a situation.

Am I doing the same thing again?

"I don't think I need that," I whispered.

"I think you do," Bronwen said, putting it in my hands. "It's a reminder of the power you hold. This man built you a crown from rock and gems and metal. You were able to vanquish him with a single thought."

I shuddered, the ghost of that power a vivid memory. But perhaps Bronwen had a point. Not that I wanted to go around murdering people, but…the stone only worked *for me*. I was the only person in this world who could tap into its power. I shouldn't fear Ramira or anyone else because I had the power to destroy anything I wanted to.

With your sister.

I dismissed that voice. I was teetering on the edge of a full-blown meltdown, and I didn't need qualifiers. What I needed was to pack this beautiful blue dress and the tiara, along with whatever courage I had at my disposal, and be ready to fight to the death for my kingdom, my people, and myself.

Even if it was just a battle of political wills.

Chapter Twenty-Two

Ward

"You are such a hypocrite."

Elodia watched me with pursed lips as I explained what I'd seen and the plan to gather soldiers. As expected, when I came to the part about how I'd learned all this information, Elodia pounced on me.

"It's fine."

"It's not fine," she said, ticking off her fingers. "You could've been *captured*. You could've been *killed*. You have a responsibility here to these soldiers and *this* castle. If you don't want to be captain, why the hell did you take the job?"

"I do want to be captain," I said, furrowing my brow. "And I was careful."

"Didn't you just say you were almost seen by the Konevellian queen and her general?"

I huffed. "And if I *hadn't* gone, we'd be blind to an invasion and caught completely off guard. Now we have a chance to end it before it begins. So all's well that ends well, right?"

She crossed her arms and frowned.

Beside her, Rutley gave me a thumbs-up. "What do you want us to do, boss?"

"Orapus has been told to be on high alert, but..." I didn't know how much I wanted to tell Elodia and Rutley. To say Captain Treen was dubious about my claims was putting it lightly. I'd asked her to send scouts along the river and watch the bay for new ships, and she'd all but laughed at me, calling me delusional. "It's imperative we get there as quickly as possible."

"We're not that many soldiers," Rutley said. "Maybe a hundred at the castle?"

"I've already sent riders out to the other cities." I walked to the map on the wall, one of the few things Gabhann had left. "All in all, it should take about two or three weeks to amass our forces." I sighed, staring at the small dot that represented the city. I didn't know if that would be fast enough. "Ayla wants to go to Orapus and invite the queen to a summit. She thinks she'll be able to convince the queen to call off the invasion."

"Is that even possible?" Elodia asked.

"I don't know." I exhaled. "But we should try to avoid bloodshed if we can."

Rutley sat back. "Or we just bring Riona down to the border, give 'em a good scare, and they'll never think of crossing the border."

"Would be nice." I didn't like leaving the fate of our kingdom up to whether Riona would make an appearance, but I didn't have much of a choice at the moment. "I want to leave in the morning."

Elodia made a noise. "With the royal guard?"

"Obviously, who else would I be leaving with?" I turned to frown at her. "Why? What's happened?"

"Well, as *someone* told you would happen," she said, "they didn't take kindly to their new boss—who most of them think slept his way to the job—leaving on a holiday the moment he got the position."

I sputtered. "I didn't go on a… I went to—"

She held up her hands. "*I* know that you decided to go on a selfish mission to Konevell to hand-deliver a letter to the queen, but they see what they want to."

"Don't you mean selfless?" I asked.

"I said what I said," she replied. "And now you come back bearing news of an army gathering on Pennlan's borders and want everyone to get ready to march on Orapus? How do you think that's going to go over?"

"It doesn't matter how it's going to go over," I said. "It's the truth, and we have to be ready."

She shrugged. "Don't say I didn't warn you."

>―» >―» >―» >―»

I called for the guard to assemble on the green that afternoon. Word traveled fast in the barracks, and I was sure I wasn't going to be sharing any new information with my soldiers. But Elodia's comments had rattled me—and not just because she'd described a guard unmoored. It was the caustic way *she'd* spoken to me. Since the day she'd arrived at the castle, we'd had a casual friendship with an undercurrent of respect. That seemed to be gone, and I wasn't sure what I needed to do to get it back.

She didn't look at me as she stood at attention with the rest of the soldiers, and I tried to shake it off.

"You've probably heard the rumors," I began, raising my voice so it echoed off the stone walls on either side of us. "Konevell is poised to invade Pennlan near Orapus. They've called every able-bodied person to join them at an encampment a day's ride from the city. In the morning, we are marching with Her Majesty there."

"To what end?" a voice called out from the ranks.

I snapped around and scanned the faces, looking for someone who'd stepped out of line. "Hopefully, just a show of force," I said. "The Pennlan stone still provides us a great amount of protection—even against a few thousand soldiers."

"If it's so protective, why did you send riders to call more soldiers to battle?"

Again, I searched for the person who'd spoken, unaccustomed to my soldiers speaking like this. "We're preparing for all options. Including the remote possibility the stone doesn't work like we want it to."

Concern rippled across their faces, and I didn't blame them.

"We'll bring every weapon we have," I said. "Pack only what you need."

Someone cleared their throat—Rutley was making a face. I couldn't read him so he nervously spoke up, "Should we perhaps think about gathering tents, bedrolls, food, too? Considering there probably isn't enough room for us within the city itself. Especially if we're expecting more soldiers."

I shifted as a low chorus of chuckles rumbled through the group and hoped the warming of my cheeks didn't show. "Yes, of course. That's what I meant. Now get to it. We leave at daybreak tomorrow. Dismissed."

They saluted in unison (thank goodness for that) but the dispersal was a lot slower. They stood in groups talking with one another and casting me angry looks. Did they think the army on the other side of the border was somehow my fault?

"Good job," Rutley said, coming to stand beside me. "Sorry about talking out of line…"

"You weren't the only one," I said, watching Elodia disappear into the barracks. "At least Elodia didn't outright call for my resignation."

"She's annoyed, for sure, but she'll get over it," he said with a wave of his hand.

I folded my arms over my chest. "Do you feel the same way she does?"

"Of course not," he said, a little too quickly.

"Rutley."

"Look, we're all gonna probably be dead in a matter of weeks anyway," he said with an affable smile. "No use worrying about it now."

"We're not going to…" I huffed, but I couldn't even finish that statement. "It'd be really nice if Riona showed up right about now. Or that damn wizard."

"Maybe Ayla shoulda just leaned into it and kissed him after all," Rutley said.

I bristled at the notion before I could stop myself, earning a chuckle from Rutley.

"Just get ready," I said, gritting my teeth. "I'm going to move these jokers along."

I felt his amused stare on the back of my neck as I marched up to the first group of soldiers. They turned to me, almost surprised to see me, and saluted as an afterthought.

"Did you mishear me? We're leaving tomorrow," I barked.

"We've got all afternoon," the soldier said then hastily added, "Sir."

"And you've got a lot to assemble," I snapped. "*Go.*"

I had the same conversation three times until the soldiers finally got the message and dispersed on their own. Everyone except a trio of older soldiers who leaned against the wall, talking. They were from the same mold as Platt, having been around over a decade, and tended to converge around him.

"What happened to our buddy?" Kavan, tall and hook-nosed with sallow skin, looked down at me with an unabashed glare. "Did you send Platt to greener pastures?"

"He's in Orapus," I said. "Overseeing the transfer of goods. As I said. Now get packing."

"Do we have to go?" Parrish seemed to have enjoyed castle life a little too much, as his uniform strained against his buttons. "I think the three of us should stay behind and guard the queen's jewels."

"The queen's jewels will be the least of our problems if Konevell invades," I snapped.

"But you said her gem is working, yeah?" Severn was short and sickly, and I never could figure out why he'd been chosen for the guard. "So why do we have to schlep all the way to Orapus just to look pretty behind her?"

"Seems like a waste of time."

"Agreed."

"Because I ordered you to." I shoved my finger into Severn's chest. "Now if you don't want to *actually* be sent to greener pastures, I suggest the three of you get moving."

Reluctantly, they peeled themselves away from the wall and

disappeared into the barracks.

"I hate to say I told you so," Elodia said from behind me.

"Then *don't*," I barked, brushing by her.

⤐ ⤐ ⤐ ⤐

At daybreak, I rose, washed my face, shaved, and donned the captain's uniform I still didn't feel comfortable in. I stared at my reflection in the small mirror and wished I saw someone who exuded confidence. But it was just me. Farm boy turned soldier turned captain. What the hell was Gabhann thinking, leaving me in charge?

But I couldn't show fear. Not to Ayla, and definitely not to the soldiers, who already doubted me. Not to Konevell, who seemed to think they could just waltz into our country like they already owned it. No, I needed to keep an air of confidence, if only to fool myself into thinking I wasn't leading our country off a cliff.

When I walked out onto the green, I was relieved to see every soldier there, along with packs of bedrolls and carriages of weapons, carrying large hunks of dried meat they must've purchased from the nearby village. I'd had nightmares the day before of Ayla walking out into an empty field because all the soldiers had quit.

But as I scanned the green, there was an ornate carriage decked in dark blue and gold, carrying a Pennlan flag on each corner. Ayla's own horse was hooked up to it, stomping the ground and whinnying as if she were annoyed to be put to such a use. There was also a large trunk next to the carriage—carrying Ayla's dresses and things, I assumed.

I let out a breath, staring at the sky.

"By the look on your face, I can tell you didn't approve...this?" Elodia said.

"Inconspicuous was the phrase I used," I muttered as Ayla walked out of the castle wearing a simple traveling outfit and talking with Bronwen.

"Go get 'er, Captain," Elodia said. "You're doing so well with everyone else these days."

I glared at her then walked over to Ayla, clearing my throat loudly. "Is this your idea of a disguise? Now everyone's going to know the queen is on the move."

"I changed my mind," she said.

"Is that so?"

"Yes." She leveled a glare. "That's so."

"Are you really going to argue with me the whole trip again?" I asked.

"Are you?" She put her hands on her hips. "We have a hundred royal soldiers marching with us. I'm in no danger."

I pointed behind her. "Bronwen—"

"Is not coming," Ayla said. "I'm able to handle my own upkeep. But we needed certain items, and it sends a bad message for a queen to be skulking around her own country—especially one that remains, as far as I know, uninvaded." She palmed the gem. "Besides that, we need Ramira to know I've come to town. You said they wanted the element of surprise? Let's take that away from them."

I hadn't liked the idea of her coming in the first place, and being so open about it seemed like asking for trouble. But she did have a point about the soldiers. There were at least a hundred, each armed to the teeth.

"Fine," I said through gritted teeth. "I hope you packed a tent and bedroll."

"I did, Your Majesty," Bronwen said, giving me a haughty look. "Are you sure you don't need me?"

"I'm sure. I'd rather you stay here where it's safe," she said, giving her attendant a long, firm hug. "Hopefully, we'll be back within a few days."

"Be careful," Bronwen said, releasing her and stepping back.

Ayla turned toward the carriage, and I opened the door. Out of habit, I held out my hand to help her in. As her fingers grasped mine, that familiar surge of electricity surged between us, and it took everything in me to remain stoic. Once she was seated, I all but slammed the door shut and whirled on the troops, all of whom were watching with interest.

"Move out." I barked, stomping toward my already-saddled horse. "We're not stopping until nightfall."

Chapter Twenty-Three

Riona

Once again, I'd crisscrossed the fae realm in butterfly form back to the wildlands, though I'd allowed myself to collapse in exhaustion for one night in my own bed before making the return journey to retrieve the troll king for whatever mysterious thing the Erlking wanted. Said king was unimpressed to see me, unimpressed by my task, and didn't seem eager to join me on another jaunt back to the Erlking's castle.

"I mean…" I hesitated. "The Erlking invited you. Practically insisted. Surely…surely, you feel some pull to heed his edict?"

"We're busy here." It was a far cry from the grateful troll who'd prostrated himself at my grandfather's feet. But perhaps that was just a show.

"It'll take a day, at most," I said, exasperated. "Please? I don't think I can come back empty-handed."

"Fine." He gave instructions to some of the trolls, and they nodded, casting me a wary glance, before disappearing into the stone. Then Lynton returned to me. "A day. Then I return."

"So…" I shifted my weight. "Are there *fewer* houses here than when I was last here?"

"Yes."

"Is that…did they…"

"I thought it best to spread our people out," he said, his tone even but his eyes flashing. "Makes us less of an easy target for wayward *daoine maithe* menaces."

I took to the sky and Lynton to the ground, and I kept a watchful eye on the zip of white magic as it moved through the rock. Lynton had never had much faith in the *daoine maithe*—for that matter, neither had Edric—but he seemed much more resolved now. Like the decimation of their people was an inevitability.

Of course, that was preposterous. The Erlking would never allow such a thing. But then came the small fear…what if Birch was no longer the be-all and end-all of magic in this land?

No. If he thinks whatever he's called Lynton to do will work, it will work.

I landed at the front gates, and Lynton materialized beside me. "Let's just get this over with."

We walked inside, and from the first moment, I could tell Lynton was uncomfortable. He was jumpy and suspicious of every fae who walked by. But as we passed a pair of brownies, he seemed to relax a little.

"There are many more…lesser fae than I anticipated here," he said.

"See?" I said with a smile. "Birch is different. He's got the love of all creatures, not just the gr…the um…" I cleared my throat. "The…um…"

"Greater fae?" he finished with a sardonic smile.

"It's such a dumb name," I said, my cheeks flushing. "There aren't greater or lesser fae. There should just be fae."

He snorted but the ghost of a smile remained on his face. Lynton was always hard to read, but the more time I spent with him, the more I was beginning to understand him. He was a man who'd lived in a time when the trolls had to keep to themselves to avoid the wrath of their neighbors. Kindness from a "greater" fae was foreign to him, and even now, after being granted clemency and access to his homeland, Lynton was still skeptical.

As we came to the Erlking's hallway, my feet stuck to the ground. Panic flooded through me as I tugged at my feet, worry that Aldrick had ascended the throne in the hours I'd been gone. But there was a fluttering magic black crow in front of me. Birch's magic.

"What's this?" Lynton said.

"I think we're supposed to go somewhere else," I said, and as I did, my foot unstuck. "C'mon."

We followed the single crow down the hall, around the large receiving room. Although the room was full, the Erlking wasn't in his chair.

The crow led us to a wall, which melted away, revealing the front of the receiving room and the empty chair. I walked inside, ignoring the roar of anger from the crowd that almost seemed predictable now, and Lynton followed silently.

We were led to a spot behind his chair, and once again, the stone melted away, this time, revealing a dark hallway. As soon as Lynton and I were past the threshold, it closed behind us.

"Fascinating," Lynton said. "I wasn't aware the Erlking had access to stone magic. Perhaps some remained from the trolls' departure."

I frowned. "Does that happen? The Erlking gets power from the clans? Like their *actual* magic?"

"No. But a troll's magic could endure in the stone for centuries." He sniffed. "I doubt it was a gift, in any case."

The hallway ended in a small, circular room with magical fire dimly lighting the space. The Erlking was seated at the largest chair, his fingers steepled together as he stared into space. There were two other chairs, so Lynton and I stepped forward to take them.

"I'm afraid those chairs aren't for you two," he said with a bit of an apologetic smile. "At least, not yet. You'll have to stand for the moment."

"What is this?" I asked, looking around.

"It's the most powerful place in the fae realm," he said, tilting his head back to follow my gaze. "The place where each of the leaders of the fae clans bestow power on the Erlking. The *Arwein*."

Lynton took a step back, a shocked gasp leaving his lips. "The *Arwein*? Why am I here?"

"Because I'd like to formally include you and your clan," he said.

"When Riona told me that Aldrick and his friends were defying my edict, I realized that my power hasn't been as absolute as it used to be. I believe it's because the trolls have returned and not formally accepted me as their Erlking."

Lynton made a noise as if he didn't believe him. "And so that's why you've brought me here?" He glanced at me. "What about her?"

He hesitated. "There's a…very small chance that the other members of the *Arwein* won't accept a troll speaking for his people. In that very *rare* instance, Riona will serve as your representative."

I frowned. They were less likely to approve of me than Lynton.

"I don't think it'll be an issue, in any case." He tapped his hands on the intricately carved table, with several moat-like beveled edges that started at the chairs and ended in the center of the table.

"This is a lot of effort just to include the trolls," Lynton said.

"Well, as I'm sure a troll like you knows, magic can wane," he said.

"Troll magic doesn't."

He cracked a wry smile. "*Daoine maithe* magic, then. Every couple of years, it's a good idea to call the members together to bestow power on the Erlking. We just happen to be solving two problems at once." He tilted his head. "The others have arrived."

It wasn't much of a fanfare. A puff of white snow heralded the arrival of my grandmother, and a rustle of autumnal leaves the arrival of the king of the forest kingdom. I waited for more, but there weren't any. Only the greater fae were allowed a seat at the table.

"This had better be good, Birch," the king of the forest realm huffed. "I was in the middle of my dinner."

"It's always necessary," Clíodhna responded.

"You're only saying that because you slept—"

"*Ahem*," Birch said, glancing at me. "We have guests, Coednin. Please mind your manners."

He turned and noticed Lynton and me for the first time, his face sliding into disgust. "What's the meaning of this? We don't allow guests to the *Arwein*. At least, not in my experience."

"King Lynton has come at my invitation to formally be inducted into the *Arwein*," Birch said with a confident smile. "They have returned to their lands and thus should have a seat at the table."

Coednin sneered but didn't argue. "And the halfling bastard?"

"Watch it," Clíodhna snarled.

"Riona is here as an alternate representative for the trolls, in case there are dissents on allowing a troll onto the council," Birch said. "Are there?"

"Perhaps," Coednin said, unsurprisingly, as he looked at Lynton. "Your kind stole a piece of the *seod croí*. Have you returned it to the rightful owners?"

He shifted. "No. It was given…given to the wizard Eoghan by my predecessor."

"Well, isn't that just lovely?" Coednin said, sitting back. "And you want him to have a seat at the table? He's no better than brownies or hobgoblins."

Lynton bared his teeth, but I stepped forward. "And a *daoine maithe* can wipe the floor with you, *king*, so watch yourself." Of the three beings at the table, Coednin was surely the weakest.

He turned to me, a curl on his lip, but Clíodhna spoke up. "Can we just get on with the *Arwein*, Birch?"

"I'm not sure I agree," Coednin said, after a long pause. "These trolls betrayed the fae realm. They deserve to be punished. I don't think it's fair to simply let them off the hook because it's been a thousand years."

Birch's smile tightened. "You're not the one who decides what is and isn't allowed, Coednin."

"Is my magic not part of what fuels you?" he asked. "My magic and the will of every creature in this land? Take care, Birch, that you don't forget: Erlkings come and go just like any other fae."

My heart seized in my chest, but Birch was unfazed. "As do kings of the forest. I don't think you'd like to pit yourself against me at even two-thirds my strength, would you?"

Clíodhna snorted. "I, for one, would welcome some fresh blood from the forest kingdom at the table."

"You're older than me," Coednin shot back. But the threat seemed to have worked. "Fine. The forest kingdom gives their blessing for the vermin to sit at the table with us as long as it means we can get on with things."

Clíodhna lifted two fingers. "As do the *sidheog*."

Birch rose and pressed his hands on the table. "Lynton, come here and place your hands next to mine."

He crossed the room and put his hands on an empty space at the table. Immediately, the white magic in my veins hummed. I tamped it down, not wanting to cause a show in the middle of this dark room.

"Lynton, king of the trolls in the wildlands, do you pledge the unyielding fealty and power of your people to the Erlking?" he asked, his voice barely above a whisper.

"I do," he said. Power seeped from his fingers, slipping down the divot and resting there.

The Erlking then asked the same question to Clíodhna, who agreed, and Coednin, who took a heartbeat to respond affirmatively as well. The table glowed as the power drained from each of their hands, joining Lynton's in the center. Finally, the Erlking reached toward the center, picking up the magic as if it were something solid.

He molded it in his hands then pressed it to his chest. He winced as the magic absorbed, illuminating the veins around his temples and sending his gray hair upright. Then…then it was over.

"Thank you for your—"

Coednin left before he could say another word, while Clíodhna let out a breath. "Riona, we should continue our training now that you've returned. Meet me in the ring in—"

"Riona must return Lynton to his homeland," Birch intervened.

"And remain there until they're fully settled."

Clíodhna made a noise but didn't argue—and disappeared into a puff of snowflakes.

"I don't need an escort," Lynton snapped when she was gone. "Nor a guardian."

"It would please me," Birch said.

"If, as you say, trolls are an equal member at the table, there should be no threat," Lynton said, his light eyes dancing in the dark. "Right?"

Birch took a few minutes to answer. "Riona has been tasked with ensuring your safety. I would like her to continue doing it."

"Very well." Lynton straightened. "I will begin my journey now. Catch up, Riona." He walked out of the room.

I exhaled. "You didn't answer his question, Erlking."

"No, I didn't," Birch said with a heavy sigh.

I opened and closed my hands. "Erlking...I'm not the protector you think I am."

"You have more magic—"

"Only when my sister is near," I interrupted. "It's the same for her stone. We need each other to make our respective powers work." I paused. "Do you...know why?"

"I don't," he said with a shake of his head. "Many of the specifics of the *seod croí* have been lost to time. And some might not have been known by anyone other than Aoibheann herself." He tilted his head toward me. "Didn't you say the trolls could pull memories from stones?"

I nodded.

"Then I think it might be time for you to return to the *aos sí* and find a memory," he said. "If there's a memory stone, it would be there."

I swallowed hard. "You want me to...*what*?" A cold sweat broke out on the base of my neck. "Don't you remember what happened the last time I went there?"

"The monsters were drawn to the wizard," he said. "You should have no such trouble with him gone."

I didn't believe that. The creatures—undead, decaying things that made unearthly sounds as they slithered up from the grave—hadn't really cared about Cade. Or Ward, for that matter.

"I won't go," I said quietly. "It's too much of a risk."

"We won't have an answer to your magic until we do," he said. "And as much as I hate to do this…" He stared at me. "Riona, you will go to the *aos sí* in search of a memory stone."

My pulse throbbed as my neck burned. "Don't make me do this, Grandfather."

"We all have to face our fears, eventually," he said.

Chapter Twenty-Four

Cade

The crew slept well into the next day, giving me ample time to try to create a portal to H'sipotu. But every time I followed the maps I'd imprinted in my mind, something stopped me before I could get to the island that had appeared in ink. Over and over and over again, until the sun was high in the sky and the crew started to make their hungover appearances.

I tried to assure myself that Eoghan had managed to figure it out, so I surely could as well. But Eoghan was far more powerful, clever, and determined than I was.

Though I couldn't help but wonder *what* had brought him to the island. Was it, as I'd always suspected, my wizarding abilities? Had he cast a spell to be alerted of any new wizards born in the entire world? So much of my childhood remained shrouded in mystery still. As much as I never wanted to see his face again, part of me longed to simply sit down with him and get the truth.

But that was as likely as me getting to the island magically. I tapped my finger on the staff, debating if I should come clean and just ask Aldonza. But considering she was snapping at everyone who spoke to her, I doubted she'd be in the mood to forgive me for breaking into her quarters and snooping.

We set sail around mid-afternoon, with Aldonza not needing me as she pointed the ship in the direction they wanted to go. She was tight-lipped about what they were doing next, so I assumed it was something of the illegal smuggling variety and kept myself scarce.

We reached an island a few hours later, and after some negotiations, Aldonza returned with instructions for the crew to retrieve crates and load the ship.

"We'll be taking it to Pyready," she said, giving me a once-over. "The wizard will help us along, I'm sure."

I nodded. "Another star map lesson?"

"Absolutely."

As darkness settled around us, the crew loaded the illegal goods, then we took off. I created a portal halfway across the sea to deliver them. They unloaded them at night, Aldonza got paid, then she asked me to create a portal back to Al'ocasep.

"Didn't we just come from there?" I asked with only a bit of annoyance.

"It's quite the place," she said. "Maybe you should join us tonight. You're practically one of us now. Time to break you of those innocent ways."

"I think I'll stay on the ship, thanks," I replied with a tight smile.

They meandered off, still as eager and excited as the night before. This time, I had no desire to return to Aldonza's cabin, so I stretched out under the stars and named them. But that exercise only lasted a few minutes before boredom caught up with me.

Once more, I attempted to create a portal to H'sipotu, and yet again, found myself only on the edge of the place, unable to continue farther via magic.

But what about via ship?

I pushed myself to sit up, looking around. I'd been watching the crew, but how they managed to find the wind and move the water still eluded me. Even when I conjured wind, it was all I did—they configured everything else to ensure the ship went where they wanted.

I still needed them for that part. But if I were to figure out how to get the ship nearer to H'sipotu, maybe I could get close enough to swim or magic myself there. But Aldonza would never go for such a thing—and trying to pull a fast one on her would be difficult. She would know if I took us off course if I attempted anything at night.

But if I attempted during the day, when Aldonza couldn't read the stars...

It was a long shot, and came with the risk that Aldonza would know something was up. But I had to try.

>–» >–» >–» >–»

As predicted, the crew slept until mid-morning then lazily woke and pushed off, and Aldonza navigated us east this time. I glanced at the sky, bright blue and cloudless, and whispered to the wind. The breeze picked up first, and the crew moved to adjust the sails. Then I summoned a few more clouds to fill the sky, blocking out the sun.

"Storm's coming?" Cluny said with a frown. "Odd."

The clouds grew darker, full of rain, as the winds picked up and a light drizzle began to fall.

The ship bobbed in the gradually increasing waves, and, having terrible balance on this ship anyway, I headed toward the mast to hang on. My magic had just stirred up the weather; now it was worsening all on its own. Rain was coming in sheets buffeted by the wind, and it was hard to see.

As the thunder crackled above, regret seeped into my mind. Would the ship's integrity hold under these conditions? And yet...yet the crew didn't look scared at all. In fact, even Volker was still in his perch, hanging off the side of the crow's nest and whooping loudly to the wind.

"Don't worry, wizard," Cluny said, coming up beside me. "We've seen worse storms. We'll make it out in one piece."

I wiped the water from my face, a little annoyed. "You don't want me to create a portal and get us out of here?"

"Not a chance," Aldonza said, walking by to grab a loose piece of rigging. "Don't know where we'll end up at this rate. And we have a lucrative deal waiting for us if we can complete the job today."

I huffed, torn between not wanting to add to the fire and needing to be asked to create a portal in daylight. I wouldn't have a chance at night; Aldonza would catch on too quickly.

So with a small whimper of prayer, I called upon more wind and rain. The sky turned darker, and the gales went from howling to almost moaning. The rain came sideways, stinging as it hit my face and eyes. And yet, the crew kept their posts, still wearing smiles as they held the sails and rigging together.

Hm. If I couldn't create a storm powerful enough to scare them, maybe they would feel differently if their sails were torn.

It was hard to do without showing the magic, but I managed to conjure a lightning bolt at the same time I magically ripped a large hole in the mainsail.

"Onor!" Aldonza cried.

He moved like a spider, crawling up the mast and sewing the sail. Within minutes, he had the whole thing mended.

"Son of a..." I muttered, glancing up. What was it going to take to scare these stupid pirates?

Another rush of seawater came across the bow, seeming to knock Cai off, but when the water receded, she was soaked and hanging on, her fist aloft with joy. Aldonza called back with a loud yell of her own and the rest of the crew joined in.

After a few minutes, I accepted that rough weather wasn't going to break their spirits, even if I kept at it for another hour. Or five. So I let the weather clear, the rain dissipate, the sun come out. And I tried not to look disappointed as we sailed into port, intent on carrying more goods to smuggle so they could pay for their philandering later that evening.

>–» >–» >–» >–»

Once again, as the sun set, Aldonza asked me to create a portal to *Al'ocasep*. But as the crew piled off, eager for another night of wasting their gold on flesh and alcohol, Aldonza hung behind, a smirk on her face.

"Are you finished with the pirate life, wizard?" she asked. "You look positively glum. Which is a feat, considering this island is designed to meet every desire you have in life."

"The one pleasure I want can't be found here," I replied dryly.

"H'sipotu is a far-off dream. You're better served—"

"That's not what I meant," I snapped, pushing myself off the railing. "I suppose I'll go to sleep."

"Lover trouble?" Aldonza asked with a quirked brow. "Girl or boy?"

"Girl— Wait," I sputtered. "None of your business."

"Girls are tricky." Aldonza grinned at me. "C'mon, tell your ol' captain about the one who broke your heart. I'm assuming that's how it went, considering how mopey you are about it."

"I'm not mopey."

"You're from Pennlan, right?" I nodded. "That's a far way to travel unless you've got a broken heart."

"I didn't travel far because I have a broken heart. I'm looking for something. And I'm not going to find it here…" I gestured to the island before us. "I'm just frustrated that my search has been stymied. It's not as if I have a lot of time to waste."

"See? Mopey." She chuckled. "C'mon. Spill. I don't like to have someone on my ship and not know at least one secret about them."

I licked my lips. "Her name is…Ayla. She's the queen of Pennlan."

Aldonza whistled. "You certainly aim high. Queens are trouble, though. Best avoided."

"She's not like that," I said. "We grew up together. Her father was killed when she was very young, and she had no one else. I arrived at the castle unable to speak to anyone, but somehow…somehow, we figured it out."

Aldonza said nothing but nodded.

"Anyway, I felt something for her the moment I laid eyes on her," I said. "And I waited too long to say something, because she fell for someone else."

"See, that's where you're wrong," Aldonza said. "Girls don't operate like that, you know? Some do, of course, but I have a feeling that if someone else caught her eye, you were never in the picture. At least not in the way you wanted to be."

"You don't know that," I said, my cheeks flushing. "You don't know how she looked at me."

"Probably like the only thing left of her childhood after that wizard tore everything away from her, right?"

I snapped my gaze to hers, stunned. "What? You know about that?"

"*Everybody* knows about that," Aldonza said with a chuckle. "I mean, until I saw your magic for myself, I was skeptical that a wizard could've pulled off half the stuff they said he did, but now I believe it. No wonder the fae are scared of them."

It was odd to talk about Eoghan and fae after so long away from it all. "Yeah. It happened. Eoghan was my master, and he betrayed us."

"Look, I'm not going to tell you how to soothe your broken heart. But having had a few of my own, and having broken more than I care to count, I'll give you a bit of advice: Love takes many forms. Sometimes, it's that deep, soul-touching connection that you read about in books. Sometimes, it's just one night with an ample-bodied woman in a short skirt. And sometimes, you can love someone with your entire soul but not want to hop into bed with them, ya get me?"

"That's not..." My face was now burning hot. "That's not what—"

"No, of course not. But you get my point." She pushed off the railing. "And maybe, just maybe, if you look past your wounded pride, you might find that you really didn't love her the way you thought you did, either. She wasn't the only orphan in that castle, after all."

"Of *course* I loved her," I snapped. "You have no clue what you're talking about."

"Sure." She stepped away from the railing. "Anyway, enjoy your evening. We'll see you in the morning." She cracked a smile. "Unless you'd like to forget about your queen the old-fashioned way..."

"No, I'm good." My entire body was hot from anger and embarrassment. "See you tomorrow."

As she walked away, I found myself glowering at her, hating her with every fiber of my being. She had no clue about my past, or Ayla, or what we shared. Or what I thought we'd shared.

"I love you. But as a friend. As my brother. Not as..."

And just like that, the hurt began anew.

Chapter Twenty-Five

Ayla

If someone had asked me a few weeks ago whether I thought it was better to travel on foot or via carriage, I would've vehemently said carriage. But having done both in the past month, I found myself wishing I could get out and walk more. After riding all day nonstop, my legs were stiff, my rear sore from sitting on the uncomfortable bench as I was jostled around on the uneven road.

For the millionth time, I glanced at the red box sitting across from me, hoping it would light up with Riona's answer at any minute. It was easy to fall into a spiral of thoughts about why she hadn't responded already, but I had to hold out hope that everything was fine and she'd just gotten busy. Besides that, I didn't *need* her quite yet, despite what Ward might think. Even just fearing the stone might be enough to change the course of Konevell's invasion.

But—I opened the box again, just to be sure—it would also be nice if I could *actually* put on a light show to prove my power.

I dropped the stone and scooted toward the window, leaning out to let the warm sun shine on my face. Nearby, a soldier named Esmond was walking, though he seemed to have a limp.

"What's wrong with your leg, Esmond?" I asked.

"Gives me a bit of trouble when I'm on it a lot," he said with a grimace. "I'll be all right."

"You should be on a horse, then," I said. "I'll find Ward to—"

"No need, Yer Majesty. I'll be fine."

But his pace slowed even more, and he fell behind my carriage. I had to lean out of the window completely to find him, and I was annoyed that his fellow soldiers didn't seem to care about his limp. But then again, everyone looked miserable. Based on the sun in the sky, it was midafternoon, and Ward hadn't even told them to stop for lunch.

I pursed my lips and leaned even farther out of the carriage, searching the crowd for his silhouette. He'd been riding back and forth all day, though he hadn't stopped to say two words to me, of course. After a few minutes, I heard the thundering of his horse.

"Ward!" I called as he rode by.

"What is it?" he snapped, slowing and turning to look at me with a disgruntled look.

I made a face. *Is he that angry with me?* "I just wanted to ask when we're planning to stop."

"We aren't."

"Oy, what?" The soldier nearest to me almost stopped short and would have had it not been for the soldier behind him pushing him forward. "What do you mean we aren't stopping?"

Ward cleared his throat. "We'll stop at sundown. But not until then. We have to get to Orapus as fast as we can."

"Don't see why," a nearby soldier muttered. "If they got a few thousand, we're as good as dead."

"That's not true," I said, earning a look of surprise from the soldier. He clearly hadn't noticed I was there.

"Save your strength for the march, soldier," Ward said. "And A—" He cleared his throat. "Your Majesty, please stay inside the carriage and quit bothering the soldiers."

I scowled. *Bothering?*

Before I could snap at him, he spurred his horse and rode away.

"What's up his butt?" I said, leaning on my elbow.

"Lover's quarrel?" the soldier said, smirking at me.

I straightened, my face flushing red. "We would have to be lovers for that to be the case. And we're not." I cleared my throat. "Do as your captain says, and save your strength for walking."

⤞ ⤞ ⤞ ⤞

It took at least until sundown for me to ignore the way the soldier had said *lover*. Rumors had swirled around Ward and me for months, but I'd always thought them of the innocent sort. Just castle gossip. But there was something…unsettling about the way the soldier had spoken so plainly.

Finally, I heard the soldiers call for the carriage to stop, and the door opened, revealing Rutley's sunburned face. "Evening, Your Majesty."

"Hello there." He helped me out of the carriage, and I had to awkwardly stretch my legs to get them to work again. "Give me a moment."

"Of course." He smirked. "Cooped up all day will do that to you."

I smiled at him. I was glad a friendly face had come to retrieve me. "So where are you taking me?"

"To your tent. We've got it all set up for you."

He led me through a smattering of bonfires, tents, and people. Most were lying in bedrolls, but some had just fallen asleep on the grass, their mouths open with exhaustion. I felt another surge of annoyance at Ward for running them so ragged. After all, what good was our army if they were exhausted?

"Your Majesty?" Rutley prompted.

"Sorry," I said, turning back toward him. "Lead the way."

Mine was the largest and most ornate tent with the Pennlan flag sitting on top of it. Bronwen had described it to me, saying that in years past, kings would march from one end of the kingdom to the other to meet and mingle with their citizens. Perhaps one day, the world would stop burning long enough for me to do something like that.

"Dinner will be served shortly. You're to stay here until then," Rutley said, bowing and disappearing.

Alone in my tent, I inspected the trimmings and found them to be excellent and fit for a queen. My things were still in their trunk, but all I grabbed was my nightgown, which I laid out on the bedroll to put on later. I brushed and rebraided my hair, missing Bronwen just a bit for her companionship and the neat way she plaited my hair, and sat with my hands folded across my lap.

But after hours of sitting still, I was too antsy to be in one place. I crossed the tent to open the flap, peering out. Everyone seemed to be sharing food and drink, and they at least looked in a better humor than on the road.

I stepped outside, closing the flap behind me. My shoulders back, chin tilted up, I walked the short distance to the next tent, where a pair of soldiers were sitting over a small fire. They glanced at me disinterestedly before looking back at the fire. Then, a heartbeat later, they scrambled to their feet to bow.

"Y-Your Majesty."

"A thousand apologies."

"What can we do for you?"

"Nothing, nothing." I held up my hands in surrender. "I just wanted to make sure you had everything you needed."

They shared a look of confusion. "In what way, Highness?"

"Food? Bedrolls?" I lifted a shoulder. "Water?"

"Yes, of course. We made sure to bring what we needed." The soldiers stared at each other. "Are you in need of anything?"

"No, I'm fine. I just wanted to make sure you were." I inched away. "Have a good night."

"Wait!" One took a hesitant step toward me. "Captain... He wanted you to stay put tonight. Asked us to..." He swallowed nervously. "Make sure you stayed put."

I pursed my lips. "He did, did he?"

"Only passing on our orders, ma'am."

"Then consider them overruled," I said, walking a few steps before stopping. "I'm just going to stretch my legs around the camp. I should be back within the hour."

They bowed, though it didn't escape my notice that they followed me from a very safe distance. I didn't argue with them. Whatever they needed to sleep at night.

I found more of the same. Makeshift tents, small fires, soldiers scrambling to attention as I passed to check in on them. There were some who seemed in awe of my presence—ones who hadn't really spent much time in the castle. Others weren't impressed by my presence but begrudgingly showed their respect. I didn't stay long at any one spot, eager to reach all the soldiers. There were so many I hadn't met yet—and I'd thought I knew most of them.

"What are you doing?" Elodia walked up as I was getting to know a pair of twins from the east.

"Just taking a walk, checking on the soldiers," I said. "Is that not allowed?"

She peered behind me to where my bodyguards were loitering. "I think you know the answer to that."

"I'm staying within the camp," I said. "I just wanted—"

"To your tent. Now."

I didn't argue with her, though I probably could have, considering I was the queen and all. But the look on her face told me it would be useless, so I let her lead me back to my tent. Before ducking under the flap Elodia held up, I waved goodbye to my two bodyguards who waved back, only to wilt under Elodia's glare.

"Now don't let me catch you wandering around again or else I'll park myself in here to watch you."

"Yes, ma'am," I said, mock saluting her.

She muttered something under her breath.

"Can you have Ward come by?" I said as she turned to leave.

"These are his orders. You don't have to complain—"

I shook my head. "Nobody's in trouble. I just want to talk with him."

"Fine."

She left me there, and I shivered under her chill.

Over half an hour later, I changed into my sleeping gown, hoping it might make me tired. But I just paced a hole in the grass in my slippered feet, counting the minutes as they passed.

Finally, footsteps. "Can I come in?" Ward asked.

"Yes, of course."

Ward brusquely marched inside. "You can be mad—"

"I'm not mad," I said with a small laugh. "And I'm sorry for…well, disobeying you, I suppose. I just wanted to make sure everyone was okay."

He stared at me. "Why wouldn't they be?"

"Because you marched them nonstop through the hot sun," I said. "They didn't even get a chance to have lunch."

"This isn't a nice walk across the countryside," Ward replied. "The longer we dawdle, the greater chance Konevell has to make their move before we're ready."

"You said that Orapus was on high alert," I replied. "They should be able to offer some defense."

He made a noise. "Let's just say that I don't have the greatest confidence in the local captain, and I'll feel better once our soldiers are within striking distance of the city."

I sat up. "What do you mean? It's still Captain Treen, isn't it? She's served well and for many years. Gabhann spoke highly of her."

He shifted. There was something he wasn't telling me. "Is that all?"

"Ward, stop. Whatever's bothering you…"

"First of all, you're in your nightgown."

I looked down, warmth spreading across my cheeks. My shift was shapeless and made of thick wool, but it was the most undressed Ward had ever seen me. "So I am." I crossed my arms. "You can't see anything."

"Ayla, we can't… We have to stay focused."

His cheeks were quite dark now, and I almost felt bad at how uncomfortable he looked. "I am focused," I said.

"Are you?" He finally met my gaze. "Because you seem to be back to your old tricks of defying me every step of the way when all I'm trying to do is keep you safe."

I bristled. "A queen doesn't cower when she's threatened. If that's what you want me to do, I might as well just hand over the Pennlan stone right now."

He exhaled, his nostrils flaring. "Have you heard from Riona?"

I shifted. "No. Not yet."

"Then you don't have any defenses to speak of, other than the soldiers out there, and they…" He trailed off, a flash of worry crossing his face. "We have one more day of travel until we get there. Just try to… Try to be the one person in camp who listens to me, will you?"

"I'm listening to you," I said, throwing my hands in the air. "And I'm trying to abide by your rules. But you said yourself I'm safest amongst my soldiers. These men and women have been protecting me since I was a child. They're my friends. I should—at a minimum—be able to walk amongst them without being frog-marched back to my room. And they should be given a break at midday, at least, to catch their breath. Captain Treen is more than enough to handle Orapus for a day or two—even if Konevell invades."

I expected more of a fight from him, but instead he shook his head heavily. "We're leaving at sunup," he said, sounding much more tired than he had before. "Get some rest."

Chapter Twenty-Six

Ward

I had the unenviable task of rousing the camp the next morning. I was called every brand of insult I knew—and some new, creative ones, to boot—but I kept plowing along. Even Ayla cast me a dirty look when she walked out of her tent wearing the same traveling clothes from the day before.

It took some time to break down the tents and pack up the wagons, so it was midmorning before we were finally on the road again. The delays were starting to itch at me—I'd wanted to be near Orapus by sundown, but it looked like it might be closer to midnight at this rate. The soldiers were moving much slower than the day before, and there didn't seem to be much I could do to goad them on. We performed drills and training all day long, but this hours-long slog was a different sort of exhaustion, especially laden with gear and weapons. I didn't blame them for cursing my name.

"We can't even stop to piss half the time," a soldier grunted at me.

"We're starving."

"Gabhann would *never*—"

"Well, Gabhann wasn't facing an invasion from a foreign country, so there's that," I snapped, adjusting my reins. "Now save your breath for the road. I promise a hearty meal from Orapus when we arrive."

Once again, I rode the length, but this time, a pale hand shot out from the carriage window and nearly pulled me off my horse.

"*Stop*, you blithering idiot." Her green eyes were on fire. "I've been trying to get your attention all morning."

"Have you?" I shifted in my saddle. "It can wait—"

"No, it can't," she said, practically hanging out of her carriage window. "You're going to run these soldiers into the ground. We need to stop and rest. Have lunch."

"What we need is to pick up the pace," I said, peering at the sky. Mid-afternoon now. We'd only get perhaps another four or five hours of sunlight.

"You pick up the pace," Ayla snapped. "Easy for you on your horse and me in my carriage. These people are tired. They'll be no good to us if they're dead on their feet."

So we stopped, against my better judgment, and the soldiers had an hour to rest and relax. As expected, it was that much harder to rouse them and get them moving again, so all in all we lost two hours of travel time—and no one looked to be in any better humor.

As I rode up to the front, Elodia got my attention. "What's with this pace, eh? Are you trying to beat a record or something?"

"Oh, are you no longer mad at me?" I snapped. "Eager to speak with me?"

"Eager for you to pull that stick out of your ass," she replied with a quirked brow. "I mean, I know we're all facing an invasion from Konevell with an army that outnumbers us significantly, but what is *wrong* with you? You said yourself the army was still assembling. You've set the guard in Orapus to be on the lookout. At the very least, they should be able to delay the invasion until we get there."

I was too tired to lie to her. "I'm worried the captain in Orapus didn't believe me."

She cleared her throat and didn't look at me. "And why is that?"

"Because she all but laughed at me when I told her," I said. "Thought it was ridiculous. Said it was delusional. I told her it was a direct order, but..." I shook my head. "Somehow I don't think my orders carry as much weight as Gabhann's did."

"Maybe because you're out questing when you should be leading your troops." Elodia smirked.

"Did you have that ready to go, or…?"

"Been waiting for the opportune moment," she replied. "Look, *this* is why you should've brought someone other than Platt with you. Me, Rutley—literally *anyone* else. We could've stayed behind and enforced the order. I highly doubt Platt's doing anything to help you." She sighed and shook her head. "I'm too tired to yell at you right now."

"That's a relief."

"But you seriously need to start using that head of yours," she said. "Especially now. Especially going into Orapus where nobody's taking you seriously. You need to make sure the *right* people have your back." She sat back in her saddle. "Because we do. You know that, right?"

"I know," I said. "And I'll feel better once I see the city and make sure it isn't already under attack."

"Look, if you're that worried about Orapus, why not send riders ahead to make sure it's fine? We're within a day of arriving, yeah?"

I shifted in my saddle. I perhaps should've thought of that. "Yes."

"The soldiers won't make it there at this pace," she said. "Send a couple ahead to make sure all is well so you can sleep easy tonight. In the morning, we'll continue and make our camp. *Then* you can bring Her Majesty with you to Captain Treen and make the old bird listen to you."

I chuckled. "You have a lot of good ideas lately, El."

"Which is why you should always listen to me." She quirked a brow. "Because I'm always right."

⤞ ⤞ ⤞ ⤞

Elodia had one of the fastest horses, so I sent her and two others ahead. The sun was sinking in front of us, so I made the call to stop and set up camp. This time, I was met with sighs of relief and gratitude as they leisurely moved to set themselves up for the night.

"How much farther, do you think?" Rutley asked as we patrolled through the camp.

"Half a day, maybe," I said. "As soon as Elodia gets back with a good report, I'll feel better."

I'd filled him in on what I'd told Elodia about the captain not believing me, and he'd had nearly the same advice. Except, of course, he was nicer about it.

"I can't say I blame her for not believing you," Rutley said. "I wouldn't want to believe you either." I glared at him, and he held up his hands. "I do, don't get me wrong. But I don't really want to."

I supposed he had a point. "I wish I knew where they were planning to come ashore. I think the best we can do is be nearby and move quickly when we do find out."

"You could send me or El to Konevell and we could spy on them?" he offered.

I shook my head. "Too dangerous at this point. They're picking people off the streets and sending them to the encampment."

"So why'd you go?"

"Because I didn't know that at the time," I replied, waving my hand. "Can you stop? I'm getting flack from all angles, and I don't need it from you, too."

He chuckled. "I'll tell you one person you aren't hearing complaints from, and that's the queen. Mostly because you won't talk with her."

I cleared my throat. "Nothing to say right now."

"I mean, I think there are a few things you might want to let her know about. Namely that the captain of a major city isn't following orders."

"She has enough to worry about."

"Well, you're about to have a lot to worry about," Rutley said, opening the flap to a nearby tent. He'd led me to Ayla's tent without me noticing. "Because she *insisted* I bring you to see her."

⇥ ⇥ ⇥ ⇥

I stepped inside, mentally practicing what I was going to say. But she was nowhere to be found.

"Ayla?" I said, panic rising in my chest.

"Out here."

I squinted, making out her silhouette on the far side of the tent. I crossed in three steps and pulled the bottom up, ducking underneath. She wore her traveling clothes still but was gazing up at the stars with a look of wonderment.

"Why didn't you just go around?" she asked.

"Because…" I didn't really know why. "I don't know. I'm tired."

"We're all tired," she replied with a look. "Which is what I wanted to talk with you about. But, of course, it's been impossible to do that since you've been avoiding me all day."

"Trying to keep morale up," I said. "No news to share with you."

"Ward." She turned to me, annoyance plain on her face. "I thought you and I were friends, that we could speak freely, especially after all we've been through." She smiled, and my heart flip-flopped. "You're allowed to yell at me. I'm allowed to yell at you. But it seems like you aren't telling me something, and that worries me."

Could I lay bare my fears about what was waiting for us in Orapus? That not a single soldier took me seriously, not out there, not in Orapus, and perhaps not even in the cities beyond? That I'd lain awake the night before, my pulse in my ears as I thought about what might happen if *nobody* answered our call because they thought me an inept captain—or worse, that I was out of my mind?

"We're facing an invasion," I managed, hoping I didn't look too guilty. I told myself I was sparing her my worries as she had enough to concern herself with. But even in my heart, I knew that was a lie.

"Yes, we all know that." She pursed her lips. "There's something else. I can tell. Something beyond just the pressure we all feel." She gestured to the camp behind her. "You've been running the soldiers to the breaking point. We didn't need to march so hard, so fast. Orapus has plenty of defenses."

I couldn't lie to her again, so I just remained silent.

"Look, if you want to be a leader, you at least need your followers to like you," she said. "Like Captain Gabhann—"

"I'm doing the best I can," I snapped, a little too loudly.

Ayla's brows rose, and my face warmed.

"Sorry."

"Fine." She stepped forward. "Be that way. But I hope you know you can tell me anything." She reached down to take my hand. "Even if it scares the daylights out of you, I want to know. We can help each other."

My heart skipped at our joined hands, though I knew on some level she was manipulating me into coming clean. Perhaps it was the exhaustion or the way her hand fit perfectly in mine, but I found myself unfurling to her.

"Why did you pick me to be captain?" I asked.

"Because I trust you," she said. "You always seem to have the right answer."

My heart sank. "But what if I don't?"

"Then we'll find the right one together." She released my hand. "I have all the faith in the world in you, Ward."

My heart lightened as we turned to watch the sky together. But there was something…off about it. The horizon seemed to have a red tint to it, almost like the sun was about to burst through for a new day.

"It's too early to be sunup, isn't it?" she asked.

"It is. And that's west," I said. "The sun would be coming from the other side."

The hair on the back of my neck stood up as the faint scent of smoke wafted in the air. I could've chalked it up to the bonfires in the camp, but the wind was blowing the other way.

"Do you smell that?" Ayla asked, looking at me.

Before I could answer, Elodia's voice rang out across the camp. Ayla and I ran toward the sound, finding her riding into the camp.

"Boss," she said, breathless, "there's a fire in the city."

"Is it Konevell?" I asked.

"No clue," she said. "I was on my way back and heard the explosion and saw the fire."

"Ward..." Ayla's eyes widened as she thumbed the stone.

"Everyone on your feet," I called to the camp. "I want twenty riders with me, *now*. El, get the rest of the troops geared up and head toward the city." I glanced around as the soldiers slowly got to their feet. "That's not a request. That's an *order*. *Move!*"

"You heard him," Elodia barked. "Orapus is under attack. We have to *go*."

Annoyingly, Elodia's goading seemed to spur them faster. My horse was brought to me, and even he looked annoyed at me. I hoisted myself into the saddle and was about ready to go when Ayla asked.

"What about me?"

I turned to her. "Stay here. El—get Rutley. Have him watch her. Leave a couple extra soldiers just in case."

She frowned. "I want to go. Ward, what if I can help? What if Ramira's there—"

"If she is, I'll send for you," I said. "But right now, you need to stay here until I call for you."

And with that, I took off toward the city.

Chapter Twenty-Seven

Riona

The Erlking's edict to search the *aos sí* was stronger than most, and every passing minute I remained in his castle, the burning sensation increased. So without even stopping to rest, I marched to the front of the castle and took to the sky. I hadn't a clue how I'd find a memory stone, but that was the least of my worries.

"We all have to face our fears, eventually."

Easy for him to say. He was the damn Erlking.

I materialized in the center of the small village and—in a bit of good news—found a pile of opened crates. Fiadh and the rest must've returned with the goods from the border. I'd been so distracted with Aldrick and Ayla that I'd forgotten about them.

"Riona, good to see you," the troll said, bowing. "Your friend Ward was most helpful."

"I'm glad to hear that," I said. "Seems you were able to gather as much as you needed."

"And then some." Her face fell as she looked south. "I fear the news isn't all good, though. There's trouble brewing just beyond the border."

"What?" I said with a frown. I hadn't had a chance to check our red box in a few days, what with the flitting back and forth. "What kind of trouble?"

"I'm not sure," Fiadh said. "But the ground is unsettled."

"If it is, it isn't our concern." Lynton materialized beside me, his face hard and unforgiving. A moment later, his daughter Aniline appeared next to him, watching him as if he were about to explode.

"I see my guardian has arrived," he drawled. "Took you long enough."

"I thought you didn't want me," I said with a half-smile.

He snorted and looked at his daughter. "See to it that she has a place to sleep. After all, the Erlking *insisted* she stay."

"I will, Da," she said with a small bow.

He disappeared into the ground. Fiadh and Aniline shared a look before turning to me.

"Sorry about him," Aniline said. "I think he's still getting used to his position as king."

"The kingdom of Pennlan has done too much for us not to come to their aid should they need it," Fiadh said, more to Aniline than to me. "You should remind your father who made sure our people survived the mountain."

"I will," Aniline said. "Go get some rest. You deserve it."

The other troll made a noise before melting into the ground. Then it was just Aniline and me. My neck burned with the Erlking's edict. I wanted to swat it away, telling it that now wasn't the right time to ask for favors since Lynton wasn't very happy with me, but it insisted.

"So, um…" I cleared my throat.

"Right, you need a house, probably?" Aniline said, turning to look at the village. "How about—"

"Before you do that," I said. "I have a question. A couple of questions, actually. About memory stones."

"Oh." She frowned. "What about them?"

"How are they created?"

"Well, when a big event happens, the energy it creates is stored in the rock. Trolls can reach in and retrieve those memories," Aniline said. "Why?"

"Is it any rock?" I asked, my gaze moving over to the *aos sí*. "Or specific ones?"

"Specific," she said. "Why?" She followed my gaze, and her already translucent skin paled even more. "What are you thinking?"

I rubbed the back of my neck. "The Erlking wants me to find some answers supposedly lost to time, and he thinks they might be in memory stones." I nodded toward the *aos sí* to the south. "Probably in there."

"Answers about what?"

I hesitated. "The *seod croí*. Specifically, the memories around when it was split. And potentially how to use the pieces."

She took a step back. "You want to *use* it?"

"Cade said the only way to destroy them is to use them against each other," I said, holding up my hands. "Trust me, none of us want a repeat of Laughlan. But maybe…maybe that memory holds an explanation for what this white magic is, and why it seems to be more active around the stones." Again, my gaze drifted toward the dark cemetery. "And my grandfather has…well, he's tasked me with searching the *aos sí* for that memory."

"You won't be able to find them," she said. "It's a magic only trolls possess."

"Great." I huffed. "I was afraid of that. I guess I'll have to ask your father for permission. I'm sure that conversation will go really well…"

"Or…" She grinned devilishly. "You and I could go. What he doesn't know won't hurt him."

"Absolutely not," I replied with a nervous laugh. "I'm already on thin ice with your da. I'm not going to make things worse by dragging you into a dangerous cemetery full of ghosts and monsters."

And yet, as I said it, my neck burned. I balled my fists, angry that this edict didn't seem to care about the consequences.

"You wouldn't be dragging me anywhere," she said. "Look, you're *daoine maithe*. You can evaporate into butterflies should they re-emerge. I can sink into the rock. They can't follow me there, right?"

I didn't like that logic. "I suppose…"

"So there's no danger. We can escape if we need to." She turned toward the south. "And if it helps you understand this power that protects us, all the better."

"Aniline, I can't—"

Before I could finish what I was saying, she evaporated into the ground, the little light of magic zooming toward the *aos sí*.

"Great." I glanced behind me to where the sun was beginning to dip below the horizon. "Guess we're going now."

>--» >--» >--» >--»

"This place is…" Aniline said as I landed beside her. She looked green, if possible, and her golden eyes widened.

"We can go back," I said, gesturing to the wildlands a few feet from where we stood.

"No." She straightened her shoulders. "Let's go. I'm sure there's one around here somewhere."

The *aos sí* was quiet, void of the usual sounds of nighttime activity from bugs and birds and other nocturnal creatures. Memories of decomposing fae creatures rising from the ground came to the forefront of my mind. I couldn't believe I'd willingly returned to this place, to chance the disturbance of the creatures of the night. Each step seemed as loud as an explosion, a dare to the mounds of dirt that held the remnants of the army who'd fought Laughlan. Louder still was the beat of my heart in my throat, and my body was ready to take to the sky at any moment.

The Erlking said it was Cade who drew the monsters, not you. Relax.

I just wished I believed him.

I let Aniline lead the way, though it didn't seem she was doing anything except looking around with wide eyes. Maybe she was pretending she could find the stones to prove herself tough—

Gasping, she pointed into the distance. "Right there. That's one." She bounded forward, scooping up something dark and bringing it back to me. I didn't see anything extraordinary about it.

"Are you…sure?" I asked.

"I gotta dust off the memory first." She covered the stone with her other hand and magic glowed between her fingertips. When she released her grip, the stone was almost alive.

"What memory is it?" I asked. "Does it have anything to do with Aoibheann?"

Horror came over her face.

"Aniline?"

"S-sorry." Her voice was thick. "It's just…it's part of the battle. Nothing…nothing important."

My heart twisted. This was a bad idea. "We should go. I'll search the Erlking's library. There's no need to subject you to more of this—"

"No!" Her voice echoed, and I flinched, listening for the ghosts' awakening. "No. I want to help you. I can handle it."

We continued our search, and though we found more memory stones, none were the ones we were looking for. What I'd hoped would be a quick retrieval was turning into a much more involved effort. With every stone Aniline picked up, her voice grew quieter and more strained —but she kept refusing my attempts to leave.

"I'm fine."

"You sound like—"

"I promise, I'm okay," she said, a little annoyed.

I opted for another subject. "So…is it one memory per stone or…?"

"Here, yes. Only one major event happened in this space," she replied, the tension in her shoulders relaxing. "But in other lands, courts and borders, where lots of things happen…a stone could hold a thousand memories."

I nodded. "We should get back to safety before—" A guttural sound echoed in the darkness and my heart dropped into my stomach. "Aniline, we need to get *out* of here."

"But—"

The mound beside us exploded, raining dirt and the stench of rotting flesh on us, followed by the roar of a ghoulish creature.

"Go!" I screamed, turning into butterflies.

A decomposing hand reached up and *grabbed the magic*, throwing me back onto the ground. The wind knocked from my lungs, I reformed, looking up as more creatures emerged. They were exactly as I remembered them—gray, decaying skin, with long, stringy white hair that barely hung onto the patches that covered their skulls.

The pointed ears, though—couldn't miss those.

I searched for the white magic, but panic was overtaking my senses. I tried to form into butterflies again, but my heart was racing too fast for that. My body shook as I scooted away from the advancing creatures, only to find them behind me, too. I was surrounded.

"Riona!" Aniline was watching from a distance—

"G-go!" I cried. "Save yourself!"

But in the haze of my terror, I realized the ghouls hadn't even noticed her. In fact, they were walking right by her to get to…me.

So much for your theory, Birch.

With that moment of sanity, I transformed into butterflies again and launched toward the sky, but once more, the creatures were able to grab me. I pulled as much as I could, casting attack butterflies at the ghouls in a futile attempt to get them to release me. But they knocked them harmlessly away, pulling me back down to my corporeal form on the ground.

The one right above me stared down at me with eyeless sockets, his jaw opening with unspoken words. A shiver of revulsion echoed through me as he reached down with skeletal fingers to lift me up by the neck. I struggled, kicking at the air as I frantically cast spells hoping to knock myself loose. But the darkness was starting to close in, and I—

Something white and bright rose from the ground, severing the hand holding me and sending me tumbling. I landed hard and looked up just in time to see another zing of white magic shooting through the ground, knocking a creature into pieces.

"Aniline!" Lynton's voice rang out in the darkness.

"Da! Over here!"

Before I could say another word, the rock beneath my body rose into a cradle then zoomed away from the monsters toward the wildlands. I barely had time to register what was happening before I was unceremoniously dumped onto the rocky ground, my head spinning and my nose still filled with the putrid smell.

Lynton materialized in front of me, followed by Fiadh and several other trolls, each of them furious. Beside me, Aniline scrambled to her feet, squaring her shoulders as she faced her father.

"What is the *meaning* of this?" Lynton barked, his voice echoing in the night air. "Was I not clear that the *aos sí* was not to be disturbed?"

"Da, it was—"

"Not a word out of you, Aniline," he said, holding up his hand. "You've done enough."

"But I told her I'd go," she said. "She told me not to. I insisted."

He turned to her, his eyes wide. "Why would you endanger yourself like that? And for this…this *daoine maithe*?"

"Because she's trying to understand the *seod croí* so she can destroy it," Aniline said. "We were looking for a memory stone that would tell us what happened and how—"

"You fool," Lynton said with a shake of his head. "She can *lie*. She has no desire to destroy the stone. She and her friends only want it for themselves."

"That is *not* true," I snapped, jumping to my feet. "The only one who wants that thing put back the way it was is…" I swallowed, forcing myself to say his name. "Eoghan. And the sooner we figure out where all the pieces are, the sooner we can face him, get the piece *your* king gave him, and destroy the stupid thing."

Lynton's nostrils flared. "I think it's time for you to return home."

"I have an edict," I said.

"Then go to your grandfather and get it reversed," he said, turning away from me. "Because you aren't welcome in these lands anymore."

CHAPTER TWENTY-EIGHT

CADE

Another day, another smuggle, another portal back to Al'ocasep. At least tonight, Aldonza hadn't stuck around to try to tell me about my heart.

As the moon glowed down on me, I paced the ship, desperate for a solution.

I needed a way to H'sipotu.

The last place I could reach magically was the middle of the ocean.

I'd already tried moving *this* ship across the water, but there was a delicate balance between the sails and the wind and water that I didn't have time to learn.

Next, I considered stealing a small boat, using magic to propel me forward until I reached the island. But I had no way of knowing how far it was to H'sipotu. I could be stuck on a boat for ages. And considering my magic was shaky even just magically gazing upon that area… I couldn't count on having it, and I didn't want to be stuck in the middle of the ocean.

So I needed a crew who could sail a ship.

I looked around the island at the other boats. They might have crews willing to help, but would they be able to get me the final stretch to the island?

No. I needed *Aldonza*.

I huffed, sitting down on the stairwell leading to the quarterdeck.

I put my head in my hands, continuing my thought exercise. The crew came back at sunup every morning—either by design or bad luck, I didn't know.

I couldn't sail the ship without the crew.

Nor could I create a portal during the day and demand they sail through it without Aldonza—

I stopped, rubbing my chin. *Aldonza* would know if we weren't in the right place. Her crew, however, would not. They didn't seem to have her depth of knowledge about the stars and how they related to the maps in her cabin.

If I could get them back on the ship and somehow…convince them to follow my lead?

But none of them trusted me as far as they could throw me. That seemed a dead end.

I continued to daydream and scheme and kept coming up empty until finally, the sun began to rise in the distance and the crew made their noisy return to the ship. They ignored me, talking amongst themselves about their conquests and games they'd won.

Aldonza was the last one, always, to return to the ship, and she looked a little more droopy-lidded than usual with a grin on her face.

"You're up early," she said, her words running together.

"Just eager to get a start on things," I said, watching her. "Where are we headed today?"

"Oh, I dunno," she slurred. "Got a couple leads. Might just do a run between islands." She scratched her belly. "Just gotta ride this wave until it ends."

"Would it be more efficient for me to create a portal to that island so we'd be there when you woke up?" I said, glancing up at the stars. "Shave off a few hours?"

She snickered. "You think I'm that dumb? If I let you do that, we'll end up in H'sipotu. Go to bed, wizard."

She stumbled off, and I scowled at her retreating back. Another plan foiled. If only I didn't need this stupid ship and her stupid crew and stupid captain to get me where I wanted to go. What good was magic if…

A devious thought slid through my mind, one that would require good timing, finesse, and perhaps borrowing a bit of fae trickery I wasn't sure I could pull off. But at this point, I needed to try whatever I could, or I'd be stuck as their errand boy forever.

⤞ ⤞ ⤞ ⤞

My plan was carefully formulated and timed. It would require the crew to be adequately drunk, and for me to be able to magic them back without them understanding what was going on. That night, I followed them off the ship, making sure to keep enough distance that they didn't know I was there.

I followed Cai first as she paved a weaving path from bar to bar (there were more than I could count on this island). Once she was having a hard time keeping her head up, I struck, sliding into the place and walking at her side.

"C'mon," I said, throwing her arm over me. I had to use magic—she was heavy, but I managed to walk her out of the place and into the darkness where I could create a portal back to the ship. Then I pushed her onto her hammock, closed the portal and set to finding the next one.

It took me some time (and a little magic) to locate everyone. Volker was the hardest, but I eventually found him underneath three women. Again, with effort and magic, I pulled him out and brought him back to the ship.

Finally, it was time for Aldonza.

I'd seen her several times that evening, always with the same guy, always at the same place. But even though the rest of the crew was too drunk to stand, she seemed to have her wits about her. Time was running out, and so were my chances of completing this crazy task.

Finally, I could wait no longer and cast a small sleeping spell her way. She blinked heavily for a few minutes before falling forward, her head landing with a clunk on the table. Her companion stared at her, aghast, then rooted in her pockets.

"Can I take her from you?" I asked, appearing by the table.

The companion stared up at me, narrowing his gaze. "You must be the boy Donza told me about. The virgin."

I cleared my throat. "I don't particularly… Fine, yes. What else did she say about me?"

"That you're a lost soul, and she feels sorry you'll never get home." The companion rose as he stuffed the gold pouch into his pocket. "I don't know what your plan is, but rest assured, Donza will make you pay for it."

I helped the captain to stand, practically throwing her over my shoulder. "It's worth it."

>⇥ >⇥ >⇥ >⇥

With everyone back on the ship, it was time to enact the second part of my plan.

First, I had to make sure Aldonza stayed asleep—at least until we were past the portal. I cast a quiet spell around her quarters and made sure to block the windows and doors.

Then, I crossed the room to her washbasin and mirror, with her sleeping form behind me for reference. I'd never attempted this before, but nothing said I *couldn't* use glamour. Wizard magic seemed to be much grander and vaster than fae magic, so…

Stop thinking. Just do.

Clíodhna's voice came filtering through my mind, and I had to smile. I gathered magic in the tip of my staff and closed my eyes, remembering what it had felt like when Riona cast a glamour on me once upon a time. How the scent of her magic had lingered in my nose and on my tongue, reminding me of honey. A pang of sadness rose as I caught a faint whiff of it. I hoped she was all right in the fae realm.

I shook myself. No time to dwell on that.

Closing my eyes once more, magic slid down my face, growing my hair out, changing the shape of my nose and lips. My clothes, too, shifted as I took on the form of Aldonza in my mind. It was as if a blanket of magic came over my body, covering me from head to toe.

In the mirror, Aldonza's face looked back at me, almost an exact replica of the woman sleeping not ten feet from me.

Riona would certainly be proud, I thought with a smile.

Now that I had my disguise, I strolled outside and created a bubble around the ship then cast a vision of the daytime sky across it. I squinted in the light, letting my eyes adjust. It wasn't a perfect replica, but the crew would be too drunk or hungover to notice.

Last but not least, I closed my eyes and drifted up to the stars, flying to the very edge of the map leading to H'sipotu. Then I opened a portal, revealing the dark sea beyond. Something strange called to me, like the air itself knew I was trespassing. Probably a good sign.

I let out a calming breath. Time to see if this crazy plan would work.

"Get up, you idiots!" I called, walking down to the bottom of the ship. "Time to move."

They grunted and groaned, most of them still drunk, but didn't argue. I kept my gaze steady and focused, the exact way I'd seen Aldonza do every day in the past week.

"Where to?"

"The wizard already made a portal. Just need to sail through it."

I held my breath, waiting for them to argue, but they just got to work. And within minutes, we'd found a breeze and the current and sailed through the portal. I'd disguised my staff as a small pocket watch and waved the portal closed behind me.

"Onward," I said. "To the west."

Chapter Twenty-Nine

Ayla

"Well, this is ridiculous."

I sat with my arms crossed over my chest as Rutley and three other soldiers played cards by a small fire. The last of the troops had just disappeared over the nearby hill, leaving the five of us in quiet solitude. Ward and the fastest riders had been gone at least an hour—though it was hard to tell time with the sun gone.

I'd already chewed my nails to the quick, paced the grass until it was flat, and argued until I was blue in the face with Rutley about whether I should go. He and I usually got along well, but I was starting to resent him a little.

"Just relax, Your Majesty," he said, throwing another card down. "There's nothing you can do down there anyway."

"But what if there is?" I said. "What if Ramira is there, and the two of us can negotiate a ceasefire?"

"Then I'm sure the good captain will send someone to fetch you," he said, not looking up. "Why don't you get some rest?"

"I'm not tired." How could I be? My city was under attack, and I was sitting here like a bump on a log. I checked the red box *again* for a letter from Riona (*where is she?*) and huffed angrily. Perhaps I should've asked her to leave a little blood.

Something echoed in the distance again—could've been thunder, could've been cannon fire. Had the royal guard arrived yet to help? Was Ward fighting an army of Konevellian soldiers by himself?

"Hah!" Rutley cried. "You lose. I win."

I scowled at him. There was a distinct lack of concern from them. But I supposed they had it easy. Safe with the queen, who was supposed to keep her distance like a good little girl.

Too bad I never liked that title.

They were engrossed in their game, and neither noticed me slipping away into the darkness. I walked through the empty camp until I found my carriage, and my horse by herself in a makeshift pen. I climbed over the fence and landed in the soft grass, my heart racing in my chest as I approached her.

She neighed but quieted when I shushed her. "It's me. Just me."

It had been a while since I'd ridden bareback, but I could do it. I hoisted myself up and hung onto her mane.

"We need to help Ward," I said.

She let out a breath and pawed the ground. I kicked her in the barrel and she seemed to know exactly what to do, jumping the fence and heading straight toward Orapus.

>-»>-»>-»>-»

The city rose from the road, a line of buildings welcoming me inside. They were, at least, intact. Perhaps the fighting was closer in.

Fighting. And me without a weapon. Perhaps running headfirst into the city under siege was the wrong thing to do.

But I kept going, the scent of smoke and the bright light in the sky drawing me down this street and that one, until we finally came to it. A building engulfed in flames, surrounded by a crowd.

I jumped off my horse and waded through the people. They were passing buckets of water to one another before dumping them onto the fire. Some had even climbed to the top of nearby buildings and were dumping water there, too, perhaps to keep the flames from spreading.

There was a loud crack and the ceiling of the burning building fell in on itself, sending shoots of embers into the nearby crowd. But it only deterred them for a moment before the pail-passing resumed. I found a spot to join the effort and nearly fell over with the weight of the full pail. But I handed it to the next person, and when a second pail came by, I was better prepared. One after the other after the other, I kept the water moving, almost rhythmically

Finally, the fire ran out of fuel, the flames growing smaller and smaller until there was nothing but the charred remains of the building. I prayed no one had been inside; it was lucky the fire hadn't spread beyond the one building, as close as they all were.

"What was in there?" I asked a nearby soldier.

"Crates of food, mostly." He shrugged. "Never seen a building go up in flames so fast."

"I—"

The sound of an army approaching drew everyone's attention. For a moment, my heart seized—was this Konevell? But no, they carried my flag and Elodia was leading them. Still, they were armed to the teeth, ready to fight, ready to defend Pennlan. But as they drew closer, bewilderment replaced stoicism. There was no enemy for them to fight, at least not tonight.

"What is all this?" An older woman wearing a dressing gown and a nice robe marched to the front of the soldiers. "Who are you people?"

"The royal guard," Elodia said. "We were told the city was under attack."

"Preposterous," the woman replied as a murmuring grew in the crowd. "It was a business fire. Nothing more, nothing less." She laughed nervously, as if afraid the crowd would turn on her. Then she moved closer to Elodia. "Where did you come from? And on whose orders?"

"Mine." Ward's face and clothes were smeared with soot. He walked right up to the woman and got in her face. "Or did you forget our conversation before I left?"

"I didn't forget. I just didn't think it had merit."

My jaw dropped. This must be Captain Treen.

Ward leaned in until I could no longer hear their conversation, so I pushed my way closer.

"…nothing to be worried about. Absolutely insane."

"I know what I saw," Ward said. "And I'm *very* concerned that you aren't taking it seriously, considering it was a direct order from Her Majesty's captain."

"I didn't think you'd really bring the entirety of Her Majesty's guard here," she said. "Orapus has more than enough force to keep the city safe. That's our job."

"And how are you going to keep the city safe by not patrolling the river or shore?"

"I haven't seen your lieutenant in a couple of days," she replied. "Perhaps he's been monitoring things for you?"

Based on Ward's face, he clearly didn't think so. "Elodia, get patrols going along the river. I want a full report by morning. Neal, find out who started this fire. It can't have been a coincidence. And—" His face went slack when he saw me standing a few feet from him. "And what the hell are *you* doing here?"

"Helping?" I said with a small lift of my shoulder.

"Where the hell is Rutley?" he said, coming to stand next to me.

"Playing cards, I'd wager," I said. "But I'm not going to sit around when my city's being invaded."

"We aren't being invaded," Captain Treen said, a little too loudly. "It was just a fire in one of the warehouses."

"A warehouse that had been earmarked for the trolls," Ward said. "Suspicious."

"You're not from here," Treen said. "These things happen all the time." She glanced at me. "And who is this?"

"You don't know?" Ward said, his brows rising. "You don't recognize…" He lowered his voice. "Her Majesty?"

Treen's eyes narrowed then widened. "Are you… What in the world are you doing here?"

"Look, why don't we head to your office and talk there?" Ward said, looking around. "Or at least somewhere more private."

>→ >→ >→ >→

I rode my horse to the barracks, led, of course, by a grumbling, angry Ward who was threatening to string Rutley up by his toes for dereliction of duty. But based on the angry looks he was shooting Captain Treen, it seemed he was more put out with her than me.

"Did nothing. Konevell could've already invaded," he muttered to himself.

"It's fine," I said. "They haven't."

"You don't understand," he said. "Clearly, Treen thinks I'm..." He trailed off.

"Why did you pick me to be captain?" The question hung in the air and took on new meaning.

"You know," I began quietly, "nobody seems to take me seriously, either."

"What?" He turned to look at me. "Yes, they do. You're the queen."

"And how much is that worth?" I said with a sad chuckle. "But I keep trying. Perhaps respect comes with age and experience. Neither of which we have in spades. But what we have is the truth." I smiled at him. "And it's our job to convince the naysayers of it."

We arrived at the barracks, and Treen greeted us with a tight smile as she led us to her office.

"Your Majesty, I apologize again for not recognizing you," Treen said.

"How would you recognize me?" I asked.

She gestured to a painting on the wall, and it took everything in me not to bark an unqueenly laugh. I remembered sitting for that portrait when I was perhaps thirteen. The painter was an old man with thick glasses whose fingers shook as he brushed the canvas. To say it was unflattering was generous.

"I'll have to commission a new one," I said a little weakly. "But I'm not concerned about that. What I'm concerned about is my captain telling you there's an army amassing forces across the river and you doing nothing about it."

"Your Majesty, I've lived here a long time," she said. "Squabbles with Konevell are nothing new."

"Closing the border is," I said.

"Yes, but it's just a misunderstanding. There's no reason Konevell would upend hundreds of years of peaceful coexistence."

I thumbed the stone around my neck. "There are reasons you don't know about. But even if there weren't, the captain of my guard is my mouthpiece. What he says has my blessing. Ergo, you disobeyed an order from your queen."

I expected her to wilt under my words, but she just folded her hands on top of her desk. "Your Majesty, with all due respect, you are new to your job. We can't just say things like 'Konevell is invading' without proper cause. Half the people in this town are Konevellian citizens or married to one or have a cousin who lives on the other side of the river. So even *if* they were to invade, which would be the height of insanity, we would have to be careful we don't cause panic."

"Gonna cause panic when Konevell starts lobbing cannonballs into people's houses," Ward muttered behind me.

"I understand the position you're in," I said, forcing a smile. "But it can't be too much to ask to send riders along the river. In fact, you probably should've been doing that all along."

"Nothing can cross the river," she said. "It's too fast and too rough. They would have to… Well, I don't know, because even in peaceful times, we've yet to figure a way across."

Ward made another noise of concern, but I shook my head. "Until we can resolve the crisis, I'll remain in town."

"And we need it to stay under wraps," Ward added.

"No." I shook my head. "There's no need to hide my presence. In fact…" I gave him a look. "It might help move certain things along if the other side knew I was here."

"Might help them send someone to slit your throat in your sleep," he replied through gritted teeth.

I smiled sweetly. "Then good thing my captain has a plethora of soldiers to keep me safe."

"I will…see to it that you're taken care of," Treen said, watching our back and forth with interest. "And you will be quite safe. This city is very well protected by our soldiers."

"Except that you let a warehouse burn down," Ward said.

"Accidents happen," she said with a forced smile. "Now, it's quite late. Let's find the queen a place to rest and we'll continue our conversation tomorrow."

Chapter Thirty

Ward

Ayla was set up in the nicest inn in the city with heavy security, and I made sure the Orapus guards knew that if anything happened to her, I would personally see to their gruesome punishment. She promised me she would stay put and implored me to remain in the city to get some rest. But as tempting as that sounded, the camp was where I needed to be.

So despite my exhausted body protesting, I rode nearly two hours back to camp. The sun was starting to come up over the horizon, but no one was stirring. I was grateful for that; I wasn't ready to face them yet.

My own tent hadn't been set up, so I headed toward Ayla's. She wouldn't need it, after all. I stepped inside and stumbled toward the bedroll, falling face-first into the pillow and blankets. They smelled faintly of her, and somehow, I found the energy to smile as I drifted off to sleep.

The next thing I knew, it was morning and the sounds of the camp echoed around me. I rolled onto my side and walked to the flap, cracking it just enough to check the position of the sun. Midmorning. Beyond, the royal guard was up and about, tending to their bonfires and talking amongst themselves.

I had no clue how I'd face them today.

Most of them probably knew they'd been dragged into the main city for a warehouse fire, and, if they hadn't already thought me an idiot, they surely would now.

And yet…the warehouse that had gone up in flames concerned me.

It seemed too coincidental that it was the same one full of goods purchased by the trolls. I assumed Fiadh had taken as much as she could, but that didn't mean it wasn't suspicious.

I heard Elodia's voice in the distance and rubbed my face. Better to get up and get it over with than delay things. They already thought me an idiot, I didn't want to add coward to the list.

Before I could leave, however, the flap opened, and Elodia walked in holding a small biscuit. She snorted.

"Treen brought some provisions this morning," she said, handing me the food. "You look rough, Boss."

"Thanks." I took a huge bite then stuffed the rest in my mouth. "How's it looking out there?"

"Do you want me to sugarcoat it or no?"

That told me enough.

"I think it's probably best that we stay here," Elodia said. "We're not as close as we could be to Orapus, but it's close enough to ferry messages and if we need to scramble, well..." She cleared her throat, clearly trying to avoid the subject.

Unsaid was the mutiny that might occur if I demanded the soldiers pack up and move. "Treen never sent riders to patrol the coast or the river. I want a report that no one's come ashore by sundown."

"Treen said they haven't seen anything out of the ordinary," Elodia said. "In fact, there've been fewer ships on the river than usual since they know they can't unload in the city. And coming in from the sea isn't an option because we have cannons there."

"And we've checked every one of those ships sitting in the bay for Konevellian soldiers?"

She gave me a look. "Boss, you're starting to sound a bit paranoid."

"They're coming, El. And I'm getting a little tired of being the only one who's taking this seriously."

"Don't shoot the messenger," she said, holding up her hands. "I'm on your side. But if you start telling soldiers to search the merchant ships, many of whom have been sitting there for over a month, you might get some pushback."

I sighed. "And have we checked the coast north of here? Do they have cannons?"

"No, but they're just mostly small fishing villages. It's pretty shallow close to the shore, hard to get big ships in." I gave her a quizzical look and she shrugged. "I asked these same questions, and this is what Treen told me. She also said it would be ridiculous for them to come ashore that far from Orapus just to march in."

"Ridiculous, but not out of the question," I said. "I want a pair riding north within the hour. They can go all the way to the border with the fae realm for all I care. But I want to know there are eyes on the ocean."

To my surprise, she nodded. "Consider it done."

"After that," I said, rubbing my stubbly face, "I want you and Rutley to sneak into Konevell and find the camp. Find out what their plans are."

She quirked a brow. "Are you actually delegating?"

I nodded. "I'll show you the small stones I used to cross. If you leave at sundown, you'll reach the camp by midnight at the latest. But I want you back here by morning. Understood?"

"Understood."

⇥ ⇥ ⇥ ⇥

Elodia left to carry out my orders, and I figured it was time to face my soldiers. I stepped outside the tent to whispers, which I ignored. I was in need of a shave and somewhere to wash up, but based on the looks of the soldiers, there wasn't a pond to be had nearby. So I'd have to make do with stubble.

Treen had already left for Orapus, but a few of her soldiers remained behind. As I walked among the troops, I considered perhaps she'd offered her assistance because she knew that my leadership had come into question.

Everywhere I went, snickers followed. They were at least smart enough to stop when I got close enough to see who was being insubordinate, but it really didn't matter. I couldn't punish an entire camp.

Loud, raucous laughter drew my grumpy attention and my gaze narrowed. The usual suspects—Kavan, Parrish, and Severn—were standing around a tent with a pot of something that smelled rancid over the fire. I almost passed them by, except there was a fourth among them.

Platt had returned, it seemed.

Swallowing my annoyance that his first stop hadn't been to see me, I walked up to the group and cleared my throat loudly. None stood to salute me, staring instead at their chosen leader, who lazily got to his feet and half-heartedly brought his hand to his forehead.

"*Captain*," he said, smugly grinning at his friends. "What can I do for you?"

"Glad you could make it back," I said. "How long have you been at camp?"

"A bit. Had to rest, catch up on the news, that sort of thing." His eyes crinkled with mirth. "I hear you brought the entire cohort of soldiers into town."

"There was a fire," I snapped. "We thought it might be Konevell."

"So instead of, I don't know, seeing what was wrong, you just thought you'd cause a panic and bring a whole parade into town?" He chuckled. "Hopefully, no carriages lose a wheel."

"Or rescue a cat from a tree."

"Or pull a baby out of a well."

"Or—"

"Enough," I snapped as they dissolved into giggles. "Show your captain some damn respect. Get your asses up and get going. You're on patrol duty now. All of you."

They let out a cry of protest. "We just got off patrol duty—"

"Perhaps you should've thought of that before disrespecting me," I barked. "Now, *go*."

I was ready for them to argue with me, to roll their eyes and tell me to pound sand. But they slowly rose and stalked away, glaring at me and talking amongst themselves.

Platt, however, stayed where he was, leisurely scratching his stomach. "Not making many friends in your new position, are you?"

"Did the trolls get what they needed?" I asked, ignoring his jibe.

"Suppose so. They left pretty quickly. Speaking of, I didn't get to pocket any of their jewels. The merchants took them all. I feel kind of duped, you know?"

I glared at him. "Your reward is your continued employment with Her Majesty's royal guard, in case you forgot."

He shrugged.

"Did they say if they were coming back?" I asked. "If so, we need to find them another set of goods."

"Oh, was that the one that burned down?" He didn't actually sound concerned. "Maybe word got out that the merchants were selling to the evil fae, and someone didn't like it."

"Is that what you heard or what you're theorizing?" I asked.

"Eh, just a guess." He held up his hands. "You know, you're awfully jumpy. Maybe you should have a drink, calm down—"

"I'll have a drink when the threat of invasion is gone," I snapped.

"I mean…" He rubbed his belly. "Is there *really* a threat? And if so, where are they coming in? Orapus?" He snorted. "We'd know they were coming. Got cannons in the armory ready to blow ships out of the water."

I didn't feel like having the same conversation with him, mostly because it wouldn't do any good. "Ride into town and check on the queen."

"But I just got back—"

I narrowed my gaze. "That's an order, soldier. And if I hear more about it, you'll be headed out of camp permanently."

>→ >→ >→ >→

At sundown, Elodia and Rutley followed me out of the camp to the small thicket near the river where Fiadh had created the crossing point. The tide was low enough that the stones were visible again, but it was still somewhat dangerous.

"Couldn't have made them bigger?" Rutley grunted.

"Just be careful," I said. "Remember, if you're caught on the road, say you're on your way to the camp. But try not to get caught—"

"I mean, that's usually the best plan," Elodia said. "Look, we'll be fine. And back by morning. Hopefully with a good report."

They climbed down the rocky bluff to the small, slippery, rocky shore of the river. Elodia went first, her long legs easily reaching each stone until she was safely across. Rutley, being much shorter, had a more difficult time but was soon on the other side. They turned to salute me before climbing up the other side.

I stood on the edge of the river even after their shadows disappeared. But eventually, I returned to camp.

The first set of riders had come back from their patrols with a good report. As Treen had said, there were nothing but fishing villages and small, quiet towns. As it would take a week to reach the very northern border of Pennlan, Elodia had sent six riders, one arriving at the end of each day with a report. It was quite a clever system, and one I wouldn't have thought of myself.

"Get some rest," I said to the rider. "Thank you."

He saluted and left the tent, and I sank into the canvas chair, rubbing my face. It was late, and I should've considered going to bed. But I wouldn't be able to rest until Elodia and Rutley returned with news of the Konevell camp.

Something caught the corner of my eye. Ayla's red box was glowing.

I scrambled to my feet and ran over, throwing the top open and ripping out the letter inside. But as I read, my heart sank into my stomach.

> Ayla,
>
> Sorry it took me a few days to respond. Things are getting weird around here, too. The fae have been causing trouble in the wildlands under Aldrick's goading—even though the Erlking expressly forbade it. The Erlking is acting weird, too, and something tells me I need to stay here until things settle.
>
> I hope you can find a way to negotiate peacefully with Ramira. If not, let me know and I'll be there as soon as I can.
>
> Sincerely,
>
> Riona

I considered my response. My gut told me to implore her to come as quickly as she could. But if Riona was concerned about the situation in the fae realm, that meant it was serious. I wasn't sure I could forgive myself if I called her down to sit around for nothing while the trolls were in trouble.

> Riona,
>
> It's Ward. Long story, but Ayla's in Orapus and I'm in a camp just outside. I'll bring her the box tonight so you can continue to communicate.
>
> I'd sleep better at night if you were here, but I get you need to stay close. As soon as things settle, please hurry.
>
> Ward

Then I put my response inside the box and closed the lid. It glowed for a moment then dimmed, and when I looked inside, the letter was gone.

Saying a small prayer, I tucked the box under my arm and walked outside, intent on finding Platt to send him, yet again, into the city. But I slowed, looking at the box. This was too important to hand to someone else—especially to Platt.

So with a sigh, I made my way toward my horse to ride into the city.

Chapter Thirty-One

RIONA

I stared at the dark ceiling, Ward's letter swimming in my mind. It was a nice distraction from the shadows that crept inside my mind, the smell of decay that permeated my nostrils. The sadness in my chest from the way Lynton all but banished me from the wildlands.

Technically, he had no right to do that. The wildlands still fell under the purview of the Erlking, and they lived there at his pleasure. But I hadn't felt like rubbing salt in the wound, so I'd returned to the *daoine maithe* lands and my own bed.

That was when I'd seen the glowing box, which I'd stupidly left here in my back-and-forth. Ayla's letter about Ramira's pending invasion had sent a jolt of concern down my body, and Ward's follow-up hadn't done much to assuage it. But at least I had a *little* time to figure things out here.

Morning came too soon, and groggily, I pulled myself from under the covers. I desperately wanted some hot tea or—

A fluttering sound came from under the door then a swarm of *bwdbachon* had appeared, drifting over to my bedside table. They circled around it and before my eyes, a large carafe and small saucer appeared.

"Uh…" I blinked. Sure, the servant fae brought food and drink, but one would have to *ask* for it. Not just *think* it. "Thank you?"

"Our pleasure, m'lady."

"I'm not a lady," I said. They'd left me some biscuits and clotted cream as well. "Why did you bring me this?"

"Because it's our job."

As a collective, they bowed then disappeared under the door.

"Well, that was…weird."

I poured myself the tea and devoured the biscuit anyway.

>→ >→ >→ >→

I couldn't shake my curiosity from my face as I ventured down the halls in search of Clíodhna. I wasn't even sure she'd be around, but somehow I knew that if I showed up in our training room, she would as well.

"So, I suppose the trolls are all settled?" she asked, materializing.

"More or less." It wasn't a lie if I withheld the truth, so my tongue didn't burn. "I had a curious morning. The *bwdbachon* brought me breakfast."

"That's what they do."

"But they've never…" I cleared my throat. "It was like I thought about it, then they brought it. Usually, you have to find one and ask. They don't just show up in your room."

"I suppose that is new." She nodded to the letter. "What's that?"

It didn't escape my notice that she hadn't answered my question. I showed her Ayla and Ward's letters and told her about Konevell. "A part of me that wants to go help, but I can't help feeling that if I do, I'll be leaving something much worse." I looked around the room as if the walls themselves were speaking to me. "There's something weird in the air. And my gut says I need to stay here."

"You are very astute, granddaughter," Clíodhna said. "Which is why it's *imperative* that you learn as much as you can from me before that something moves from the air to reality."

"Clíodhna," I said quietly. "What I saw in the *Arwein*. The disagreements between Birch and the forest king. Is that…normal?"

She watched me for a moment. "Things are shifting, granddaughter. The whole world seems to be moving as each new piece of the *seod croí* is found. Your grandfather is losing his grip on his power."

218

"What happens if he does?" I asked quietly.

"Someone else will take his seat," she said. "I don't have to hazard a guess as to who it might be."

Aldrick. "Birch doesn't seem worried."

"That makes one of us." She shook herself. "You had explicit instructions to stay in the wildlands, and yet, here you are."

"Not exactly." I winced. "There was an update to my instructions. He wanted me to go to the *aos sí* to find a memory stone that would explain the white magic. Lynton's daughter volunteered to take me." I rubbed the back of my neck. "The creatures woke up again."

Clíodhna started. "They did?"

I shifted uncomfortably. "I think they were attracted to the *daoine maithe* blood. They didn't notice Aniline at all."

My grandmother grew quiet, her expression unreadable. "Do you know what those creatures are?"

I shook my head. "Other than terrifying?"

"In the battle of the *aos sí*, Laughlan used every tool at his disposal to fight against the armies. Including..." She sighed. "Including reanimating the bodies of dead fae to fight against their fellow soldiers."

I shivered, reality veering a little too close to my dreams.

"When Laughlan died, so the legends go, the creatures returned to their graves, buried themselves, and went to sleep. There they've rested, waiting for their master to return." She looked at me. "When you told me about your first venture into the cemetery, I thought perhaps it was your wizard who'd brought them back to life. Now...now I'm not so sure."

"The Erlking said the same thing," I said. "But you're right. I haven't felt the edict since I've been back. Maybe it's because I went to the *aos sí*, and I just wasn't successful?"

She made a noncommittal noise. "For the best, I'd wager. You wouldn't find anything but memories of death and destruction in the *aos sí*," Clíodhna said. "You're better off searching for the place where the stone was split."

"And where's that?"

"I have no idea. If I were to guess, it would be in the *Arwein*."

"Like, in the room itself?" I straightened. "You think there'd be a memory stone there?"

She lifted a shoulder, and Aniline's words came back to me.

"But in other lands, courts and borders and places where lots of things happen…a stone could hold a thousand memories."

I frowned. "I guess it doesn't matter where it is. Lynton's all but banished me from the wildlands, and I think if I show up again, he'll probably bury me in rock. So finding a memory stone isn't really in the cards right now."

"I'm sure he'll come around eventually," she said. "Now, until such time that your grandfather is deposed, we will continue as normal. To the training ring?"

I groaned.

>⇥ >⇥ >⇥ >⇥

It was way past dark when I finally dragged my bruised and battered body to my room. I made sure the box from Ayla had nothing inside before crossing the room and falling—

—onto a new bed. I lifted my head off the pillow, finding the sheets made of silk instead of cotton. The pillow, too, had more fluff inside. The quilt was thicker. Everything seemed to be upgraded.

"Huh."

Things happened in the Erlking's castle all the time, and I'd learned young that it was best not to question it. I flipped onto my back gingerly and stared at the new drapery hanging from the four-poster bed, replaying the day and how very poorly I'd performed in the training ring. But for once, Clíodhna hadn't seemed upset with me. Rather, every time I fell, she wanted me back on my feet for another round. She wasn't looking for the white magic anymore, either. Whatever was on her mind…she wasn't sharing it with me.

But she *had* given me something to think about. Namely, finding a memory stone in the *Arwein*. It was a small room, full of lots of magic and memory and history. Surely *any* rock on the floor could be used as a memory stone, right?

Yet I hesitated. First of all, I wasn't sure Birch would even let me take a stone to the wildlands for a troll to read. There was a chance it had the secrets of the *seod croí* but also probably a thousand others over the years. What if the trolls learned something they weren't supposed to? Asking him for permission seemed like a bridge too far…even to find more information about the *seod croí*.

But if I could sneak inside…

I scoffed at myself. The Erlking's chambers were never empty, not when people waited months to get an audience with him. But *he* wouldn't be there. So it wasn't impossible to think…

What am I saying? Break into the Arwein*?*

I rubbed my grumbling stomach. I was starving, but I'd missed the big midday meal and I didn't have the energy to search out a servant fae to bring me something—

But just as before, a flurry of activity heralded the arrival of the *bwdbachon*. This time, they offered up a thigh of roasted bird, potatoes, and dark root vegetables, along with a large pitcher of water.

"Say," I picked up the thigh and tearing off a piece, "why do you keep bringing me food?"

"Because you're the mistress," they replied in one unified voice. "And what you demand, we deliver."

"But I'm not really…*demanding* anything," I said. "I'm just thinking it would be nice if—"

Again, they shimmered and swirled around the table, and before I could say another word, a raspberry tart appeared.

"I mean, thanks, but this is a bit disconcerting," I said. "I'm not trying to abuse whatever new power's been bestowed on me. So like, how do I just…not think about what I want when I'm musing?"

They remained stationary in the air. "We don't understand, m'lady."

"I don't want you to have to act on every thought I have," I said, pulling my legs underneath me. "Otherwise, you'd be here all day and all night. And that's not fair."

"We don't understand, m'lady. We exist to serve."

That was true. *Bwdbachon* liked to be helpful; it was why they were so well-suited to this task. But it still felt like I was taking advantage of their generosity.

"Listen, can we make a deal?" I asked. "Can you guys just…wait for me to *ask* before you provide me with food? That way, I'll feel a bit more intentional about it."

"Whatever the mistress desires."

I didn't like that "mistress" title either. What had changed? Had the Erlking released an edict I didn't know about? Still, I wasn't about to look a gift horse in the mouth.

"Thank you for bringing me dinner," I said. "And dessert."

"If you need anything else," they said with a bow, "just ask."

"Actually," I said, watching them, "you guys know everything about the castle, right?"

They nodded in unison.

"How does one get into the *Arwein*?" I asked.

"Mistress, you just need to ask the room to open."

I frowned. It couldn't be *that* easy, could it? "I'm sure there's something else, some other piece of information I need. Like a code or a spell or—"

They bristled. "We do not lie. All you need is to ask the room to open, and it will open itself to you."

"Right, sorry, didn't mean to offend," I said, holding up my hands. "Thank you again."

This time, they disappeared without another word, leaving me with more questions than answers.

Chapter Thirty-Two

Cade

The ocean was smooth and the sun shining as Aldonza's ship cut through the water. Of course, that was thanks to the magical bubble I'd cast around the ship. The sun had risen in the real world, but I couldn't figure how to transition to the world beyond without alerting the crew that something was afoot. I handed off steering of the ship to Cluny which raised some eyebrows, but nobody said anything about it as I stood on the deck silently. Aldonza was quiet most of the day anyway.

Speaking of our captain, the sleeping spell would be wearing off any minute, and I couldn't redo it without risking losing my glamour and the bubble around us. But as my magical eye kept searching the horizon; there wasn't an island in sight for miles.

"You sure you know where we're going?" Cluny asked, his voice full of doubt.

"Of course I—" The magic transforming my voice into Aldonza's had stopped.

"What the…?"

Below us, the doors to Aldonza's quarters burst open, and she came barreling out, her eyes wide and clothing askew.

"What in the *hell* is going on? Where the hell are we?" Her gaze landed on me. "And what the…"

The crew stared between the two of us before their angry gazes landed on me. "Wizard…" Cluny growled. "What is this treachery?"

"Well." I allowed the glamour to fade along with the bubble, and night fell on us once again. "You wouldn't take me otherwise."

"You…" She walked up to me, pulling her knife from its sheath and reaching for my neck. "Take us *back*. Now."

"No." I crossed my arms over my chest. "I didn't get us this far just to turn around."

"Take. Us. *Back*." She actually looked scared. "You don't know what you've done. You don't know what—"

There was a loud echoing in the distance, almost like a horn blowing, but it sounded like nothing I'd ever heard before. Based on the way the blood drained from Aldonza's face, she had.

"I'm begging you," she said. "Get us out of here. My life is forfeit if they catch me. We are running out of time."

Her terror was obvious, but I couldn't find it in me to be sorry. "What I need to do in H'sipotu is more important than whatever you fear from them. If I don't find the—"

Something whistled through the air.

"Head's up!"

I ducked just in time as the railing ten steps from us exploded into splinters. I spun, searching for the assailants and saw nothing. Where had that even come from?

"I don't see—"

Aldonza left me behind, barking orders at her crew to turn the ship and head back. They didn't need to be told twice, springing into action and rushing around. Another whistle, another explosion—still no sign of whomever was attacking us.

"What's going on?" I asked. "Where are they?"

"You won't see them until it's too late," she snarled. "Now, create one of those portals and get us *out* of here."

"So we're close?" I grinned madly. "Give me the dinghy. I can—"

The deck exploded under my feet, sending me flying. I only just had the wherewithal to cast a spell around myself so I landed neatly on the ground, but Cai wasn't so lucky. She splashed into the ocean, unconscious.

"Leave her," Aldonza barked.

Two explosions, on the front and back of the ship.

"We're taking on water!" Cluny cried.

"Then plug the hole!" Aldonza said, taking the steps two by two to disappear under the deck.

Another blow of the horn, but this one was a little different. Somber. Like a death knell.

The crew seemed to understand it and slowed, almost as if welcoming death.

"Well, this is ridiculous."

I cast a spell gathering Cai from the ocean and depositing her on the deck. I patched all the holes in the ship, stopping the water from flowing in. Then I walked up to the quarter deck and raised the volume of my voice.

"We have no quarrel with you," I called. "Show yourselves, or I'll make you show yourselves."

Proving my point, I cast a spell, blowing a gust of wind across the top of the water. It hit something solid. So there *was* something I couldn't see. But what kind of magic was this?

Then, the air shimmered. One ship appeared then another—no fewer than ten of them. They'd surrounded us. They were unlike any boats I'd ever seen: tall, round-hulled with ornate decorations. Their sails seemed to be made of thick, purple leather, as was their armor, which was draped along their breastbones. But I couldn't tear my eyes off them.

My hair, my eyes, my skin. Just like with Aldonza, something pulled me to them, a kinship. I almost forgot they'd been blowing holes in our boat until one of them, a tall, muscular man, banged some sort of a long, cylindrical object on the deck.

He spoke in a language I almost understood, but I still had to use magic to translate it through my ears.

"What is your name, *re'nal'sef?*" he called. "And why do you seek

H'sipotu?"

"My name is Cade," I said. "I'm… I believe I'm from this place. I'm in search of information about a powerful object. I was hoping you might be able to assist me."

"The last time we trusted one of your kind, we suffered greatly."

Damn you, Eoghan. "I'm not like him."

"You are his apprentice," he replied. "You were taken from us at a young age and now you seek to finish what your master began."

I opened and closed my mouth. "That's not why I'm here. I'm one of you—"

"And you've brought another *re'nal'sef* with you." He tilted his head. "Are you too scared to show your face, A'onzal?"

The captain's footsteps came slowly up the walk until she appeared on the deck, giving me a death glare before she faced the main ship and the man who'd called out to her.

"I'm scared of nothing," she replied, though that was a bald-faced lie. "But we have no quarrel with you. The wizard is the one who wanted to come. You can take him and let us be. We will go in peace."

The man chuckled. "And if I let you go, the queen would have my head on the end of a sword." He turned to the others. "Chain them up. Anyone who fights gets thrown overboard. Bring the ship with us. And alert the queen. I'm sure she will be *very* happy to hear that A'onzal has finally returned."

⤳ ⤳ ⤳ ⤳

They parted me from my staff, and although it was an easy feat to summon it, I wasn't planning on fighting them anytime soon. I was exactly where I wanted to be, and with any luck, I could reason with the queen, and she would see that I meant no harm.

The *e'potu* soldiers did as they were instructed, and none of the crew made any move to disagree. Soon we were all chained by the wrists and herded onto the main boat. As soon as I set foot on it, something drew up inside me, something familiar from long ago.

"Move it," the *e'potu* soldier said, pushing me forward.

I stumbled to sit next to Iga, keeping a wary eye on my staff. It complained at the distance, but as I'd anticipated, there seemed to be something in the air—even on board this ship—that was coming between me and my ability to wield magic. It wasn't as bad as under the mountain, more like when I'd first stepped into the fae realm. Not gone. Just different.

A few *e'potu* soldiers manned Aldonza's ship, and once it was ready to go, the main soldier walked past us to the front of the ship and brought an oddly shaped shell to his lips. The sound that had preceded the attack echoed around us and I winced at the volume.

But the winds picked up and the ship's sails billowed out, pushing us forward. The air shimmered and my lips parted as what appeared to be a nearly invisible veil swept across the front of the ship. As it touched my skin, magic rushed through my veins to reach out to it. It felt like coming back to Pennlan, except…except *more*.

Before my eyes, a smattering of large islands appeared out of nowhere. Tall, green palms swayed in the breeze along the white sand beaches. The water was shallower here, green and beautiful and calm. As we drew closer, docks, small houses, even a village came into view. It was so much to take in I couldn't figure out where to look first.

Behind me, Aldonza let out a heavy breath.

"It's not so bad," I said to her. "There are worse places to be held captive."

"You say that…"

The main ship pulled into a dock that seemed built for it, and the soldiers on board forced us to stand and disembark. The magic in the air that called to me was growing stronger, and nearly knocked me off my feet as I set foot onto the squeaky, white sand.

"Keep moving, wizard," the *e'potu* growled, pushing me along.

"You know, I'm one of you," I replied.

"You're a *re'nal'sef*," he said. "Once you leave H'sipotu, you can never return."

I frowned as he pushed me through the small village. The homes were made from the materials of the island, built with the logs from the palm trees, covered with the fronds as roofs, most of them open in the front. There were few people out, and they stared openly at us.

Or rather, at Aldonza.

"Are you famous or something?" I asked.

"I told you," she said through gritted teeth. "There's a bounty on my head. And thanks to you, it's about to come due."

"Look, once we get inside," I said, "I'll get my staff back. Create a portal and get you out of here. Okay?"

She snorted. "Good luck with that." She quirked her brow. "Try to summon that staff to you."

I opened my hand, reaching for my staff that was in the hands of a soldier far behind us. I felt the tug, sensed it stretching against the bounds, but it stayed put.

"You made a grave mistake coming here," she said. "The last wizard who set foot here couldn't wield magic either. That's why he did what he did."

"The last wizard who…" I swallowed hard. "Eoghan? You were here when he—" I blinked, my mind reeling. "You *knew* who I was?"

"What I do or don't know doesn't matter," she replied evasively. "The fact of the matter is: I told you what would happen if we showed up here. And now you get to live with the consequences." She paused. "For however long the queen allows you to."

CHAPTER THIRTY-THREE

AYLA

Movement in my room awoke me suddenly, and my heart was in my chest as I sat up quickly.

"Who are—" I recognized the shape. "Ward. It's you."

"Sorry," he said, his voice low and gruff. "I was hoping to drop it off without waking you."

He had something rectangular in his hand—my letter box. I must've left it in camp. "Did Riona send a letter?"

He nodded and brought the letter to me, sitting on the edge of my bed. I read through it in the dim light and chewed my lip.

"I sent her a response. Told her we needed her as soon as she could get away." He toyed with the edge of the quilt. "But this seems like another *coincidence* I just can't believe. There seems to be chaos coming from all corners."

"Right now, the chaos is outside our borders," I said, folding the letters.

"But that can change in a heartbeat."

He looked so weary, so beaten down. We both had a lot riding on our shoulders, but his burden seemed especially weighty right now. I wanted to take it from him, but I didn't know how.

"I should be getting back—" He rose, but I grabbed his hand and pulled him back to sit on the bed.

"Stay here," I whispered.

"Here?" His dark eyes glanced at the bed.

My face warmed. "In the inn, I mean. It's late. You need your strength, and we need to talk about what to do next. Join me for breakfast in the morning."

"I need to go," he said, looking toward the window. "I sent El and Rutley to Konevell and gave them explicit instructions to be back by sunup."

"And when you return to camp, you'll get all the information," I said, gently covering his hand with mine. "You're no good to anyone when you're running yourself ragged."

He must've really been tired, because he agreed. And didn't even make it to the door, falling onto the small couch in the sitting room and snoring within seconds.

Smiling, I stepped out of bed and took one of the many blankets with me to cover him. I allowed myself a moment to run my fingers over his short, coarse hair, something I'd wanted to do for ages. But I stopped myself from drifting down to his sharp cheeks, his shapely nose, his lips…

And I forced myself to go to sleep.

⤜⤜⤜⤜

The sound of movement woke me again, but this time, I smiled, knowing it was Ward. The sun was barely up, casting a beautiful early morning glow over the city outside the windows. He was standing over my wash basin, shaving his stubble with the small knife he always carried. He caught my gaze in the reflection and stilled, like prey caught in a predator's stare.

"Good morning," I said, pushing the covers off and grabbing my dressing robe. "Did you sleep well?"

He nodded, his discomfort clear from across the room. "How do you…um….get food?"

"Order breakfast?" I asked, stretching a little. "I'll take care of it."

"You should get dressed first." Another uncomfortable shift. "People are going to talk. More than they already do."

"We have bigger things to worry about than people *talking* about you sleeping on the couch." But to put him at ease, I closed the door to the bedroom and changed into some respectable clothes. When I emerged, Ward had figured out how to ask the attendant for breakfast, as there was a carafe with two cups of coffee and a small assortment of pastries.

"This is a lot," he said.

"Are the soldiers getting provisions in the camp?" I asked. "I told Treen to make sure you were taken care of."

He nodded, rubbing the back of his neck. "Does she still think I'm out of my mind?"

"If she does, she wouldn't say a word to me, because I believe you," I replied with a look as I sipped the coffee. "Now, what's going on in camp?"

He told me about sending Elodia and Rutley across the border, and how he was hoping they'd be waiting with news, about sending the riders north and how the first had returned with a promising report about peaceful villages.

"And the soldiers? How are they faring?"

Just as he was about to answer, there was a knock at the door and a soldier walked in carrying a letter on a silver platter. "Your Majesty. Captain." He bowed then juggled the tray to salute me. "We've just received this."

The Konevell seal made my heart leap into my throat. I took the letter quickly, ripping open the seal and holding my breath. My hopes were dashed when I read the signature line first.

"It's not from Ramira. It's from Lord Galliford." I looked up at Ward. "He wants to have tea."

"Who is that again?" Ward asked.

"Ramira's envoy. The one who proposed I marry an eight-year-old," I said, folding the letter. "Well, it's not what I wanted, but it's a first step."

He nodded. "I'll stay. Just in case he tries anything."

"Ward, I doubt Lord Galliford's going to pull a knife from his belt and slit my throat over tea." I shook my head with a chuckle. "But if you insist…

I wasn't about to ask him to leave.

>⇥ >⇥ >⇥ >⇥

Suddenly, I was very grateful for Bronwen's suggestion of the blue dress and tiara Edric had made. I'd requested an actual handmaiden to help me dress and add rouge to my cheeks. The girl who arrived didn't do as great a job as Bronwen, but it still made me feel much more capable of having this meeting.

I was adjusting my tiara in the mirror when Ward walked in, resplendent in his captain's uniform. It had been a while since I'd seen him in it, and the dark blue brought out the light-colored flecks in his eyes. He seemed similarly taken with me, his gaze raking over my body in a way that brought more color to my cheeks.

"Um. That's…" He sounded strained. "Is that the tiara Edric made for you?"

I nodded as the handmaiden smirked and pinned it in place. "I figure it will be a good reminder of what I'm capable of."

"You should already know," he said with a tone that made me a little weak in the knees. But he seemed to notice we weren't alone, and the dreamy look he had in his eyes evaporated. "Galliford will be here in twenty minutes."

At five minutes past, the doors opened, and Lord Galliford strolled in. He was older, tall, lanky, with grayish skin and a sour demeanor, though today he seemed more chipper than usual. I remained seated as he approached the table and reached out for my hand.

"Your Majesty, it's so nice to see you out of the castle." He leaned down and kissed my knuckles sweetly. Already, I was on edge. Our last meeting had been disastrous, and he'd left in a snit. An odd change of behavior to be so effusive with pleasantries.

"I just wish it wasn't under such dire circumstances," I said, gesturing to Ward. "I'm sure you've met my captain."

"Yes, Captain…" He stopped, perhaps realizing Gabhann wasn't there. "No, we haven't met."

"Ward." He held out his hand, gripping the envoy's with perhaps a little too much relish. "I've heard so much about you."

"I'm sure." Galliford sat. I couldn't help noticing something in his gaze when he looked at Ward. Something that made me even more nervous. "Well, now. We do have lots to discuss, don't we?"

"More than a little, I'd say," I replied. "Starting with why Queen Ramira thought it wise to close the border."

"From what I hear, Pennlan's found new trading partners," he said. "I had no clue the fae could travel through rock and create gemstones from pebbles."

"Trolls, actually," I said. "And yes, they can." I gestured to my tiara. "Their late king made this for me, in fact."

"Pardon… Late?" Galliford frowned. "What happened to him?"

Ward ducked a smile and for once…for once I felt like I had the upper hand. "Well, he tried to kill us so I blasted him into next year."

I expected Galliford to react with shock and awe, but he merely chuckled. "Another in one of the tall tales you're eager to tell these days. You seem to have a lot of them. First, Eoghan—"

"Would you like a demonstration?" I hoped not, because I had no way of making my stone come to life without Riona.

Luckily, Galliford held up his hands. "I believe we've gotten off on the wrong foot."

"If we have, it's no fault of ours," I said. "I sent a letter to Queen Ramira, and it was sent back unopened. Now how are we going to negotiate if we can't even talk?"

"That's precisely why she sent me," Galliford said. "These sorts of delicate negotiations are best had face-to-face, instead of in writing where things like *tone* and *intent* can be misconstrued."

I glanced at Ward, who was watching the Konevellian with murder in his eyes. "Then why isn't the queen herself here? Surely, she has nothing to fear from me."

"She's back in the capital. It's quite an event, as I'm sure you know, to move a queen from here to there. Though one doesn't have to bring their whole army." He chuckled. "I believe that might be what they call overkill."

Beneath the table, I twisted the fabric of my skirt. Was he trying to suss out information? Did he know we knew about their gathering army across the river?

"Well," I said, after a long pause, "one can't be too careful when one's neighbor is making hostile moves like closing borders. I wanted to make sure my forces here in Orapus had all available resources…should they be needed."

He laughed a little too loudly. "Your Majesty, you're talking about us as if we're mortal enemies. Have the fae addled your brain so much that you've forgotten what race you are?"

"My brain is fine," I said. "But what isn't fine is the army you've got situated across the river or the lies you've told since you walked in the door."

"Ayla," Ward said with a shake of his head.

But whether by intent or accident, Galliford's words had triggered something deep and angry inside me. "I know Queen Ramira is across the river. I know she's planning an invasion of Pennlan. What I don't know is what Konevell wants that they think they can only get through bloodshed."

His entire demeanor changed, like a mask of wax melting off his face. "Bloodshed isn't necessary, of course. Surrender your kingdom to us, and no harm will come to a single citizen of your country."

"Absolutely not," I said.

"Then I suppose our discussion is at an end," he said, rising. But Ward was faster, pulling his sword and putting it to Galliford's neck.

"The queen hadn't dismissed you yet," he snarled. "And if you think you get to walk out of here after threatening her, you have another think coming."

"If you arrest me, Ramira will see it as an escalation," Galliford said.

I barked a sardonic laugh. "And how could our relationship get any worse?"

"Your country is as good as ours, Ayla," Galliford said. "What you should be focused on is your own salvation. If you renounce your throne without a fight, Her Majesty will grant you asylum and allow you to leave in peace. But if you arrest me or..." He eyed Ward. "Or worse, I can't guarantee that offer will be on the table."

"Ward," I said.

Begrudgingly, he lowered his sword.

"I will allow you to crawl back to your queen, but you will bring a message," I said. "Pennlan will not bow to you or anyone else. We will defend our borders against all enemies, including those we long considered friends. If your queen would like to prevent the destruction of *her* army, please tell her I'm eager to resolve our conflict without causing harm to anyone." I smiled. "But I will remind you who has the most powerful object in history hanging from her neck and who only has a few thousand soldiers."

"From what I hear, Your Majesty, that little stone is nothing but a trinket without your little sister running around," he replied. "And I don't see her."

Something cold slipped down into my stomach. *How the hell did he know that?* "Ward, see him out."

"With pleasure."

Chapter Thirty-Four

Ward

I wasn't gentle as I pushed the old envoy out of the inn. His personal bodyguards were waiting for him, though they didn't seem to care that I'd roughed him up a little. The old man adjusted his jacket, glared at me then stepped into the carriage.

"Your queen is making a grave mistake," he said. "And just signed your death warrant."

"I'm sure." I nodded to his guards. "Get him out of here before I arrest him."

The carriage rolled forward, and I turned to the two guards behind me.

"Follow him and tell me where he goes," I said.

They looked like they wanted to argue—they were Treen's after all —but saluted and followed the carriage on foot. With a sniff, I turned and marched back upstairs to Ayla.

She was staring out the window, twisting the gem in her hand, her gaze unfocused.

"He's gone," I said. "I—"

"How did he know about the stone, Ward?" She whirled around, concern evident on her face for the first time. "How did he know I needed Riona? There's only…" She swallowed, taking a step back. "Not many people knew that. You, Elodia, Rutley, me, and Riona."

"What are you saying?" I asked, stepping forward. "We can trust El and Rutley. I trust them with my life. They wouldn't have shared that.

I'm sure some other soldier overheard. Or maybe they found out some other way."

"What other way, Ward?" She turned back to the window.

"You always have a pair of guards at dinner," I said, after a minute. "Maybe they overheard your conversation."

She sighed. "That doesn't make it better. Someone in my ranks who can't be trusted. And now…now my one tool in keeping Konevell off our shores is gone. I wanted to use the threat of the stone to keep them at bay until we could negotiate. But it's clear they know we're outmatched. And they're coming whether we're ready or not."

"Maybe not," I said. "Riona—"

"And what if she doesn't come? Or can't?" Ayla said. "What then?"

Even though this was the scenario I'd been trying to get Ayla to consider for at least a week, my stomach turned at the finality of her tone. But I didn't want her to know she'd unnerved me.

"They haven't come ashore yet," I began. "El and Rutley should be back in camp now with a report from Konevell. And the riders should be back, too."

"You didn't answer me." Again, she turned to face me. "What are we gonna do if Konevell invades and I don't have the power of the stone to push them back?"

"Then we'll have to do it the old-fashioned way, with steel and strength," I said. "We number two hundred with Treen's soldiers. Reinforcements should be arriving within the week. If we can keep them at bay that long, we'll be able to fend them off."

She looked at her stone. "All this for a stupid little gem."

"I've seen that stupid little gem in action, and it's nothing to sneeze at," I said. "Let's not lose hope yet. Write to Riona again. Let her know we're getting desperate. I know she'll come as soon as she can."

"I did write to her, just now." She glanced at the box. "But something tells me… Ward, we need to be prepared for the worst possible outcome."

The words hung in the air for a moment, and it was all I could do to try to keep her spirits up. "Maybe Cade will make a surprise appearance."

She didn't respond. After a few minutes, I took that as my sign to leave.

>→ >→ >→ >→

I wanted to head back to camp, but first I decided to make a stop at the barracks. Both to thank Captain Treen for her generosity and to give her the latest update. I hoped, at least, this time would go better than the first. The sound of her laughter still rang in my ear as I walked the halls toward her office. I rapped on the door and let myself in before she answered.

"Ah. You again."

"You again, your superior officer," I reminded her with a thin smile. "Or do I have to find your replacement?"

"You'd have a hard time finding someone who takes you seriously," she said. "Considering your track record thus far." She sat back in her chair. "Find any invaders in your patrols of the river? What about the shore?"

"I'm sure I'll have an answer when I return to camp and find the soldiers I sent across," I replied evenly.

"And how did you manage to sneak them across?" she asked.

"Same way I snuck across." I tilted my head. "It pays to have some magical friends, Treen."

"I don't see them around anymore. Have they returned to their caves?"

"Her Majesty just met with Lord Galliford," I said. "I assume you know who that is?"

She shook her head, that self-satisfied smirk on her face.

"Envoy to Queen Ramira of Konevell. He asked Her Majesty to consider surrendering before he brought his army to rain destruction on Orapus." I watched as the smile faded and found no joy in it. "She, of course, declined. But we find ourselves in a very precarious position. My hope is that the soldiers I sent across the river were able to get more information about their plans and exactly where they mean to come ashore so we can be ready."

"Why in all that's green and good would Konevell want to invade Pennlan—and why Orapus?" Treen asked, more to herself than me. "It makes no sense. There are Konevellian citizens here. Why would they risk destroying their own people?"

"Because they want the Pennlan stone," I said, walking toward the door. "I suggest you inform your troops and start preparing for battle. Who knows how much time we have until they strike? We need to be ready for anything."

"Where are you going?"

"Back to my soldiers," I said, a little heavily. "And hopefully, to some good news."

⤜ ⤜ ⤜ ⤜

"What do you mean, *they haven't returned yet?*"

I'd ridden as fast as my horse would take me back to the army camp, intent on finding answers the moment I hopped off. But when the soldier informed me that neither Elodia nor Rutley had returned that morning, my stomach dropped. They should've been back hours ago.

I walked the length of the camp, talking to nearly every soldier I found, just to make sure they hadn't snuck in and gone to bed. But their bedrolls were empty, their gear still gone. What could've been holding them up?

Instead of focusing on the nightmare scenarios, I gave the sentries at the front of camp explicit instructions to send the two of them straight to me when they returned. Then I sent word to all corners of the camp that I wanted the soldiers to assemble on the field outside the camp at three sharp.

I stood in my tent, rehearsing what I was going to say. Treen had finally believed me; would my own soldiers?

"Someone in my ranks can't be trusted."

A chill ran through my body. I had a hard time believing anyone would betray their kingdom—their queen—like that. Even Platt, with all his failings, was a loyal soldier and did what was asked. With more than a little complaining, of course. And he hadn't even been near the castle when Ayla and Riona had their discussion, so it couldn't have been him.

Elodia and Rutley haven't returned yet. Maybe one of them—

No. Absolutely not. They'd been as thick as thieves from the moment they'd arrived. They would die for each other—and for this kingdom. They'd be back soon, and I could dismiss these ridiculous thoughts.

There were footsteps outside my tent. "Er. Sir?"

"Have they returned?"

"No. But it's nearly three. Thought you'd want to make your way to the green."

I nodded to no one and rubbed my hands together. I couldn't find the mole in the guard *and* prepare ourselves for battle. A sad loneliness rose up in me for Elodia and Rutley. There was no one else I could trust to handle such a delicate task.

Perhaps Elodia had been right. It would've been better for me to stay with my troops and earn their trust than to go off on adventures to prove myself to Ayla.

"Sir?"

"Coming."

⇥ ⇥ ⇥ ⇥

I gazed out on my assembled soldiers and couldn't help but notice just how few there were. Myself, Elodia, and Rutley were the youngest by at least five years, and the rest seemed to hover around middle age. They were supposedly the best of the best, but perhaps I should've done more to swap out the older soldiers for fresh blood. Maybe then I wouldn't feel like we were so woefully inadequate.

"Negotiations with Konevell failed," I said, raising my voice to echo across the field. "They will be moving to invade sometime in the coming days, we think." I debated mentioning that I'd sent Elodia and Rutley but decided against it, considering the loose lips that seemed prevalent. "We hope to know exactly where soon. But until we do, I want every single one of you to be ready for war at a moment's notice. Soldiers from the other cities should be arriving soon to bolster our numbers but..." Did I tell them we were outmatched? "The day the Konevellians arrive is going to be a tough day for us all. But we can and will—"

"What about the stone?"

"Yeah—the queen is powerful. Can't she do something?"

I flexed my hands. Konevell already knew our greatest secret, but I feared what it might do to morale. "The stone has certain restrictions on it. It can't be used by the queen alone. Her sister must be in her presence and, thus far... she's been detained."

A chorus of angry cries echoed up from the soldiers and I felt myself losing them.

"We will remain optimistic," I said, holding my hands up. "The tide could change on a moment's notice. But I want us to be prepared in case it doesn't—"

"Prepared to be slaughtered?" Platt had broken formation to stand apart, his arms over his chest. "Because it sounds to me like that's what's going to happen."

"Then it's a good thing you were all hand-picked by Captain Gabhann to be the bravest and most talented soldiers in the country," I replied, giving him a death glare. "Or did she choose wrong? Are you going to leave us in our time of need?"

I waited for them to break ranks, to pack up and leave. But they stood firm. Even Platt stayed where he was, shifting uncomfortably as he, perhaps, waited for someone else to make the first move.

"That's what I thought," I said. "Now I know I haven't been the best captain or earned your loyalty. But I also know that whatever comes, I will stand shoulder to shoulder with you to fight this aggressor. And I'll do everything in my power to see to it that Riona gets her pointy-eared butt here as quickly as possible."

They let out a half-hearted cheer, which gained steam, and soon they were pumping their fists in the air as they yelled. My spirits lifted with them, hoping that the change in the wind meant help was on its way.

They got even higher when I saw Elodia and Rutley crest over the hill.

>-» >-» >-» >-»

"What took you so long?" I barked as soon as we were back in the tent. "You had explicit instructions to—"

"The camp was gone," Rutley said.

"G-gone? Like it was never there, or…?"

"No, it was definitely there. We saw the remnants of the bonfires, all that," Elodia said. "But we didn't see anybody. They've moved on. We tried to follow their path, but…"

"They reached a big, oceanside city and we didn't want to risk asking around," Rutley said. "I think they've gone to sea."

Headed here. I rose and paced behind my desk. "Treen's been told that negotiations have stalled and they're making their move. If they try to come in from the bay, we're ready for them."

"What about from the north?" Elodia asked. "You were right, boss. There were hundreds of soldiers—maybe even a thousand. If they meet us head-on, we're goners."

"Then we'd better hope Riona's waiting for them with Ayla," I said, after a long pause.

Chapter Thirty-Five

RIONA

Riona,

It's certain: Konevell is preparing to invade. I know things are strained in the fae realm, but I believe you and I could stop the madness with our combined powers without any loss on either side—and could perhaps force Konevell to abandon their ridiculous plans. Otherwise, I fear we're heading into a war that will leave hundreds dead.

Please let me know soonest.

Sincerely,

Ayla

The letter was waiting for me after another brutal day of training with Clíodhna. There was also a healing draught on the bedside table with a steaming cup of stew, courtesy of the servant fae. I seemed to have offended them during our last encounter because although they'd been delivering food and other goodies to my room, I hadn't actually seen them to talk with them about it.

After studying the letter and slurping down the last of the soup, I decided on a plan. I would flit down to Orapus, help Ayla erect a barrier, then flit back and hopefully…hopefully the fae realm wouldn't descend into chaos. Then I'd—

My neck burned so hot that I cried out in pain. "*Are you kidding me?*" I bellowed to no one in particular.

There was fluttering again as the *bwdbachon* scooted under my door. "You rang, m'lady?"

"I didn't," I said, wincing as I sat back down on my bed and the burning subsided. "Just wondering why my neck is on fire."

"It's the Erlking's edict, of course. Are you unfamiliar?"

I glared at them. "No, I'm quite familiar. But what I don't understand is why it's reappeared. I went to the *aos sí*. I didn't find a memory stone. The burning stopped. Why is it bugging me again?"

"Because you have a new thread that hasn't been pulled," they responded, as if it were obvious. "Did you not ask about the *Arwein* last night?"

I scowled. "Are you telling me this edict decided to revive just because I had a new idea where to find a…" I huffed. Damn fae magic. "Fine. But I have to get to Pennlan. My sister needs me." Even thinking it scorched my neck like the worst sunburn I'd ever had. "*Ugh!* I'm going!"

>-» >-» >-» >-»

It was highly suspect that the Erlking was, in effect, goading me into breaking into the most sacred space in his castle. I mean, he *had* to know the consequences, right? Or was the notion so completely ridiculous that the Erlking never even considered such a thing?

"All you need is to ask the room to open and it will open itself to you."

Though the *bwdbachon* couldn't lie, I parsed their words as I walked the quiet, dark halls. There didn't *seem* to be any double meaning, any ulterior motives that would change the context of what they were telling me. But I still needed to tread carefully.

There wasn't a creature stirring—except, of course, the servant fae. Now that the halls weren't so crowded, they were busy scrubbing and dusting and changing the curtains and statues around. They paid me little mind as I passed by, but it was difficult to keep from accidentally stepping on them, especially as small mouse-like fae pulled on the rugs beneath my feet to clean them.

As predicted, the Erlking's room was packed. Many of the fae were asleep on their feet, some slumped against the wall, and still others curled into tight balls on the ground. But more than a few were wide awake, watching each other warily as they ensured nobody would get between them and their spot.

When the Erlking had opened the doors for Lynton and me, it had been in plain view of the throne room. Somehow I didn't think I could repeat that without being seen, so I'd have to figure something else out.

Noise drew my attention toward the front of the room. A tall *sidheog* fae had a small pixie in its long fingers with a murderous look on his face. "I was here *first*, you little peon!"

"No, *I* was here first!" squeaked the tiny fae. "You just didn't see me!"

I waited to see if anyone would intervene, but no one did. And with a huff, the *sidheog* hurled the tiny fae toward the back of the room. He landed with a loud noise and sank to the floor, his eyes unfocused. I crept over to him, gently cradling him in my hands.

"Are you all right?" I whispered.

The pixie shook himself, rattled his wings, and took back to the air, but hovered over my hand. "Who does he think he is, big bully? I've been here for *weeks* hoping to get an audience. And this guy thinks because he's big, he can just shove me out of the way?"

"Do you want me to get you back to the front?" I asked.

The pixie stopped grousing and turned to look at me warily. "Why would a *daoine maithe* help me?"

"Because I think we can help each other," I said with a smile. "And with any luck, you'll be ready to meet with the Erlking first thing."

He grinned. "What do you want me to do?"

⇥ ⇥ ⇥ ⇥

The pixie moved subtly, so quietly that I almost lost track of him, but for the loud cry of pain as he yanked on an ear of a nearby forest fae.

The fae woke up, spinning around in search of his aggressor.

Without anyone to blame, he shoved the nearest creature. "What's the big idea?"

The *clurichaun*, a red-haired, rosy-cheeked fae, who'd been fast asleep standing up, with drool running down her face, snapped awake and snarled at the forest fae. "What was that all about?"

"You started it!" The forest fae pushed her again.

The *clurichaun* pushed back, sending him into a nearby forest fae, who was also still asleep. He woke up, shoved the forest fae back into the *clurichaun*, sending *her* into the nearest *daoine maithe* who was asleep. On and on it went, until the entire room was awake and brawling with each other.

"I think that worked," the pixie said, returning to sit on my shoulder. "Now what?"

I held my breath and waded through the ruckus. I could've transformed into butterflies, but I didn't want to risk being seen. Down here, everyone was too busy fighting everyone else to see me sliding between them.

"Wait a minute—" A hand clamped on my shoulder and spun me around. The forest fae who'd gotten into it with the pixie in the first place leaned down to put his face within inches of mine. "Don't think I don't see what you're—"

The pixie jumped off my shoulder and blew a puff of dust into the forest fae's face. He blinked heavily for a minute before falling backward, dead asleep.

"Serves you right, you big oaf," the pixie huffed.

We'd made it to the front, a brawling room of fae behind us and the Erlking's empty throne room in front of us. I turned to the pixie and nodded.

"Thanks for your help. Hopefully, he sees you in the morning first thing." I paused, before leaning toward him. "Can you not…tell anyone what I'm about to do?"

He lifted a shoulder as he sat on the ground, crossing his legs with a satisfied smirk.

With that, I turned and dashed toward the throne, searching for the door to the *Arwein*. It had just *opened* for Lynton and me, without any sort of spell and—

My stomach dropped as the stones pulled apart, as they'd done before. The room was…

It was letting me in. Just like the *bwdbachon* had said it would.

"This is weird," I whispered, walking into the darkness. But I didn't relax. Just because the room had let me in didn't mean that it wouldn't tell the Erlking I'd trespassed.

And why are you doing this by sneaking around instead of just asking the Erlking?

My reasons seemed flimsy as my heart pounded in my chest. But might as well keep going…

I reached the end of the hall and the circular table where Lynton had officially joined the *Arwein*. There *was* palpable magic, lingering long after the powerful fae had left. Clíodhna was probably right; there were probably a ton of memories stored in the rock.

I bypassed the table, falling to my knees to run my hands along the stone floor. The pieces were cemented in place or held there by the pressure of brick. I crawled along the floor, feeling for a pebble or—

My heart seized in my chest as voices echoed down the hall, and I dove under the table as the door opened and two sets of feet came into the room. I held my breath, praying they couldn't sense me, but from the agitated way they walked around the room, perhaps they were too distracted to notice an interloper.

The Erlking's booming voice was uncharacteristically quiet and full of worry as he spoke. "We need to prepare for the worst to happen. Aldrick seems to be sneaking around, gathering alliances where he can. I can't be sure he doesn't already have the forest realm in his pocket."

"Psh. Coednin has always been cantankerous." Clíodhna was with him. "His behavior isn't new. I think Aldrick's merely stretching his legs. I don't believe he'll make a play for the throne."

"You don't know my son like I do," Birch replied. "He's relentless—ruthless. I fear what he'll do to the lesser among us if he takes the throne. The wildlands might be a desolate graveyard when he's finished."

"I've already told Riona to come to my castle should it happen," Clíodhna said, her voice low. "I worry about her. There's something… something amiss with her."

"The training isn't going well?"

"This special magic—her mother's magic—she can only access it when near a piece of the *seod croí*, which makes me wonder…" She paused, and I held my breath. "And the creatures in the *aos sí* were drawn to her, too. I feel like it's this magic in her veins."

"Drawn to her, you say?" Birch asked softly.

"She says they were attracted to her and only her. Left the troll alone." The table creaked as she leaned on it. "Birch, I feel there's something…something about this magic that might be beyond us both."

"There's no doubt of that," he said. "Perhaps it's a blessing Riona can't summon it the way her mother could…"

"Then Aldrick would have a challenge for your throne."

"And she would be targeted. She's already in danger thanks to that damn wizard thinking he can use her for the Pennlan stone."

They remained silent for a beat.

"What do you think it is?" Clíodhna asked. "This magic."

I bit my lip, leaning closer so I could hear.

"I have no idea. Theories, yes. But nothing…nothing that makes sense. There was, perhaps, a good reason for the *daoine maithe* and *sidheog* to remain separate all these years. Because until Leandra appeared, no such magic existed in our people."

Disappointment settled in my chest. I'd hoped—prayed—the Erlking had some great answer he was keeping from me to *protect* me. But he was as in the dark as I was.

"Perhaps I should take her to my castle now—"

"No." Birch was firm. "I would rather keep her here until there's no option left. The *bwdbachon* have been instructed to keep a close eye on her. If she has even an inkling of leaving, she will be burned and told that it's because of the edict to find a memory stone that probably doesn't exist."

Clíodhna chuckled. "That's quite devilish of you, Birch."

"It's important she remain close," he said. "I wouldn't put it past Aldrick to use her to get to me."

"All the more reason she should go where it's safe," Clíodhna said. "Perhaps to Pennlan? She said her sister is facing an invasion. Together, their powers are unstoppable."

"She must remain here, Clíodhna," Birch said in a tone that suggested he would entertain no arguments. "And in the meantime, keep working with her. Try to pull this magic from her, even if it brings her to the brink. Something tells me she's going to need all the power she can get in the coming weeks."

"As you wish, Erlking."

The sound of her magic whipping through the air heralded her departure. I waited for the Erlking's magic to do the same, but he took a few moments, silently contemplating (or so I assumed). Then, with a heavy sigh, he dissipated into his magical form and left the room.

I crawled out from under the table, my heartbeat echoing loudly between my ears. And without another word, I used a butterfly to pry a small piece of stone from the floor and pocketed it.

I didn't want to come back here again. No telling what I'd overhear if I did.

Chapter Thirty-Six

Cade

The *e'potu* soldiers kept mentioning the queen, but instead they put us in what I assumed was a prison. But there were no bars on the window, no guards at the door. Nothing was keeping us inside.

"Because there's nowhere to go," Aldonza said, lying flat on the floor and staring at the ceiling. "And now they're content to let us wait and stew before they bring us before her."

"Can you manipulate the world the way they can?" I asked, turning to her. "Can I, for that matter?"

"I could, once upon a time," she said. "But once you leave…your connection to the land is severed forever. Now it just feels like a memory."

I looked at my hands. "I feel it. It's reacting with my magic. If I had my staff…" It hadn't been destroyed—I doubted they could, even with their weird magic. It was somewhere on this island, calling out to me, like a piece that had been ripped from my soul.

"Maybe you're special, then," she said. "As for me, I'm glad to be rid of the curse."

"Curse?" I shook my head. "This magic is a curse?"

"This whole place is a curse," she said, sitting up. "Everyone here's bound to the rules and one step out of line, gone. Tossed into the ocean lest you anger the so-called magic of the island. No one's brave enough to stand up to the magic, so they all just live in fear of breaking rules." She nodded toward the door. "There are no exceptions."

I watched her, deciphering the emotions on her face. There was hatred of this place, for sure, but there was sadness, too. Like the choice to leave had been made for her.

"Why did you leave?"

"That's my business," she snapped.

I could've asked more, but the doors opened and the *e'potu* lead soldier walked inside, his face a mask of indifference.

"You two," he said, pointing to myself and Aldonza. "Come with me."

>—»>—»>—»>—»

Aldonza walked with her head held high, and I kept pace, though I felt naked without my staff. But took in as much of the island as I could. The magic Aldonza spoke of *was* everywhere. The dirt had it, the leaves had it, the air. As I took a breath, I felt it bouncing against my lungs, unable to penetrate my body, and rushing out through my mouth as I exhaled.

My fingers danced by my side, trying to capture the magic, which was almost tangible, like millions of pieces of sand. But just like sand, I couldn't hold it for more than a moment before it slipped through. There would be no wielding it—at least for now.

We came upon what I assumed was the queen's castle, though it was really more like a larger version of the houses dotting the island. Even on the inside, there was nothing but a single room with a woman seated on a chair. She was older, with gray hair and a severe look about her. And all her ire was focused on Aldonza.

She rose slowly, taking her time to walk down the ten or so steps to meet us on the ground.

"Kneel before your queen," the *e'potu* soldier demanded.

It was as if the air itself knocked my knees forward and I fell, landing hard on my hands. Aldonza, at least, had expected such a thing and her bow was much more graceful.

"Well, well, well," the queen said, her voice low and scratchy. "You certainly have aged poorly, girl. But I suppose a life of whoring, drinking, and pirating will do that to you."

"Better than being a prisoner," she replied, her lips barely moving.

"Is that what you think this place was, daughter?"

I spun toward her sharply. *Daughter?*

Aldonza shifted uncomfortably under my gaping stare but kept her focus on her…mother? "It was."

"You are in luck, then," the queen said. "The island came together in your absence and has selected a new line. The M'on'u family will take over when I die."

"Those drunkards?" Aldonza snorted. "Good luck."

"I would have preferred it to be my only child, but you saw fit to break our rule." She straightened. "And leave our island. You know the rules, A'onzal. Once you leave…" She softened. "You are dead to us."

My chest tightened. "That's not… That can't be true, can it? Even your own daughter?"

Finally, the queen looked at me. "It is true. Even for those who were forcibly taken. You are lost to us. A *re'nal'sef.*" She tilted her head. "You have grown, Cad'reugam."

I blinked at the sound of…my name. My real name. The one Eoghan had effectively wiped from my memory.

"It's perhaps been a while since you've heard that, hm?" She softened. "We welcomed the wizard into our fold—the first *re'nal'sef* in an age to be so honored. And he left us with ruin and misery."

"Why?" I asked. "Why did he come here?"

"Because of you, boy. Your special bond of magic called to him. He came promising to teach and mentor you within our walls, while also asking to learn about the way we wield magic. But instead, he killed half our soldiers and stole you in the night."

"I promise you I mean no harm," I said quietly. "But Eoghan continues to threaten the safety of the continent. He's searching for the *seod croí*, which is—"

"I know of the stone," she said. "And I can tell you without hesitation that the stone has been lost for at least a thousand years."

I stepped forward. "I know who has it. The *fuath*, a type of fae."

"I'm quite aware of the *fuath*." She turned to the *e'potu* soldier standing guard. "Take my daughter back to her…crew, T'adlos. It seems I must educate our young *re'nal'sef* about our history."

>⇥ >⇥ >⇥ >⇥

"There is a story all children are told on this island," she said, walking me toward the tall wall on the left. I hadn't noticed, but they were covered with colorful paintings of events—mostly on the water. "I suppose you were too young or have forgotten it. I also told the story to your former master, but apparently, he didn't absorb the message."

I furrowed my brow, but didn't speak.

"A thousand years ago, a group of magical creatures came to our island seeking refuge," she said, pointing to the tapestry in front of us.

"That's…" I took a step forward. "That's them. That's the *fuath*." My heart soared. They *had* come this way. And as I drew closer, my pulse quickened. The fish-headed creature in question had a *brightly colored stone in her hand.*

I could've cried. I hadn't gone on a wild goose chase—I was one step closer to finding another piece of the stone. And if it was here, in this bubble, Eoghan couldn't get to it.

"Where did they go?" I said, turning around excitedly. "They had the *seod croí*. I have to find it."

The queen chuckled. "You will be searching until the end of your life."

"What does that mean?"

She joined me beside the painting. "The stories my ancestors told was that the fish-headed people arrived in a brigade of chaos. They were running from something—or someone—and sought protection from our people. We gave them safe haven in our reefs and underwater caverns, but…" She pointed to the stone. "The power they brought corrupted them. They began to fight each other for control of it. Our seas ran red with their blood. Until..." She lifted an unconcerned shoulder. "There was no one left to kill."

I turned to her. "Surely, there's someone...some of them left?"

She shook her head. "Gone. All of them. The ocean tells us so."

I wasn't sure how a body of water could communicate, but she spoke with such finality that I had to believe her. "And the...stone?"

"Gone as well," she said. "Buried in the depths of the ocean. Perhaps for the best that it remains there." There was a look of challenge in her eyes, as if daring me to contradict her.

"You said you told this to Eoghan," I said softly. "Did you mention it was the *seod croí?*"

She chuckled. "I can tell an ambitious man when I see one, so no, I did not mention the name of the powerful object. I believe he thought it just a tale, not based in reality. I doubt he even remembers much of his time here, except for taking you."

"I hope for your sake that's true," I said. "Because he will be back for this piece, if he hasn't already."

"Didn't you hear me, boy? It's *gone.*"

"It can't be," I said. "It's too powerful. The only way it can be destroyed is by using the other three pieces against it."

"Then it's buried at the bottom of the ocean," she said. "And the ocean is keen to leave it that way. A stone that powerful shouldn't be held by any one person—"

"Which is why we need to find it. So we can get rid of it," I said.

"Hm." She turned away from me. "I suppose that's a noble goal. But I warn you—ambitious *e'potu* have searched for the stone, and they have never been successful. There are forces keeping it from being found. I won't be able to stop you from looking, but..." She smiled. "I doubt even your dangerous wizard mentor would be able to overcome the entire ocean."

You'd be surprised.

"I have to keep looking for it," I said. "I can't stop now."

"Unfortunately, you're my prisoner," she said. "The moment you left, you became a *re'nal'sef,* and never allowed back on this island again. As was…my daughter. That you both crossed into our territory without permission means you must be punished."

I opened and closed my mouth. "Surely, you can make an exception for—"

"If it were up to me, I would. But the magic that powers us, sustains us, keeps us alive…it is very clear on the rules. If I were to break the rules, even for my beloved daughter…there is a chance the entire island could sink into the sea, never to be seen again."

"This whole island is a curse." Aldonza's words came back to me. I'd thought it an exaggeration, that perhaps it was just a dogmatic person or two. But the way the queen spoke, it was as if she physically could not turn away from the rules of the island.

"So that's it, then?" I asked. "We'll just be your prisoners? Or are you planning on killing us? Does the *magic* have a preference?"

She cracked a wry smile. "You must be punished in accordance with our laws. But the punishment is at my discretion. There is something I need you to do for me. Something even my promiscuous daughter can help with. The mission is dangerous, and will probably result in your collective deaths, but…" She lifted a shoulder. "If you survive, you are free to go and continue your search for the stone."

"What is it?"

She smiled. "In due time, Cad'reugam. I have asked the island if they might allow me to delay your punishment by a day. The winds have agreed to my request, so long as you are return at the end of tomorrow's sunset."

"Well, that was awfully nice of them, but I'd rather just go ahead and get it out of the way," I snapped. "Why are they deigning to give me such a gift?"

"I lost my child fifteen years ago," she said softly. "She was willful and stubborn, refusing to follow our traditions and assume the throne. She was called to the sea, to adventure, to the world beyond our safe barriers. And she left without caring what she did to our people, or how they would suffer." She walked toward the door. "You, on the other hand, were stolen by an evil man. Your childhood should've been spent here, learning the magic both in your veins and in the world around you. Instead, it was spent in a cold castle with no family, no friends, no love."

"I had…a friend," I said quietly.

"You should've been surrounded by your people. And since that was taken from you, I believe you deserve a second chance, or as much of one as our laws will allow."

We stepped out into the light and she gestured to the left. I followed her gaze to where a beautiful, older woman stood. Her hair was straight, raven, loose down her back. Her deep brown eyes held warmth and tears of joy. The smile on her face was so familiar…because it was mine.

"M…Mama?"

Chapter Thirty-Seven

Ayla

Ayla,

I've hit a snag and am unable to leave quite yet. But I'm working on it. I'm going to meet with the Erlking to see if he can grant me a small reprieve tomorrow, at least long enough for us to create some sort of strong barrier to keep the Konevellians out.

Expect another letter this afternoon.

Sincerely,

Riona

I'd awoken in the middle of the night to that message. Sleep was impossible after that, staring at the quiet city beyond my windows and wondering what it would look like when Konevell invaded.

I twisted the stone in my hand, searching for the magic I knew would be out of my reach without my sister. A snag. What in the world could that mean? I was fairly sure I'd been clear we were facing certain death without her. How could she leave us in our hour of need?

But even as I thought that, my heart softened. Riona wasn't that sort of person. She was seeking approval from the Erlking in the morning to leave, anyway. I just had to hold out hope that no one would invade before then.

I paced my room, consumed with worry. About Riona, about what was coming, about Galliford knowing that the stone was useless without her. How he'd come across that information.

The thought slithered around my brain like a snake, making my skin crawl. Any of the soldiers under Ward's command could be a spy. As impossible as it seemed, considering they were all hand-picked by Captain Gabhann. They'd all sworn an oath to the crown, to the throne, to me. They'd promised to protect me until their dying breath.

Perhaps if you were a stronger queen, they'd want to keep their oath.

Eoghan's voice filtered through my mind, sending shivers down my spine. Galliford's comment about my addled brain… It had sounded too much like Eoghan. Too much like another man trying to pat me on the head and tell me the things that I saw and experienced were wrong.

But what could I do? Until Riona arrived, nothing. Sit in my nice little room and ruminate over the world crumbling all around me.

Riona,
Please hurry.
Ayla

Somehow, I fell asleep, and when I awoke, the sun was bright and the city alive. They didn't seem the least bit rattled or worried about an impending invasion. I, on the other hand, couldn't help envisioning the streets engulfed in flames like that warehouse had been, and I worried for the people going about their day.

I walked to the door and had the guard deliver a message. An hour later, Captain Treen was in my room, looking a little unsettled but not nearly as concerned as I wanted her to be.

"Your Majesty," Treen said, bowing. "You summoned me."

"Ward informed you of what's coming, yes?"

"He...did." She shifted uncomfortably, and I gave her a look that dared her to disagree with me. "And we have started making preparations. But as I told Elodia, there are very few places they could come ashore nearby, and it doesn't make sense for them to invade somewhere north just to have to march two or three days south. I know Ward sent riders in that direction, but I think that's the wrong place to look." She took a step forward. "I know you've made him your leader, but—"

"How many battles have you fought in, Captain?" I asked, tilting my head.

"Um…" She cleared her throat. "None."

"Are you aware of the events that happened in the castle six months ago?" I asked, keeping my same even tone. "When the wizard Eoghan tried to make himself king in order to get to the Pennlan stone?"

"Um…" She cleared her throat. "To an extent, yes."

"Do you know who was responsible for thwarting that plan? Who managed to command the soldiers and extract the stone from my bewitched sister and put it in my hands so we could defeat the monster?"

Again, she shifted. "I'm guessing the one you promoted to captain."

"Indeed." I sat back. "Despite what rumors might suggest, I'm not some silly little girl who made my crush my captain. I chose Ward because he's proven himself time and time again. And it's high time you start respecting him and trust that he knows what he's doing."

"Of course." Her cheeks had darkened. "My apologies."

"In any other time, I would relieve you of your duties," I said. "But the threat we're facing is great, and we need everyone at our disposal." I paused, giving her a haughty stare. "Now. Can I count on you to do your job and prepare for battle?"

She nodded and bowed. "Yes, Your Majesty."

"Good." I rose and walked to the window. "Orapus might be well-protected, but I'm concerned about the people in it. We must keep the casualties to a minimum. I think it's best to give the order to evacuate the city."

"E-evacuate?"

"Yes." I smiled thinly at her. "And you will ensure it's done. After all, the people know you—they're familiar with you. And they will listen to you. I hope." I dropped the smile. "The less blood spilled, the better."

"I recommend perhaps holding off on evacuating the city. The last thing we want is a panic."

"Is it? I would think the last thing we want would be for the citizens to die in the crossfire."

She licked her lips. "The troops were saying your stone is useless without your sister," she said. "Is that true?"

I nodded, running my finger along her last letter. "I believe I'll hear from her soon with news that she's on her way. And in the meantime, I expect that the captain of Orapus will do her duty and listen to her superior officer when he tells her what to do."

"Yes, Your Majesty."

She bowed and stiffly walked out the door, passing Ward, who wore a look of surprise as he stepped past her to enter. He didn't say a word until he closed the door behind him then smirked approvingly.

"How much of that did you overhear?" I asked.

"The part about you having a crush on me, I think," he said.

I wanted to melt into the floor, but I kept my composure. "If I recall, I said that I didn't choose you because I had a crush, but because you've proven yourself."

His smile faded a little, and I knew it had nothing to do with the qualification I'd just made. "El and Rutley returned."

"And?" Based on his face, I assumed it wasn't good news.

"The Konevellians are on the move."

Dread settled in the bottom of my stomach. "So I suppose the conversation with Galliford was just a formality. He knew I had no intention of surrendering."

"Probably," Ward said. "I've sent more riders north, this time with scopes to look out on the ocean and try to spot their ships. If we know where to expect them…" He glanced down at the letter Riona had sent. "Really wish your sister would hurry up and get here."

I nodded, walked to the red box, and turned it over. Nothing.

"What's going on?" he asked. "Did you hear from her again?"

"Yes. She said she's hit a *snag*, whatever that means. But she was seeking an audience with the Erlking to get permission to leave. She said I'd hear from her as soon as she was on her way but…" I glanced at the box. "Nothing yet."

"She'll come," Ward said, but there was less conviction than usual. "She has to—"

Hurried footsteps echoed up the stairs, and Elodia and Rutley burst into the room. "Boss, come quick."

"Is it Konevell?" he asked.

"No, but a rider's returned," Rutley said. "Just, come on."

We took the stairs two by two until we reached the front steps of the inn, where a soldier was lying on the ground, sucking down water onto his parched lips. His horse looked just as exhausted, frothing at the mouth.

"Where did you come from?" Ward asked, kneeling beside him.

"This isn't one of yours?" I asked with a frown.

He shook his head. "I've never seen him before."

"I'm from Gleddol," he said. "We got the call to come down to Orapus. A hundred of us left right away." He swallowed more water. "We were walking along the main road when we saw an explosion in the distance. It was…"

Ward swallowed. "Konevell?"

"I don't know," he said. "I was told by my captain to hurry here to seek help."

"How far?" Ward's tone was even, but I could hear the panic.

"A few hours," he said.

Ward jumped to his feet. "Rutley, with me. You two." He pointed to the soldiers standing on the steps. "You're coming as well. Get four horses ready within the next half hour. Elodia, head back to camp. I want everyone ready to march when I give the signal."

"What if it's another false alarm?" the soldier behind us asked.

"It's not," Elodia said, her tone quiet. "Are you sure you don't want us to start marching now?"

"No," Ward said. "We need to find them, figure out where they're going, then make a plan to engage."

"Ward." I twisted my hands. I'd never felt so useless in my life.

"If they come here," he said, looking me dead in the eyes, "you run. Understand?"

I nodded.

"I said *move*," he barked, and within seconds, the four soldiers scattered. Then his shoulders slumped. "I hoped this wouldn't happen."

"Maybe it's not as bad as you think," I offered, not believing my own words. "Maybe it is just another false alarm."

He reached for my hand and squeezed it. "I'll be back as soon as I can."

Chapter Thirty-Eight

Ward

Hoofbeats thundered against the ground as the three riders and I pushed north. I couldn't see any sign of smoke in the distance, but that didn't mean anything. To my left, the bright blue ocean glittered as it rushed toward the shore. Every so often, I'd see small fishing villages with little rowboats out on the water. They were quiet and peaceful, and as Treen had said, it was too shallow to come ashore. The quiet soothed my nerves, and some part of me envied them for their blissful ignorance. Tomorrow, they'd get up, hop on their boats, cast their nets, and spend another day on the water without a clue of the impending disaster.

The smell of something burning hit my nose, and I spun in my saddle to search for the source. Rutley seemed to have scented it as well and slowed his horse. The other two soldiers followed suit and we stood there, listening, smelling, and perhaps praying that we were wrong.

But as we crested a hill, the scene before us was too real for words. A bloody valley, filled with swords, spears, and other weapons sticking out from all angles. Beneath the red was the familiar blue the others and I wore. Pennlan soldiers.

"They must be the soldiers from Gleddol," Rutley whispered. "Guy's lucky he got out when he did."

I urged my horse forward, though neither of us really wanted to. I forced myself to look at each face, not knowing any of them and at the same time…they were painfully familiar. I'd once been like them. Signed up to join the Pennlan guard because it paid good money and offered a bit of prestige in a town where nothing seemed to shine.

And now, their blood was strewn across the country they were sworn to protect.

"They didn't even have a chance," I said. This didn't look like the haphazard attack of an untrained army; rather, it looked like the work of demons. Even the battle of the *aos sí* hadn't seemed this...one-sided. I didn't see a single red-uniformed corpse amongst them.

"I still don't know where the burning smell's coming from," Rutley said.

"Over there," I said, nodding toward the west where a column of smoke was rising.

"Do you think..." Rutley hesitated. "Do you think the Konevellians are there?"

"No." The trampled grass said they were going southeast. Toward Orapus. It was a miracle we hadn't come across them yet. "But we should look for survivors."

⤞ ⤞ ⤞ ⤞

As we approached the village, the sound of hooves on cobblestone was eerily loud in the absence of any other noise. It was a bit bigger than some of the others we'd passed along the way—or it had been. Now it was just a charred skeleton, void of life, of happiness, of hope.

I stared at the remains of a small rag doll nearby, unable to tear my mind away from the fate of its owner. How bloodthirsty were the Konevellians? Had they allowed survivors to flee or had they decided there would be no witnesses to their carnage?

A few more steps told me the answer I hadn't wanted to know. More bodies lined the main street, a sickening trail of would-be defenders who hadn't had a chance. None of them carried any weapons—I hoped, at least, it meant the invaders had taken them and not that they'd been unarmed and attempted to fight an entire army. I stopped counting after the twentieth body, my heart too heavy to continue.

I turned back toward the ocean, and my mind tormented me. I

began to second-guess every decision I'd made. If I'd brought Elodia or Rutley with me to Orapus in the first place instead of Platt, they could have stayed with the Konevellian camp, giving us a better idea of their plans and positions.

But no. I'd wanted to *be the hero*, to get the glory and save the day as I'd always done. What did it matter if it cost us precious time and intelligence on the enemy?

Ayla. What was she going to say when I told her? She'd never look at me the same again.

"This is my fault," I murmured.

"It's the Konevellians' fault," Rutley said, coming up beside me. "And right now, we have more important things to worry about. I don't think they torched the village and got back on their ships to go home. The Konevellian army is somewhere in Pennlan, and we need to figure out where before they torch another town."

His words made sense, but the only thought in my mind was how completely I'd misread the situation. The fishing village hadn't even had a warning.

"Ogled is about two hours from here," Rutley continued. "They have what, a hundred-fifty soldiers? They should be on their way to us, and if not, I'll get them."

"It's not going to be enough," I said. "Konevell is much more prepared for war than we are. We don't have a fraction of the people they do. We don't even have a navy."

"Yeah, but we have a stone, don't we?" Rutley said.

"Didn't help these people." My mind raced with questions, theories, fears, anxiety. Up until now, the threat of invasion had seemed somewhat…abstract. But standing in this city, surrounded by the ashes of…of people. Citizens. Innocents. The abstract had become a harsh reality.

I left Rutley behind, walking down a wide street that led right to the water. From the posts sticking out of the water, there'd been docks here, but the Konevellians had seen fit to set fire to them, too. A few remained, but everything else had fallen into the water.

They needn't have bothered. Pennlan didn't have a navy, nor did they have ships at their disposal to move soldiers. It seemed unnecessary, destruction for destruction's sake.

I turned and stared at the village from this vantage point, imagining the invaders pulling up to the docks. Perhaps the locals thought the blockade was over and met the invading army with open arms. Then perhaps the cannons died and the army jumped out from the ships to start burning their way through Pennlan, and we hadn't a clue where. It wouldn't take long to find, of course, but how many innocent civilians would be caught in the crossfire? I thought of the peaceful boats in the inlets, of the fishermen who I'd hoped would remain ignorant of the threat coming. Would they be next?

"Boss?" Rutley called from down the street.

"We found some people."

I swallowed. "Dead?"

"Alive. C'mon."

>-» >-» >-» >-»

There were more than a few—it seemed the survivors were coming back to survey the damage. Some were injured and bleeding, and all were covered in soot. Each one that still breathed air was a blessing, a life that hadn't been taken.

No one wanted to talk with us except for a pair of women picking through the remains of a house. They turned when they saw me, and I didn't miss the look of disgust on their face when they raked their eyes over my uniform.

"What happened here?"

"Five ships," the older woman began. "Came one right after the other—had Pennlan flags. Loaded up on the dock and soldiers started streaming out. They lit everything on fire." She shuddered. "We don't have guards here, so it was just us with our fishing spears against their swords. Wasn't very fair. But we weren't important enough, I guess, for the queen to protect us."

"Then what happened?" Rutley said, ignoring their barb.

"Some escaped. Some tried to fight." She shrugged. "A group of locals burned the docks down so no more ships could come ashore. But the bastards made sure everything was good and destroyed before they marched away."

"Where'd they go?" Rutley asked.

"That way," she said, pointing southeast.

"How many did they have?" I asked.

"More than we had here, that's for sure," she said. "We didn't have a warning or nothin'. Just showed up and started firing." She made a noise. "Those ships, too, they looked too much like Pennlan ships for my liking."

"Pennlan doesn't have ships," I said.

"Not ones owned by the queen," she said. "Merchant ships. They go up and down the coastline. That's probably why nobody thought anything of them. Haven't seen one in an age—hear the border to Konevell is closed and none of the other countries want to travel all the way up here. So we all got excited when we saw five of 'em coming ashore."

My mind snapped to that merchant—Róisín. She'd been more disgruntled than the rest with the troll's solution. But had she really betrayed her kingdom and thrown in her lot with the Konevellians?

I wouldn't put it past her.

"Suppose it would be too much to ask the *queen* to send some supplies here, eh?" she asked, looking at my captain's pins again. "I know we're a small fishing village. But you know, people lost everything and—"

"As soon as we can spare them," I said, my voice hoarse. "Or you're welcome to come down to Orapus and we'll—"

"Probably not Orapus," Rutley said with a low cough. "Maybe send them north? Away from the chaos?"

I nodded. "Rutley, see to it that these people are taken care of one way or another."

"Where are you going?" he asked.

"I have to inform the queen and prepare our soldiers," I said over my shoulder as I walked back to my horse. "After you get them settled, I want you to find the Konevellian army and report back on their location." I stopped, glancing at the sky. "And say a prayer that Riona can get back from the fae kingdom to help us prevent this from happening again."

Chapter Thirty-Nine

Riona

I couldn't get the conversation between my grandparents out of my mind. There was a lot to digest—that they were even talking about me, that I differed from my mother in that I couldn't access the white magic the way she could, the concern about Aldrick. I was at least relieved that the Erlking *was* worried about him and wasn't brushing it off. Not that it made much of a difference in my world.

Also weighing heavily on my mind was Ayla. But just as he'd said, every time I tried to leave, the pain in my neck kept me within the castle walls. And even worse—as I tried to go to his throne room again, the burning returned. I couldn't leave, and I couldn't get a reprieve.

But I couldn't share bad news with Ayla until I'd exhausted every option.

Clíodhna had summoned me to the training room, and as I told her the situation, and pleaded with her to get the Erlking to change his mind, she unsurprisingly shook her head. "If he wants you here, it's for a reason."

"But my sister is—"

"Your sister has an entire army at her disposal," Clíodhna said. "They can fight their little squabbles."

But I wasn't about to take no for an answer. "Do you really want to risk Pennlan losing? What happens to Ayla's stone if someone else is on the Pennlan throne? We know she can be trusted. Can the Konevellian queen?"

"Presumably, the Konevellian queen wouldn't be able to use it alone, as your sister can't," Clíodhna replied evenly.

"But we have no idea *why* I'm needed to unlock the stone," I said, throwing my hand in the air. "Maybe it's the fae blood, but maybe it's something else. Maybe if the stone goes into the Konevellians' hands, whatever loopholes currently hamper us won't hamper them."

"I sincerely doubt it."

"But can you be *sure?*" I stepped closer to her. "Can you be absolutely, positively, ready to lay the lives of all the *sidheog* on the line *sure?* Because with that evil wizard, there's no telling what sort of tricks he has up his sleeve."

She watched me for a moment, and I could sense her resolve breaking.

"All I'm asking is…a day. Day and a half maybe. Just to get down there, turn on the stone, push out whoever needs pushing and save the day. Then I'll be back, and we can deal with," I gestured to the air. "whatever madness is going on here. But if I don't…" I swallowed. "My sister could be in real danger."

Finally, a sigh. "Fine. We'll go see your grandfather to ask for his permission."

I let out a silent cheer of victory. *Hang on, Ayla. I'm coming.*

➻➻ ➻➻

But as we walked into the Erlking's throne room, there was a new energy, this one raising the hair on the back of my neck. More fae than I'd ever seen within the castle were streaming toward the Erlking's chambers, already bursting at the seams.

"What's going on?" I muttered.

Clíodhna wore a frown. "Something unsettling. Come."

She grabbed my wrist and practically dragged me toward the chambers, once more bypassing the usual door I went through and walking through the secret one. Birch was seated on his throne, wearing his nicest crown for once. His gaze was focused on the other end of the room, waiting for something—or someone.

"Clíodhna—"

"Hush, child."

The fae at the very back made room for someone to pass. My heart seized as I saw the white-blond hair and I resisted the urge to grab Clíodhna's hand in fear.

The last two fae moved out of the way, revealing my uncle wearing a black tunic and a smug smile. He continued toward the front of the room where he stood, not bowing or showing any deference. Father and son stared at each other, neither speaking. There was an expectant energy in the room, almost a relief, as if the tinderbox of emotion was finally about to come to a head finally.

"Aldrick," Birch said, his smile tight and firm. "What news from the border?"

"We both know I'm not here to talk about the border," Aldrick replied, his voice low and even. "Your magic grows weak, old man. It's time you step down and let me take your place."

Birch rose from his seat, and the room filled with crackling energy. My whole body shivered as I swallowed hard, unsure if they were going to go at it here in the room with all the witnesses or move it somewhere else.

"Is this really how you want to die, son?" Birch said, his eyes soft. "It will give me no pleasure to dispose of you."

Aldrick snorted. "Consider this an official challenge to your throne."

Another echo of energy zapped through the room, leaving me breathless. If Aldrick had misgivings, it was too late.

"Clíodhna…" I said, looking at my grandmother. "What's going to happen?"

"I don't know," she said, putting a comforting hand on my shoulder. "But we must be prepared for the worst."

"Absolutely not," I snarled, facing forward. "Birch *will* win. Then we'll all be better off without Aldrick."

She made a noise, and I couldn't help but notice how my throat itched as I spoke.

>→ >→ >→ >→

In the time it took me to travel from the Erlking's court to my former training ring, it had been transformed into something more like an arena. Fae creatures—mostly the greater variety, but some lesser—poured into the stands, eager to watch the show. There was a jovial mood amongst them, like they were getting entertainment for the first time in ages.

"What's going on?" I whispered to Clíodhna, who hadn't left my side since the pronouncement was made. "What is all this?"

"Birch taught you nothing," she muttered. "When an official challenge is given to the Erlking's throne, the challenger and Erlking meet before the clans. They will engage in a fight to the death—non-negotiable, so you'd better have your affairs in order before you challenge the Erlking." She pointed to the rings where she and I had been practicing not a few days before. "They will fight in there and will be unable to leave until one of them is dead."

I swallowed. "Aldrick, I hope."

She took my hand and pulled me into the crowd. "Come. I'm expected to sit with the other leaders."

I followed her up a long staircase to a box that had plush seats with brownies offering wine and chocolates. "How was this put together so quickly?"

"Much of this is driven by the old magic of the Erlking," she said. "But anyone who's been paying attention would've known this was coming." She nodded to the brownie, who brought by a tray of chocolates and plucked one for herself. "Especially the staff. They hear everything. They've long been Birch's greatest asset."

I frowned. "Why are you—"

Silence descended in the crowded stadium as Aldrick and Birch materialized in the center of the ring. Birch held up his hands, and, when he spoke, it was as if he was right next to me.

"Fae creatures from near and far, welcome to the Erlking's challenge." He wore a smile but even from this distance, I could tell it was strained. "This day, you will see two fae enter and one fae leave. Whoever leaves will be your new Erlking and should have your support."

I waited to feel the edict, but it didn't come. Then I realized he said *should* not *will*. Clíodhna caught my eye with a nervous look, and the others began murmuring around us.

"Well, well!" Coednin's voice boomed behind me, making me jump. "It's finally time to see a change in the weather. I'm looking forward to a rousing good fight."

I scowled at him. "You could look at least a little cowed. Try not to be so obvious as to which side you're pulling for."

"And you should take care," he said, leaning forward. "Because once Aldrick is king, you won't be able to speak so freely. Or maybe even speak at all. I hear he's reinstating the drowning of halfling bastards."

I narrowed my gaze and turned back around.

The fighters stood on either side of the ring, as I'd done in my training. I held my breath as the Erlking began the fight, and the crowd erupted into cheers as light and magic flew. It was a class in fight mastery, far beyond what I could ever do. Aldrick had more magic than I'd given him credit for, but he was still no match for the Erlking's raw power. Aldrick's strategy was apparent from the outset: he could not match power-to-power with his father, so he did his best to dodge direct blows and set to weakening the old man.

But the Erlking was not nearly as powerful as I'd thought, either. And as the fight carried on, I found myself paying more attention to who received more applause. When Birch landed a particular blow, there were cheers, to be sure. But nothing like when Aldrick hit his father.

And it seemed with every cheer, every applause, the Erlking's magic was growing weaker. Almost as if everyone in attendance was slowly losing hope in his abilities and switching their fealty to Aldrick.

"C'mon, Birch," Clíodhna whispered, her knuckles white as she gripped her skirt. "Don't let him win."

I turned to my grandfather, noticing how very old and tired he looked now. And as much as I could, I redoubled my fealty to him, promising him silently that if he won this fight, I would never disobey him ever again.

The magic show grew quiet once more, and it was the Erlking who was on his knees and panting and not Aldrick. In fact, Aldrick looked… looked like he hadn't even been fighting.

"It's time, Father," he said. "You've had a good run."

"Aldrick," Birch panted, "you are not fit to hold my throne."

"Unfortunately," Aldrick raised a powerful ball of magical moths, "that decision is no longer up to you."

The moths tumbled through the air, gaining speed. I expected Birch to put up a fight at the last minute, to disappear, to do *something* to defend himself. But the sparrows cut a perfect hole through his chest, exiting the other side.

A hush came over the crowd, and my hands came to my mouth.

The Erlking, my grandfather, the man who'd been infallible in my young eyes…fell to the earth. Dead.

A wave of power flooded through me. For the first time in my life, I felt…untethered. Like I could do anything and everything I wanted without anyone looking over my shoulder. The freedom was exhilarating and petrifying and made me want to run to the hills and dance naked under the stars while also digging a hole and burying myself so I would never be seen again.

"Look at me." Clíodhna wrenched my gaze toward her. "Look at me, Riona. This is very important. I need you to swear fealty to the kingdom of Pennlan."

"I…what?"

"*Do this now*. Swear your fealty to Pennlan."

Something in her eyes terrified me. "I swear loyalty to Pennlan."

As the words left my lips, a sensation of grounding washed over me. I was once again tethered to a ruler, though one without the magic to compel me to do much of anything. I wasn't sure what I'd just done, but Clíodhna seemed pleased.

"Good." She lifted her gaze. "Now leave this place. As quickly as you can. You are no longer safe in the fae realm."

I did what I was told without asking, turning to leave. But before I could, two of Aldrick's men appeared in front of me.

"Halfling bastard, you're coming with us. By order of the new Erlking."

Chapter Forty

Cade

The woman before me was so familiar it *hurt*. It wasn't just her face, which mirrored mine in the shape of her nose and the curve of her lips. But it was the way she stood, the air surrounding her. She was on the other side of the room, but I could almost smell her, a memory of home and love and everything that had long been forgotten under Eoghan's tutelage. My magic reached for her, desperately wanting to bring her to me and never let her go.

She stepped forward, watching me as if she wasn't quite sure she believed her eyes.

"My boy," she whispered. "I knew you would come back to me one day."

I had a thousand questions, too many thoughts to get them in any sort of order. So I just buried my head in her neck, squeezing my eyes shut.

She stroked my hair. "Thank you, Queen Nigino'k for your mercy."

"T'en," the queen replied, "I will need the boy to accept his punishment at sundown tomorrow." She paused as she turned. Out of nowhere, she procured my staff and handed it to me. "I trust you won't use this against our people?"

I didn't want to let my mother go, but my staff was *very* happy to be back in my hands. "Why would I want to hurt my own people?"

She smiled, but it was tinged with sadness. "Tomorrow at sundown, you will be sent for. I hope you…enjoy this time with your family while you can. Because you will never get it again."

>-» >-» >-» >-»

"You don't speak much," T'en, my *mother*, said, her voice melodious in my ear. I longed to turn off the magic so I could hear it unfiltered, but I wanted to understand every word she said.

"I don't know what to say," I managed, after a moment. "I never expected... I thought... I don't know..."

She took my hand and kissed it gently. "I understand, son."

I had no doubts that she did. She wasn't magical in any way I'd ever come across before, not like a fae, certainly not like a wizard, but even so, there *was* something magical about her. She seemed to understand the movement of the air, the ripple of the water under the dock as we walked, even the way the clouds moved with the wind. It was an understanding I would never have, no matter how long I studied.

"You might."

I stumbled over my feet. "Can you...can you read my mind?"

"No, not in so many words, but I sense your feelings. Your uncertainty," she said. "My poor son." She spoke it so confidently, like she didn't have a doubt in the world who I was.

"Am I the only wizard?"

"Are you the only one with magic like yours?" She nodded. "Yes. It's not unheard of for our people to be born with magic in their veins, but it's rare. The day you were born, the entire island was eager to see what you would become."

"And how did...how did I come to be with Eoghan?" I asked.

"He showed up asking for 'the boy.' The queen negotiated the deal. Supposedly, she wanted something in return that he didn't provide. Because one morning, you both were gone, half the island was decimated, and the queen was raving mad." She paused. "It was as if he'd fought the magic of the island itself to leave the confines, and it took many years for it to recover. Since then, we've never allowed a single person past our barriers. Until you."

"Did the queen let me back in because she wanted me to finish what Eoghan started or because..." I swallowed. "Because she felt pity on me?"

"Perhaps both. But she's still bound to the island."

"So is the queen in charge or is the island?" I asked. "Because it sounds pretty interchangeable."

She smiled. "Our queen is merely a conduit. She has feelings and opinions, of course, but she must do the bidding of the magic of the island. It's the most beautiful blessing and the most demanding curse." She paused. "She didn't even get to mourn the loss of her daughter. The island was too angry at the betrayal to allow even a single tear to be shed."

This place is a curse. I was beginning to see why Aldonza had opted to leave instead of being forced to do the bidding of a sentient island. But as the queen said, she'd chosen to leave. I was stolen.

"Did you...did you try to look for me?" I asked.

She tilted her head. "I missed you with all my heart. But I knew you were safe."

"How?"

"The leaves told the sea," she said. "And the sea told me."

"I don't understand the magic here," I said. "But you never even... Nobody came looking for me?"

"If I could," she whispered, "I would have. But the moment any of us leave the safety of this island, we become *re'nal'sef* and can never return home again. Our connection to everything is severed. It is a fate worse than death."

Aldonza seemed to be getting on just fine. "But I was your son." I stopped and looked at her. "Surely...surely I meant more to you than this magic?"

"You mean the world to me," she said, her eyes filling with tears. "But if I left this island looking for you..." She inhaled deeply and gently took my hand. "I have lived with this choice my entire life. And I will live with it until the day I die. But there was more than just you to consider."

"What does that mean?"

She cupped my cheek. "Come. Let me introduce you to them."

>⇀ >⇀ >⇀ >⇀

T'en walked me toward a house on the edge of the island. There were purple shirts and pants hanging on a line outside, with a large, soapy tub nearby. Several chicken-like creatures pecked at the ground, though they were green and purple, with long beaks. One of those long-snouted pigs was in a pen, along with a creature that looked like a goat, except for its wings.

"What is this place?" I asked.

"Home," she said, softly.

She didn't let go of my hand as she led me through the front opening, though I stopped short as my eyes adjusted to the inside.

"Look who's come back to us," she said with a smile.

Five bodies rose to their feet immediately. A brother, older by a year or two and *taller than me*, came running over, grabbing me by the face before crushing me to him. A sister who shared my cheekbones and the shape of my ears was next, tears falling down her face as she cried out in pure joy. Another sister, maybe ten, hugged my midsection. And a small boy just toddled over and stared at me as if he wasn't sure who I was.

Then…

"It can't be."

The man who stood was like my missing half. What I didn't inherit from my mother was plain on his face, the chin, the shape of his hairline. Even the way his black locks fell around the nape of his neck. He strode over to me as my siblings (*my siblings!*) parted.

"You're…" My father stared at me with tears in his eyes and, like me, seemed completely overwhelmed. So he just hugged me and I hugged him back, squeezing my eyes shut as I thanked the fates that I'd come home.

"Come, come," the older of my sisters cried, pulling me toward the table. "You're starving, I'm sure."

"Look at that," my brother said, examining my staff. "You've got a real wizard staff and everything!"

"What is the mainland like?" my younger sister cried.

"Where did you go?"

"What did you learn?"

"Why are you home?"

"Children, children," T'en said with a gracious smile. "Give your brother time to catch his breath. He wasn't expecting all this, I'm sure." She beamed at me. "But yes, it's time to feed you."

It happened in a flash—almost by magic, except for the quick movement of hands and feet. The once-bare table was immediately covered in all manner of foods I'd never seen before (that I could remember, anyway). Succulent fruits that tasted tart and sweet, salty fish and crustaceans, and the pungent taste of spices that seemed to cover everything else. I tried a little of everything and found it all delicious.

My siblings (*siblings!*) peppered me with questions about the world. I told them about my life in Pennlan, about Eoghan's treachery, and taking off in search of the stone. When I got to the part about Aldonza, and how she was the first *e'potu* person I'd seen, my mother covered her hand with her heart.

"It was the magic, I'm sure of it," she said. "Of all the ports that A'onzal could have arrived at, she was at that one, the same day as you, my dear son. You were meant to come home today. By the fates or magic, you were meant to be here."

I let out a breath. "I still have to find the stone the *fuath* stole. It's imperative we get to it before Eoghan does. He has one already, given to him by the trolls. Ayla has one, but it's not always assured that it'll work. There's this one, buried somewhere in the sea. And a fourth…that we have no clue about."

"It's better to let the stone lie, then," my father said with a shake of his head. "The ocean will keep it safe."

"The ocean is no match for Eoghan," I said. "And I think… There's something that's…" I ran my hand through my hair as I gathered my thoughts. "You say it's because of the magic that I found Aldonza. But what if the magic wanted me to find the stone, too? What if there's something or someone else pushing me toward finding it so we can finally rid the world of this horrible thing?"

My parents stared at each other and my mother shook her head. "The stone the *fuath* brought to this island…it was their ruin. Their death. They were so consumed with the power of it that they slaughtered each other until there was no one left." She put her hands in her lap. "And the ocean buried it deep."

"But how do you *know*—"

"The ocean told us."

I sat back, shaking my head. "Everyone keeps saying that. But how is the ocean sentient? How can you communicate with it? For that matter, how do you communicate with the island?" I was rambling now, but I wanted to know. "I can feel the magic, but I can't wield it. I can't even hold onto it."

My father's smile widened. "How is it that you speak with the magic in your veins?"

I shifted. "It's not so much a communication as a feeling. Thoughts. Emotions. I can concentrate on what I want it to do, and it does it." I glanced around the room. "It doesn't *talk* to me. More like I tell it what to do."

My brother chuckled. "It sounds like you're quite the bully."

"I'm not…" I twisted my grip on my staff. "That's how I was taught. By both Eoghan *and* the fae."

"And I wonder how you would fare if you were taught something else?" he asked. "To use magic as a partner instead of a slave."

"I'm open to new experiences," I said.

"Then in the morning," he said, "we will see if we can't reteach you the basics of how *e'potu* live in this world. You've been a *re'nal'sef* too long."

Chapter Forty-One

Ayla

Something cold slipped into the bottom of my stomach as I read my sister's letter. The Erlking…was dead? In the brief moments I'd spent with him he'd impressed me with his power. I'd put him on par with Eoghan in terms of magical ability—for whatever that was worth. That someone was able to kill him—that *his own son* was able to kill him…

I read it again, a hundred different worries swirling at once. My sister's life was in danger. The trolls were in danger, too. She was trapped in…

I sat back, staring out the open window. She was trapped in the fae realm. The trolls were as well. Neither would be able to come when and if Konevell made their move across the river.

Three times, I attempted to write a response, but there was nothing to be said that hadn't been said already. Finally, I settled for:

Riona,
Please stay safe.
Ayla

I folded the letter and placed it in the box, waiting for it to glow…

But it didn't.

I opened and closed it again, wondering if maybe I'd missed the latch. Once more. Perhaps the letter wasn't set in right. But every time I opened the box, the letter was still in there. My pulse pounded between my ears. My one line of communication to my sister, the one person who might be able to help us…

Gone.

I sat back, my hand over my chest. I prayed this didn't mean she was dead (though logically, the box should've worked even if she was). Three more times, I tried to send my letter, and three more times, I opened the lid to find the letter staring back at me.

Closing my eyes, I rested my forehead on the table. "Cade. I don't know if you can hear me, but if you can…come home soon. We could really use you right about now."

A moment later, I rose from the table. I went from window to window, catching glimpses of the ocean and wishing I could dive into the blue abyss. It would be something more productive than this incessant *waiting*. Waiting for news, waiting for chaos, waiting for the world to end. Waiting to find out what I should do. Now, waiting to find out what had happened to Riona. Waiting. Waiting. Waiting.

I paced the length of the room more times than I could count, stopping only to peer down at the street below, looking for Ward to arrive with news of what he'd found on the coast. And as I stood there, staring over the city, resignation set in.

We were most likely on our own. We wouldn't have magic or trickery or anything except our swords and our people. For some reason, accepting this lifted some clouds in my mind. At least some of the uncertainty was over. We would meet Konevell on the battlefield and we would…

I swallowed. I didn't know what we'd do then.

As the sun was crossing into the afternoon sky, Ward turned the corner. He took his time handing the reins of his horse to the soldier at the front. Every step up the stairs took an impossibly long time. I had half a mind to march downstairs and accost him in the front hall, but I merely stood by the window with my arms crossed as I tapped my foot.

My door opened, and he walked in, his gaze on the ground.

"What is it?" I said. "What's wrong?"

He wouldn't even look at me. "Ayla, I…"

I inched forward. "What? What's happened? Has Konevell—"

"They came ashore in a small fishing village a few hours' ride north of here," he said, his lips barely moving. "The town was destroyed. I'm not sure how many…are dead. The army is on the move somewhere in Pennlan."

I swallowed—another wait over. "I see. What about the Pennlan army that came from Gleddol?"

"Gone." The sound barely left his lips. "Obliterated. There were a hundred and fifty, and they were…" Again, he swallowed.

I shivered. We had a hundred from the royal guard, another hundred from Orapus. But somehow…somehow, I guessed that the extra fifty bodies wouldn't make much of a difference.

"Rutley is looking for them and will report back," he continued, finding his voice again. "As soon as we find them, we'll meet them head-on." He glanced at the open box on my desk, his eyes lighting with hope. "Have you heard from Riona?"

"It's not good news," I said, turning away from him. "The Erlking is dead, and Aldrick's forbidden Riona to leave the castle. Her…uncle is now in charge."

I didn't need to look to sense the hope evaporating from his body. "What?"

"We will have to meet the Konevellian army…with the forces we have," I finished, though it was difficult to speak. It was even harder to turn back around and look at him. "What preparations have you made?"

He stared at me like I'd spoken a foreign language. "What do you mean?"

"What…what have we done to prepare for them?" I asked. "I know we have weapons, but—"

"I haven't done anything," he said, his voice low and distant, like something had stunned him into silence. "I came here first."

I gripped my skirt. "Fine. What *are* your plans to prepare for this?"

"I have…no idea." He sank into the nearest chair, his head hanging. "Ayla, two years ago, I was walking the border gate in Críoch, grateful to be more than a street rat. And now you expect me to be a military mastermind? To know how to lead an army to victory? I have no training in this, no idea where to even begin. The best I can do is walk our troops to their slaughter. Because that's what's waiting for us."

It was the first time my calm, confident Ward seemed unnerved. "What happened in that fishing village, Ward?"

"People died," he said, his voice growing more panicked and unhinged. "Fishermen fought spear against sword and were slaughtered. The Gleddol army met them head-on and didn't stand a chance either. Those who escaped have lost *everything*. It's my job to protect the border, and I—" His voice cracked. "I failed. I'm not the right man for this job. Someone else…someone else needs to take over. I have no idea what I'm doing."

"That makes two of us," I said with a firmness I didn't realize I had. "You, at least, had a choice. You chose to take the mantle from Captain Gabhann. That—"

"That doesn't mean anything," he said. "Except that I'm a complete fool."

He gripped his head in his hands, the picture of a broken man. And something moved me to cross the room in three steps to stand before him. He wouldn't look at me, his faraway gaze on the floor. I held my breath and gently took his stubbled face in my hands as I knelt in front of him. I'd never touched him like this before—never touched *anyone* like this before. But with calm breaths, I tilted his face up so I could meet his gaze.

"I'm so sorry—"

"What's done is done," I said, my voice barely over a whisper. "And now we have to move forward with what we have. You are my captain. I chose you for a reason."

"It was a bad reason," he said.

"It's because you *always* seem to know the right thing to do." I rubbed the pads of my thumbs against his cheek, bringing his head closer to mine. "You can command a room to do exactly what's necessary. When we were in the troll realm, and all looked to be lost…you told everyone what to do, where to go, what to look for."

"And Lynton showed up at the last minute," he admitted. "Had he not, we'd probably still be in that prison."

"You would've figured it out," I said. "I believe in you."

"You shouldn't."

He lowered his gaze, unable to look at me. Before my eyes, my brave, infallible Ward was falling to pieces, the facade of his bravado falling away to reveal a young man as overwhelmed and scared as I was. Seeing him like this, watching him fumble over his words and be unsure, it somehow emboldened me—the way knowing that magic wasn't going to save us had. It was time I stopped waiting for someone to save my kingdom and figured out how to save it myself.

"Ward," I whispered, pressing my forehead to his, "it's as you said: we're in this together, whatever happens. There's no one else I'd want by my side."

He met my gaze, something shifting. "Even though I failed you—"

"You could never fail me," I said. "Not when I've failed you so many times, and you've given me more chances than I deserve."

Finally, the ghost of a smile appeared on his lips, and relief swept through me. "I have given you a couple, that's true."

"Now dust yourself off, get it together, and let's figure out what we're going to do," I said. "Together. Deal?"

"Ayla, we could…" He covered my hand with his. "You could die. You understand that, right? We have no magic, no stone. No wizard, no fae, no troll. It's just going to be Konevell's army against ours—and we don't have the numbers to beat theirs."

I again rubbed his cheek. "Don't lose hope until the bitter end, Ward. I'm not."

"I suppose it's time you gave me a talk instead of the other way around," he said, a chuckle emitting from deep within his chest. I became aware of the warmth of his hands over mine, the feel of his cheeks under my hands, the earthy scent of his musk from riding all day. We were close —so close his breath tickled my lips. Just an inch or two closer and we would meet.

"Ayla, I—"

"I thought I told you two to quit doing that."

We sprang apart, but not from the shock of being caught in a compromising position. The voice—that beautiful voice—was a beacon of light in our doom and gloom. And I couldn't hide the tears that came to my eyes as I took in the sight of my dear Captain Gabhann, wearing the same traveling clothes she'd left us in, standing in my doorway, a frown on her face.

"W-what are you doing here?" Ward stammered. "Where did you come from?"

"Got wind that there was an army about to invade," she said. "What kind of soldier would I be if I didn't suit up and protect my kingdom from those damn sea-dwellers?"

I took a step forward, but Ward was faster, throwing himself onto his former captain with such force she took two steps backward.

"I'm so glad you're here," he whispered, his throat tight.

"Well, I didn't come alone, either," she said with a grin. "I brought about two hundred of my closest friends."

(HAPTER FORTY-TWO

WARD

I was so happy to see Gabhann that I didn't argue with her when she said the safest place for Ayla was the army camp. So the three of us set off immediately, meeting up with the two hundred troops from Cymorth and Arwyr who were waiting just outside the city.

"I've never been so excited to see my own soldiers," Ayla said with a joyful smile. "Is it going to be enough?"

I didn't have the heart to wipe the happiness from her face. "I hope so."

There was a loud, raucous cheer as we rode into the camp, and it grew even louder as the troops followed us. I didn't even mind how the royal guard practically swooned at the sight of their former captain; considering I'd shed more than a few tears at her return, I was feeling much the same.

The old bird didn't waste much time, calling a de facto council meeting of the captains of each of the cities so we could all understand what we were up against.

"They came ashore here," I said, pointing to the spot on the map. "Rutley's scouting their current location, but my guess is they're marching toward Orapus."

"Just as you said, Ward," Ayla replied with a haughty look toward Captain Treen.

"Now's not the time for I-told-you-sos, Ayla," Gabhann said. "How many are we looking at?"

"I didn't get a good count," I said. "But Konevell recruited every able-bodied person they could find. Hardened soldiers they're not."

"How's that going to help us?" Captain Nevins, from Cymorth, asked.

"Our soldiers train and drill every day with their swords. A farmer might not have the ability to lift their sword as fast," Gabhann said. "Where they may outnumber us, we might have an edge on the skills."

"Are any other cities coming?" Kilwin, from Arwyr, asked.

"They should be," I said. "Unfortunately, our forces from Gleddol were…" I couldn't dwell on it, not in front of the other captains.

"When are we expecting Konevell to strike?" Nevins asked.

"Within two days." Rutley walked in without introducing himself, his face dusty and red from being in the sun. "We found them marching along the main road." He glanced toward me. "They seem keen to torch every city in their path. And…leave no survivors."

The group let out a collective breath, and I was a little relieved that Kilwin and Nevins looked just as unsettled as I felt.

"We have to stop them before they hurt anyone else," Ayla said, breaking the silence.

"Rutley, did you get a count?" Gabhann asked, her gaze fixated on the map.

"A thousand, at least. Maybe more."

"How many soldiers do we have at present?"

"Four hundred or so," I said.

"Plus the stone," Rutley said. "And Riona, right? Isn't she coming to our aid?"

Ayla made a noise, and it was her turn to blush. "Riona is… detained."

"Detained—" Rutley began but I shook my head to quiet him.

Gabhann looked at me. "When did you say our reinforcements would arrive?"

"Hard to say," I said. "We sent out riders over a week ago, but I don't know how quickly they'd be able to scramble."

"You scrambled in what, a day?" She nodded. "They're prepared to do the same. Or should be."

I ran my hand along the back of my neck. Would the old captain in Críoch be as quick as I was? I couldn't be sure. "I don't think it wise to count on them."

"Perhaps not." Gabhann straightened. "Have we sent word to the surrounding villages and Orapus for volunteers to fight?"

"Yes," I said. "We've gotten a few, but…"

"But what?"

My face burned a little. "I don't think anyone's taking me seriously. Nobody believes that Konevell's about to invade or has invaded. They think…" The room became uncomfortably hot.

She snorted. "They're full of it, all of them. Got the same sort of feedback when I'd come into town looking for potential candidates for the guard. Treen."

The captain snapped to attention. "Yes, ma'am."

"You will put out the call for volunteers. Tell them that if they value their lives and homes and property, they will join us." She paused. "And while you're at it, evacuate the city. Go now."

Ayla cast another haughty glance at the captain as she nodded and walked out of the tent. "I told her to do that yesterday."

"Then it's a good thing I showed up to remind her of her job," Gabhann said with a wink. But the levity was gone as she leaned over the map. "The longer we wait, the more damage Konevell can do along this road. It's not vacant, you know. Villages, farmlands…people live there." She met Ayla's gaze. "We don't really get to decide when we'll get attacked, either. They could move tonight and surround us, and we'd have no recourse but to surrender."

She nodded, her face growing pale. "We can't let them take this country." She grasped the stone around her neck. "Too much is riding on this stone remaining mine to wield. And if there's even a chance that

Ramira…"

"We won't let that happen," I said. "Because you're going to run like hell if they show up. Got it?"

She met my gaze and nodded curtly.

⸺ ⸺ ⸺ ⸺

The meeting ended shortly after that, and we were all given our orders to prepare for the coming battle. But even though it was my job to whip them into shape, I couldn't bring myself to discipline my own troops. They wandered around, many of them drinking more than they should've been. But I didn't stop them, even joining an older soldier in taking a sip from a flask filled with a spicy whiskey. But one sip was all I allowed myself, knowing I needed my wits about me tomorrow.

I lay down in my tent, but I couldn't sleep, so I got up and wandered more. Eventually, I found myself in front of Ayla's tent, debating if I should go inside. But the decision was made for me as Ayla came out, jumping a little when she saw me standing there.

"Oh!" She smiled. "I was coming to look for you."

"Here I am," I replied. "What did you need?"

"Just…to talk," she said, rubbing her arms. "You?"

I could've come up with a different excuse, but I didn't have it in me. "Same."

"Do you want to talk somewhere else?" she asked, glancing at the other tents. "Maybe somewhere more private?"

I shouldn't have, but I nodded. "Sure."

We walked side by side in silence until we left the perimeter of the camp. Every so often, our hands would brush, but neither of us made any attempt to take the other's hand. Wordlessly, Ayla sat down under a tree and leaned against the bark, releasing a heavy sigh as she tilted her head upward.

"Pretty night," she murmured.

"Yeah," I said, settling next to her with my hand touching hers. "You know, the stars look different in the fae realm."

"Do they?"

I nodded, pointing to a bright star near the horizon. "That bright one there was higher up. It helped us find our way out of an impossible maze."

"I remember you telling me about that," she said with a smile. Turning to me, she asked, "Why do you think Eoghan sent you two on a trip when he could've just made a portal right to the lake to get the stone?"

"He could get to the stone, sure. But he couldn't get it *out*. That's what he said, anyway," I replied. "The only person who could get it without drowning was Riona."

"I see." She rubbed her hands. "I hope she's okay."

"She's a survivor," I said. "But...it's a little concerning that she hasn't managed to sneak out of the fae realm yet."

"Maybe there'll be a miracle tomorrow," Ayla replied softly. "Maybe she'll appear in a puff of butterflies, telling me the crazy way she managed to escape her uncle." She chuckled. "Stranger things have happened, you know?"

"Maybe."

We settled into silence again, and her hand inched closer to mine.

"About what happened earlier today," Ayla whispered.

"Please never speak of it again," I said with a groan. "Especially to Elodia or Rutley. They'd never let me live it down."

"It was actually kind of...nice," she said with a soft smile. "Seeing you so...human. Vulnerable. Honest."

I bristled, making a noise of protest but not responding.

"I've never seen you show any weakness," she said. "Even when we were in that cave, when we were about to be crushed, you just..." She made a gesture. "You never wavered. I used to think *nothing* could get under your skin. Except..."

I furrowed my brow. "Except what?"

"Except..." She cast her gaze down. "Me, I guess."

I swallowed hard, the memory of her hands against my cheeks warming me from head to toe. The whisper of her words against my skin, how she'd cradled me at my weakest moment, it was the kind of intimacy that exhilarated and terrified me at the same time. If Gabhann hadn't returned, we might've taken things a step further.

"You know we can never be, right?" I said, my voice soft. "You and I…"

"I know," she said, looking down at her hands. "That's…what I wanted to talk with you about. If things go south, or maybe even before we…" She twisted her fingers. "I want you to get a message to the other side. I'll marry whomever they want. Just as long as…as long as no one else gets hurt."

"I think that ship might've sailed, Ayla," I said with a half-smile. "If they're invading, the time for peaceful negotiations is pretty much over. Why would they stop now when they already have their army inside Pennlan? All they need to do is find you, take the stone, and claim Pennlan for their own."

"Maybe a bloodless solution would appeal to them?"

"Why would you think that?"

"Because it would appeal to me," she whispered. "I can't imagine anyone willingly sending their own people to die."

I cast her a sideways look. For all the horrible, backstabbing things Eoghan had done to her, there was one silver lining to Ayla's sheltered upbringing: she was impossibly, adorably optimistic about people. And no matter what happened in the coming days, I hoped she always remained that way.

"What?" she said. "What's so funny?"

"Nothing," I said, looking up at the dark sky. "I'll make sure the message is delivered. And when you marry that eight-year-old boy, I'll be there in my shiniest shoes and pressed uniform to celebrate."

She made a noise that bordered on disgust. "Where's Cade when you need him?"

"Probably still moping," I said. "Maybe we'll find him at the bottom of a cask of ale at some port city in the south. Bet he hasn't even left yet. You broke his heart, his soul, his—"

"Stop," Ayla said with a gentle nudge. "Don't make me feel worse than I already do."

"But you don't…" I cast her a sideways glance. "You really don't love him?"

"Of course I love him, but it's not like that," she said. "And maybe I was…I was unfair for leading him on a little in the troll realm."

"What, by throwing yourself on him?" I asked with a snicker as she protested more. "'*Oh, Cade! You'll share a room with me because I hate my sister—wait,* half-*sister!*'"

"Stop!" she said, shoving me again with an uncharacteristically loud giggle. "I wasn't *that* bad."

"Please."

"Fine, maybe…" She wore a smile I hadn't seen in days. "But I feel like since he first went on the quest with you, I've just gotten moments with him. He was my best friend my entire life. Then one day he was just…gone." She sighed. "I just wish he hadn't left without saying goodbye. I miss him terribly."

"Yeah, I kind of do, too," I said. "And Riona. And the trolls. And anyone else with magic…"

Just like that, the reality of our situation came back to both of us. She looked at me with a mix of fear, sadness, and uncertainty, and I couldn't muster a single word.

"Look, Ward—"

Whatever she was going to say was lost in the loud explosion that happened fifty paces from where we stood.

Chapter Forty-Three

RIONA

Whether the Erlking's death had caused mass panic or met easy acceptance, I hadn't a clue. I'd been marched from the arena to my bedchambers and locked inside. I'd managed to get a letter out to Ayla before my guards realized what the box was and confiscated it. So all there was left to do was sit and pray that my sister was able to figure out how to avoid war with Konevell. Because it didn't look like I was going to make it to help.

"Please be okay," I whispered to the wind.

I wasn't sure how much time passed, but it felt like a lifetime. Finally, a *bwdbachon* arrived with a piece of bread and cheese and a goblet of water. She placed the food on the floor and turned to go.

"Wait!" I said. "What's going on out there?"

"Ma'am." She bowed then said, her voice small and high. "I'm not allowed to speak with you."

I bit my lip. "Are you mandated or just told?"

She cast a furtive glance around. I was thinking the latter because she *had* spoken with me.

"Look, just tell me: Is Clíodhna still queen of the *sidheog*?" My worst nightmare would be for Aldrick to have taken both my grandparents from me. She was smart—she didn't like him, but she wouldn't overtly go against the new Erlking. Not when she had all the *sidheog* people to consider.

"Y-yes," the brownie said. "I have to go."

She disappeared through the crack in the door, and I sat back, picking up the bread and taking a big bite. Clíodhna had said Birch used the servants in the castles as his eyes and ears in the castle. So perhaps I could do the same.

Thinking about my grandfather drew a dark cloud over my head. It was easy to get distracted worrying about the future, but in the moments of quiet, I let myself mourn. Not just the stability he'd brought to my life —and that it had continued at all after my mother's death—but Birch himself. My grandfather.

More time passed, and I began to drive myself crazy with the lack of news and activity. I'd tried to pick the lock, but it kept reconfiguring itself once I'd managed it. My next target—the window—was met with the same difficulty.

I looked at the glass, and the chair seated at my desk.

Worth a shot.

I lifted the chair with my butterflies and drew it back so it would have a running start. Then as fast as my magic would carry it, the chair went zooming toward the glass. Too late, I realized it wasn't going to work, and the chair exploded into splinters, showering me with pieces of wood.

I waited for someone to come check out the noise, but no one did. They must've just enchanted my room to keep me inside without needing to monitor me closely.

That, I might be able to work with.

I busied myself trying to find a weakness in the room—some stone I could squeeze my butterfly form through. Some way out. This lasted well past the sun's disappearance until, finally, I sat back, exhausted and defeated.

I crawled up to the window and peered out at the dark night and stars above. I closed my eyes and dug for that damn white magic that would've been *so helpful*…and couldn't reach it. What good was this ability if I couldn't ever *use* it?

Suddenly, Ayla's obsession with being able to use the Pennlan stone without me made more sense.

I slid down to sit once more, staring at my hands and trying to talk myself into believing that my sister was fine. That Aldrick was a much different Erlking than master of the border and all was well beyond my bedroom. That everyone was at peace. That there was a perfectly logical reason they'd locked me in this room.

Actually, why *had* they locked me in here?

If I were Aldrick—who hated my very existence—mine would've been the first execution I ordered. Or I would've sent my minions to do the dirty work. At least come rough me up a little. But they hadn't just left me alone, they'd seen fit to feed me, too. Surely not something they'd bother with if they were planning to kill me.

So what were they gonna do with me?

I sat with my gaze on the door, willing something or someone to come and bring me news. I even tried sending little butterflies under the door and around the edges, but they were rebuffed. Still, I kept at it, even as my eyes drifted closed…

Something was staring at me. I jumped to attention and was blinded by a bright light. My eyes adjusted and I blinked.

"*B-bwdbachon?*" I blurted before I could stop myself. "S-sorry, do you have a name?"

The creature who'd brought me food earlier rubbed her hands anxiously. "Rief, m'lady."

"Not a lady," I said with a wave of my hand. "What are you doing here?"

"You asked me to bring you news," she said. "And I have news."

I grinned. "Share!"

She painted a grim picture. Aldrick's ascension to the throne had been swift and absolute. After they'd taken me to my room, they'd all but dragged Clíodhna to the *Arwein* to officially name Aldrick the Erlking. Some part of me had hoped she'd refuse to give her blessing, but the *bwdbachon* confirmed she had.

"Self-preservation and all," I muttered. "I can't blame her, I guess. Where is she now?"

"I'm not sure," the brownie said. "I don't believe she's left for the *sidheog* yet."

"Because of me?"

"I don't believe she's been…allowed. The new Erlking has declared that the members of his *Arwein* should remain close to him."

I snorted. That was sure a vote of confidence for him. "Did you find out what they have planned for me?"

"N-no," she said. "They have told the servants to say nothing. But it appears they're preparing for something. I don't know what."

"Something that involves me?" I asked.

"I believe so. But it's hard to hear sometimes. There are lots of charms around the Erlking these days." She bowed. "That's all I know."

"Thank you," I said. "Might I ask one more favor of you?"

"It's no favor, m'lady," she said, looking a bit taken aback. "The Erlking invited you to the *Arwein*. Therefore, we of the castle are bound to serve you as we serve the others."

My jaw fell open. "I'm not… He didn't…"

That sly son of a… So he wasn't senile. He'd known exactly what he was doing inviting Lynton and me into that room.

"What is the…request?" she asked.

"Can you help me bust out of here?" I asked. "I need to reach my sister in Pennlan."

She nodded. "It will be hard, but I can try."

"Thank you, Rief," I said, reaching forward to offer my finger to her small hand. "Your help is appreciated."

"It's no trouble, m'lady," she said, bowing again. "It's our calling."

>→ >→ >→ >→

It was well past midnight when my *bwdbachon* friend returned, this time bringing with her a collection of her friends. They said nothing to me as they went to the window and began hammering with tiny little tools. I walked toward them, not wanting to tell them I'd tried that already, but hopeful they had some clue I didn't.

"M'lady, we're almost done replacing the glass," Rief said, flitting over to look at me. "You'll have to be quick."

"Quick?" I shook my head, not understanding.

"I believe you'll see better as your magical form." Her voice was strained, as if she were skirting very close to saying something she wasn't supposed to.

So I transformed into butterflies and zoomed over to the window. At this size, I realized that they were replacing small fragments of the window. There would be a moment when they had one section removed and hadn't yet replaced it, and that would be my moment to escape.

I watched one come off, and zoomed toward it, squeezing myself through and out into the night sky. With one butterfly out, the rest of me followed, and I was free.

My form spun back to the bright lights in the window, still diligently working, and my heart swelled with gratitude as I reconsidered every interaction I'd ever had with them.

"Thank you," I said. "I won't forget this."

They didn't acknowledge me, continuing their work with almost fevered focus. So I floated toward the sky, eager to get to freedom, safety, my sister…

…but I couldn't just…*leave.*

I turned back around, watching the castle under the moonlight. Clíodhna was still in there, perhaps under lock and key as I'd been. The *bwdbachon* who'd just freed me from my prison might be punished for helping me escape. And the trolls…

My neck didn't burn—the edict was gone with my grandfather's last breath—but I felt the pull of duty toward the creatures in the wildlands. They'd been helpless against the *daoine maithe* who had come to terrorize them, and I wasn't holding my breath that Aldrick would suddenly forget about them.

Still, what good could I do? My sister's stone was on the other side of the continent, and the white magic was dormant unless someone beat me within an inch of my life. Which was…entirely possible, should I engage in a fight with ten fae stronger than I was.

But…maybe I could sneak the trolls across the border to Pennlan.

The idea sounded more appealing the more I thought about it. I could go to the wildlands, gather the trolls, and take them with me. Together, we'd probably be able to sneak across the border (I hoped) into Pennlan. Then we could continue south to meet my sister and help her with the Konevell problem.

I glanced south, my heart aching for my sister. "Hang on a little longer, Ayla. We'll be there as soon as we can."

Chapter Forty-Four

Cade

The sound of the *neh'nhah* (the chicken-like creatures) woke me the next morning with loud braying that sounded more donkey than fowl. I'd spent the night in an open window, on a hammock made of the purple leather and couldn't remember a day I'd woken up more refreshed. I looked around this room, shared by my brothers, and had a moment of sadness for the life I might've had if Eoghan hadn't taken me.

I wouldn't know Ayla, or Riona, or even Ward, who'd grown on me, apparently. I wouldn't know the green hills of Pennlan or the cold tundra of the northern fae realm. I wouldn't have a staff, either—Eoghan had given me my first one.

But I would've awoken in a room with my brothers every morning. Would've known what it was like to *have* a brother, to live amongst my peers instead of constantly feeling like an outsider. Was that life better? It was impossible to say.

"Oy!" My eldest brother Nire'huf stretched and sat up in his hammock. "Good to see you there, *ren'elk*. I never took it down, you know, after you left. I had a feeling you'd be sleeping in it once again."

I smiled at his optimism and the pet term for "little brother." He must've been six or seven when I was taken. "If only for one night. The queen has a plan for me."

"I know." His expression softened. "So we should make the most of our day today, eh? Why don't you come out on the boat with me? Find ourselves a fish or two."

Before I could argue, I found myself in a humble fishing boat laden with nets and fishing lines. Nire'huf seemed to understand the current and waves in ways I couldn't fathom, sticking his hand into the water and pushing the sail this way and that.

"What are you doing?" I asked.

"Searching for fish," he said, pulling his hand out. "Do you want to try?"

I leaned over and stuck my hand in as he did. But all I felt was the cool water along my palm. "Maybe I don't have the magic—"

"You do," he said. "You used to out-fish me. But you've forgotten how." He closed his eyes. "Can you feel the magic in the air?"

I followed suit and quieted my mind. There was magic—I'd felt it since the moment I'd set foot on this island. "I can't do anything with it."

"That's your problem, *ren'elk,* you're trying to do when you need to be. The magic you're used to wielding exists only when you demand of it. The magic here is in control, and we must be careful how we approach it. The first step toward being able to use it is to understand that you have no power over it. You must simply allow it to rule over every aspect of your life."

That sounded absolutely terrifying. "I don't think I can do that."

"You used to. And if you want to survive whatever task the queen has for you, it's a good idea to be able to understand the magic of the island."

I couldn't argue with that point, so I set my staff down at the bottom of the boat and relaxed into my seat.

"Let go," Nire'huf said.

It was a simple request, and yet it forced me to realize just how tightly I held onto my magic at any given moment. Eoghan's voice filled my head, barking orders, demanding things of me in my youth. Criticizing my unwieldy use of magic before I'd had a staff that was actually made for me. He'd made me so terrified that I would hurt someone—hurt *Ayla*—if I didn't keep a tight control on my magic that

I'd forgotten what it was like to just relax into it.

I loosened the grip on my body, feeling the tension leave my shoulders, my arms, my stomach, my legs, even down to my toes. With as little movement as I could, I slipped my hand back into the water.

In my relaxed state, the magic in the water was now able to flow *through* my skin, sending messages to my brain. There was sand beneath the water and nearby, some coral housed a thousand multicolored fish. A larger fish lay in wait, ready for its morning meal. Even further, a shark lurked deep in the ocean, hoping that the predator would become the prey.

And as my consciousness expanded, I found a school of gray fish—the ones that my brother, whose energy was palpable from across the boat—was also looking at.

"Very good," Nire'huf said softly. "You haven't completely forgotten, have you?"

I opened my eyes and exhaled loudly. "That was…" I shook my head. "What else can I do?"

He smiled. "First, you can help me cast some nets. Then we'll see how you do on navigating our path home."

⤞⤞⤞⤞

We caught so many we had to let some go. Nire'huf said it was because I was so pure of heart that the island was being so generous.

"Do you *actually* believe the island is sentient like that?" I asked. To his frown, I added hastily, "I'm not trying to be blasphemous. I'm just… There's nothing like it anywhere else."

"Which is why it's so special," he said. "We are a blessed people here. You, of course, are doubly so. You can wield magic here and take it with you to the mainland and beyond. We can't do that."

Aldonza certainly couldn't. "But how do you *know* that if you step out of line, you'll be punished?"

He smiled sadly. "Because that's what happened when you were taken. The queen allowed the wizard to cross our barrier, against the wishes of the island. He betrayed us, and the island did nothing to protect us from him. Then he took you."

I pursed my lips. "But that's not... Eoghan is just evil. That has nothing to do with the island *letting* you—"

"You might know magic in a different way," he said, a little sadly as the boat hull reached the soft sand of the beach. "But this is the way we were raised, how we see the world. It makes us feel safe to know our purpose and path in life. To question it...like A'onzal did...is to follow a path away from family. And that's not a path I want to go down."

I nodded. "Understood."

Together, we carried in the fish, which our eldest sister H'ierf'ih took from us, putting some in barrels and others hanging out to dry on the line.

"We share what we catch," she said with a bright smile. "The villagers will be pleased to have this bounty today!"

She'd hooked the cow-like creature up to a wagon, and she and Nire'huf hoisted the heavy barrels on top.

"Let me help," I said, my staff alighting.

"No need, brother," H'ierf'ih said. "It's our pleasure to serve the island and the people."

"Nothing warms my heart more than seeing you and Nire'huf together," T'en said, coming to stand next to me. "The two of you used to sneak out on that boat and find all the fish. Come home smelling of the sea and little boys." She smiled sadly. "After you left, Nire'huf wouldn't touch the boat for months."

My siblings finished loading the fish, and my sister set off toward the main town, a whistle echoing back toward us.

"What troubles you, son?" T'en asked softly. "Your heart is unsettled."

"Do you think my abduction was punishment for breaking the laws of the island?" I asked.

She let out a deep breath. "I believe it's more complicated than that." She turned to look at me. "Why?"

"I suppose I'm looking for a reason to help me sleep better at night," I said. "Because right now, it seems wildly unfair. I didn't ask to be born with this magic. I didn't want to be taken by Eoghan. And to see what life could've been like had I been born normal…"

"And what is normal?"

"Like my siblings," I said, nodding to Nire'huf.

"You were given a blessing."

"A blessing, huh?" I kicked the ground, unsure where this anger had come from. "A curse is more like it. Nothing good has come from this magic."

"Your friends on the mainland would feel differently, I'm sure."

My mood soured as Ayla's face flashed before my mind's eye. I did my best to hide it, but I couldn't help the snappy way I responded, "They like me because I can save them. Nothing more."

She tilted her head, reading me. "You've been nursing a broken heart of your own, haven't you, son?"

I nodded, my face warming. "Just before I left, I told Ayla that I had feelings for her. She didn't reciprocate."

"Oh, my sweet boy," T'en said, taking my arm. "It hurts now. But one day, you will understand that she did the best thing for you. Would you rather she'd let you love her knowing she didn't feel the same?"

"I wanted her to love me back," I said, allowing myself to be stubborn. "And I don't know if I can stand to watch her love someone else instead."

"But my dear son, she *does* love you. You are the most precious person in the world to her," T'en said softly. "Even today, I can feel her heart pining for your return, the same way I felt its love for you your entire life. *She's* the reason I didn't leave to find you. Because she became your family in a way we couldn't."

Family. "But that's not what—"

"What is it you want from her, son?" She tilted her head at me.

I wanted her all to myself, to be the hero of her story, to save her from the dangers of the world and have her fawn over me like she fawned over Ward. To know what it was to kiss her, to feel her body. To make her cheeks red the way the women on that island did.

"Sweet boy," she said with a small smile. "If that's all you want from your greatest love, you need to reconsider your thoughts on the matter. She's not a prize to be won or a possession you can use for your physical needs."

My face warmed. "I know that."

"One day," she said, "you will grow past this and see why she's not meant for you."

Because I'm unlovable. It was as if my mother's words had unlocked something deep inside me, a fear I'd carried unspoken since the moment I'd shown up in Pennlan. I was always different, always the outsider. When Ayla had chosen Ward, it had made me so angry because some part of me felt it inevitable. Why would beautiful, perfect Ayla choose the foreigner when she had brilliant, handsome, *normal* Pennlan-born Ward instead?

"Your feelings are valid," T'en said softly, as the wind blew by us. "And the more you examine them, the more you'll see that they're not the reality. Your differences don't make you unlovable. They make you exquisitely perfect. And one day, you *will* find the happiness you are so desperately seeking in your Ayla. When you do, you will understand."

"But what if I never find anyone?" I whispered.

She put her hand on my arm. "Happiness comes in all forms, my dear son. From knowing oneself. Seeing our friends for who they are and not what we want them to be. And most importantly, once we learn to love ourselves exactly as we are, true happiness comes from within. We need no other person or thing in this world or the next to see the beauty in every moment." She lifted a shoulder. "And should another person come along, then that's just a bonus."

"I don't think that's how it works," I said. "But it's a nice sentiment. Like telling someone who lost a race that they did their best."

She just smiled. "You're still hurting. Once it fades, you'll understand. I—"

She turned suddenly, her brow furrowing. Walking up the beach was that *e'potu* soldier, flanked by five others. They carried their weapons and didn't look to be in a mood to argue."

"The wizard's been summoned," he said.

"We have until sundown, T'adlos," my mother said, putting her arm protectively on me. Behind me, Nire'huf came running, standing in front of me.

"The queen promised we'd have the full day," he said.

"The island has demanded differently," T'adlos said. "We lost another group of fishermen today. Nothing back but a few boards and limbs. The queen feels it was a mistake to allow the time."

"What's going on?" I asked. "What do you mean you lost another group of fishermen? To what?"

My mother's face paled. "You can't be serious. You aren't sending him to face *Law'ek'ub*."

Law'ek'ub. Why did that sound familiar?

T'adlos nodded. "It is the task set upon his master that was never completed. And so the apprentice must uphold his end of the bargain. Then the island will be satisfied."

"What is *Law'ek'ub*?" I said, turning to my mother and brother.

"The queen will explain everything," T'adlos said. "Come with me."

CHAPTER FORTY-FIVE

AYLA

It took a few moments for my ears to stop ringing, for my eyes to adjust to the bright flames, for the pain of being thrown backward and falling on the ground to ricochet through my body. I moved slowly, shaking my head to come back to my senses. There'd been an explosion. There were soldiers running all around us, both wearing our blue and a foreign red.

"Ayla…"

Someone had taken my face. Ward. He was saying something.

"What?"

"Ayla, listen to me." His eyes were wild—terrified. "You need to run."

"What?"

"Run."

At once, my reality snapped into focus. The Konevellians had gone on the attack first. Ward and I had been thrown twenty feet from the tree we'd been sitting under—and the tree was now on fire. Everywhere I looked, red outnumbered blue. The Konevellian invaders moved like possessed creatures, overwhelming our camp in moments.

"*Ayla!*" Ward shook me. "Do you understand?"

"No," I said, finally looking at him.

"Find Elodia, Rutley—someone you trust. Or a horse, I don't care. *But get out of here.*" He picked the stone hanging from my neck and tucked it under the neckline of my dress. "And *do not let anyone see this thing.* As far as they know, you're just a civilian. *Got it?*"

"W-wait, where are you going?" I asked.

"I have to find a weapon," he said. "I don't want you to look back or to stop until you're far away. Do you understand?"

I stared at him, fear seeping over every inch of me like black ink spilled on the page. Would I ever see him again?

"Be careful," I whispered, intertwining our hands. "Come back to me."

He tore away from me then stopped, turned, and came back. Before I could stop him, his mouth covered mine—hot and wanting, tasting of ash and musk and desperation. He broke the kiss before it really began, searched my eyes, then ran into the fray.

I sat there on my hands, watching him knock a Konevellian soldier from behind before they could kill the Pennlan soldier they were fighting. I squeezed my eyes shut as the Pennlan soldier moved to pierce the Konevellian soldier with his sword. When I opened them again, Ward now had the bloody sword and was barking orders I couldn't hear.

Get out of here. As far as they know, you're just a civilian.

His orders drew me to my feet. I was wearing a simple dress, no tiara, and with the stone hidden in my bosom, I did look like a common maiden.

Find someone you trust.

I moved my feet one after the other. It was still the middle of the night, and the burning trees illuminated the smoky skies. The sounds of battle were everywhere: panting, screams of agony, cries of vengeance. My eyes burned, but I kept wandering, knowing I would—

Something hard caught the bottom of my foot, and I fell forward, landing on something wet. A dead Pennlan soldier. Campbell. His dark eyes stared up, unseeing at the black sky. He'd never see the grandson he was so proud of again.

I swallowed a scream, pushing myself away and staring down at my hands. They were covered in blood. This time, my stomach came all the way up, and I retched into a tuft of grass. Not a moment too soon, I jumped out of the way as a pair of soldiers tumbled in my direction, tussling and fighting. I watched, powerless, until my fingers closed around a rock.

Without thinking, I cracked the rock onto the Konevellian's forehead. But all it did was draw his attention to me.

The Pennlan soldier—Erna—gasped. "Get out of here, Ayla!"

The Konevellian's eyes lit up with recognition as he drew something to his lips—it appeared to be a shell of some kind. But before he could blow it, Erna ran him through, and he slumped forward, dead.

"*Get out of here,*" she said. "If you're captured, we're all lost."

Slowly, I nodded, jumping to my feet and running.

It was hard to orient myself. Most of the tents had been trampled or set on fire, and the smoke was getting hard to see through. The battle was moving away from the camp, though, which was a good sign.

A horse was approaching. Without thinking, I dove behind a trampled tent and covered myself in the canvas as the horse came to a stop. I barely drew breath, my heart as loud as a thunderclap in my chest.

"Fan out." The voice was new and through the slit in the canvas, I could make out a red uniform. "She has to be here somewhere."

"She could be back in the town?"

"No. They said she was here." He turned his horse. "Now go."

They left, and I lay there under the canvas, counting the seconds in my head. When I hadn't heard anything for a few minutes, I pushed the canvas off and sat up. A voice in my head that wanted me to call out to the man, to surrender myself to stop the bloodshed. To sacrifice myself for the greater good.

But Erna's words rang clear in my head. *If you're captured, we're all lost.*

I pressed my hand to my bosom where the stone sat between my breasts and rose to my feet. I needed a horse—my horse. I would ride to Pennlan castle, then… Then what? To the fae realm, where Riona's uncle would most likely have me killed? To the wildlands, perhaps. Ward and Cade had been able to walk through the fae realm; perhaps I could, too. First, I had to survive the day and *find a horse.*

Two Konevellian soldiers emerged from the darkness, overtaking a Pennlan soldier. One raised their sword and swung it toward the soldier's neck. I looked away but I couldn't avoid the sound of metal slicing through flesh, nor the sickening *thump-thump* of two somethings falling.

Then it was silent, except for the slow chuckling.

"What do we have here?" one said, wiping the splattered blood off his mouth. "Looks like a young woman. Pale skin, auburn hair."

"Fits the bill, yeah," said the other, twirling his sword. "Now why don't you make like a good little—"

A third figure emerged from the smoke on horseback, swinging a sword. Down the Konevellians went, one right after the other, as the figure rode up to me and held out her hand.

"Let's get you out of here," Gabhann said, a nasty gash on her face.

My knees nearly buckled in relief as I climbed on the horse in front of her. "What's happening out there?"

"Nothing to concern yourself with," she said, her tone even. "They want you and that stone—so we need to get you as far away as we can. To Orapus—"

"No." I spun to look at her. "No, not Orapus. They're looking for me there."

She nodded, understanding. "Then where?"

"To the fae realm," I said, swallowing. "We'll deal with what we find when we get there. But at least if I can get to my sister—"

She slumped into me, a strangled noise coming from her lips. I turned as she slid off the horse onto the ground….an arrow sticking out of her back.

Someone screamed, perhaps me, and within seconds, I was on the ground next to her. I pulled the arrow from her back, earning a grunt of pain, but I was able to roll her onto her back. Blood trickled out of her mouth as she stared at the sky, gasping for breath.

"W-what c-can I do?" I whispered. "What do I do?"

She said nothing, blinking up at the sky.

"C-Captain." I was shaking, my hands covered in her blood now. There was so much blood. "Captain, what do I do?"

Maybe a bandage? I tore at my dress. If I could stop the bleeding, we could get back on the horse. I could find someone to help her. Someone in the fae realm would surely be able to heal her. She just had to hang on until then. Surely, she could do that…

"A-Ayla."

Her soft voice stopped my rambling thoughts, and I bent closer to listen.

"I-it was an h-honor."

Her eyes became glassy as her hand fell from mine. Slowly, her breathing ceased, and she exhaled one last time.

My face was wet—tears. They came in waves, sobs coming from somewhere deep inside of me. With shaking hands, I smoothed the gray hairs on the top of her head. What had she planned for her retirement? Was she going to plant a garden and tend to it? Perhaps start a new hobby that would take up all her time? The possibilities would've been endless.

Instead, she'd turned right back around and come to the front lines in our hour of need. And paid the price for it.

Hatred like I'd never felt for anyone except Eoghan roared through me. The damn Konevellians had caused this—and for what? A stupid stone they wouldn't even be able to use? No amount of power was worth all this.

My hands gripped my dress now, a furious yell threatening to escape. I wanted to hurt something the way I hurt. I wanted to find a Konevellian soldier and beat them until they didn't move anymore.

But Ward's voice in my head broke through the anger. Run. I had to run. I had to keep going until I made it to safety. I couldn't let them get their hands on me or this stone.

"Your Majesty, I'm so glad I found you."

I looked up slowly, barely recognizing Platt as he emerged out of the shadows. His uniform was singed, but he seemed to be all right otherwise. He didn't even look at Gabhann as he helped me to my feet, pulling me back toward Gabhann's horse.

"The Konevellians are everywhere. Looking for you. We've got to get you to safety."

I nodded, numbly, unable to tear my gaze away from the captain's body. She looked so peaceful, lying in the grass and flowers.

"Now, get on, and we'll get you to safety," Platt said, motioning to the horse.

Safety. Trust. Ward's warning rang between my ears. I'd known Platt for years, but did I trust him?

"I'll ride alone," I said, finding my voice. "You go back and help the fight."

"The fight is lost, Majesty," he said, though I didn't hear any hint of mourning in his tone. "You are the most important person now. Getting you to safety."

He put his hands on my waist to lift me up, and I twisted out of his grip. There wasn't a single Konevellian soldier in sight. If someone had shot Gabhann, intending to keep us from escaping, wouldn't they have been here to claim their prize by now?

"You." I balled my fists. He didn't have a scratch on him—not even a hair out of place. "You did this, didn't you?"

"What are you—"

This time, he wasn't gentle, grabbing me by the waist and pulling me to him. Before I could say a word, something cold and sharp pressed against my throat.

"Now, I'm supposed to bring you back alive," he breathed against my cheek. "And the moment they have you, they'll call off the fighting, understand? So if you want to prevent more deaths like poor, retired Captain Gabhann…I suggest you keep your mouth shut and follow along like a good little girl."

"You're despicable," I snarled. I hadn't thought I could hate anything more than Eoghan, but Platt was vying for the top spot. "What did they offer you? Gold? The captain's spot?"

"They recognized the value of my presence," he said. "And yeah, a lot of gold. More than even that troll could make."

"So you're the one who told them about my stone?"

"Stone?" He snorted. "What about it?"

I opened and closed my mouth. "So you didn't tell them that—"

"Enough talk." He pushed me forward. "Move."

Chapter Forty-Six

Ward

The scent of blood was thick, mixing with smoke. It was hard to see, harder still to know where I was. My head pounded from where I'd knocked it on the ground, but soon enough, I forgot about the pain. Survive—that was the only thing that mattered.

The Konevellians had come from everywhere, outnumbering us by even more than I'd anticipated. Or maybe their attack had been so surprising that they'd been able to slaughter us before we even knew what was happening.

A cry of pain drew my gaze. Esmond was fighting three Konevellian soldiers and losing badly. I gripped my sword and ran over, knocking away a blade then another. But it didn't do any good, as the third blade found him in the front. He fell forward, blood gushing from his open wound, and lay still.

The three soldiers then looked at me, grinning evilly. I tilted my head and smirked. In my youth, I'd been in more than a few scraps with rival gangs—a past I'd nearly forgotten.

"Come on," I said. "Let's see what you got."

They came at me, and I dropped my sword, knowing I'd be faster without the heavy metal. I skidded across the wet grass, pulling my short knife from under my arm and cutting the back of one of their legs while shooting my leg out to trip the other one. Down my knife went into his shoulder, and while he was screaming, I ripped his sword from his scabbard and ran it through the third.

I yanked my knife out and picked up my sword, leaving the incapacitated and dying enemies where they lay as I wiped my forehead and continued.

Severn was firing off arrows while standing in front of our weapons carriage. His leg seemed to be broken, but he was standing firm against an advancing crowd of red-coated soldiers.

"You ain't getting our weapons!" he cried, firing another. But with his unsteady leg, his aim was off, and it landed harmlessly in the ground—his last arrow.

The Konevellians rushed him at once, and I ran after them. I pulled them off, one by one, fighting, knocking, or hacking away. But before I could get three of them off, Severn was in pieces on the ground, and the Konevellians were pulling cannons, swords, shields, and whatever else out of the wagon and sprinting away with them.

I gripped my sword and moved to follow, but another strangled cry caught my attention. Another outnumbered Pennlan soldier. Before I could reach him, he was dead.

Another cry. This time I was quick enough to reach her and together we fought back the enemy, leaving them on the ground. She breathed a sigh of relief, thanking me with a nod, then we both heard another cry, and she took off running to help.

I turned to keep running when I spotted a gray-haired figure on the ground.

Captain Gabhann.

I stumbled over to her, kneeling and touching her still-warm hand. She was staring at the sky, still.

But there was no time to mourn, not when I had soldiers fighting for their lives. Another cry, another soldier in need of help. Again and again, I careened from fight to fight, helping my blue-uniformed brethren where I could before moving on to the next. The battle seemed endless and fatigue was starting to set in. My arms ached from the vibration of steel against steel, my legs from walking through muddy ground, and my heart…my heart was growing tired of all the death. Especially by my hand.

In the distance, a low, loud noise echoed through the air. Another joined it then another, until the entire battlefield was filled with the sound—followed by a raucous cheer. My heart sank to my stomach. That hadn't come from our side—so what did it mean?

The skirmishes continued, but those without an opponent began walking away. Red uniforms across the battlefield seemed to be moving as one, punctuated by the sound of that *horn* again. I stumbled as I followed, a moth to a flame.

The red in the sky wasn't just the fire—the sun was coming up in the distance. And as I crested a hill, my stomach dropped into my shoes.

The field below was littered with blue-clad bodies. The red soldiers walked by them without a care in the world, some stopping to drive their swords into those who moaned as they bled out on the ground. My throat went dry as I stumbled down the hill. As I approached the first bodies, I expected to see Elodia or Rutley's face staring back at me, but…

Berdine. She liked to play the piano.

Parrish. One of Platt's lackeys.

Haslett had given me a nip of whiskey just a few hours ago. Did he still have his flask on him?

I tilted from right to left, watching the strongest men and women I'd known lying still in a field, in their own blood. Was this how the *aos sí* became the haunted graveyard? Would the trolls come here and take a memory stone? If I ever saw one again, I'd ask them to. These soldiers deserved to be remembered for their bravery—even if Pennlan was lost to time.

Up ahead, the red soldiers had gathered, hooting and hollering.

A pair of arrows came sailing into the crowd, finding two of the Konevellian soldiers. Then two more. Three more. Someone—

Elodia.

She was up in a tree, firing off as many arrows as she could, fury on her face. Down below, Rutley was handing her more.

Renewed hope and anger roared through me. I would be honored to die amongst my soldiers, taking out as many of those bastards as I could. Rutley saw me, his eyes lit up with relief, and he grabbed his sword from the ground. Elodia climbed down the tree—she was out of arrows—and took her blade as well.

We would fight an unwinnable fight with everything we had. A feral yell came from somewhere deep in my chest.

"Calm yourself, Captain. Or you might hit the wrong person."

I skidded to a halt, almost sliding on the blood-soaked ground.

Platt.

I knew, without explanation, that he'd had a hand in this. He wore plainclothes, and his hair and skin were mussed, but not from battle. He didn't have a scratch on him.

And he was standing amongst the red-tunic-wearing bastards without a sword sticking out of him.

I gripped my sword and inched closer but he pointed to the left. "Before you run me through, you might want to see what's happening over there."

I almost didn't listen, expecting it to be a ruse, when my heart sank to my toes. In the throng of red soldiers, Ayla was bound and gagged, fury on her face. She seemed to be whole and unscathed, and for that I was grateful. Next to her, a tall, pale woman with raven-black hair was examining something dangling from a necklace. The Pennlan stone.

"See?" Platt said. "No use killing me now. But if you lay down your weapons, I'll make sure you three aren't killed on sight. After all…" He smirked. "Something must remain of the so-called elite royal guard."

"You… You *traitor*," Elodia screamed.

Rutley took a step forward. "You sold us out!"

"Perhaps so," he said.

"Your friends are dead," I spat. "Kavan, Parrish, and Severn. Don't you care?"

He lifted a shoulder. "I can make new friends. The queen of Konevell has promised a handsome reward if I—"

It happened in a blink. The Konevellian soldier broke ranks and shoved his sword through Platt's stomach without a second look. He fell forward, sputtering and coughing blood as he writhed on the ground. All I could do was stare, knowing justice was done…but angry I hadn't been the one to mete it out.

"Now, as for the rest of you," the soldier said, walking forward. "Are you gonna do this easy—"

I lifted my sword, baring my teeth. "You'll have to kill us if—"

"No!" Ayla's voice echoed over the plain. Her face was wild, frantic. Terrified. It was hard to believe that mere hours ago—was it even an hour? Time had moved so strangely—I'd kissed her for the first time. It had been a moment of insanity, knowing I might not see the sunrise and not wanting to die before I knew what she tasted like. The look in her eyes had been worth it. A look that was long gone now.

I wanted to tell her to be brave, to let us die honorably as so many others had done, but she tore her gaze back to Ramira, her lips moving quickly in words I couldn't hear. Ramira gazed down at her as if she were bored then pointed to the stone and asked her a question. Ayla nodded meekly, her gaze darting back to me as she bowed her head.

Don't give up, Ayla. Not for my life. It's not worth it.

But whatever deal they'd made was struck, and Ramira balled up the necklace and slipped it into her pocket as Ayla was dragged away. Ramira turned to face us, walking in long strides. Her black boots came up to her knees, her legs thin and willowy as they disappeared under a red tunic. She even wore a tiara with a red gem in the center.

I raised my sword, and the Konevellian soldiers advanced, but Ramira held up her hand as she passed them, silently telling them to stand down. Then she continued until she stood twenty paces from us.

"Your queen has promised to cooperate if I spare your lives," Ramira said, her voice as velvety and deep as when I'd heard it under the table. "Put down your weapons, and we will honor her wishes."

I hesitated, especially as Elodia and Rutley came up beside me. But perhaps we all thought the same thing—we were no good to Ayla dead. So with a sick feeling in my stomach, I dropped my sword and put my hands in the air. Rutley followed suit, and after a pregnant pause, Elodia dropped hers as well. We were surrounded immediately, our hands bound behind our backs, and marched toward the throng of red soldiers.

Ramira came closer. She had crow's feet around her eyes, thin lips, and a near constant-looking sneer. She glanced at Rutley then at me.

"Hm. I suppose I see the appeal." She straightened and said nothing else but walked over the field as if nothing were amiss. And together, Rutley, Elodia, and I were frog-marched behind her.

But I made sure to kick the dying Platt hard in the gut as I passed.

CHAPTER FORTY-SEVEN

RIONA

"I thought I was clear. You're not welcome here."

Lynton hadn't even let me set foot in the village. He'd planted his feet, crossing his arms, and glared me down from the sky. He was the one I needed to talk to anyway, so I landed in front of him with an equal amount of stubborn annoyance.

"The Erlking is dead, Lynton. We gotta get you guys out of here."

He lifted one shoulder. "I figured."

I waited for more of a reaction, but there was none. "Aldrick is in charge now."

"I figured."

I threw my hands up, helplessly. "Don't you understand what this means for you?"

"Nothing it didn't mean before," Lynton said. "The politics in the Erlking's castle don't affect us. We are in danger by our very existence regardless of who sits on the throne. We have already made preparations for the coming storm and are ready to weather them."

"Are you?" I blinked. "Because I don't know if you realize—"

"We have survived a war before, child," he snapped. "And we will survive another. Our greatest asset is that we never underestimate the ruthlessness of our tormentors." He glanced toward the sky. "Now leave. If they're as deadly as you say, you are in as much danger as we are. Perhaps even more, with your heritage." He turned his back to me. "We aren't in need of your *protection* anymore. You have no edict. You are free to go."

The ground swelled up around my legs and began to carry me backwards toward the *aos sí*. I flailed my arms, panicking at the thought of setting foot in that horror story again, and used a few butterflies to pry my feet from his grip. It was…easy. Which made me even more nervous.

"Lynton," I said, landing back where he stood. "Listen to me. Pennlan is safe from them. You can set up in any of the open fields. Ayla won't mind at all, I promise—"

"We are not leaving our land again," he replied. "We will stay and defend it to our death—"

"But there's no *reason* to do that! Why are you so intent on the decimation of your entire race?"

"Because it will come whether we are in Pennlan or in our homes. It will come whether we fight or lay down our weapons. The only choice we have is where we spill our blood. And we choose our home."

And with that, he melted into the ground and zoomed away in the rock. I didn't follow him, too stunned by his declaration. Too sad that he'd already given up on even trying to fight.

But maybe he was right. The Erlking's edicts didn't end at the borders. If Aldrick had a mind to, he could summon the trolls and they wouldn't be able to fight…

…unless they disappeared into the mountains again, like they'd done a thousand years ago.

I screwed up my face, exploded into butterflies, and landed square in front of him.

"You're a coward," I snarled. "You'd rather roll over and accept whatever the fae want from you—"

He brushed past me, walking toward his hut. "I told you, we have no control—"

"Then how come Edric was able to?" I barked. "How come he could cut ties with the Erlking?" I lifted my hands in the air. "You've made no such allegiance to Aldrick. Maybe your dissent will—"

"Don't you understand what happened?" Lynton said. "The trolls *never* needed to be at the table. The reason the Erlking's power waned was because others at the table had already turned against him. The moment we set foot back in these lands, we were already back under the Erlking's control."

"Then go back to the mountain!" I said. "Why are you—"

He stopped me, the blood draining from his translucent face. I turned as the approaching burst of power raised the hair on my skin. A cloud of creatures floated over the air with all the foreboding of a dark storm cloud. I readied myself for a fight, knowing it would be woefully one-sided unless a miracle occurred.

"Spread out," Thorstan barked. "They're scattered across this land like the vermin they are. I want every last one brought to the Erlking's castle."

"For what purpose?"

He turned to me, surprise on his face. "Aren't you supposed to be under lock and key, halfling?"

"You should've had a better lock," I replied with a nasty smile. "Now what are you doing with the trolls?"

"The Erlking has demanded they return to his castle to face punishment for their crimes," he said with a sneer. "I believe they'll be executed."

My chest seized. "You can't... They've done *nothing* wrong!"

"And what are you going to do about it?" Thorstan asked. "Fling a halfling butterfly at me? We know your little secret. You can't wield that powerful magic without your human sister present. And to my knowledge, she's nowhere around here."

My pulse pounded between my ears. *How does he know that?*

"If you have a problem with what we're doing, halfling, take it up with the Erlking." He smirked. "I'm sure he would *love* to remind you of your place."

>→ >→ >→ >→

I knew Aldrick well enough to trust that the trolls would remain alive until they reached the Erlking's castle so they could be killed publicly. He did enjoy a spectacle, and slaughtering a few hundred trolls was the perfect thing to showcase his new might.

Going back to the castle was risky, but I had no other choice. Aldrick would sooner kill me than listen, but maybe… I didn't know. Maybe inspiration would strike. It usually did when I was about to do something incredibly stupid.

I landed near the front doors and took a breath as I stared up at the castle. It no longer felt like home, more like…like a bad dream. Evil seemed to seep from every window and door, and there was an ominous feeling about the way the sun hit the stone. I shook myself, gathering my courage, and started walking in when I noticed my reflection in a nearby mirror. Perhaps not the best idea to walk inside looking like myself.

It had been ages since I'd had to use glamour. There was, of course, the risk that someone would see right through it. But the chaotic energy of the castle was on my side, so I would take that risk. I made myself a few inches taller, turned my green eyes golden, and lightened my hair until it was the color of my sister's. Then I walked right back into the prison they'd left me in.

The walk to the Erlking's chambers was as unfamiliar as the castle, and it didn't escape my notice that the only fae walking the crowded halls were of the so-called greater variety. Gone were the odd little creatures. I didn't even see a servant flitting across the ceiling.

Unsurprisingly, the crowd thickened as I drew closer to the Erlking's chambers. I could have continued toward the back, but now I knew the secret entrance. Aldrick would probably have me killed for even approaching him. But I was a dead girl walking either way.

I held my breath as the walls parted, revealing the front of the chamber. Clíodhna was seated in a chair, her hands tied to the armrests as she looked out on the room with a stoic sort of resignation. And there was Aldrick, resplendent in a gold tunic and the Erlking's crown, sitting in my grandfather's chair.

The sight drew fury from parts of me I hadn't known existed.

Holding my head high, I walked into the room via the secret entrance. Clíodhna's eyes turned to me, wide and fearful as her mouth opened. As powerful as she was, she could've seen through my glamour immediately.

"Who are..." Aldrick's eyes shifted from confused to furious. "What are you doing out of your room?"

"You should know your locks can't hold me," I shot back, releasing my glamour. "I'm here to formally request that you *leave the trolls alone*."

He snorted then threw his head back and laughed. The rest of the room joined in. I stood there, waiting for them to finish, my hands balled into fists as I kept my breathing steady.

"Oh, you are quite the humorous bastard child," Aldrick said, wiping his eyes. "No. Now go back to your room until you're called upon."

I took a step forward, shocked I was able to. "I will ask you *again*. Leave the trolls alone. They're innocent."

He stared at me, shock flitting across his features. "How is this possible? I gave you a direct order."

Clíodhna caught my gaze, and I suddenly realized the importance of the oath I'd sworn to Pennlan. "No. I'm not yours to command anymore. I'm a princess of Pennlan by birth and swore an oath to my sister, the queen."

He snorted. "Whatever, worm. The trolls will be executed because I said so. Just like the *bwdbachon* will be punished for helping you escape."

"They didn't..." I shook my head, but my tongue burned, and he smirked.

"You may be able to lie, but that doesn't mean it's not plain on your face," he said, gripping the throne. "Bring the *bwdbachon* to me. The vermin of this castle need to understand who's in charge these days."

There was something familiar about the way he said *vermin*—

mainly, because he'd used it against me more times than I could count. I looked around the room. It was all *daoine maithe*, forest fae, and a few *sidheog*.

"I fear what he'll do to the lesser among us if he takes the throne."

Birch's words echoed in my mind as I kept searching for signs that he was wrong. But Aldrick had shown me—shown everyone—who he was from the start.

Aldrick gestured to the *daoine maithe* nearby. "Take her back to her room. And this time, *watch her* and make sure she stays put until—"

"Until what?" I dared, taking a step forward. "You'll kill me? Why haven't you already? Aren't I vermin like the rest of them? Expendable? Easy to get rid of?"

He hesitated, only for a second, before turning his nose up at me. "I've tired of this conversation. Get her out of my sight."

The fae stepped forward, but I held my ground.

"I won't let you hurt them," I snarled. "Any of them. The trolls. The *bwdbachon*. Any other lesser fae in this land."

"And what are you going to do about it?" he asked with a sneer. "I'm the Erlking. If I want to destroy the pests, all I have to do is say the word."

He was the Erlking, but there was *one* way I could stop his reign of terror. One very stupid way. But there was something stuck in my mind —the conversation between Birch and Clíodhna where my grandfather had spoken of me so highly, as if I held this magical power deep in my veins.

"Something tells me she's going to need all the power she can get in the coming weeks."

Birch had known exactly what he was doing. He'd all but predicted this day would come, from the moment he first put me in the training ring with Aldrick to insisting to Clíodhna that I stay here instead of leaving for Pennlan when Konevell first threatened.

He'd had one last task for me.

"I challenge you," I whispered.

A hush came over the crowd as Aldrick stared at me. "What did you say?"

"Consider this an official challenge for your throne," I said, my heart pounding wildly in my chest. "If you won't see reason, and you won't leave the weaker amongst us alone..." I swallowed. "I have no choice but to fight for them."

The magic was immediate, a binding that I couldn't wriggle out of no matter who I swore allegiance to. Aldrick knew it too, and to my surprise, there was *fear* on his face. Was it because he thought I had a chance of beating him, or something else?

"V-very well," he said, struggling to keep his composure. "In the morning. We will duel." He rose, his face paler than it had been. "Feel free to use this evening to say your goodbyes."

I lifted my chin, unwilling to show my unease. "Give me my box back so I can communicate with my sister."

He waved me off, and the red box appeared in my hands—dormant. There wasn't a letter from Ayla inside.

I prayed that didn't mean bad news.

"Problem?" Aldrick asked.

"No," I said softly, lifting my gaze to meet his. "I'll see you in the ring tomorrow."

And as I turned, the room parted and allowed me to leave. But before I did, I couldn't help noticing the look of triumph on Clíodhna's face.

>—» >—» >—» >—»

I'd spent most of the night staring at the moon, but as the morning dawned, so did the realization that I probably wasn't going to last the day. It was impossible for me to leave—the challenge I'd uttered kept me in this castle. The only thing I had to give was my blood...and I wasn't even sure that would work.

But I could do nothing else for my sister.

I conjured a vial and a knife, and sliced a red line across my arm, allowing the blood to drip into the glass container. I didn't know how much was needed, so I filled as much as I could then put it in the box. Then I penned a short letter.

> Ayla,
>
> I pray this letter reaches you before Konevell does.
>
> I've challenged Aldrick for the Erlking's throne. This probably won't go well. So I've included a vial of my blood. It's the best I can do, under the circumstances.
>
> It's been an honor to know you,
>
> Your sister,
>
> Riona

I folded and placed the letter next to the vial of blood, closing the top and holding my breath as it glowed then went dim.

"Please get there in time," I whispered. "Please be safe."

And as I closed my eyes, I said the same for myself.

CHAPTER FORTY-EIGHT

CADE

Nire'huf and T'en insisted on coming with me, flanking me on either side. I was sure the rest of my family would've come, too, had they been around. But there wasn't time to summon them, as the soldiers weren't taking no for an answer.

"So what, exactly, is *Law'ek'ub*?" I asked my brother.

"He's a demon *law'ua'b*," he replied, pointing to a set of purple leather clothes hanging from a nearby line.

I slowed my steps. *That* was where I'd heard it before. On the first island Aldonza had taken me to, where I'd seen the thick purple skins that were so prevalent on H'sipotu as well. The old man had told me a tale of a monster twenty times the size of the already sizable creatures.

"Oh." I cleared my throat. "So what am I supposed to do about him?"

"Kill him, I'd guess," Nire'huf said with a dark expression. "Never mind it's been attempted over the years, and *no one* has gotten close to defeating him."

"The queen intends to send you to your death," my mother whispered.

"Aldonza, too," I said as we approached the castle. "And her crew."

My mother's grip on my arm tightened as we stepped inside to where the queen stood, comforting a grieving family. She nodded to them, and they walked out, casting an angry look in my direction as if *I* were at fault.

Which, based on their superstition, I supposed I was.

"Wizard, it's time for your punishment to be meted out," she said, though she didn't look pleased to be saying it. "Some years ago, when your master came to our borders, demanding to see you, we made a deal. He could cross into our lands and train you but only if he promised to help us defeat *Law'ek'ub*. He said he would, but as you now know, he wasn't a man of his word. And our island punished us, and the creature that hunts our fishermen still takes what he wants from us."

She walked toward another tapestry on the wall, pointing to a monstrous whale that seemed larger than the entire island we currently stood on. He had rows and rows of teeth open to consume the unsuspecting boat floating into its mouth.

"*Law'ua'b* of the normal variety are fearsome hunters, but normally do not bother our fishermen. If the island sees fit to allow us to have one, which is very rare, we use all the pieces of the creature. Their skin is impenetrable while they live—yet useful for many different applications from our sails to the clothes we wear. The meat is nutritious and dries well for us to eat for many months. The teeth serve as useful weapons for arrows and spear tips." She paused, nodding to the soldiers who carried spears tipped with what I now realized were teeth, each one bigger than my hand. I tried not to think about them chomping down on my extremities.

"How do you kill the normal ones?" I asked.

She offered a tense smile. "We don't. When a creature dies of old age, they sometimes wash up on our shores, then we take what the island has offered us."

"So…" I turned, looking at the group gathered. "None of you have ever actually killed a regular one…and you want me to kill the demonic one?"

The queen nodded. "We do not expect you to be successful. Therefore, on the very slim chance that you are, you and the rest of the crew will be free to continue your search for the powerful stone that first brought you to the island."

I turned to look at the whale in the painting, dread filling the bottom of my stomach.

"To ensure that you stay on task," the queen continued, "I will be sending an escort of our best sailors. Should you try to escape before finding the creature, they have instructions to destroy your ship and leave no survivors."

"I won't run," I said defiantly.

Beside me, Nire'huf puffed out his chest. "I ask to be included on this mission."

The queen raised her brow as my mother let out a cry of protest. "You can't, Nire'huf."

"I allowed that wizard to take my brother and did nothing," he said. "I won't stand idly by and let him die if I think I can help. I'm the best fisherman on the island. He needs me to find the creature."

I shook my head, but the queen nodded. "If you insist."

"I do."

My mother bit her lip and looked away. I covered her hand with mine and squeezed. "I won't let anything happen to him."

"But who will make sure the same is true for you?" she asked softly.

>→ >→ >→ >→

We pushed off from the safety of the dock and headed out of the veil surrounding the island toward the deep ocean. I couldn't wipe the image of *Law'ek'ub* eating a ship larger than this one from my mind. At least he'd swallow us in one piece.

Beside me, my brother—who'd insisted on being on *this* ship with me—stared toward the sea with unwavering courage. I'd tried to convince him that he didn't need to come, that our parents didn't need to lose two sons together, but he shook his head and stared at me with an intensity that was so familiar it hurt.

"Let him kill himself if he wants," Cluny had muttered. "Two idiots for the price of one."

So I hadn't argued and kept my silence as we said our goodbyes to the family. My parents couldn't stop crying, and my sisters clung to me like this was our first separation ever. I tried to keep myself from being swept away by their emotion, but it was hard.

"I've just gotten you back and now you have to go again," my mother whispered, holding my face as she kissed both my cheeks over and over.

I wanted to tell her I'd be back, but I didn't want the last words I said to my mother to be a lie.

Trepidation filled me as H'sipotu disappeared behind the horizon. Lightly, I tried to convince myself Eoghan could've defeated the monster, but simply chose not to. Perhaps I had the sort of magic that could easily dispose of the creature, save the day, and return everyone back to the island safe and sound.

Don't fool yourself. You never get that lucky.

"I feel it," Nire'huf said beside me. "It's..." He shivered. "It's more than what's natural."

I turned to him, not sensing much. "From where?"

"Everywhere. Nowhere." He licked his lips, looking nervous for the first time. "How are you expected to slay such a thing?"

"I'm not," I said with an unhelpful smile. "I think that's the point." I cleared my throat. "Not too late for me to move you to one of these other ships."

"Won't matter," Aldonza said, coming to stand next to us. "*Law'ek'ub* won't leave a ship unscathed. He'll swallow us before he's done. Maybe in one chomp, if we're lucky."

"Have you seen him before?" I asked.

"No. But I've heard stories from survivors who only managed to get away because they turned around." She nodded to the other ship, which was so close, I could practically step across. "They've got their orders to stay on us until we're dead. Which probably means they're going to die, too."

"Have a little faith," I said, though I didn't have any in myself.

"Why should I?" She put her hands behind her head. "Unless you want to create one of those portals and get us all the hell out of here..." She wagged her brows. "I'll even help you find that powerful stone, eh?"

It was tempting.

"If you do, the queen will ask our family to accept your punishment," Nire'huf said. "And they won't have a choice."

I turned to him, my brow furrowed. "But they're innocent—"

"Someone must pay a price for your misdeeds," he said. "Or the island will make us all suffer. That's how it's been and that's how it will always be."

Aldonza snorted. "That, or the queen's got a damn complex and doesn't want everyone to know her entire existence is a lie."

"You might've left the island, but you need to watch your tongue," Nire'huf said with a steely gaze. "Because the island will mete its punishment even..." He spun around, his eyes widening. "*Ren'elk!* It's coming!"

I felt it too, the massive surge of power as it moved closer—faster than a creature that big had any right to be moving. I gripped my staff, scanning the ocean for which direction it was coming from. But it was so big the entire ocean seemed filled with its power.

East. I turned just as the shadow came up from the dark ocean. First it was a single row of teeth, then another, then another, then another, as the creature rose from the water, pushing the ocean back toward us.

I moved fast, using magic to encircle all the soldiers within striking distance and move them to a nearby ship just as the massive jaw split the vessel in two as it dove back under the water.

"This was a bad idea," Aldonza whispered. "The queen's sent all these people to die."

"Not if I have anything do with it," I said, running toward the bow of the ship. The monster was everywhere and nowhere at once.

A chorus of screaming turned my head. A tail three times the size of

H'sipotu had two ships in its flapper. With a snap, it flung the vessels as if they—and the crews aboard them—weighed nothing. I caught as many as I could, but it wasn't enough as the soldiers landed in the water.

"Swim to a ship!" I cried to them. "Get out of the water!" I looked toward T'adlos. "You need to get these soldiers to safety. *Leave!*"

"We were given a job," he said. "If we leave, you will, too."

"You can't—"

The distraction was enough, and I watched in horror as the monster reappeared, and this time…his massive jaws closed before I could save the sailors. I dashed forward, sending magic toward the creature, searching for the soldiers to bring them to safety. But my magic bounced harmlessly off the skin.

"This isn't going to work," I said, running my hands through my hair. "These soldiers will die."

"What do you suggest, *re'nal'sef?*" Aldonza said, lazily leaning on the wheel of her ship. "Should we just go ahead and sacrifice ourselves or should we hope that *Law'ek'ub* likes the taste of the islanders' ship more so we can get out of here?"

"We should…"

My heart stopped. Another ship was now in the monster's mouth. Without thinking, I created a portal and stepped through. Mustering all the magic I had at my disposal, I sent the nastiest attack spell toward the roof of the monster's mouth.

It did nothing.

"*Ren'elk,*" my brother cried from Aldonza's ship as the jaws came down.

"Everyone hurry!" I created another portal and magically grabbed all the soldiers to push them through it to safety. I barely managed to get through myself before the jaws closed.

And to my horror, the portal disappeared, the magical connection from here to there severed.

"That's…not good," I whispered.

"What do you mean?" Nire'huf said. "What happened?"

"It's not that I can't wield magic against it," I said. "It has the ability to stop my magic inside of its body. This is... I've never faced a creature with this sort of power before." I turned to him, fear coursing through me. "I don't know how to fight it."

"You'd better figure it out," Aldonza said. "Because it's coming for us."

The shadow moved through the water, clearly trying to decide between us and the other ship. But as it emerged behind us, it didn't have to decide—it could swallow us both. But I only had time to create one portal.

Knowing it was us or them...I made my choice.

I created a portal around the other ship, pushing it through and sending it back toward H'sipotu. And before the jaws closed completely, trapping me inside, I created one more portal and shoved my brother through.

Then everything went dark.

CHAPTER FORTY-NINE

AYLA

I was captured, but I was still alive.

Ward, Elodia, and Rutley were alive. Or so Ramira had promised. Until I knew otherwise, I wouldn't waste my energy worrying.

They'd transported me back to Orapus—which was now flying a Konevellian flag—in a barred carriage and stuck me in the barracks' prison. I didn't see a single Pennlan soldier as I passed. The red Konevellian uniforms were as sickening as the red blood on the battlefield. But as they threw me inside a dark, musty cell, all I could do was remind myself of my very important truths.

I was alive. Ward, Elodia, and Rutley were alive.

Riona was…perhaps alive.

Cade might show his stupid wizard face at *any moment* and help. My anger at his abrupt departure was a nice momentary distraction from the situation I found myself in.

When that faded, all that was left was the tidal wave of emotion.

Reliving the battle was harder than living it had been, because in the solitude of my jail cell, I could recall every gasping breath, the scent of blood on the air. Nearly every soldier who'd served at my castle was lying dead in a field outside the city. I saw their faces in my mind, heard their cries of anguish. The only ones left…the only ones left of my soldiers were Ward, Elodia, and Rutley. Even the traitorous Platt hadn't survived the day. But it wasn't until my mind replayed Captain Gabhann's end that the tears came.

Unfortunately, that coincided with the sound of approaching footsteps. I sucked in a breath and quickly wiped my eyes, coming to stand like the monarch I still was. The good captain would've expected me to be strong, and I would do my best to honor her sacrifice.

The door groaned open, and I held my breath as Ramira ducked under the threshold. She was two heads taller than I was, at least, with a sour-looking face and a quiet kind of disdain that made me dislike her immediately. But I did find it curious that she would come to speak with me herself.

"Are your accommodations to your liking?" she asked, without a hint of sarcasm.

"Wonderful," I replied, just as evenly. "I thank you for your generosity."

She cracked a smile. "You're as feisty as Galliford said, I see. Even in defeat, you don't seem to understand your place."

"I'm quite aware of my place." I gestured to the room. "Can't miss the bars, you know." I folded my arms across my chest. "What do you want?"

She tsked. "You shouldn't be so rude to your captor."

"What are you going to do, slaughter my army and take me prisoner?" I shrugged. "You have my stone. What more do you want from me?"

"How do you make it work?" she said.

It took everything in me to keep from barking a laugh. "I'm sorry?"

"How do you make it…turn on?" She didn't seem to have it on her —smart. "What magic word do you need?"

"There isn't a magic word," I replied, the corners of my mouth threatening to betray my amusement. "You took over Pennlan. You are its queen. You are now the one who makes the stone work." I sat on the filthy bench as if it were my throne. "I don't have any wisdom to impart."

"I will *kill* your soldiers," she snarled, taking a step forward.

"I'm well aware of that," I replied evenly. "And there is no magic word, no magic potion. There's just…"

Your stone doesn't work without your sister around.

Lord Galliford had said that to me the last time we'd met. Which, presumably, meant that Ramira knew as well.

"You just need my sister," I said slowly. "Which you knew."

"We have that taken care of, trust me," she said, waving her hand. "It still won't work."

"*How*," I said, worry breaking through my facade. "How do you have it covered? What do you have that—"

"We're getting off track." She brushed her dress. "So you're not going to cooperate?"

"I…" I held up my hands. "If you have my sister…then you have everything I know to give you." I let out a morose laugh. "Other than to be the queen of Pennlan. Which, I assume, you now are."

I waited for her to contradict me, to argue, but she merely sniffed and walked out without another word.

I sat there, staring at the floor. Riona was stuck in the fae realm because of Aldrick. Was he somehow in an alliance with Ramira, too? Had there been some larger game of chess afoot that I had no idea about?

"Oh, Riona, I hope you're safe," I whispered to the stillness. "Please be safe."

➻➻ ➻➻ ➻➻ ➻➻

More time passed, and without a window, I hadn't a clue how much. A meal was provided—bread and cheese with water. I caught a moment of rest here and there, my dreams plagued by memories of blood, death, destruction. Of Ward being amongst the dead. Of Riona, too. Even Cade, so I clearly wasn't *that* mad at him. Each time, I woke with a start, expecting to see someone in the prison but finding myself alone.

After a time, I paced nervously, chewing my thumb until it was raw. There were exactly twenty steps from one end of my cell to the other. Nineteen if I widened my stance a bit, twenty-one if I took smaller steps.

It became a game to get to the other side in twenty steps and when I won ten times in a row, I tired of it.

Finally, more footsteps approached. I readied myself as Ramira walked through the door, wearing a different outfit.

"We have discovered the problem with the stone," she said.

"I'm all ears," I replied.

"It wasn't enough to take Pennlan for ourselves," she said. "Because the curse on the stone isn't about the country, it's about the bloodline."

I opened and closed my fists. "Fascinating."

"Guards." She called behind her. "Hold her down."

Three guards raced inside, and I held up my hands to protect myself, but they were stronger. Two grabbed me and pinned me against the bench while the other pulled out a dagger.

"W-what are you doing?" I said, panic seeping into my voice. "You don't need to—"

But instead of going for my throat, the dagger sliced across my arm. I bit my tongue instead of crying out. Crimson red blood pooled and slid down my arm. The soldier pulled out a small vial and held it to my skin

"Fill it up," Ramira said. "We don't know how much is necessary."

I watched my blood fall into the vial, steadying my breathing. But I needn't have worried—every eye was glued to the blood dripping from my arm, slowly filling the glass container. This must be how Riona had felt when Edric did the same thing to her.

Once two vials were full, they released me and left without another word, not bothering to offer me a tourniquet or bandages. So I finished tearing the hem off my dress, pausing as I remembered when I'd made the tear in the first place, in a futile attempt to bandage Gabhann's wound. I stared at the hem, an odd numbness coming over me. Instead of crying again, I wrapped my arm as tight as I could until the bleeding stopped.

I exhaled, grasping the edge of the bench and staring at the floor. Could it be so simple? It was bad news for me if it worked—they would no longer need me. I was as good as dead.

Please don't work, I whispered to whomever might be listening.

>_* >_* >_* >_*

The next few hours (minutes? days?) dragged on. I sat there, counting my heartbeats and breaths as if they were precious commodities. Every slight sound was a death knell in my mind, every faint footstep the executioner coming to end my existence. They might just mop my blood from the ground if they needed more.

Though, what, *exactly* was Ramira going to use the Pennlan stone for? Take over the other kingdoms? The fae realm? Just to have it and say she was the most powerful human in the land?

This new mystery kept my focus when the footsteps returned. I prepared myself for the end, for the worst news, for these precious breaths and heartbeats to become even more so. The door swung open, and Ramira walked in, her face a mask of fury.

"Didn't work?" I asked with a hint of a smirk.

"You will marry my son this afternoon."

That certainly wasn't what I'd been expecting. "I'm sorry?"

"Blood isn't enough. We need a member of the bloodline themselves to wield it. So, this afternoon, you will marry my son." She cracked a smile. "After all, the wife of the king could wield the stone. Your husband will be able to, as well."

I kept my face expressionless. If Riona and I were correct, Leandra hadn't actually been able to use the stone. Clearly, this information hadn't reached Ramira. Eventually, she'd come to the truth. But until she did, I could delay as long as possible.

"And if I refuse?" I asked softly, keeping up my air of defiance so as to not arouse suspicion.

"We will kill your trio of soldiers, including your precious *Ward*."

The way she said his name made my entire body itch. "He means nothing to me."

"Doesn't he? Not the story I've been told."

"By *whom*?" I asked, narrowing my gaze.

"Platt, for one."

"You'd trust the word of a traitor?"

"I would when he's been given a wagonful of gold," she said. "He was quite chatty. And he said that you've become quite attached to the captain of your guard. Perhaps even romantically involved."

I devoted all my energy into keeping my face passive. "No. He means nothing. Kill him if you like."

"I thought you might say that," she said. "So for every day you refuse, we will obliterate a Pennlan village and kill everyone in it."

The air left my chest before I could stop it. "That…You would kill hundreds of innocent people?"

"I would do whatever it takes to have this power," she snarled, taking a step toward me. "I've already made it abundantly clear that I care very little for your citizenry. Now will you comply or do you want more blood on your hands?"

I stared at her, searching for signs of weakness, for something that would give me a leg up into her mind and help me outsmart her. But she was a blank slate, focused on power.

"What do you need the stone for, anyway?" I asked. "What possible reason could you have to need something so powerful?"

"I wouldn't expect a child like you to understand," she replied, straightening. "Now will you marry my son, or do I have to start slaughtering more people?"

I weighed my options. If I agreed, I'd presumably be let out of this cell to get ready. That would give me a little more opportunity to actually *do* something instead of worrying about my own fate.

"Yes," I said, tilting my head up to look at her. "I will."

Chapter Fifty

Ward

"I have to piss."

"Do it somewhere else."

"Kinda hard, El."

I tilted my head against the tentpole they'd tied us to. We'd been here for hours, based on the sun shining through the canvas above our heads. Ayla had been taken somewhere else in a carriage, but we'd been marched the relatively short distance to the Konevellian camp. I didn't really understand why they hadn't killed us—surely, Ayla's cooperation didn't have that much pull. But as the hours wore on, and no one came for us, the real reason became painfully obvious.

We weren't a threat.

How could we be, when our entire army lay dead in a field and our queen was held captive?

"Think they're going to bring us dinner?" Rutley asked, breaking the silence again.

Elodia made another dismissive noise. "No. And quit asking."

"Are you getting annoyed with me or something?"

"Yeah, I am." She twisted as much as her bonds would allow. "Shame you didn't—" She stopped, but we all heard her unsaid words. "Sorry, Rut."

"'S okay. I'm being annoying. Better than sitting in my own thoughts."

As captain, I should've said something rousing and inspiring to cheer them up. But it was hard to be hopeful when the world was so bleak.

"You alive over there, Captain?" Elodia asked.

"Not captain," I said, my voice quiet. "Not anymore."

"You still have us," Rutley said. "For whatever that's worth."

I closed my eyes but regretted it. The battle played on repeat in my mind, along with the bone-crushing guilt. It was hard to be in my own skin, harder still to know that somehow, I was still alive when everyone else was gone. I hadn't fought less valiantly than anyone else.

"What do you think they'll do with us?" Elodia murmured.

"I've always wanted to see Konevell," Rutley replied. "Maybe I'll become a sailor."

"You get seasick on a rowboat."

"So? I could learn."

I tilted my head to the side, glancing out the sliver of canvas as another red tunic walked by. "What do you think they've done with Ayla?"

They both grew silent. "We have to assume they kept her alive, yeah?" Elodia said, after a minute. "They need her to use the stone."

"They need her *and* Riona," I replied. "And they know it."

"You said Riona's stuck in the fae realm?" Rutley said. "So she's safe, then, right?"

I didn't know. I didn't have any answers, and as much as habit wanted me to search for them, I was tired. It was stupid to think I could be of any use in the games of wizards, fae, and queens. I was a simple farm boy, turned soldier, turned captain. Perhaps, like Rutley, I could disappear into the sea, change my name and try to forget the grand failure I'd become.

Rutley sure made it sound appealing. "Maybe we can buy a boat. Head all the way to Forcadel or any of the other far-off nations."

"Forcadel has its own problems," Elodia replied. "None of which we want to be part of."

"I'd go," I said, after a minute. "I'm sure we can steal a boat if we need to."

"That's what I'm talking about!" Rutley said.

"You'd leave Ayla behind?" Even though I couldn't see Elodia's face, I could picture her expression. That raised eyebrow, the smirk dancing on her lips that said she knew the answer to the question she was asking.

"I'm not much use to Ayla anymore," I said, allowing sadness to seep into my voice.

"Aren't you?" Elodia said. "Pennlan is lost, but she's alive. Surely, she'd want to spend the rest of her exiled days with the man of her dreams, eh?"

I could've argued that man wasn't me, but the ghost of her kiss told me differently. She'd been eager for it, ready, even as the world ended around us. I was the one she wanted by her side. And she was the one I wanted by mine. We could start a new life together as double failures. At least we'd have each other.

Again, I craned my neck to look outside. We didn't look to be heavily guarded.

"We need to get out of here," I said, after a minute. "That's step one."

"I thought you'd never ask." Elodia stood up, her hands free of bonds.

Rutley and I stared at her, shocked.

"How long have you been free?" Rutley asked.

"Hours. Just waiting for the two of you to quit bellyaching." She flashed the small arrowhead between her hands she'd used to slice our bonds.

"You mean to tell me we could've left hours ago?" I said, standing up.

"All you had to do was say the word, *Captain*," Elodia said. "I was just waiting for you to pull your head out of your ass and do it."

⤝⤝ ⤝⤝ ⤝⤝ ⤝⤝

Getting out of the camp was easier said than done. We were free of our bonds, but there were still hundreds of red tunics to contend with. They didn't seem to be looking for us, which was good for us, but there were still too many for us just to walk out amongst them.

"We need to find out where they're hiding their uniforms," Rutley said.

"Or knock a couple on the head and steal them."

We didn't have to wait long for an opportunity. Two soldiers who were getting off shift walked into a tent. We made quick work of them; three punches and they were out. I was secretly pleased neither Elodia nor Rutley wanted them dead; there'd been far too much bloodshed already. Rutley and I donned their uniforms and set out in search of a third, which we found in the next tent over.

None of us were comfortable in the red uniforms, but no one gave us a second look as we strolled through the camp. I forced myself to stare ahead and not look for recognizable faces. My only goal was getting out of this camp, perhaps finding a horse, getting Ayla, and…

And after that, we'd figure it out.

"Horses, three o'clock," Rutley said.

I led the way, expecting the three soldiers on post to say something as we walked over and got them ready to leave. But they simply waved us off.

"Wish we could get out of here," one said. "Just waiting for the word to go home."

I hated him, his red uniform, and everything about him, but something prompted me to ask, "What are you waiting for?"

He shrugged, leaning against the post holding the horses in the pen. "No clue. No clue why we were even here. Just seems like…like a dream."

I furrowed my brow as the other two set to finishing the horses. "What do you mean by that?"

"I've never killed a person before, but last night…" He shuddered.

"It's like something evil came over me. Made me into something I wasn't. I just kept fighting. I never got tired until...until just now. You know?"

"C...Um, Sir," Elodia said, already atop the horse. "We have our orders."

But I wasn't quite ready. "Something evil, you say? What did it feel like? When did it start?"

"You didn't feel it?" He finally lifted his gaze to look at me. "You... you don't look..." His eyes widened. "You're the—"

I reared back and punched him in the face, and he toppled backward.

"Well, see, that's why I wanted to get out of here," Elodia said. "What was so important that you had to ask him?"

I stared at the soldier on the ground. They *had* seemed like they were otherworldly. Much like Pennlan's soldiers, Konevell hadn't really engaged in warfare in a few hundred years either. That they'd been so ruthless...

"Ward," Elodia said. "If we stand here much longer, our exit's not going to be so easy. *Let's go*."

⤞ ⤞ ⤞ ⤞

Elodia shouldn't have worried much. Most of the soldiers seemed on the verge of falling asleep—understandable after the night they'd had. But it seemed more than the usual amount of exhaustion. They'd managed to kill everyone in our army without suffering the same casualties. Even outnumbering us...more of them should've been killed.

Was magic involved? And if so...was it fae or something decidedly more wizardly?

But any thoughts I had on the subject evaporated when we crested a hill and saw what lay below in the valley. I'd thought the battlefield was much farther away—and much larger. The twisted, mangled bodies were even more grotesque in the light, and the flies and vultures had begun swarming.

"Guess we have to ride around that," Rutley said, his pale face a little green.

"C'mon," I said, silently urging my horse forward. I had to fight dual urges to scream in fury and descend back into darkness. I kept my gaze glued to the horizon, knowing if I looked down, if I recognized the faces of my soldiers, I would lose it.

But a soft sob came from beside me—Elodia was crying. Strong, stoic, unflappable Elodia was crying. Rutley was as well, his lip trembling under his bushy red beard.

"We won't fail them," she said, hastily wiping her cheeks. "I swear that we'll make sure their sacrifice isn't in vain."

"How are we gonna manage that?" Rutley asked. "We're three people with no weapons or magic."

"I don't know, but we're gonna." She tilted her head up to the sky as we passed a particularly gruesome pile on the ground. "Because we can't just let this be forgotten."

"We won't," I said, after a moment. "I—"

Something caught my eye in the distance—something…glowing.

"What's that?" I said, dismounting before I could stop myself. I walked through the charred grass until I recognized the remains of the tree. My tent was right here. Which meant…

I rushed forward, hope lighting through me. It was Ayla's box—she'd kept it near her at all times, just in case another update arrived from Riona. I frantically threw open the box and dove for the letter inside.

I read it three times in quick succession. Riona… Riona was going to die? Questions, theories, anguish, sadness, fury, grief, despair…they all melded in my mind until I didn't know what to think. She'd written that she was brave, that she'd accepted her fate, but was that true?

It fit, of course. But she must've been scared. Alone.

"What is it, boss?" Rutley asked.

I handed him the letter and he and Elodia read it. I reached into the velvet box and pulled out a small glass vial filled with red liquid. The only thing left of Riona, perhaps. I cradled it to my chest as my heart ached.

Another promising life snuffed out without reason. Ayla would be devastated when she found out.

"But this is… Well, it's not good news," Elodia said. "But it's not… She sent the blood, didn't she? If we can get that to Ayla—"

"And find the stone—" Rutley added.

"Then we can…I don't know, do something, right?" Elodia finished.

Slowly, I nodded, looking at the vial again. Riona would want me to do everything to save her sister and put things right. And Ayla was pretty powerful when she had that stone turned on. Maybe she'd know what to do.

Elodia was right. We couldn't let our fallen soldiers' deaths be in vain. We had to keep fighting until there was nothing left to give.

"Yes," I said. "We have to find Ayla."

Chapter Fifty-One

RIONA

The sun was creeping over the trees when there was the sound of voices beyond the door. My chest seized with fear for a moment before the door opened and Clíodhna walked in. She adjusted her tunic as if she'd been pushed around but stepped inside as cool as a cucumber.

"Did he want me to do this?" I asked.

"Nobody wants these things, child."

"But he thought I could do it." I walked toward her. "That's why he wanted me to stay close, wasn't it? He knew Aldrick would be making his move and—"

"Your grandfather had his secrets, most of which he never shared with me."

"Why didn't you challenge him?" I asked. "Why not fight him the way he fought Birch?"

"I'm old," she said. "Old and not as strong as I used to be. More importantly, if I'm killed, then my people will be at the mercy of whomever Aldrick puts in charge. Somehow, I doubt he would make a choice I'd agree with." She nodded to me. "You're the only one capable of defeating Aldrick."

I nodded, rubbing my hands together. "Not without my sister, I'm not."

"There is the alternative," she said. "You said when you're on death's door…"

"And what's to stop Aldrick from shoving me through it, hm?" I said, running my hand through my hair. "It's far more likely that I die today, Clíodhna."

"I have faith that you'll prevail." She walked to the door. "My time is up. Good luck, Riona."

Then she was gone.

>→ >→ >→ >→

The path to the arena was familiar but like so many other things, there was a strange aura. As if the very air itself was unclear on the future. I should've taken comfort in the fact that it didn't feel like my death was a foregone conclusion, but my hands still shook as I counted the seconds before my challenge.

Still, I found myself lacking regrets. I wouldn't have been able to live with myself had I sat back and let Aldrick kill the trolls. I wasn't just fighting for myself, I was fighting for every creature Aldrick deemed lesser than him, the ones who were expendable and ignorable. Who'd been given a seat at the table by Birch only to have it ripped away.

The roar of the crowd vibrated against my skin, and I tilted my head back to take in the sight. The stands seemed even bigger than when I'd watched the fight between Aldrick and Birch, almost overwhelming in the number of faces jeering down at me. They didn't seem all that friendly, and I wondered what they might do if I *did* kill him.

That was a big *if.*

I felt Aldrick before he materialized, a large wave of power that washed over me like the ocean. He was showing off.

"Fae creatures from near and far, welcome to the Erlking's challenge," he said, his voice booming across the stands. "This day, you will see two enter and one fae leave."

The crowd roared as my stomach turned uncomfortably.

"The victor will become your new Erlking and will have your undying support."

The edict zipped across the crowd and stung the back of my neck. It was done.

"Now, worm." Aldrick opened his hands. "Shall we begin?"

I didn't get a chance to respond. The onslaught was fast and relentless. I'd thought he was doing his worst in the training ring, but it was a pale reflection of the power he now held. I barely had time to breathe, each magical hit finding a new, unbruised part on my body until all I could do was lie there, struggling to breathe.

There was a pause, and I heard his footsteps coming toward me. I couldn't even lift a finger as he knelt beside me.

"Surrender," he whispered.

"W-what?" I lifted my head, finding a little strength to push myself up.

But another flash of magic came and knocked me back.

"Stay down, you moron," he said. "If they think I'm letting you live, they will ask questions."

"You're letting me…" I must've been delusional. "That's not… Why? How? I challenged you. There's no escaping."

"You heard me," he said, rising to his feet again. "One fae will leave. I said nothing about a *half-fae*."

My gaze snapped to his, unable to contain my shock. This was… Had I hit my head harder than I'd thought? Aldrick had never shown anybody compassion, least of all me, and I'd openly challenged him in front of the entire fae realm.

"Why?" I asked.

He shifted, almost looking…uncomfortable? Nervous? "Because as insufferable as you are, there's a purpose for you, and I'm not going back on my deal."

My stomach dropped. "Deal? What kind of deal?"

"One that requires you to still have a pulse," he said. "So if you value your life, you will do as I say and stay on your back."

But who? Who could want me alive? My thoughts immediately went to my sister, but that made no sense. Cade, perhaps? Was there some agreement he'd made with Birch to keep me alive? Or was…

A cold shiver came over me.

"Aldrick, you didn't…" I whispered, slowly meeting his gaze. "You didn't make a deal with…with…*him*, did you? What could he *possibly* have given you that…" Realization dawned. "Did he help you kill Birch?"

"He might've given me a potion or two," he said with a small twitch. "Enhanced my focus, allowed me to tap into more magic. He's quite good at what he does."

"And in return, you hand me over?" I said, finding more strength as the moments passed. "I think you got the raw end of the deal."

"How's that?"

I opened my mouth to respond but thought better of it. I hadn't a clue how the future would play out and telling Aldrick—or anyone—that I wasn't able to use the Pennlan stone seemed like playing a card I should keep close to my vest.

"Because he's not to be trusted," I said, after a moment. "And whatever he's promised, he'll be sure to take it away just as fast."

"I'm not going to discuss it with you," he said. "Now lie down and pretend to die or else I'll have to—"

"You'll have to what?" I barked a laugh. "You played your hand too soon, Uncle. Now that I know you need me alive, I have the upper hand."

"I highly doubt that. I said alive, not conscious." He smirked. "And after Eoghan is finished with you, I'm sure you'll be eager to meet the same fate as your mother. So call it a delayed execution."

"No." I balled my fists. "I refuse to be a pawn in Eoghan's games anymore. If you want out of this ring, you'll have to kill me, or…" I cracked a smile. "Die yourself."

"Very well," he said with a sigh. "I tried to be merciful."

The attacks began anew. But as painful, as horrific, as twisted as my body felt, I could tell he was pulling his punches. I needed to remain conscious, in this realm, in this arena. As long as I could stand and fight, he'd have to push me closer and closer to death.

And if he pushed me over the edge, then Eoghan would take care of him.

Aldrick was relentless, his blows aiming for my head in ways I had no hope of fighting against. If I lost consciousness for even a moment, Aldrick would claim victory and my chance to escape Eoghan's plans would be gone.

Crunch, crunch, crunch. I was walking in the garden.

Bam. I was flung back to the edge of the arena.

There was a cold breeze on my cheeks.

There was unimaginable pain as another bone broke.

I opened my eyes into the dim light of the garden and turned around, looking for a way back to reality.

"Riona."

Aoibheann stood behind me, somewhere between the dream world and the afterlife. She was clearer than she'd ever been before, though the edges of her form were still blurry. Her golden eyes were framed by thick dark lashes, her long black hair braided as it had been in the troll's memories.

"I have to go back," I called. "Aldrick is—"

"I know," Aoibheann said. "I will be back when you've taken the throne."

She opened her hand, revealing the white magic again. Immediately, the same magic in my veins reached for it, turning on like a flame on a pile of dry kindling. I smiled for a moment before…

…cracking open my eyes to the gray sky. The roar of the crowd was deafening; Aldrick must've declared himself the winner. But there was white magic warming my fingers, my toes, my legs—healing me. I flexed my fingers and moved my head slowly from side to side. Then I rolled onto my side and gingerly pushed myself onto my knees.

The crowd grew silent. Aldrick, whose back was to me, turned slowly as I came shakily to my feet.

"Not gone yet," I whispered, my throat scratchy and parched.

Whatever Aoibheann had done, however she'd unlocked this magic, it was fully at my fingertips, as if Ayla and the Pennlan stone were right next to me.

Aldrick seemed to know it, too. "W-what is this... You aren't supposed to be able to—"

I didn't let him finish, knowing that my time with this magic was short. I let it explode from my body, flying toward him with all the ferocity and anger I felt at his multilevel betrayal. He hadn't just killed my beloved grandfather, he'd done so at the bidding of a man who'd demonstrated his capacity for evil time and time again. And Aldrick thought himself to be *above* treachery, like he had a chance against Eoghan.

My fury grew deeper, thinking of how he'd tortured the trolls for his own amusement, how within hours of his ascension, he'd terrified every lesser creature in the castle. How he considered himself better than everyone, when he was nothing more than a traitor.

And when my fury was gone, and the light faded, there was nothing left of my uncle but the Erlking's crown.

The white magic escaped my grip and disappeared back into the aether where it lived. Without it keeping me upright, I fell to my knees, my hands grasping at the dirt. A cold breeze brushed my ear, and Clíodhna whispered:

"Get up, Riona. Show them no weakness."

Gathering strength from places I didn't know I had, I pushed myself back to my feet. I walked as best I could on stinging legs toward the crown and used a butterfly to pick it up. I held it in my hands, staring at it and marveling at how something so...simple could signify so much.

And without a second thought, I shoved it onto my head.

Chapter Fifty-Two

Cade

It was dark and smelled of acid, but my mind and body were intact. I opened my eyes and saw nothing, but my staff reached my hand, and it lit up with a soft glow. The cavernous stomach was all around us, and there was…

Screaming. Someone was screaming.

I jumped to my feet, the magic in my staff growing brighter until every inch of the stomach was illuminated. Then I saw it…

The ones who'd been swallowed before us. Screaming as they flailed and paddled in the acid of the creature's stomach. Three were already still, their eyes wide as they floated in the yellow muck. But the rest were slowly, agonizingly…

Movement to my left as Cluny appeared with a bow and arrow. In three movements, he fired off arrows into the surviving soldiers, killing them instantly.

"Why did you—?" I asked.

"Mercy," he said, shaking his head. "Too bad there won't be anyone left here to do the same for us."

I turned around to look at the crew, most of whom were staring over the edge of the ship with determined faces. Aldonza shook her head, moving from one side to the other.

"It's already eating through the hull," she said. "We won't have long."

A drop fell from the top of the stomach, landing on the deck of the ship and eating a hole in the wood almost instantly.

"Now might be a nice time for you to use your wizardly magic," Onor said, glaring at me. "Or maybe create us one of those portals to safety?"

I tried, but I already knew what would happen. "I can't. Something about this creature is keeping me from reaching the outside world." I lifted my staff toward a spot on the upper stomach and fired off a ball of energy. It bounced harmlessly off before landing with a splash in the acid. I held onto the railing of the ship as it bobbed in the waves.

"Nothing," I said with a sad shake of my head. "There's nothing I can do."

"Well, then I guess we should just drink until it takes us," Aldonza said, walking down the steps to the bottom of the ship. "No use wasting good ale."

⤐ ⤐ ⤐ ⤐

The crew followed and within moments, I was alone on the deck. It was eerily quiet, save the random sounds of *drip-drip-drip* of the acid falling into the bottom of the stomach. I could, at least, deflect those from falling onto the deck of the ship, but it was just delaying the inevitable.

I found myself thinking of home—but not the island. Of Pennlan. Ayla, Ward, Riona. Sadness that they'd never know what happened to me threatened to bring tears to my eyes.

Shaking my head, I cursed my bad luck. If only I'd kept my focus on the *seod croí* and not on trying to find H'sipotu.

You were, a kinder voice than I deserved reminded me. *Aldonza knew about the* fuath.

Of course she had, and she'd neglected to tell me that they'd killed each other off a thousand years ago, and the *seod croí* was lost to the depths of the ocean. If she'd only been a bit less reticent with information, we could've skipped *all* of this.

But your mother...

I scoffed. My sweet mother was too enamored with this island and the superstitions to see the reality. There was just plain old magic here, and they had the power to manipulate it. There was no sentient part of the island that wielded punishments for bad behavior. There was no greater design to my life. I was just a kid unluckily born a wizard and whose life would unluckily end in the stomach of this monster.

A monster who'd been terrorizing the people of H'sipotu for a thousand years.

A monster who was the most powerful creature I'd ever encountered.

My eyes popped open. "It can't be. That would be…"

That would be too much like fate.

But I couldn't shake this feeling, this *notion* that maybe I wasn't just bounced around from place to place. That maybe I *had* met Aldonza for a reason. That I was meant to be here, in this stomach, because… because…

I held my breath and relaxed my body, the way Nire'huf had taught me. I let go of my agitation, my dismissal of the island's superstitions, my grip on magic. The desperation that I was seeing the end of my short life. All of it floated away from my body as my shoulders dropped and my hands relaxed on my knees.

I let my magical eye drift in the abyss, desiring to go nowhere in particular, but allowing myself to be drawn to the powerful. To the magnificent. To the source that had turned this fearsome creature into a monster the size of a mountain.

Then…then I saw it.

Pulsing, giving unnatural power and strength to this creature, deeply embedded in the stomach muscles.

"Cade…"

My concentration shattered as my eyes opened. "What?"

Aldonza and the crew had reemerged. She pointed to the back half of her ship, which was starting to tip farther into the acid. "You need to figure yourself out here quick or else we're going to be in trouble."

"I'm going as fast as I can," I snapped.

Again, I closed my eyes and let the magic of the air touch my skin, whispering truths to me. It still had my last query in its grasp, rippling through the space as it reached the edge of the stomach. Like a drum, it throbbed against the stomach, searching, looking, finding…

"Cade—"

"Shut up."

I didn't mean to be rude, but I couldn't break my concentration again. Not when I could feel the pull of power.

There.

It was buried deep, and there was a good chance I wouldn't be able to get to it, but there was no other option but to try. I jumped to my feet, casting a protective spell around myself and walking toward the edge of the ship. Then I jumped into the acidic pool—earning screams of concern from the crew.

"You aren't going to leave us, you—"

Whatever Aldonza called me was lost as my bubble sank into the acid. Even protected by magic, the acid burned the edges, promising a painful death should my concentration waver. I let myself sink, holding my breath as my head dipped beneath the yellow liquid.

With my staff in my hand and most of my concentration on keeping myself from being melted, I kicked and swam toward the source of the magic. Toward the thing calling to me on an almost visceral level. In the back of my mind, I could hear the shrieks of concern from the crew, and I just prayed I could be fast enough to save us all.

My magic-protected feet reached the bottom of the stomach, softly pressing against the taut surface. Once more I closed my eyes, searching for the source of the power. It was right near here.

I gathered as much magic as I could muster and attacked the stomach muscles. But just like before, the creature was too strong. I wasn't powerful enough.

I was running out of air, so I kicked my way back to the surface, taking in a big gulp of air. There wasn't much left of the ship now, and Aldonza and the rest were clinging to the mast wearing panicked looks. She caught my gaze, and I shook my head.

I could cast a protection spell on them, as I'd done for myself, but I wouldn't be able to hold it forever, and I didn't see a way out of here otherwise. With a deep breath, I steeled my resolve and dove back into the acid, kicking down until I came to the spot I'd been attacking.

I hit it with everything I had while still maintaining my own protection. And when I couldn't hold my breath anymore, I returned to the surface. And back down. Again and again…and I accomplished exactly nothing. Not even a mark on the stomach.

The next time I came to the surface, there was nothing left of the ship except a small piece the crew was huddled on. But they no longer looked panicked—in fact, they almost seemed resolute.

And before my eyes, Cluny let go and fell into the acid.

I moved quickly, casting a protection spell on him and nearly losing mine in the process.

"What are you doing?" he called.

"I'm not giving up yet," I barked. "Just give me… Give me a little more time."

"We don't have any more time," Aldonza said. "Whatever you're doing… It's not working. We just have to face facts."

"Let me try one more thing," I said.

I dove back under, but this time…this time I returned to that peaceful state where I was no longer in control. The magic in my body floated like a leaf in a river, and for the first time in my life, I didn't ask of it. I simply let it exist.

And as I did, the magic surrounding me—the magic in the air, the magic in the stomach acid, the magic in the stone itself—came to join it. Like a gathering of torchlights that illuminated a dark space, they mingled and understood each other in a way I wouldn't have thought possible. And as I lay there, my lungs burning from lack of air, I simply asked it a question.

Will you help me?

The magic exploded from my body. Even though I could see nothing, I felt the layers of the monster's stomach rip away, rivers of blood mixing with the yellow, until finally…finally the pulsing object came dislodged and floated toward me.

I reached toward it, closing my fingers around the jagged edges—then the whole world went white.

➻ ➻ ➻ ➻

I was still me, still in my body, and yet, there was something *otherworldly* coming from the thing in my hand. It was as if the entire world was at my fingertips, and my own magic was an amusement in comparison. I barely needed to think for it to move at my whim, rising in a tidal wave of power to disintegrate the creature around us.

Cool water rushed over me as I sank into the water, but I somehow didn't need to breathe anymore. As long as I held onto this thing, this potent, *powerful* stone.

The *seod croí*.

Holding the Pennlan stone had never felt like this, though I could sense the magnitude of power swimming beneath the surface. That piece wasn't meant for me, held back by a myriad of charms and spells to bind it to the Pennlan line. But *this* was mine, unbridled, untethered, uninhibited by anything but my own imagination.

You could make her love you.

The thought came unwelcome from the deepest, darkest depths of my soul. And I believed, though I had no clue how, that the power in this stone was enough to turn her heart, should I ask it to. Whether by fear, or by show of force, or by threat or—

What am I thinking?

I could never hurt Ayla. Not in a million years. The other voice came fast and furious, staring at these dark thoughts with the sort of incredulity that they deserved. The darkness fell back, biding its time but not disappearing. Promising to return when the moment was right.

With effort, I wrenched the stone from my hand and stuffed it into my pocket.

The spell broken, I opened my eyes into a dark world. I was sinking into the ocean, the light from the sun too far for me to see. My chest was burning, and I was starting to see spots. The call of the *seod croí* was tempting, promising to allow me to remain under water as long as I wanted, that I would never die, that I would live forever… Even through the fabric of my pants, it was calling to me again.

But I didn't need it. I didn't *want* it.

My staff lit up, pushing me up, up, up, up. I burst through to the surface, coughing and gasping for breath as the sun warmed my skin. The waves were high, and it was only after several washed over me that I realized it was because of *me*. Because I'd disintegrated *Law'ek'ub*…and hopefully not the rest of the crew.

"Aldonza?" I called, turning around in the ocean. "Anyone out there?"

First, nothing. My heart sank into my boots. Had I taken them in the process?

Then, "You sure do put on a show, wizard."

I turned toward the source of the voice, where I found Aldonza hanging onto a piece of her ship that had survived—and the rest of her crew was, too.

I smiled at Cluny, who nodded his thanks. "Did you get what you were after?"

I shivered, feeling the weight of the *seod croí* piece in my pocket. "I did. And I want to get this as far away from me as possible."

"Well, better start swimming," Aldonza said. "Long way back to shore."

I smiled at her. "Maybe I can help you out."

I started with the mast, raising it out of the ocean. Then I formed the deck beneath it, the hull, the sails, even down to the ropes. Then I gathered each of the crew and myself and put us back aboard the ship.

"See? I knew it'd be handy to have a wizard around," Aldonza said with a smile.

CHAPTER FIFTY-THREE

AYLA

As predicted, I was released from my prison cell, but I was escorted by five guards so I couldn't call it freedom. They stuffed me inside a carriage and brought me back to the nice inn where I'd been staying before the attack. They marched me up the staircase to the top floor suite, which was empty save a boy roughly nine years old.

The boy who would be my husband already matched me in height —perhaps all the Konevellian royal family were giants. But his face was youthful, still sporting baby cheeks and smooth amber skin. I might've found him somewhat adorable if he hadn't worn his mother's trademark sneer.

"So you're to be my wife?" he said, spitting the word as if I were a new toy he didn't want. "You're ugly."

"And you're in need of manners," I replied. "Which I'll be happy to teach you once we return to Pennlan castle."

He smirked. "You aren't going to live long enough. Once we're married, and I can use the stone, you're as good as dead."

I assumed that might be the case, so I shrugged. "Your mother says they have my sister. Is that true? Because, you know, the stone is useless without her."

"I'm sure I don't know the details of who we have and don't have," he said, brushing his hands on his tunic. "All I know is I have to say the vows then test the stone. Then we'll be rid of you."

I should've known he wouldn't have the information I needed. But

I'd still try to wheedle it out of him. "I'm sure if your mother has her, you would've seen her. She looks like me, just, you know. Fae. Green eyes. Black hair."

"I don't care to even notice the servants who bring me food. I don't know why I'd notice some disgusting creature from the north."

Well, that was a dead end. The urge was strong to pull him over my knee and spank him for his attitude, but I doubted I'd be able to manage it, considering he was as big as I was. So instead, I walked to the window and looked out, toying with different ideas.

The door opened and I braced myself—but nothing could've prepared me for who walked in with Ramira and Galliford.

Roísín.

Anger flared from somewhere deep inside, but I took it out on the inside of my palms as I dug my fingernails into them. I took a deep, calming breath, making sure to get one good glare in before I let my attention shift to Ramira and Galliford, the latter of whom was carrying something in his hand.

My blood.

Why would they still have my blood? I watched him hold it carefully, as if it were a precious jewel.

"Your Majesty, I understand the haste, but how do we know this is going to work?" Galliford asked. "And how will we *know* that it's working and not just some magic trick?"

I started, turning fully around.

"He's shown himself to be trustworthy thus far," Ramira said, walking to her son and adjusting his tunic. "After all, we were victorious, as he promised. There's no reason to doubt that this will work as he says."

My blood ran cold as I dropped all desire to mask my emotions. They couldn't be talking about...

"Tell me you didn't," I whispered. "You didn't...ally yourselves with *him*."

Ramira finally seemed to notice me and gave me a satisfied smirk.

"You know, for all your complaining about him, he's quite generous."

"In exchange for something he wants," I said, taking a step forward. "What could he possibly have promised you?"

"Isn't it obvious?" She smiled. "He came to us about a month ago and told me that if I marched on Pennlan to claim it for ourselves, he would make sure we were victorious. Our soldiers were given three days' worth of strength, as well as a warrior's edge." She smirked. "It's no coincidence only three of your soldiers survived."

My stomach was twisting. Eoghan had cast a spell on her whole army? "And what are you to give him in return?"

"He merely asked for access to my son and the Pennlan stone," she said.

I burst into laughter. "And you believed him?"

"Only those who are easily misguided would be bamboozled by him," Ramira said, finally turning to me with a sneer on her face. "He made you a weak queen because he intended to mold you to his will. Until, of course, he found someone he could more easily *manipulate*." She smirked. "Your sister, it seems, is weaker than you."

"And he took her blood so he could be rid of her," I replied. "You don't know him like I do. He doesn't want partners. He wants the power for himself. Do you even understand what you're helping him do? Do you know about Laughlan and—"

"I'm tired of listening to you," Ramira replied with a wave of her hand. "Galliford, do the honors so we can be rid of her."

Galliford walked over, nervously placing the blood on a table twenty paces from me, before plucking a book and flipping through the pages. It was then I realized the blood wasn't mine—it was *Riona's*. Another vial from Eoghan, most likely.

The stone was around Ramira's neck, and she was a healthy distance away from the blood. If I moved from this spot, I would have only seconds to combine them. The soldiers lining the room wouldn't give me much time. But once I had the stone and Riona's blood… Maybe I had a shot at saving myself after all.

And if it didn't work, they'd probably just shoot me with their arrows.

Please work.

"Now," Galliford said, clearing his throat, "Dearly—"

"Expedite it," Ramira barked.

He gave her a look. "If we want to be sure the marriage is binding, we'll have to do this the right way."

She rolled her eyes, and he cleared his throat, beginning again. I scanned the room, planning my attack while trying to channel Ward's brilliance. What would he do if he were here?

No use thinking like that. You can't fight the way he can.

I would have to do it my own way.

"Now, Manfred, repeat after me," Galliford said. "I, Manfred—"

I released a gasp as I buried my head in my hands, faking loud sobbing. Between my hands, I checked to see if anyone had bought my sudden distress. Galliford seemed confused, Manfred bored, Ramira... Ramira rolled her eyes.

"What is it?" she said.

"I just... I'm sorry. It's all just hitting me." I took a step away from the de facto altar, waiting for someone to come for me. But they just watched. "Gabhann, my soldiers. It's happening so soon. So quickly. I just..." I took another step. "I haven't had time to process all of it. I'm just so..." Another step—I was within striking distance of the table with Riona's blood now. "I'm so devastated. Another betrayal by Eoghan."

Galliford lowered his book. "Understandably so, you—"

"Enough of this," Ramira said. "I don't care if you're hysterical. You aren't going to live long enough for it to matter anyway. Get back here and *marry* my son."

I swiped the vial, slipping it inside my tunic sleeve. I turned back to them, waiting to see if anyone had noticed. But as I walked back over to the would-be altar, no one said a word, too focused on me.

I nodded, wiping my eyes. "I'm s-sorry. Please c-continue."

Galliford watched me with something like pity in his eyes. "Your Majesty, surely we can spare a moment for her to get herself together. It's not becoming for a bride to be crying on her wedding day."

Ramira released a growl of frustration and marched over to where Galliford stood, ripping the book out of his hand and snarling at him. "If you won't get on with it, I will do it myself. Now—"

I snatched the necklace around Ramira's neck and yanked as hard as I could. The stone released from its chain. Ramira grabbed for it, but I dove to the ground. With a cry, I smashed the vial of blood with the stone.

The world went white.

Voices exploded between my ears, singing and demanding to know how I wanted to use the power within my hands. Did I want to exact revenge? Did I want to destroy everything in Konevell like they'd done to us?

No.

First, the magic sought out those in the battlefield, and I held my breath, hoping it might find someone alive. But there wasn't a soul still stirring in the bloody grass. So I asked the magic to erect a graveyard, to honor each of the Pennlan soldiers who'd given their lives. I didn't know if that was possible, and yet…yet it happened exactly as I'd asked.

Then, this gentle power found every single Konevellian on Pennlan soil and transported them over the border—even Galliford and Manfred. I wasn't in the business of being a bloodthirsty queen like Ramira. They would live to see another day—as long as they stayed on their side of the border.

The only thing left was Ramira.

I opened my eyes to the sight of her cowering on the ground, blinded by the light of the magic. "You've crossed a line no queen should ever have crossed."

She lowered her hands, gazing up at me as if I were the most fearsome thing she'd seen. "P-please…s-show mercy."

"Why should I show you *mercy* when you showed none to my people?" I said, stepping forward.

"It was the wizard," she stammered. "It was him. He made me do it."

I chuckled. "He promised you the world, didn't he? Said as long as you delivered the stone to him, you could have dominion over the humans. Or something along those lines?"

Her silence was damning. "Please, spare my son, at least."

"He was already spared," I said. "Perhaps, in time, Konevell can regain Pennlan's trust, and we can be friendly. But Konevell has much to repent for. And for now, we have much bigger concerns."

"S-so you're going to let me live?"

I could've killed her. Obliterated her the way I'd killed Edric. But I found myself unable to stomach more bloodshed. Like Edric, she was but a pawn in Eoghan's games. He'd find out she failed him and mete out his own punishment. My guess was, he wouldn't be as kind.

"I won't be the one to end your life," I said. "But if even *one* Konevellian soldier sets foot in my kingdom again, I will destroy everyone in your kingdom. Do you understand?"

"Y-yes…" She bowed. "Your Majesty."

Then she was gone, returned to her castle alongside her son.

The power died down, and the room returned to normal. I was standing, the stone in my outstretched hand, covered in blood, panting loudly as I came back to myself.

"So…"

I nearly jumped out of my skin, turning to the left where Ward, Elodia, and Rutley were waiting with wide eyes and open mouths. Ward opened his fist, showing another vial of blood in his hand.

"I take it you don't need this?"

"No," I said weakly. "No, today… Today I think I saved the day all on my own."

CHAPTER FIFTY-FOUR

WARD

"She's...*what?*"

There was plenty to catch Ayla up on, but I was pleased Riona's update had come before I'd had to tell her otherwise. I was sure the story was both long and ridiculous, and involved Riona bravely doing something incredibly stupid. But I couldn't deny that the dark world had seemed a little brighter when the box lit up and there was good news inside.

Ayla's magic had completely emptied the city of Konevellian soldiers and anyone who allied themselves with the enemy country. A magical barrier had also been erected along the riverfront, preventing anyone not allowed from setting foot on Pennlan soil.

"Including, I hope, Eoghan," she said, staring out the window of the inn. "But he's made it clear that he doesn't really need to be here to cause problems."

She confirmed my theory that he'd bewitched the Konevellian soldiers to fight more ruthlessly, and I thought perhaps he might've done the same to the queen.

But she shook her head. "Ramira was twisted in her own mind. The sort of power-hungry person Eoghan found easy to manipulate."

"Yet, you spared her."

"Eoghan will find her," she said definitively. "He'll probably be very angry that his little plan was foiled again." She cracked a smile. "I wish I could see his face when he finds out."

Down below, two Pennlan soldiers patrolled the streets. We'd finally gotten our reinforcements from the other cities, and they'd fallen into line under my leadership almost immediately. They'd had to pass the battlefield; they knew what had been lost. Even the old captain from Críoch had deferred to me, telling me how proud he was of his former subordinate. But it fell short. I couldn't shake this feeling of failure, that every headstone in that cemetery was my fault.

"Eoghan's declared war on us," she said. "We've got to find as many allies as we can before Eoghan takes them for himself." She shook her head. "Maybe the other kingdoms will listen." She shook her head. "And if they don't, my captain needs to prepare my army."

Captain. It seemed like such a ridiculous title, considering. That anyone was even listening to me anymore was a miracle. That Ayla still wanted to be in the same room, even more.

"Ward?"

"Do you still think I'm the one who should be leading them?"

"I told you, Ward, I want you by my side," she said, walking up to me. "Whether that's as my captain or just as…" She slipped her hand into mine. "I don't want to face what's coming without you."

I stared down at her, at the glimmer of green in her gaze. There was a new confidence about her. Almost like she'd aged twenty years in the past day and a half. When she stared into my eyes as she told me she wanted me by her side, I knew she no longer *needed* me the way she had in the past. She'd finally come to realize her own potential, as I'd seen all along.

But wanting? That made two of us.

So I leaned down and captured her lips in a sweet kiss.

>⇥ >⇥ >⇥ >⇥

There was a certain air of nerves amongst the soldiers as they drilled in the barracks. Captain Treen had been killed in the battle, so Rutley was running the drills. Although these soldiers hadn't seen a day of battle, they seemed to understand what they could be up against—and if they didn't, I was sure Rutley would let them know.

But it wasn't Rutley I was looking for.

I found her deep in conversation with another captain, this one newly arrived from the far eastern city of Hillview. They both saw me, saluted immediately, and the captain dismissed himself as I called Elodia over to me.

"How are they looking?" I asked.

"Not ready."

"I'm sure you'll whip them into shape."

"Not if we're going up against a magically-enhanced army again," Elodia said, her shoulders tense. "I don't even know how we'd defend against that."

"Well, we'll have Riona next time," I said. "And get this, she's now the Erlking."

"Wait, she survived? And *what?*"

I waved her off. "I'm sure we'll find out more when we get back to Pennlan. Which brings me to what I wanted to talk with you about." I turned back toward the soldiers. "You know, I'm a terrible captain."

"Yes, you are."

I scowled. "I mean, you could've qualified that with—"

"Absolutely not," she said. "You suck at this."

"Fine, yes, I do." I turned to her. "So I'm giving you the job."

Her face shifted so quickly I was afraid she'd pulled a muscle. "I'm sorry…what?"

"Look, we have no clue what stupid thing Eoghan is going to throw at us next," I said, looking out at the ocean beyond. "But he's clearly not above recruiting people. We have to be on our guard, and Ayla needs someone out there looking for the fourth stone. I can't oversee all these soldiers and handle Eoghan and…whatever he's going to do." I turned to her. "So I'm doing that thing you told me to do. Donate? Defer?"

"Delegate," Elodia said weakly. "Are you… You haven't thought about this, have you?"

"I have. A lot, actually." I looked at the ground. "And I can't be in two places at once, as much as I want to be. I'd much rather put the guard in the hands of the *one* person who never let me forget what my real job was. I know you'll do great."

She swallowed. "If you're sure."

"I am. Ayla's already given her blessing." It took everything in my power to keep my face passive. "We had a nice chat about it earlier."

"Mm. I see a hickey on your neck."

My hand flew to my neck, even though there was no way any such thing could've occurred. Experienced, Ayla certainly was not, but I was looking forward to teaching her. Still, Elodia snickered unprofessionally into her hand.

"Very funny," I said.

"I see it now. You can't be captain and get up her skirt—"

"That's not what's going on!"

"Oh, Ward, how *scandalous* it'll be for the queen to be screwing her captain. But some farm boy? Oh, that'll just—"

"*Will you shut up?*"

⤜⤜⤜⤜

With the border magic holding strong, Ayla and I decided it was time to return to Pennlan. Elodia remained in the city to work through the reassignment of soldiers after the decimation of the Orapus- and

Pennlan-based ones. She seemed eager to complete the task, throwing herself into watching each soldier and asking about their skill set. I was happy to hand the job over to someone else.

We took a group of twenty soldiers to escort us back to the castle, and this time, I rode inside the carriage with Ayla as we plotted our next move.

"We need to find more alliances," she said softly. "Eoghan has Konevell. Does he have the others under his thumb? Should we be worried about them invading? I want to know sooner rather than later."

"We can send Rutley and others to scope it out," I said.

She shook her head. "As much as I don't want to lean on Riona, we need answers faster than Rutley can ride."

"Maybe she's figured out how to conjure a portal," I said with a wry smile. "Or maybe Cade…"

"Cade…" She sighed. "I'm going to slap him something silly when he gets back. What a time to disappear." She looked at her fingernails, but there was worry on her face. "I hope…I pray Eoghan hasn't gotten to him."

"Cade can hold his own."

"Not against Eoghan," she said. "He might've gotten better with the trolls, but he's still…Eoghan taught him everything he needed to retrieve the stone and nothing more." She sighed, staring out the window, and I read the unsaid end to her sentence.

"Cade's fine, I'm sure of it," I said, reaching across to take her hand. "But back to these other countries… What are you looking to accomplish?"

"First, find out if they've been in contact with Eoghan," she said. "Then, if they're willing to join our alliance. I fear…" She chewed her lip. "Somehow, I get the feeling history is about to repeat itself."

The thought chilled me. "That would require him to find another two stones *and* take yours."

"I wouldn't put it past him." She adjusted her legs. "I've been thinking about lines of succession. About what would happen if I were to die. Obviously, the stone didn't work when Ramira named herself queen of Pennlan. It has to do with blood." She sat back. "And right now, Riona's unable to use the stone. Because I live. But what if I die?"

"Then Riona would be queen," I said softly. "And have the ability to use the stone."

"If I were Eoghan, that would be the *first* thing I'd do," she said, meeting my gaze. "Now that he knows only a sovereign of my bloodline can wield the stone, what's stopping him from slitting my throat?"

"Me." I leaned toward her. "I will protect you."

She waved me off, as if I were focusing on the wrong thing. "If Eoghan gets the other stones, Ward, then kills me, all he'll have to do is bewitch Riona and he'll have all four pieces at his disposal."

"Riona could fight him," I said. "Maybe being Erlking has given her newfound powers?"

But even as I said the words, I recalled Birch being hesitant to go head-to-head with Eoghan, scared of the bewitchment magic and what it could mean for the most powerful fae in existence. Riona was still as susceptible as ever.

"What do you think we should do about it?" I asked.

"I don't know," she said, looking at her hands. "We need to talk with Riona. And we all need to be prepared for the very worst…and hope for the best."

Chapter Fifty-Five

Riona

Ward's scrawled name was awfully close to Ayla's. The use of *we* also gave me pause. But any joy I felt was dampened by the mention of that damn wizard and his meddling. It seemed all our chaos was coming from him, and I, for one, was getting pretty sick of it. I almost wanted him to show his face so I could do to him what I'd done to Aldrick.

Almost.

In the moments after my fight, I'd convened an *Arwein* quickly. Coednin was unsurprisingly reticent about throwing his allegiance to me, but when I threatened to find someone in his ranks who would, he clammed up and approved me. Clíodhna, obviously, was a full-throated approval, and Lynton, who I'd reinvited to the table, even wore a smile as he gave his approval as well.

I'd then gone to the infirmary where they'd patched me up so I was no longer suffering from internal injuries. Then…then I found myself standing in front of the stone door leading to the Erlking's throne.

It was very clearly mine now. The magic that permeated the space seemed to be as familiar as the hair on my head. Even the details of the door had changed. What were once thorns and roses were now butterflies and green fields. I found myself focusing on that instead of the raucous conversation happening just beyond the doors.

Clíodhna's cold magic brushed my cheek as she appeared beside me. "Looks different. But I'm sure it works the same." She nodded toward the room. "Seems like they're eager to speak with their new Erlking."

"Why do I feel like they're just waiting for me to make a mistake so they can eat me?" I whispered. "I shouldn't have done this. I'm not *powerful* enough to do this."

"I daresay you are, considering the very clear statement you made in the arena yesterday," she said with a smirk. "And that fear will keep them in line. As will the allegiance of your *Arwein*."

"Coednin is going to find someone to replace me, like he did with Birch," I said, chewing my thumbnail. "I shouldn't have—"

"What should you have done instead, then?" she asked.

I didn't have an answer. It had all seemed like the right thing to do. "There are bigger problems afoot, though."

I told her about Aldrick's deal with Eoghan, and how the wizard seemed to be behind the invasion of Pennlan.

"I wouldn't be surprised if he was messing with Cade, too, wherever he is," I said.

She nodded. "Your first priority is to the safety and security of the people of this realm."

"They won't be safe or secure if Eoghan marches across the border and kills everyone," I said. "Remember, I saw what happened when

Laughlan had the stone. And he was a nice guy to begin with. I shudder to think…"

She waved me off. "You are my Erlking, but you're still my granddaughter, so I can still give you advice. Your focus should be on your people, building your alliances in this realm, winning the hearts and minds of creatures big and small. The sooner you do that, the easier it will be to call on those alliances, should the wizard be foolish enough to show his face."

I shifted uncomfortably. "I think we would be foolish to expect him not to."

"Let your sister and her stone handle the wizard for the time being, until there's a crisis to be solved," Clíodhna said. "Or you'll find yourself an Erlking without a people."

I rubbed my hands together, disagreeing with her but not wanting to argue. Then remembering that technically *she* was my underling, and I could do what I wanted without heeding her advice. The thought was unnerving, as if I were somehow playing in a space I had no business being in.

"Thanks for the advice," I said with a smile. "I suppose it's time for me to meet my people, hm?"

>⇥ >⇥ >⇥ >⇥

The noise was immediate and deafening, starting even before I sat on the throne. It was hard to figure out who to talk with first, with all the creatures clamoring for attention. Was this really what Birch had seen all the time? It was so overwhelming.

Not to mention the worry about *who* to pick first. Did I show favoritism to a *daoine maithe*? Or did I select one of the smaller creatures bouncing around above the fray? Pick a *sidheog*?

"Uuum…" I swallowed hard and sang a counting song. "You."

It was a forest fae, and the clamoring turned into groans of criticism. He approached slowly, grasping his hands as if he thought I might blow him across the room. He spoke, but I couldn't hear what he was saying due to the clamoring.

"What?" I cried, pointing to my ear.

It was then that I realized the Erlking had to silence everyone—and I hadn't a clue how to do that. But just like the door, the magic from the chair rose to meet me. And as I pushed it out into the room, the squawks and yelling grew quieter until there was nothing but a soft buzzing.

I smiled. "That's better. Now, what's your issue?"

"Well, you see, I have this plot of land in the forest kingdom…"

Whatever the forest fae had to say was lost as the room faded around me. I would've thought I was going insane, except for the familiar brush of cold air on my cheeks, and the sound of feet crunching against dead grass.

"Am I…asleep?" I blinked.

"No, you're just much more accessible now."

Aoibheann walked out from under the portcullis, a warm smile on her face. Now she was fully formed, with nary a blur on her. She seemed almost *proud* of me as she approached but didn't come any closer.

"What is this place?" I asked. "And why can I access it?"

"This is a place between the dead and the living," she said. "You can access it when you, yourself, are between the dead and the living."

I swallowed hard. I'd been here too many times to be comfortable with that. "Can everybody?"

"No, you are…very special, Riona. Your mother was, too. But because her blood wasn't diluted, she could come and go as she pleased." Aoibheann smiled. "She and I were good friends in her youth. She would spend all her nighttimes playing with me. I never had a child myself, so she was…"

She grew somber, and I could read between the lines.

"Now that you have the power of the Erlking, you have bridged the gap created by your father's blood to reach this place as needed," she finished. "And not a moment too soon. We have much to discuss."

"What is this white magic?" I asked, trying to step forward but finding myself stuck. "And why does it seem like it comes from…you?"

She grimaced, as if she carried a heavy burden she didn't want to share with me. "There is…one more secret about the *seod croí* that has been lost to time." She paused, perhaps gathering her thoughts or maybe deciding if she wanted to share them with me at all. "The stone wasn't split into four pieces. It was split into five."

"Wait…*what?*" My heart dropped. *Five?* That meant our work was so much—

"Calm yourself," she said, holding up her hands. "And let me explain. After we gave the Pennlan stone to your ancestor for safekeeping, my half-brother, the Erlking, and I realized that even a quarter stone was too tempting. My half-brother could be trusted, but what about the next Erlking? You, of all people, have seen how ego and greed can cause chaos. Our first attempt was to destroy it, naturally, but it could not be destroyed by itself. So we split it in secret, where only he and I were aware that it had happened, and we took the secret to our graves."

"So…where are they?" I asked.

She smiled. "I would think it's obvious."

I looked from side to side. "N…no?"

"We absorbed them into our blood, into our magic," she said. "One in my *sidheog* line and one in the *daoine maithe*."

A chill skittered down my spine. Suddenly, a lot of things began to make sense.

"Alongside, there was an edict that no *sidheog* and *daoine maithe* could be together," she said. "And it was strong—so strong it lasted almost a thousand years. But unfortunately, the Erlkings who knew about the edict over time forgot why and stopped strengthening it. It persevered until about forty years ago when…"

"My mother?" I said softly.

Aoibheann nodded. "She was the first to tap into the last piece of the *seod croí* since it was split. She didn't know what it was, of course, or why she had the strange white magic she did. So we thought…perhaps it was all right." She sighed. "Then she met your father, and we became aware of the wizard Eoghan."

"So you're telling me that those two pieces of the stone are in my blood?" I asked softly, looking at my hands. "And it manifests as the white magic? Is that why the Pennlan stone only turns on when I'm around?"

She nodded. "The Pennlan stone has some magic without your presence, but it's not anything useful to a human. The same way the trolls discovered the only thing they could do with their piece was enhance the magic they already had. But when two pieces are in close proximity, the magic comes alive."

I turned away from her, my hand coming to my chest as I processed what she was saying. It had been dangerous when Eoghan thought he was using me to get to the Pennlan stone. But now there was a scenario where he'd have *three* stones at his disposal—the Pennlan stone, the troll's stone, and the one in my blood. All he'd have to do was kill Ayla and take control of me.

I prayed Cade was unsuccessful in finding the fourth.

"Riona?"

"This is…" I ran my hands through my hair, glancing at the other side of the garden. The path toward death. Suddenly, it looked a bit more enticing.

"What am I supposed to do with this information?" I asked.

But she was starting to fade. "You must gather the other three pieces. Use them to destroy each other."

"I don't know how!" I cried, trying to step toward her. "And I can't face him without—"

"You must face the wizard again," she said, her voice fading. "He will be a threat as long as he carries the stones with him."

"I…" I blinked, turning back to her. "Wait, stones—plural? Stones, *plural?*"

>–» >–» >–» >–»

But before I could say another word, I snapped back to the Erlking throne room, my hand against my chest as I tried to process everything I'd just learned.

"Erlking?" The forest fae in front of me tilted her head. "Are you well?"

"I have to get to my sister," I said, pushing myself up. "I have to get to Pennlan."

Chapter Fifty-Six

Cade

"My brother returns!"

Nire'huf screamed and thrust his fist into the air as our ship drew closer to H'sipotu. I shouldn't have been surprised to see him waiting, considering his deep connection with the sea. But the others on the dock, clearly having just returned because they were still unloading, wore looks of shock.

"You…" T'adlos said, blinking. "You couldn't have."

"Do you think we would've come back if we hadn't been successful?" Aldonza said with a knowing smirk. "Suppose your all-knowing island wanted us to live, after all."

It hadn't taken much convincing to get Aldonza to agree to return. After all, we'd completed the task her mother had set out for us. We were free to come and go as we pleased. And as if proving the point, the island had revealed itself to us as we drew closer.

"How did you manage to…" T'adlos said, coming up to face me. "It's impossible. Thousands have died trying to attempt what you did."

"Thousands aren't a wizard," Aldonza said, as if she'd personally goaded me on herself.

"It was more than that," I said with a tense smile. "I need to speak with your queen. Right away."

The piece of the *seod croí* weighed heavily in my pocket, whispering to me like the wind on the ocean. I wanted nothing more than to hand it to *anyone* else, but I kept it close for the moment.

Nire'huf seemed to know immediately that something was wrong as he walked beside me. "What is it?"

I waited until we were far enough out of earshot before I opened my pocket to show him the stone. "This. It's what I've been searching for. It was embedded in the stomach of *Law'ek'ub*."

"It feels the same," Nire'huf said. "Until I saw you, I feared the monster had followed us back and was about to eat the entire island."

It had certainly seemed large enough to attempt such a thing. "I need to talk to the queen about this. To know if she knew…or had an inkling. And perhaps ask if someone…someone can accompany me back to Pennlan."

He slowed. "Why?"

I turned to him, allowing the full range of fears to cross my face. "Because I don't trust myself with it. It speaks to me in a way… And the longer I hang on to it…" I knew I was babbling, but I didn't care. "The safest place is in Pennlan."

"Then let me come," Nire'huf said. "I can take it—"

He reached for it, and something angry roared inside me. The urge to throw my brother across the island swelled in my staff. I took a deep breath, closing my eyes to quell the thought.

"Please," I said. "I just need… I need help."

He reached for me, but this time, simply put his arm around mine. "Then I will help you, *ren'elk*."

With Nire'huf on my arm, I was a little more stable, as if his presence grounded me to the here and now and helped me fight the quiet voice in the back of my mind.

And I couldn't help but wonder…did Eoghan have these thoughts as he carried around the troll's piece? Or was it just this particular piece that whispered evil things to my heart?

"What is it saying to you?" Nire'huf said. "Perhaps if you tell me, it will help."

"It seems to be reaching for my…my worst instincts," I said. "It promises that if I give in to it, it will..." I exhaled, hating myself a little. "It will make Ayla love me."

"The queen in Pennlan?" he asked, and I nodded. "How can a stone do that?"

"It's one quarter of the most powerful object in existence," I said, finding more strength as we spoke. "It was created by a fae and a wizard to stop all the wars, all the fighting. Bring unending peace to the continent. But it corrupted the wizard, drove him mad with power. Those who finally defeated him decided to break it into pieces, as the only way to destroy it was to use them against each other. But before they could attempt it, the pieces were stolen. The *fuath* brought theirs here."

He nodded solemnly. "And it drove *them* mad." He tightened his grip. "I will be by your side, *ren'elk,* until we can relieve you of this burden."

The queen's house was up ahead, and I had no clue how I would convince her to go against the natural order of things. But I didn't have a choice; I couldn't do this alone.

We entered the castle together, me leaning on my brother more than I should have. The queen let out a gasp of surprise as she rose slowly from her throne. "Y... It can't be."

"Believe it, Your Majesty. My brother was successful," Nire'huf announced. "And he has a very important request for you."

But the voice in my head was starting to speak again, telling me I should cast a killing blow to the queen for what she'd allowed to happen. It was *her* fault my parents hadn't been able to come look for me. An arbitrary rule that...

"*Ren'elk?*" Nire'huf said.

It was all I could do to keep my magic to myself. I squeezed my eyes shut, fighting the urge and the stone's powerful pull.

There was a soft touch to my forehead, and a cooling feeling washed over me; I hadn't even realized I'd begun to sweat profusely. I opened my eyes weakly into the queen's soft, concerned gaze.

"There is great conflict in you," she said softly.

"He needs someone to help him take the stone back to Pennlan," Nire'huf said. "Someone more trustworthy than the pirates. Please…" He puffed out his chest. "Grant me permission to leave the island."

She stared back at him, her eyes wide. "That is…quite a request."

"It's important," he said. "Because if my brother holds onto this thing for much longer, I fear it will take him—then we'll have worse problems on our hands."

"If you leave, you cannot come back," she said quietly.

"That's a stupid rule, and you know it," I snarled, allowing my anger to bubble to the surface. "There is no island, no sentient being, nothing keeping everyone here except for your own arb—" I exhaled, covering my face with my hands. "I'm sorry. That just came out."

"The rules are the rules," she said softly. "If I could change them, I would."

"Then I will leave," Nire'huf said. "And join my brother on the mainland."

"Absolutely not," I managed, stepping away from him. "You belong here. Pennlan is miles from an ocean. You'd be miserable."

"If I leave, I lose my connection with the island regardless," he said with a sad smile. "But I would have my *ren'elk*. And that is more important to me than anything else in this world."

"You would break our mother's heart."

"No, he wouldn't."

My parents and the rest of my siblings had arrived. My mother crossed the room in three steps, coming to place another grounding hand on my shoulder to keep me in the here and now.

"My sons would not and could not ever break my heart," she said. "Even if I could never see them again, the sea would let me know they were safe."

I couldn't believe my ears. "You can't leave them, Nire'huf."

"I'm not leaving you, either," he said with a look. "My mind is made up."

"Then it seems there's nothing more to discuss," the queen said. "I do wish both of you the best of luck." She bowed her head. "And wizard, we are grateful to you for delivering us from the monster who terrorized our shores. We can breathe easier knowing our fishermen will be safe."

"Come," T'en said. "We need to get him back to the ship and on his way. The sooner that stone is parted from him, the better."

⇥ ⇥ ⇥ ⇥

My family walked me back to Aldonza's ship, with Nire'huf taking my left side and my mother my right. Their collective energy seemed to calm me enough to push the stone's whispering to the back of my mind.

"Wait," I said, stopping. "I feel in control now. Nire'huf." I nodded to him. "Take the stone from my pocket. Hide it from me."

"Already done." He flashed the stone between his fingers, and I exhaled a breath when the phantom urge to take it back was soft in my mind. "I figured it was best to do it when you weren't looking."

"Thank you." I smiled at him. "Thank you. That feels much better."

"What are brothers for?"

"My sons." T'en took us both in her arms. "You are the most precious things to me in all the world. There is nowhere you couldn't go where my love would not follow you. We may be parted in this life, but in the next...we will be reunited."

I pulled her toward me, burying myself in her neck and trying my best to remember everything about her so I would never forget again. I did the same for my father, my sisters, and even my little brother.

"Take care of Nire'huf," he said.

"I will," I said with a smile.

"And yourself, too." T'en again touched my face. "Give yourself grace to heal from your heartbreak, but please...don't lose your closest friendship."

Aldonza and the crew didn't seem surprised when Nire'huf walked on board with me. My family stood on the dock, all of them with tears and smiles on their faces. It was the way I wanted to remember them—to take their love and support with me, even if I couldn't be with them physically. But as T'en had said, I could just ask the leaves to ask the sea how they were.

"Ready to go?" Aldonza asked.

"Are you?"

"God, yes." She rolled her eyes. "Glad to never see this place again."

"You didn't even say goodbye to your mother?" I asked.

She scoffed, but there was an undercurrent of hurt there. "We said our goodbyes ages ago. Now we're just dead to each other."

The ship cast off from the dock, and before I wanted to, the island faded behind its protective veil. My heart broke a little as Nire'huf exhaled, putting his hand to his chest. But he turned to me and smiled broadly.

"I'm ready for our next adventure," he said with a grin. "To Pennlan?"

"Wizard?" Aldonza called. "Are you making that portal?"

There was something powerful and *familiar* coming. I spun around and only just saw the portal appear on the deck, only just saw the dark orange spell flying toward me, only just saw it pass through my brother without stopping.

He let out a breath, falling to his knees, then to the ground.

Someone was screaming. I cradled him in my arms, shock rolling over me as I tried to figure out what was going on. His eyes were staring at the sky, unseeing. No breath left his lips. He was… He was gone.

"You always did do better than I expected you to, apprentice."

My mind snapped to attention as I turned to the man standing in front of the portal. That he had the *fuath* stone in his hand was the least of my worries. I snarled as I grabbed my staff and came to my feet, ready to rip him limb from limb.

"You can certainly try to fight me," Eoghan said, pulling a small brown stone from his pocket. "But I think even you know that it's futile now."

He whispered a spell, something in a tongue so ancient that it made every hair on my body stand up straight. The two stones began to glow… then they suctioned together. Power moved through his body, causing his eyes to turn black for a moment before returning to normal. He cracked his neck and let out a breath.

"I wasn't quite sure that was going to work," he said, as if he were discussing the weather. "When I took the stone from the trolls, it wouldn't do a single thing for me. Which was odd, considering it had no restrictions on it, the way the Pennlan stone did." He tilted his head. "*And* considering that only Ayla can use the Pennlan stone, I wonder why it acted the way it did when that little half-fae bastard used it." He slipped the stone into his pocket. "I'll be sure to ask when I see her again. Which I assume will be quite soon."

And with that, he stepped through the open portal and was gone.

THE ADVENTURE CONCLUDES IN

A QUEST OF AETHER & DUST

ACKNOWLEGMENTS

So I know in the last book I said it was hard to write a book with a newborn, but let me tell you—writing a book pregnant and with a toddler is yet another level of difficult. 0/10 would recommend.

This wouldn't have gotten accomplished without my village to keep my child and my sanity. My husband, first and foremost, who continues to support my writing habit and allows me to fly even when I'm losing my mind. Also thanks to my parents and mother-in-law, who had the horrible task of spending time with their grand baby once a week.

Shout-out to the Moms Who Write Discord server for listening to my brain dumps, sprinting with me, and nodding in understanding as I vented about whatever. As I've grown as an author, it's become clear to me that a (digital) writer village is as important as a physical one.

Of course, thanks to my editor Danielle Fine, my cover designer Bianca, and my typo checker Lisa, without whom this would be a hot mess of a book.

ABOUT THE AUTHOR

S. Usher Evans was born and raised in Pensacola, Florida. After a decade of fighting bureaucratic battles as an IT consultant in Washington, D.C., she suffered a massive quarter-life-crisis. She decided fighting dragons was more fun than writing policy, so she moved back to Pensacola to write books full-time. She currently resides there with her husband and kids and frequently can be found plotting on the beach.

Visit S. Usher Evans online at:
http://www.susherevans.com/

www.ingramcontent.com/pod-product-compliance
Lightning Source LLC
Chambersburg PA
CBHW051002210726